Before I could think better of the idea, I took a step forward, rested my hands on his arms, then leaned up to press my mouth to his.

He stood frozen in my embrace, his lips soft but unyielding. Either he hadn't actually wanted to kiss me, or he'd decided rather quickly that he disliked it.

How humiliating.

I'd had to rise up onto my tiptoes to reach his mouth. In an abrupt move, I settled back onto my heels and drew my hands away from his arms.

"There. I did as you asked—"

He reached out and brushed his thumb against my lower lip, his gaze intent on my mouth. "Do it again."

My cheeks caught fire. Did I do it wrong the first time? While I debated how to do it right, he seemed to grow tired of the delay. His hand went behind my neck to cup my head, and he urged me closer.

"Again," he ordered.

I complied. This time I felt his arms go around me the moment our lips touched and he drew me closer until our fronts were pressed together and I rested intimately against his body. We both gasped a little at the contact. Being pressed against him was every bit as distracting as being picked up and held in his arms.

The hardness of his body was such a contrast to the softness of his lips that I had to concentrate to get the kiss right this time. Until his mouth opened. And then I lost my ability to concentrate on anything at all.

BY ELIZABETH ELLIOTT

The Warlord

Scoundrel

Betrothed

The Dark Knight

The Princess

THE
PRINCESS

ELIZABETH
ELLIOTT

BANTAM BOOKS · NEW YORK

A Bantam Books Mass Market Original

Copyright © 2018 by Linda Kay Crippes

Published in the United States by Bantam Books, an imprint of Random House, a division of Penguin Random House LLC, New York.

BANTAM BOOKS and the HOUSE colophon are registered trademarks of Penguin Random House LLC.

ISBN: 978-0-553-57568-2
Ebook ISBN: 978-0-345-53863-5

Cover design: Eileen Carey
Cover photographs: © Alla Samarskaya/Shutterstock (woman),
© Matt Gibson/Shutterstock (castle)

Printed in the United States of America

randomhousebooks.com

9   8   7   6   5   4   3   2   1

Bantam Books mass market edition: June 2018

CONTENTS

THE
PRINCESS

CHAPTER ONE

The German Princess

London, 1293

"MAY I PRESENT FAULKE SEGRAVE, LORD OF Derllys, heir to the Baron of Carreg." The English knight gestured for the second man to step forward, and then he cleared his throat. "May I also present Lord Faulke's cousin, Sir Richard Segrave of Hawksforth."

At my nod, Sir Roland bowed low, and then returned to his station by the door. I tried to show no outward expression as I eyed the two newcomers.

Everyone who knew Faulke Segrave claimed he was tall with dark hair and blue eyes, and a face most ladies found pleasing. What stood before me was definitely tall and blue eyed. A chain mail hood covered his hair, which made confirmation of its color difficult to determine. The color of his beard was just as mysterious, since it was caked with dried mud that was an unpleasant shade of grayish brown. Even his facial features were difficult to distinguish under the streaks of muck and dirt that covered his face and beard. As for a pleasing personality, I did not hold out much hope.

Faulke's cousin, Richard, was a near twin in appearance as well as in filth. My gaze lingered on their eyes, the whites made more vivid by the mud that surrounded them, the blue even more intense against the white. It was a rather startling effect, as if they were staring at me from behind Venetian masks. The hairs on the back of my neck stood up, and I forced my gaze lower.

The surcoats they wore might have the Segrave dragon on their chests, but it was impossible to know for certain. Everything they wore, from head to foot, was covered with dried mud. They both looked—and smelled—as if they had recently rolled through a bog.

I lifted the fingers of my right hand, just a little, and then let them settle again onto the arm of my chair. Gerhardt, the captain of my guard, recognized the signal and stepped forward to introduce me to our visitors in his painfully precise French.

"I present to you Her Royal Highness, Isabel of Ascalon, Dowager Crown Princess of Rheinbaden, Princess of England, Countess of Maldon, Baroness Helmsford, Baroness Sildon, daughter of King Edward of England, and widow of Crown Prince Hartman of Rheinbaden."

The list of titles was meant to intimidate, to make certain the Segraves understood who held the advantage between us. Gerhardt returned to his place by my side and we all waited as the Segraves stared back at us.

No one shifted their weight or cleared their throat or coughed. The only sounds were the chirps of songbirds in the gardens, and the distant rumble from beyond our walls of the beast that was London.

The longer the silence stretched out, the more I had to convince myself that I was the only one who could hear the telltale beat of my heart as it pattered out a nervous rhythm. On the outside I presented a practiced portrait to the world of a mature woman nearly twenty-four years old. On the inside I cowered like a child. I had dreaded this day from the moment I received word that my husband had drowned. An accident fueled by idiotic male pride and too much wine had shattered my ordered world just over a year ago. I had left Rheinbaden the day after my official year of mourning ended, and landed in England a month later to meet a father I had forgotten and visit the grave of a mother I could scarcely remember. And now I found myself staring into the angry face of my future.

The differences between us might be comical, under different circumstances. Their garments were covered in mud. Mine smelled pleasantly of the sandalwood-lined trunks where I stored my finest clothing. I doubt they had washed their hands or faces in the last week. I had taken a long, leisurely bath in rosewater just that morning. Indeed, I had spent hours preparing for this meeting, determined there would be no doubt in the Segraves' minds that they were dealing with a very wealthy, very powerful noblewoman.

I wore my finest jewels, my pink gown and surcoat

fashioned from the richest fabrics then liberally embellished with designs made of seed pearls. The colors were nicely offset by my dark hair and Plantagenet-blue eyes, but the entire ensemble probably outweighed the Segraves' armor. The effect was worth a little discomfort. I had greeted kings in these garments. They were seeing me at my very best.

In contrast, the Segraves looked as if someone had just dragged them from a ditch. I sincerely hoped I was seeing them at their worst.

Most people consider an audience with royalty an occasion of some importance. At the very least, they bathed and donned clean clothing. Big and broad shouldered, the two warriors looked and smelled so fierce they were more likely to be taken for Welsh barbarians than knights of the realm.

Just that morning, my friend Avalene de Forshay had surveyed us with a critical eye and claimed we were so radiant that only a religious painting could inspire greater awe. It was the effect I had hoped for, but the mocking looks from the Segraves gave me pause. My people wore their finest court clothing, which meant they were dressed in white and pink, the royal colors of Rheinbaden. And then I recalled that most English considered pink an unmanly color. They did not understand that in the Alps of Rheinbaden, pink symbolized the color of blood mixed with snow.

The uncomfortable silence was finally broken as the nearby bells of All Hallows by the Tower began to ring, a seemingly endless reverberation echoed by scores of churches across the city. The cacophony of sound made conversation temporarily impossible, unless I wanted to resort to rude shouts, which I did not.

Several strikes later, Richard leaned closer to his cousin, obviously counting on the bells to cover his words, but the ringing suddenly ceased and the silence amplified his voice. "We should have insisted—"

Faulke cut him off with a sharp look, and then he turned to glare again at me. It was a good thing I didn't scare easily.

Gerhardt, the captain of my guard, expressed my sentiments exactly. *"Sie sind beleidigend."*

Sometimes Gerhardt saw insult where none existed, but in this instance, I had to agree with him. They *were* insulting. My hopes for a civil first meeting evaporated.

Gerhardt was too stoic for foolish notions such as hope. Like most of my people, the captain of my guard bore the obvious marks of his Germanic heritage: blond hair, blue eyes, lean and tall, with absolutely no sense of humor. His steely eyed presence at my side cowed most men, and I watched his hand flex on the hilt of his sword as his mouth became a flat line.

I looked back at the Segraves. Richard watched Gerhardt as if my captain were a viper. Faulke's gaze had returned to me. His scowl left little doubt about his impressions of what he saw. I let my mouth curve into what I hoped was a condescending smile.

Faulke's hands became fists at his sides and his gaze went to Gerhardt. "Does your princess speak French?"

The room fell silent again.

His voice was deeper than I expected, and I found myself momentarily distracted by the sound of it. And then I was amazed that he would ask such a question. French was the native language of every English noble, although most could also speak the English tongue of their Saxon vassals and peasants. French was also the common language of nobles throughout the civilized world.

Except in Rheinbaden. There, visitors spoke in German or they were not heard. Even the Rheinbaden nobles who spoke French pretended ignorance, since they considered every foreign language inferior to German. As a result, very few of my people spoke French, and fewer still spoke English. Not that it mattered.

Regardless of who spoke what language, one did not address a servant when their master or mistress was present. It would serve him right if we all pretended ignorance. I actually toyed with the idea until Faulke took a threatening step toward Gerhardt. Political posturing was not worth spilled blood. Not yet, anyway.

I rose from my seat and saw Faulke's eyes widen. He stood taller than most men, but then again, so do I. The pearl-encrusted crown made me appear even taller. I answered his question in flawless French. "My subjects do not speak to *ausländers* without my permission, Lord Faulke. You are ausländers. Outsiders. If you have something to say to me, I can converse fluently in French, Latin, English, Italian, and German."

He simply stared at me.

"I believe additional introductions are in order," I

went on, my tone brisk. "The man you just addressed is the captain of my guard. Gerhardt speaks French, although my ladies and most of my soldiers and servants speak only German. That should not matter, since anything you wish to say to them should be said first to me."

I folded my hands and gave him a serene look. This was the moment I had waited for. They were men and therefore thought themselves above me. I had just corrected their thinking. Now would come the well-deserved apologies.

"An hour ago I was faced with the prospect of immediate imprisonment or a royal bride. You may be happy to know that I have just signed our betrothal papers. It seems we shall be married within the month." He folded his arms across his broad chest, dislodging a few clumps of dried mud that crumbled to the floor. "You might be a princess, but I am the man you will soon call your lord and master."

I was speechless. His arrogance made mine pale in comparison, which was not an easy feat when I was purposely trying to be arrogant. He also made my father's generosity sound like a punishment, the ungrateful churl.

Another hard-learned lesson was to know your opponent. My attention went to his shoulders, and then to his arms. His build spoke of long hours spent swinging a sword, likely from the time he could walk. Indeed, both cousins looked as if they had just been plucked from the midst of a battlefield.

In contrast, my soldiers had spent too many years guarding doorways in my court, and none at all in actual battle. There was no doubt in my mind that these two knights could do serious damage to my men, if they were so inclined, and they certainly looked inclined. And that made me wonder if my new "lord and master" would ever raise a hand against me.

Fortunately, my father had already given me reassurances on that score. If this man ever dared abuse me, I would ensure that he also learned a hard, painful lesson. That thought bolstered my courage.

"Most men would think themselves blessed to gain such prizes," I finally said, in as calm a voice as I could manage.

"Most men are not brought to the altar at the point of a sword."

My gaze went to his side and I noticed for the first time that both men had been relieved of their weapons. Little wonder they were so angry. Still, it was their own greed that formed this prison, and they were being amply compensated for their troubles.

Despite my own frustrations, I made an unexpected discovery as I watched Faulke draw in a breath and then slowly release it through tight lips. Despite the mud and wild beard, there was something appealing about the shape of his mouth. That is, if one were attracted to rude, uncivilized sorts of men with intriguing mouths, which I am not. Still, amid the dirt and anger, I saw glimpses of a strong profile that some women might find appealing.

He tilted his head to one side and slowly looked me up and down again, this time in a way that made my temperature rise and butterflies stir to life in my stomach. Some instinct warned me not to underestimate this man, even as I reminded him of his supposed good fortune.

"Our marriage will provide your family with more wealth and power than you could have ever hoped for from a marriage to Avalene de Forshay," I pointed out.

He shook his head. "An hour ago, I learned that the woman I was legally betrothed to marry has been put beyond my reach by your father's order. The day may come when I am pleased with our impending marriage, but today is not that day."

I was not particularly pleased with this day myself. Until the Segraves entered this chamber, I had hoped for a man who would be the complete opposite of my first husband, Hartman. This would teach me to be careful what I wished for.

A certain amount of resentment from Faulke had been expected. Still, I had not anticipated this level of hostility. The titles he would gain with my dowry included an earldom, several baronies, manors, and all the wealth that went with the accompanying lands. He would soon become one of the richest and most powerful men in England. All he had to do was tamp down his ambitions in Wales. Was that really such a sacrifice?

It was a stupid question. I had been surrounded by ambitious men all my life, and none of them welcomed the sacrifice of their ambitions. I knew the Segraves' history. *Ruthless Ambition* should be their family motto.

I recalled a conversation I had earlier in the day with Faulke's former betrothed. "Lady Avalene warned me that you would not be happy with our betrothal, but I did not fully comprehend the depths of your displeasure."

Something dark flickered in his eyes. "Lady Avalene was everything I wanted in a wife."

Which implied that I was not. The butterflies congealed into an icy lump. Was he trying to make me jealous of Avalene, or simply taking another opportunity to insult me?

It was difficult to be jealous of a woman who was in love with a notorious assassin. Dante Chiavari, her husband-to-be, was not even an Englishman. And that proved how little Faulke knew Avalene, if he thought he could stir my jealousy toward her.

I pretended to adjust the cuff of my sleeve as I considered my response, letting my fingers trail across the smooth bumps of the seed pearls that were stitched in tight rows from my elbows to my wrists. The Segraves were driven by their greed for power. So why was he goading me?

"You are barely acquainted with Lady Avalene," I said, "which means that what she would have brought to your marriage was more important than the lady herself. And yet she has very little in the way of lands or wealth."

He spread his hands and lifted his shoulders, a silent admission of the truth. "Surely you are aware of the reasons I sought her out."

"Aye. Our impending marriage is a direct result of those reasons," I said. "If you wed Avalene and then fathered a son on her, you could rule all of Wales through such a child."

"Those possibilities existed," he admitted as he tilted his head in a mockery of a bow. "However, now that your father has interfered, there is no longer any chance that Avalene will be my wife."

"My father is no fool."

"Nor am I," he countered. "You were married nearly ten years and yet you have no heirs. Our marriage contract is such that only an heir of your body can inherit my family's lands and titles, along with your own. Your father has found a means to extinguish my family's line, and ensure that everything the Segraves hold dear will eventually revert to the crown."

Ah, here was the true crux of his anger. The Segraves' holdings in Wales were impressive, given their recent rise to power, with a dozen fortified keeps and their main fortress, Hawksforth, the jewel that presided over them all. Now those holdings were tied to any child I might bear. I had hoped the Segraves would be so blinded by the wealth and titles my father intended to rain upon them that they would meekly accept the terms of our betrothal. Foolish hopes.

In any event, his accusation did not surprise me, and I had a ready answer. "My husband contracted mumps many years ago, just before our first child was born."

"The child did not live long," Faulke retorted.

That was brutal but true, and the truth still hurt a deep, guarded part of my soul. Hartman and I had both contracted mumps in the last month of my pregnancy. He had nearly died of his illness. I had wanted to, when I watched my babe take a few labored breaths and then no more.

Everyone knew that a case of mumps as severe as Hartman's often left a man unable to father children. Without that explanation, I would be impossible to marry off to any nobleman who needed an heir, no matter my wealth or bloodline. Even so, my father had to act quickly, before the gossip in Rheinbaden about my husband's fertile mistress followed me to England.

"Mumps is the rumor," Faulke agreed, "but it does not change the fact that your ability to produce a healthy heir is unproven."

I refused to feel guilty. It was the Segraves' actions that had led all of us to this place. Faulke was hardly the innocent victim. *Ach*, he even looked the part of a villain, with his wild beard and fouled clothes. I gazed at him with cool eyes. "The terms of our marriage are due in great part to your own matrimonial history, Lord Faulke. You are very young to have buried three wives. There are rumors of murder."

His hands fisted at his sides and his lips barely moved when he answered my charge. "I did not murder my wives."

"I do not particularly care," I lied. "The terms of our marriage are such that you now have a vested interest in my health and longevity."

"I am well aware of the terms," Faulke bit out. "I am a wealthy earl only as long as you live."

"My father feels that is sufficient motivation to ensure I do not fall victim to the sorts of unusual accidents and illnesses that befell your previous brides."

Faulke studied something on my gown, and then he

lifted his gaze to mine again. "Are you such a dutiful daughter that you would willingly enter into marriage with a man rumored to murder his wives, a man who makes no secret of the fact that he wants another woman as his wife?"

" 'Tis a daughter's duty to obey her father," I said in an even tone. " 'Tis the duty of a princess to serve her country and to obey her king. Do you suggest I commit treason?"

"Refusing a suitor is hardly grounds for treason," he countered in a low voice. "You are the daughter of a king and the widow of a crown prince. Aside from my own unsavory reputation, one of my grandfathers was in trade, the other was a landless knight in service to your great-uncle at Pembroke. My grandmothers are even less illustrious. The only reason we hold a title is because my father happened to be in the right place at the right time to save your grandfather's life on the battlefield. Will you truly be content with a man of such ill-repute, one with the blood of commoners in his veins?"

His questions gave me pause. He was the first person who expected me to voice an opinion on the matter.

I wondered why he cared.

My opinion counted for nothing. It would make no difference in our circumstances.

And then his strategy became suddenly clear. He could not refuse the betrothal without insulting his king. Men had found themselves locked in the Tower for more minor offenses. Faulke obviously valued his freedom, and thought there was another means to escape the trap of our marriage. I had to admire his strategy. "Do you think I have some choice in this matter?"

"Daughters hold a special place in the hearts of their fathers," he said with a small shrug. "Surely your father would take your happiness into consideration."

Was he jesting? The children of kings were a far different matter than the children of commoners, or more specifically, the children of a newly made barony. My father had mentioned that Faulke had three young daughters, but Avalene knew little about them.

I looked at him in a new light, recalling some of the close-knit families in the village at Grunental, the castle where I had spent the last lonely years of my marriage. I had sometimes envied them, husbands and wives who loved each other as well as they loved their children, but I always knew they were a phenomena of the common classes. And yet Faulke had just boasted of his common blood. Did his daughters hold a special place in *his* heart?

What a novel concept.

"The king is most assuredly unlike most fathers," I said before I could be distracted by the idea of loving parents. "He takes into consideration what is best for England, which also happens to be what is best for him. I am certain my happiness is a sacrifice he is willing to make, should he be forced to choose between my happiness and the good of the realm."

Faulke studied my face for a long moment, and then he tilted his head forward to rub his brow. I could almost see the fight seep out of him. His muttered words confirmed as much. "Then it seems we are to be married."

"It would seem so," I agreed. The anger in his eyes faded and I made a startling realization. He had truly believed I could refuse my father's order. I gestured toward his clothing. "Is that the reason you came to our first meeting in such a state? Did you hope I would find you so repulsive that I would cry off?"

His mouth twisted into a grim line. "Your repulsion was an entirely unplanned effect, Princess, brought about by Chiavari's determination to sever my betrothal to Lady Avalene as quickly as possible."

Faulke looked at his cousin, then down at his own garments, as if seeing their state for the first time. "We have ridden across most of Wales and southern England in the last month, and have seen nothing but rain for the past fortnight. Hours ago we were taken prisoner at the gates to London, and then brought to this palace. Richard and I were escorted to this solar under guard soon after I signed our betrothal contract." He spread his hands again, this time in a mocking gesture. "Thus, we appear before you."

He stared boldly into my eyes, almost as if he were issuing a challenge of some sort. I could not seem to look away. Nor did I want to. If he were trying to intimidate me, it would not work.

Eventually a movement at the doorway caught my attention, then Sir Roland stepped aside to allow another man to enter the solar. I gave Sir Roland a nod, and the knight announced the stranger.

"My lords and ladies, may I present Mordecai of the king's council and adviser to the royal family." The old

knight ended that announcement with a bout of coughing that had Mordecai looking at him askance.

Everyone else in the solar stared at the newest arrival,
just as we had all stared at the Segraves. Most mystics
were outright frauds, but no one rose to the rank of
royal adviser without proven skills of some sort. Still,
the only thing that appeared mystical about Mordecai
was his clothing. The long robes he wore were made of a
strange, shimmering cloth that seemed to change color
with every movement as he walked into the room, from
darkest black to deep purples and blues, with occasional
fiery streaks of red and gold.

I was certain the genial smile and innocent blue eyes
disguised a mind as devious as my father's. I fought
down the urge to back away when he stopped before me
and lifted my hand to give it a perfunctory kiss.

"Princess Isabel, you are even more beautiful than I
remembered."

Mordecai watched me process his compliment, his
lips curved in a secretive smile that set my teeth on edge.
I nodded a greeting. "You have not changed at all from
my childhood memories of you, Mordecai. I hope you
will share your secrets for retaining such youthful vigor.
Beautiful women are known to be vain."

"And still clever," he said with a chuckle. "You were
always my favorite of your parents' brood."

That was news to me. Unwelcome news, which I decided to ignore. "To what do we owe the pleasure of
your company?"

"You have many decisions to make in the coming
weeks," Mordecai replied. "The banns will be read dur-

ing the next three Sunday masses at St. Paul's, and the marriage will take place the following Monday. That gives you little more than three weeks to make the necessary preparations."

"You seem to have something specific in mind," Faulke remarked. "What preparations must be made?"

Mordecai's gaze flickered to the mullioned windows that overlooked the gardens. The late summer sun cast golden rays across the floor. "The journey to Wales will be the most pressing, of course. It must be accomplished before winter. You have more than one hundred Rheinbaden soldiers and servants in your company, Princess. How long did you prepare for your journey here from Rheinbaden?"

"Several months," I answered. "But we can be ready to move again with less work. We have all the necessary livestock, wagons, and crates. We will simply need to lay in fresh supplies."

Mordecai shook his head. "One hundred of your father's soldiers will also go with you to Wales. Some of the soldiers have wives and children, or other entanglements, so there are always the camp followers to consider. Lord Faulke arrived in London with a score of men, whom I assume will also accompany you. In all, your company will number nearly three hundred people. You will be responsible for them all."

This time I looked to Gerhardt and then to Sir Roland, but the English knight merely lifted his shoulders in a shrug of apology. I had assumed Sir Roland, the captain of my father's guard, would make provisions for his men, and I'd had no knowledge of the families and camp followers. Ach, we would be a small city.

"Aside from the journey and the eventual living arrangements you must make for the number of people who will reside at Hawksforth," Mordecai said, "there is also the matter of Maldon Castle and your other estates." He turned to my future husband. "Lord Faulke, your father will become sheriff of Maldon upon your marriage and oversee the stewards at Isabel's estates. You will be within your rights to replace them with your own appointments. However, your wife may have her own opinions about the stewards, as most are her relatives. I expect other matters will arise during those discussions that you will wish to address."

"My bride and I do, indeed, have much to discuss before the wedding," Faulke said. He gave me a formal bow that lacked any trace of insult or mockery. "By your leave, my lady, my cousin and I will depart your company. As you pointed out earlier, we are hardly fit for an audience. We will return on the morrow to discuss the preparations for our marriage in more detail, after we have had a chance to make ourselves more presentable."

I toyed with the idea of a polite curtsey and then dismissed it. I still outranked Faulke, and I did not want him to think I was softening. I gave him a syrupy smile instead. "I shall count the hours until your return, sir."

Rather than take his leave, he took several steps toward me, and that odd feeling was suddenly back in my stomach again. Butterflies. Or fear. From the corner of my eye I saw Gerhardt move forward to a protective position at my side, close enough to intervene, and yet far enough to draw his weapon without skewering me.

Faulke stood so close that I wanted to take a step back, envisioning smears of dirt on my white bliaut, but that would look cowardly so I held my ground. I barely flinched when he reached out and captured my hand in his. And then I stared dumbly at our joined hands, his so large that it almost enveloped mine completely. My natural instinct was to pull away from such an unexpected intimacy, and I allowed myself to take a step backward from the mud-covered knight, as far as his hold would allow, but he held fast to my hand.

He waited until I looked into his eyes, and then I couldn't seem to look away. He turned my hand over and pressed his lips to my wrist, his gaze holding mine captive the entire time. His deep voice was just above a whisper. "I shall endeavor to make the wait worth your while, Princess."

The words were innocent enough, but my cheeks felt suddenly warm. Before I could conjure up a witty retort, or summon a rational thought of any sort, he released his hold and backed away several steps. He bowed again, and then he and his cousin left the solar. I watched them go with a mixture of disbelief at his audacity and surprise that he had somehow managed to have the last word. He had left me speechless. Again.

Eventually I sat back down and resisted the urge to cradle my hand in my lap, to trace the imprint of his lips upon my wrist. The strangeness of my reaction to his touch baffled me. I flattened my palm against my thigh and tried to rub away the lingering tingles in my hand

and wrist without being obvious about it. Why had he done such a thing? Did he think I would somehow fall under his spell, overwhelmed by a simple kiss on my wrist? *Had* a simple kiss rendered me senseless?

I suddenly felt everyone's gazes upon me as they waited for me to react in some way to Faulke's departure. Only Mordecai was bold enough to finally break the silence.

"This marriage is of great importance, Princess. You will be suitably rewarded for your cooperation."

I glanced at the kindly expression on his face and then looked away. It was a mask, one as false as any of the masks I wore to conceal my true thoughts and feelings. I leaned my head against the back of the chair and closed my eyes. My emotions were in turmoil. I was tired. Exhausted. I hadn't slept well since I left Rheinbaden, and not at all the night before. Those were the reasons for my odd reaction to Faulke Segrave's touch. He was an insulting, uncouth, unwashed bear of a man, likely as barbaric as the Welshmen he ruled. His touch had actually repelled me. Aye, repelled. I was so on edge and out of sorts that I would have reacted the same if anyone had held my hand and kissed my wrist in that moment. It was a moment that would never happen again.

The hopes I'd had for a tolerable marriage lay in ashes. Yet Mordecai and my father both encouraged and praised my cooperation as I was swept toward a future that promised to be more miserable than my past.

Aside from counting the hours until our next meeting, I dreaded even more the day when Faulke learned the full truth of my deception in this marriage.

I released a slow sigh and wondered if I would live long enough to be "suitably rewarded" for my part in this crime.

CHAPTER TWO

Poison

THAT NIGHT I DREAMED ABOUT FAULKE SEGRAVE. The odd part was that I knew it was a dream. Pursuit and capture seemed to be the main themes of the evening, and we took turns looking for each other in a darkened forest as if we were playing a game. Several times I laughed when he couldn't find me.

"Princess?"

A hand encased in a knight's glove reached toward me from swirling mists and I shrieked in fright. The hand motioned me toward the shadows. Although this was definitely a dream, I wasn't foolish enough to go willingly into the shadows.

"Show yourself!" I demanded.

The hand motioned me forward again. "Come closer, Princess. I cannot linger long."

That voice did *not* belong to Faulke. My mind drifted through a list of possibilities and stopped on Sir Roland. I looked up to where the face that went with Sir Roland's hand should be. Shadows. I stared again at the disembodied hand. I knew this place wasn't real, but I knew just as surely that I was here for a reason. I reached toward Sir Roland's hand. Just as my fingertips almost reached his glove, another voice called out to me.

"Princess?"

Someone grabbed my shoulders to pull me away from the outstretched hand. I tried to reach out farther, even as the gloved hand withdrew into the shadows. The sight of that hand disappearing into nothingness sent shivers down my spine and I drew back, suddenly afraid of being drawn into the shadows and disappearing myself.

"Princess, please. You must wake up!"

That was Hilda speaking, one of my attendants. She sounded frightened. I struggled toward consciousness.

"What . . . ?" I was still so drugged by sleep that I could barely form the word.

"My lady, wake up!" Hilda gave my shoulder another firm shake. "Sir Roland is dead! Murdered!"

My eyes popped open just as Hilda leaned over me with a candle that was blindingly close to my eyes, so near that I could feel its heat curl my eyelashes. I closed my eyes and tried to keep my voice calm so she would not be startled and drip hot beeswax onto my face. "I cannot see with you holding that candle so close, Hilda."

"Forgive me, Princess. I am just . . . there was a murder last eve! Here!"

The golden red light behind my eyelids became marginally darker. I opened my eyes again and sat up. My bedchamber was still dark, but through the window behind Hilda I could see the pink glow of dawn. Gretchen, my other attendant and my oldest friend, stood at the foot of my bed, her hands clasped before her as she chewed on her bottom lip.

I remembered the dream and shuddered. "What happened to Sir Roland?"

"Two of the English soldiers found his body when they went to wake him," Gretchen answered, "although they think he has been dead for most of the night."

"Faulke is dead, too?" I asked, struggling to separate the fragments of my dream from reality.

"No, Sir Roland," Hilda said. She shook her head and spoke to me in a slow, deliberate tone. "The captain of your English guard is dead, not your betrothed. They took Sir Roland's body to the great hall. Gerhardt has also sent for Lord Dante."

Sir Roland. He was an old man. A sick old man. I recalled several times when he had been overcome with coughing spells in the last few days. "Why would Gerhardt involve Chiavari?"

Hilda and Gretchen exchanged a look. Gretchen said, "Ashland Palace is still Lord Dante's until he leaves for Italy, my lady. 'Tis customary to inform the host when a death occurs among his guests."

"Of course," I said as I rubbed my eyes. "I am not quite awake yet."

"Do you wish for a robe or would you like us to dress you?" Hilda asked.

I stared at the canopy above my head and tried to

gather my thoughts. I had dreamed of two men, and now one was dead. Was it possible that both had died? Or, did the dream mean nothing at all?

"We assumed you would want to view the body," Gretchen said. "'Tis your duty, my lady."

Aye, it was my duty. Sir Roland had been the captain of the English guard, and therefore the highest ranked of my father's soldiers here at Ashland. The questions were slow to form in my sleep-fogged brain. "How did he die?"

"The soldiers are not certain," Hilda said. "There does not seem to be a mark upon the body, but he was found holding his throat, as if he had been strangled."

I remembered again the persistent cough that had plagued him this past week. "He is not a young man. Indeed, Sir Roland is . . . *was* . . . much older than my father. 'Tis likely consumption. He has been ill all week."

My ladies exchanged another look.

"What?" I demanded.

Gretchen leaned closer, her voice almost a whisper. "The soldiers reported that he bled from his ears and nose, and even from his eyes. You know what that means."

A sudden shiver went through me. There was one cause of death that claimed far too many noble lives, one we were all bred to fear. "Poison?"

"Surely that is the reason Gerhardt summoned Lord Dante so quickly," Hilda said. Her hands were gripped together so tightly her knuckles were white. "Lord Dante is an expert in such matters, yes?"

"He is an expert," I confirmed, hoping to quell further speculation. According to my father, poison was Dante Chiavari's specialty, along with throat cutting and a few other murderous skills. We were living under the same roof with a notorious poisoner, and now one of my men had been poisoned. Coincidence? I wondered.

Not that I would voice my doubts to Gretchen and Hilda. Poison found those closest to a noble as often as it found its mark, although it seemed odd that Sir Roland would receive a poison meant for me. Still, my suspicions could be wrong.

I shook my head. It was all speculation. I tossed the covers back and rose from my bed. "Bring me a gown, and then tell me everything you know about this death."

MY LADIES HAD little information to share, which was another reason I hurried through my ablutions. I wanted to see the body and make my own judgment. Perhaps the soldiers had been mistaken about the poison. Sir Roland had been sick. He was old. Not all sick old men died peacefully.

The great hall was the heart of Ashland Palace, a vast vaulted room built to accommodate hundreds of soldiers and courtiers at wide benches and tables. The hall and kitchens stretched along the southern wing of the palace, with a row of windows near the ceiling to let in light and draw out smoke from the two massive fireplaces at each end of the hall.

The room was still cast in shadows when I arrived, but servants were busy lighting torches that were set into the walls and braces of candles around the head table. Dozens of English soldiers milled about the room, with more arriving by the moment. Almost everyone in the palace would soon be gathered here to break their fast, regardless of this tragedy, but few people filed to their seats this morning. Everyone faced toward the west side of the room and spoke in hushed voices. I followed the direction of their gazes.

Sir Roland was laid out on a table near one of the fireplaces. As Chiavari pulled the edge of a blanket up over the dead knight's face, my gaze went to Sir Roland's bared arms that showed beneath the narrow blanket. I knew the proud old knight would not like to be put on display this way, but what I could see of him did not look quite real. His flesh was the color of tallow, a waxen figure instead of a man. I tried to find something about the body that seemed familiar. My gaze moved to the flow of wavy, iron-gray hair that spilled from beneath the blanket and over the edge of the table. Then I noticed dark streaks in his hair. Blood.

Gerhardt intercepted me by standing directly in my path. "You do not need to see any more of him than this, Princess. His face is . . ."

"His face is what?" I demanded.

"The agony of Sir Roland's passing is apparent in his death mask," Gerhardt murmured. His eyes were somber, his jaw tight.

I glanced again at the dead knight and couldn't prevent the shudder that traveled up my spine. Sir Roland had not looked well yesterday in my solar. His skin had a grayish tinge to it and he had coughed even more than usual. I should have sent for a physician. He was my responsibility as much as Gerhardt or my other soldiers. This should not have happened. I should have recognized that he was sick.

My gaze moved from Sir Roland to Chiavari. Dante Chiavari was our host and the current owner of this palace, a tall man with dark hair. His Italian ancestors were evident in his face, his features similar to the marble busts of ancient Roman emperors that I had viewed years ago on a pilgrimage to Rome. Something about him reminded me of the gyrfalcons in Rheinbaden, his eyes cold and assessing, the unemotional gaze of a predator that was constantly scanning its environment. Not for looking for danger, but searching for prey.

Few knew his true identity, but many in England feared him. His was the last face that scores of my father's enemies had looked upon. If not for Avalene, I would have thought him immune to any bouts of humanity. She had an almost magical effect on the man, but a quick glance around the hall confirmed that she was not in attendance. I would have to face him alone.

Chiavari's startling green eyes were hooded now as he gave instructions of some sort to his steward. Our gazes met briefly as he walked to the head table and took his seat. He began to wash his hands in a basin of lemon water that a servant had placed next to him.

"I had nothing to do with his death," Chiavari said in a quiet voice as I walked toward the table. "I can see the accusation in your eyes, Princess, but I am not the cause of this loss."

"Then he was not poisoned?" I asked, even as I

straightened my spine. It would not do to look cowardly. One did not act like prey in the company of a predator.

"Oh, he was poisoned," Chiavari said, "but I did not do it."

I studied his face as he continued his ablutions, but I found nothing reflected there that would convince me of his innocence. "If not you, then who?"

He lifted his shoulders in a shrug. "That question might be easier to answer if we learn how he was poisoned. Our best hope will be if someone saw something unusual take place. I intend to learn how the doses were delivered, and then trace the poison back to its source."

"Was the poison in something he ate or drank, or is there a mark that indicates a poisoned blade?"

"There are no wounds," he said. "If my suspicions are correct, the poison that causes this type of death is a slow one, most often introduced in food over the course of several days or weeks. If it is what I suspect, the poison gradually turns the blood into an acid that eats through the body from the inside out." He pressed his lips together, apparently aware—too late—that I did not need that much detail. He said in a softer tone, "If we can find more of the poisoned food, perhaps we can trace the poison to its source."

"I see." The poison sounded ghastly. Then again, was there a good poison?

"Sir Roland's soldiers told me that no one else is ill," Chiavari went on. "No one recalls him eating foods from a particular public house or street hawker, or purchasing anything from the markets to bring back to the palace."

"My men are searching Sir Roland's chamber and the

stables," Gerhardt said as he walked up behind me. He spoke in a measured voice, as he spoke French for our host's benefit. "Sir Roland rode every day. Perhaps we will find something in his tack."

I nodded to agree with his reasoning, but my attention was drawn back to Sir Roland's body. I watched Chiavari's steward direct four soldiers to each take a corner of the table he was laid upon, and then they carried the body from the hall.

"They will take him to All Hallows," Chiavari said. "According to his lieutenants, he has a daughter in London. I sent a messenger to notify her of Sir Roland's death, and the body will then be taken to the church of her choosing."

A surge of guilt flooded through me. In all my worries about a poisoner, I had not given a single thought to Sir Roland's family. I did not realize he even had a family. Then again, I had known him little more than a month. We were cordial, but still, I should have known more about his personal life.

"Send one of our men with the *weregild* when the body is delivered," I told Gerhardt. "Better yet, take it yourself. The daughter will not speak German, and I do not trust anyone else to make the proper explanation."

"What is there to explain?" Gerhardt retorted, just as Chiavari asked,

"What is a weregild?"

"The payment for her father's death," I answered. "Sir Roland was the captain of my English guard, therefore his death is my responsibility. I must pay the price for his murder."

"Ah, blood money," Chiavari murmured. "You realize that your father is responsible for his knights and he will most certainly give the daughter Sir Roland's pension?"

I lifted my shoulders. "That is his right. This is mine."

"I will see it done," Gerhardt said. His upper lip curled as his gaze went again to Chiavari. "Your palace is not as safe as you claimed, assassin."

"Mordecai made the claims, not me," Chiavari said. His tone was mild, but I had already learned that Chiavari was at his most dangerous when he was quiet. "If I had been consulted before King Edward issued the princess an invitation to move into my home, I might have reminded the king that danger tends to follow me."

"A man is dead," I reminded them. "I would like to know how we find those responsible for the crime."

Chiavari gave Gerhardt one more look through narrowed eyes before answering. "You know that I will not be in England much longer, but if you have a poisoner in your midst, I can tell you the signs to watch for. If I leave before the culprit is found, you would do well to ask for Mordecai's help. He taught me much of what I know about poisons and the manners of their use."

His advice reminded me that Chiavari had once been Mordecai's apprentice, and the magician had trained him to be an assassin. My childhood had not been particularly pleasant, but I would not wish Chiavari's childhood upon anyone.

I watched his gaze move to the far side of the hall and he sat up straighter, even as his expression softened. I did not need to turn around to know that Avalene had come into the hall. My presence was forgotten as Chiavari rose from his seat and walked across the hall to greet his betrothed. He lifted both of her hands to his lips. *"Buongiorno, cara."*

While the two lovers cooed over each other, I looked around and realized my ladies had already seated themselves at their usual places. I took my seat next to Avalene's at the head table. Being one seat away from a creature like Chiavari was not quite so unnerving with Avalene between us as a buffer.

"I was so sorry to hear about your captain," Avalene told me as she settled onto her chair. She drew her blond braid over one shoulder to let it coil in her lap, and then she smoothed the skirts of her bloodred gown. She looked to Dante and then back to me, her blue eyes wide with concern. "Was it poison, then?"

"Aye," I said. "At least, that is what Chiavari believes."

"Oh, he would know," she said in a matter-of-fact tone. The look she gave him was filled with pride. "Poisons are Dante's specialty."

"Aye, well . . ." What did one say to that boast? "We are all thankful for his expertise."

Avalene beamed at Chiavari, and I could have sworn he blushed. He then proceeded to give Avalene a summary of all that had happened since he left their chambers, and he had her mostly up-to-date when two of my soldiers entered the great hall. One of them carried a saddlebag that they brought to Gerhardt. Gerhardt looked inside one of the leather bags, closed the flap, and then walked toward us. He placed the bag on the table in front of Chiavari.

"There are sweetmeats inside," Gerhardt said. He began to tip the bag as if to empty the contents onto the table, but Chiavari reached over and snatched the bag from Gerhardt's grasp.

"Fool! Do not foul the table where my wife breaks her bread." Chiavari opened the bag and peered inside, and then leaned closer and took a deep breath. "This is the source of the poison. Tell your men to wash their hands if they handled the sweetmeats. They are in no danger of dying, but it could make them ill. I will accompany you to check his quarters to see what was found, and interview the English soldiers to see if they know where Sir Roland came by these sweetmeats."

Gerhardt left to relay the message to my soldiers. Chiavari turned and cradled Avalene's hand between his as if it were a treasure. "You will forgive me for calling you 'wife' before the church gives me that right?"

A small sound came out of Avalene that I assumed was a giggle. "I liked it."

The smile Chiavari gave Avalene was almost frightening in its intensity. He was like a man possessed. He did not like it when another man so much as looked at Avalene. Frankly, I was surprised that Chiavari had allowed Faulke to live after Faulke announced his intentions to wed Avalene. I also began to wonder if Faulke realized his life would have been drastically shortened if he had not renounced his claim. Now Chiavari was free to wed Avalene, and Faulke was free to wed his consolation prize. Lucky, lucky me.

"I must leave you to investigate this death," Chiavari said. He murmured something else in Italian that made her blush. I turned away from the happy couple and looked at my ladies. Gretchen and Hilda both smiled behind their hands when I rolled my eyes.

Avalene sighed again when Chiavari took his leave, and the light in her eyes dimmed a little when he disappeared into one of the hallways with Gerhardt a pace behind him.

"Do you truly mean all that you say to him?" I asked. It was a rude question, but I had discovered early in our friendship that I could ask much ruder questions and get answers. Avalene had never encountered royalty before she met me. Apparently she thought there was some rule that said my rank meant she had to answer any question I posed to her.

"I mean more than I can say with mere words," she murmured. "He is my life, my reason for being."

I shook my head. "I cannot imagine it."

She gave me an odd look. "Did you not come to love Prince Hartman?"

That, too, was a rude question, but I let it pass. Love played little role in the planning of noble marriages, but it sometimes developed over time. On my wedding day, I would have answered, *With all my heart.* Now I realized that much of what I had once felt for Hartman had been infatuation rather than love, a young girl's first foray into romance.

"I was just six years old when I arrived in Rheinbaden, and twelve when I wed," I said in a rare moment of candor. "Hartman was five years my senior. Before our marriage, I made a nuisance of myself to attract as much of his attention as possible. I did not care how much trouble

I caused, as long as he saw me, spoke to me, and some-how acknowledged my presence. In my eyes, Hartman was everything that was manly and heroic."

I did not add that in his eyes I was a bothersome child. A child blinded to her hero's many faults.

"I did not mean to pry," Avalene whispered, bringing me back to the present. "Forgive me, Princess."

I made an effort to smile. "I was happy in my mar-riage."

She gave me a doubtful look. Even I had to admit there was no real ring of truth to the claim. My happi-ness had been that of a child who thought someone fi-nally wanted her. No one had ever loved me the way Chiavari so obviously loved Avalene.

I made a great show of washing my hands in the bowl of lemon water placed next to me, hoping she would take the hint that I no longer wanted to talk about my marriage.

"Did you see Faulke Segrave and his cousin when they were here yesterday?" I asked. "By the time Mordecai departed, it was too late to seek your company. This is the first chance I've had to speak with you about my first meeting with the Segraves."

"Dante would not allow me anywhere near the Se-graves," she said. "I doubt his feelings on that subject will change until we are wed. Perhaps not even then."

"No, I suppose not," I murmured. A line of servants entered the great hall bearing trays and bowls that held our morning meal.

"What do you think of them?" she asked.

It took me a moment to realize she was talking about

the Segraves, rather than the servants. My stomach growled as the morning meal came closer. "Faulke was not what I expected from your descriptions. Actually, both men were caked with mud from head to toe, and their beards looked as if they had muddy bushes glued to their faces. They both smelled like a bog."

Avalene giggled, and then clapped a hand over her mouth. "Forgive me, Princess! I did not mean to imply that there is anything laughable about your betrothed."

No, there was nothing laughable about Faulke Segrave. I waved my hand to dismiss the matter. "What did they look like when you saw them last?"

"Hm." Avalene lifted her gaze and stroked her fingertips along her throat as she recalled her last encounter with the Segraves. "When I saw them, their beards were not so fearsome as you describe, but that was weeks ago. I suppose they could look very fierce by now. Did they frighten you?"

"Hardly." I gave a snort of laughter. It was amazing how convincing my lies could sound when I put my mind to the matter. "I have faced far worse than the Segraves, my dear."

Avalene lowered her gaze. Then I recalled that she had also faced a man I deemed a worse prospect than Faulke Segrave . . . and she fell in love with him. I was such a coward.

I cleared my throat. "Do *you* think Faulke murdered his wives?"

Her mouth became a straight line. "I can only relay the rumors, my lady. I cannot judge the truth of them."

"Everyone is entitled to their opinion," I said. "What is yours?"

"Truly, I am not certain." She met my gaze and I could tell her answer was sincere. Avalene's expressions were pretty much an open book into her emotions. Subterfuge was not her specialty. "Dante thinks at least one and probably more were murdered, that the odds of all three dying of natural causes are very slim. On the other hand, I heard that he went into true mourning for all three wives, and that his first marriage was a love match."

My eyes must have given away my surprise.

" 'Tis known to happen," she said with a smile. "Faulke and his first bride were only fifteen when they wed. Jeanne's father is the Earl of Wentworth, and he did not want Faulke as a son-in-law. Indeed, he had one of your cousins in mind, but Jeanne insisted on Faulke. She died giving birth less than a year after their marriage."

"Childbirth is a common enough cause of death," I said.

" 'Tis true." Avalene gave a nod of agreement. She waited while the servants placed meats, eggs, and porridge on the table, and then leaned closer and lowered her voice. "There were rumors that Faulke's father was already negotiating with the family of his second wife, Edith, within weeks of Jeanne's death. Edith was the only child of a wealthy merchant, and her dowry was said to be richer than Jeanne's."

"Edith is the one who died from a fall?"

"Aye. Rumors say she wanted to be a nun and threw

herself from a tower rather than continue to submit to her wifely duties in the bedchamber."

"Well, that does not speak well of my future husband's prowess in the marriage bed," I muttered.

Avalene turned away as she made some sort of choking sound.

"Well, it doesn't," I said defensively. "Women with considerate husbands do not toss themselves from towers."

"Some say she was pushed," Avalene countered.

"Oh. Well. That is different, I suppose." How, I wasn't quite sure. The man was either a brute in the bedchamber or a murderer. All things considered, I supposed any woman would prefer a brute. "What of his last wife?"

"Alice was her name." Avalene pressed her lips together and gave me her prim, disapproving look. "She gave birth to her first child five months after her wedding to Faulke, a girl named Lucy, although their wedding day was the first time she and Faulke had ever met. Everyone remarked how big and healthy Lucy looked for such a short pregnancy, and how the girl looked nothing like Faulke, or even like Alice, for that matter. Alice was pregnant with her second child when she died, and few thought Faulke was the father of that babe, either.

"Alice was said to have died of food poisoning," she went on, "a bad fish that made several people sick, but Alice was the only one who died. Some say Faulke worried that she would give birth to a son. He would be forced to accept the boy as his heir, even if the child was not his own."

My gaze went to the place near the fireplace where Sir

Roland's body had so recently rested. "Do you think Faulke had a hand in Sir Roland's death?"

"Dante says Sir Roland was poisoned over many days or perhaps even weeks. If that is true, I know for certain that Faulke was nowhere near London while Sir Roland was being poisoned." Avalene reached over and almost patted my hand before she thought better of the idea. Her hand hovered impotently in the air, then returned to her lap. "Do not worry. Dante will discover how this happened. 'Tis more likely Sir Roland had enemies that have nothing to do with you or his position in your household."

That sounded doubtful. But why would someone target Sir Roland to get to me? If they wanted to make me vulnerable, they should have targeted Gerhardt. There was also the fact that Faulke's father had been in London for weeks, even if Faulke had not.

"Faulke goes to your father's court quite often to negotiate with the king as well as with other nobles," Avalene said in a hesitant voice. "He and his cousin Richard are . . . very popular with the ladies at court."

Here, at last, was a trait that Faulke shared with my dead husband. However, I could not fathom the Segraves' popularity. Even my father had cautioned me that Segrave was unlikely to be faithful, that women often pursued him, and Faulke had little aversion to being caught.

English ladies must have very strange tastes in men, I decided. Avalene's choice was proof enough of that fact. Although, I had to admit there was something strangely . . . compelling about Faulke Segrave. "Why are you telling me this?"

"The rumors about his wife Edith," she said. "If she had an aversion to the marriage bed, I do not think Faulke was the problem. The tales of the two cousins' exploits at court are quite lurid. If I were you, I would not worry about Faulke's ability to consummate your marriage in an acceptable manner."

That had not been a worry until now. Well, not the ability part. The whole consummation part was indeed a worry, but Avalene didn't need to know the particulars. "So, you are saying that my future husband has a reputation as a court whore?"

Avalene's mouth dropped open. "Ah . . . That was not . . ." Her gaze darted around and then she loaded her trencher with a mountain of scrambled eggs. "Goodness, I am starved. We shouldn't let the eggs grow cold. Mmm."

I almost laughed at her transparent attempt to change the subject. Unfortunately for Avalene, I wanted to know everything about my future husband. The fewer surprises there were in my upcoming marriage, the fewer humiliations. However, as I pictured the man who had appeared before me yesterday, I could not imagine any woman at court who would welcome him into her bed. Englishwomen must like their men coarse. Some cynical part of me wondered if he bathed for them. "What do the rumors say of Faulke's prowess with the ladies?"

"Mmph." Avalene continued to chew as she pointed to her mouth and cheeks that had taken on the silhouette of a squirrel storing nuts. She gave an apologetic shrug and then pushed a serving bowl filled with scrambled eggs in my direction. "Mmm."

"Yes, I'm sure they're very good," I said as I ladled a serving of the eggs onto my trencher. Then I turned to Avalene and fixed her with a piercing stare. "But we still have the whole meal for you to tell me everything you know of Faulke Segrave's exploits with women."

CHAPTER THREE

The Garden

THE WEATHER COOPERATED, SO THAT AFTER-
noon I had a table and stools set up in the orchard just
outside my solar windows. There my ladies and I awaited
the promised visit from the Segraves. Warm sunshine fil-
tered through the leaves as they rustled in the breeze,
and the sweet scent of ripening apples perfumed the air.
The lilting strains of a song performed by two lute play-
ers and a piper provided soft music in the background.
When I closed my eyes, I could almost imagine I was still
in the gardens at Grunental.

I frowned when they began to play a song I knew well,
one about a knight's yearning for a beautiful maiden. I
kept my eyes closed and sighed. "Gretchen, I specifically
requested no love songs. Please remind them."

There was a rustle of skirts as Gretchen left to do my bidding.

" 'Tis a popular song," Hilda said. "I know they like to play it."

I opened my eyes and gave Hilda a look across the table. "I hardly want to listen to romantic drivel when I need to keep my thoughts focused on murder and marriage."

Hilda smiled but didn't look up from her embroidery hoop. Her silver needle flashed in the sunlight as it dipped into the fabric at a measured pace.

"That sounded worse than I intended." I sighed again, and then surveyed the table in front of me.

Inkwells, thick sheets of parchment, and an assortment of quills were scattered about its surface, including a page from my current illumination project. I was copying a book that I had borrowed from my father, including the illustrations.

"Lord Dante seems to have the murder business in hand," Hilda said, still concentrating on her needlework. "He seems quite determined to uncover the culprit."

" 'Tis hardly reassuring when the dead are multiplying, God rest their souls." I stared down at the manuscript page without really seeing it.

Chiavari had appeared an hour ago with news that Sir Roland's daughter was also dead, along with her husband and one of their sons, with more of the poisoned sweetmeats discovered at her home. Learning there were more victims was hardly good news, but Chiavari said one should look first at those closest to the victims to find guilt.

The daughter's husband was the head of the fletchers guild in London, and he was in a long-standing argument with his cousin over the guild's leadership. Chiavari thought it possible that guild politics had turned deadly, and Sir Roland had simply been in the wrong place at the wrong time. It seemed possible that Sir Roland's death had nothing at all to do with me or my court.

"Any warrior, even one as old as Sir Roland, would rail at the thought of being brought low by poison," Hilda said. " 'Tis a coward's weapon."

And that was another reason I distrusted Dante Chiavari.

"Aye, a real man should fight on a battlefield, not from an apothecary," I agreed. "However, Chiavari's expertise in this matter is proving valuable."

All we could do now was await more news about the investigation, as well as the promised visit from Faulke Segrave.

I was not good at waiting.

Gretchen took her seat next to Hilda on the opposite side of the table, and soon both women were bent over their hoops again.

Now would be a good time to bring up the subject that had been bothering me since my talk with Avalene at breakfast. I glanced around to mark the locations of our four guards and the musicians to make sure only my ladies were close enough to hear my words.

"There is something I would like to discuss with you both," I began. The women's hands stilled over their hoops and they gave me expectant looks. "It has to do with my upcoming marriage."

Gretchen's gaze turned wary. Hilda simply blinked.

Now that I had their attention, I wasn't quite certain what to do with it. Instead I tried to envision what the Segraves would see later today when they looked at my fair-haired ladies in their pink gowns.

Hilda's garments were drawn tight across her bust and hips, with the neckline strategically lowered and the sleeves raised. Gretchen's gown fell in such perfectly modest lines that the dress looked as if it could have been carved onto a statue.

Even if they dressed in sackcloth, my ladies would always attract male attention, each in their own way. Men looked at Gretchen and thought of a heartbroken Madonna, captivated by her untouchable aura. Men looked at Hilda and thought of lusty sex.

"I tolerated Hartman's women the entirety of our marriage," I said to them at last. I picked up a quill and pretended to test its point, acting as if I had just commented on something as trivial as the weather. "There are rumors that the Segraves have been intimate with many women in my father's court. You are both beautiful women. I will not tolerate betrayal from my own ladies."

Gretchen was the first to respond. "Princess, we would never dishonor you in such a fashion."

Gretchen pressed her lips together and gave Hilda an uncertain look.

"What?" Hilda looked between my accusing gaze and Gretchen's.

"You have a certain reputation," Gretchen murmured, in what had to be the understatement of the year.

Hilda was also a widow, but I doubted she had mourned her elderly husband's death for the time it took to bury him. She certainly hadn't waited until he died before she found herself one lover after another at the royal court in Rheinbaden, each man more powerful than the last, until she found herself the mistress of the king himself, an affair she took few pains to conceal, once her husband had died.

Unfortunately for Hilda, there was competition for her place at court. One of her rivals made certain the king happened upon Hilda in the gardens when she was in the most compromising position possible with one of her young lovers. Banishment to my remote court at the edge of the kingdom was her punishment.

"I am a respectable widow," Hilda insisted, "although I freely admit that I enjoy the company of men, unlike some of us I could mention."

Hilda stared at Gretchen while she spoke. Gretchen simply shrugged. "Unlike you, I still mourn my husband. Even if I were like you, I would never consider an affair with Lord Faulke. I am the princess's oldest friend, and I would never betray her that way."

There was a suspicious warmth in the vicinity of my heart. Gretchen and I had grown up together, reached every milestone of womanhood together, spent nearly every waking moment with each other. We were more sisters than friends, and, like some sisters, we'd had more than our share of disagreements over the years.

The first distancing of our friendship began when my

baby died. She could not fathom the depths of my grief, and she strongly disapproved of my increasing reluctance to do what was necessary to create a second child.

And then Gretchen was married. She still acted as my companion, but she spent every free moment with her beloved, Engel. His death two years later destroyed her. She did not just grieve; something inside her broke.

Engel was supposed to be the captain of my guard when I took up residence at Grunental Castle, but he had been killed by outlaws on his way back from a scouting mission. We had all hoped the change of scenery at Grunental Castle would shake Gretchen from her stupor. Gretchen's brother, Gerhardt, even volunteered to take Engel's place as the captain of my guard, but his presence had no more effect on her than I did. Weeks turned into months as she barely ate, rarely drank, and did not sleep.

Even though years had passed, the carefree girl was now a somber woman who never laughed, and whose rare smiles never quite reached her eyes. She was simply marking time, suffering through each day on Earth to get herself one step closer to her own death and the joyous reunion with her sainted Engel.

In the meantime, I wondered if this unexpected declaration of friendship meant she was finally beginning to open up and live again. It was the most emotion I had witnessed from her in weeks. Perhaps this move to England had been good for her after all.

"I appreciate your loyalty," I said to Gretchen, meaning every word. Then I turned to Hilda with an expectant look.

"Of course I would not betray you," Hilda said with a dismissive wave of her hand, as if the entire notion were ridiculous. "You took me in when every friend had abandoned me. I do not forget my friends, either, Princess."

"Well. Who knew I was so popular?" My gaze narrowed, but Hilda simply lifted her chin and stared back at me, silently daring me to question her loyalty.

"Faulke has a reputation at court as a womanizer," I said. "I will not tolerate his mistresses."

"My lady," Gretchen began in a hesitant tone. "Prince Hartman had a reputation with women that equaled or surpassed what I have heard of the Segraves. You made your wishes known to the prince and he ignored them."

"What makes you think Lord Faulke will be any easier to geld than Prince Hartman?" Hilda chimed in.

"I am not the foreign princess here," I reminded them, "and my betrothed is no prince. My power here is considerable. He will respect my wishes . . . once we discuss the situation and come to an agreement."

Hilda made a snorting sound that she quickly disguised as a cough. Gretchen shook her head and then looked down to pick at one of her stitches.

Now that I heard my grand plan aloud, it didn't sound so grand after all. It galled me to admit it, but I said, "I would welcome your advice on the matter."

Startled, both women looked up again, their stitches forgotten. Surprisingly, Gretchen was the first to speak. "Even if Lord Faulke would swear to be faithful, I fear his oath is bound to be broken. Women pursue powerful men. Most men eventually succumb to temptation. A man of rank and wealth is rarely faithful. To my knowledge, their wives' objections have little or no effect on their affairs."

Well, that wasn't helpful.

"She has a point," Hilda said. "If a wife objects to her husband's affairs, the wife becomes a shrew in his eyes. The most likely outcome is that he will seek solace in another woman's arms. After all, it's a mistress's job to take her lover's side in all arguments with his wife, or anyone else who upsets him."

"Are you suggesting that I never argue?" I sputtered. If a docile wife was the key to a faithful husband, I was doomed.

"Not at all, but you might want to choose battles you can win," Hilda said. "When a man is known to have carnal appetites, a wise wife is realistic as to how well she can control such a man's fidelity. Rather than forbid all affairs, perhaps you might ask him to forgo the company of certain types of women, or women in certain places. Prince Hartman could do as he pleased in Rheinbaden, but here your father is the king. Surely Lord Faulke would at least agree to be discreet?"

Hm. Both women had a point. Although the thought of Faulke with any other woman was surprisingly disturbing.

"Think about what will happen if Lord Faulke agrees to your edict," Gretchen said in a quiet voice. "Are you ready for the consequences, if you forbid him any bed but your own? He will seek out your company more often, if he has no other women to . . . to relieve his manly needs." She couldn't quite disguise a shudder.

"Although, one assumes the Segraves are not always so dirty and smelly as they were yesterday."

The image of mud-streaked sheets came to mind, and the recollection of the Segraves' smell made me shudder as well. A trickle of uncertainty wound through my chest. Perhaps I was being foolish and should say nothing to Faulke about his affairs.

I recalled an image of Maria von Tyrol at the royal court in Rheinbaden, smiling at me across the great hall while she rubbed her swollen belly, knowing she could taunt me without consequence. The one and only time I had complained about Maria, Hartman had used his fist to drive home the fact that I was not allowed to question him about his women. When Maria found out about my punishment, she and her friends made my life a misery. I went to Grunental Castle as soon as the opportunity presented itself, and never again returned to the royal court. Some might say I was forced from my rightful place, but after years of torment, I went willingly.

"I have no quarrel with a servant or peasant girl who might try to improve her lot or gain a few coins in exchange for a quick tumble with my husband," I said, striving hard to sound believable. Why did the thought of Faulke with another woman turn my stomach sour? My ladies were right: I had to be realistic. "What I will not tolerate is an affair with any female who would dare to consider herself equal or above me in any way."

Gretchen and Hilda exchanged a look that I recognized. Pity. They both knew about Maria, just as they knew that many at Rheinbaden's royal court had treated me as if I were the prince's mistress and Maria were his wife. My humiliation and their knowledge of it still had the power to make me angry. God, how I hated that woman.

"What do you intend to say to Lord Faulke?" Hilda asked in a hushed voice.

"Whatever seems appropriate at the time," I said with a shrug, hoping that would dismiss the matter. In truth, I had no idea how to even bring up the subject.

"The women at court will still seek him out," Gretchen warned, "especially when he becomes a wealthy earl."

My jaw hardened. "I doubt the English ladies will be very enthusiastic about his company after I ruin the reputations of one or two of them."

In Rheinbaden, I had been powerless. Here, there would be consequences for crossing me. I just hoped I wouldn't have to set an example within my own household. "If a *friend* betrays me, the consequences will be much worse."

Gretchen bit her lip, but Hilda gave an impatient huff. "You have our pledge that we will not betray you, Princess. I will not break my promise, and you know Gretchen will not break hers, either."

Well, now I just felt petty.

"I am not so foolish as to think I can keep a man faithful," I admitted. "But I will not tolerate another Maria in my household, or any woman who reminds me of her in any way. Will you support me in this?"

"Aye," they both murmured.

"Good. Then that is all we need to say on the matter." I picked up the manuscript page and barely resisted the urge to fling it across the orchard. Just the thought of Maria von Tyrol could reduce me to helpless fury.

My grip on the page tightened, and then I set it on the table with exaggerated calm. Avalene's tales that morning of Faulke's exploits with the ladies at court had resurrected all of the ugly emotions I had vowed to leave in Rheinbaden. Here I had wealth and influence, and, as Faulke had been so quick to point out, I outranked him. Here, I was not an ausländer.

If Faulke dared to humiliate me with his women once we were married, I would make certain he felt an equal measure of shame and regret. And I *would* make his mistresses pay a price, just as I had promised my ladies, but he would pay as well.

How to inform him of these particular quirks of mine was a worry. It had been hard enough to tell my ladies that I didn't want them sleeping with my husband. How would I tell my husband that he could not continue his affairs? That was bound to be a jolly conversation.

Today was too soon to have that talk with Faulke. However, it had to take place before the wedding. He would never agree to such a stipulation after the wedding night.

The thought of my wedding night produced another small shudder before I pushed that thought away. Far away. I was getting very good at ignoring the inevitable. Instead I picked up a quill and made another effort to concentrate on my drawing.

ILLUMINATION WAS A good distraction, as it turned out. I continued to colorize each paragraph's dropped initials that were already outlined in black ink, my mind absorbed with the task. The pages I transposed were part of a collection of fables originally written by an ancient Greek named Aesop. The current pages of the fable I worked upon told the tale of a wolf in sheep's clothing. The wily wolf figured predominantly in every illumination, his face peering out from the loop in a letter "P," his body twined around a letter "S," a drawing of him seated upon his haunches with his head thrown back in a howl, the silhouette forming the letter "A." I loved watching the colored inks bring my wolf to life.

I don't know why my wolf had blue eyes, but they looked rather familiar. I tilted my head to one side to study the eyes from a different angle. Fragments of last night's dream teased the edges of my memory. Perhaps I hadn't recalled the entire—

"Lord Faulke requests an audience, Princess."

Gerhardt's announcement startled me. I had been so absorbed in my work I hadn't even heard him approach. I looked up from my page and saw two men standing next to my captain. For a long moment I just stared at them, dumbfounded. My gaze went to the man nearest me.

Here was the original version of my wolf's eyes. But that was all I recognized. If not for his eyes, I would scarce believe this was the same person I had met just yesterday. This man was remarkably clean. And just plain remarkable.

I looked down at the forgotten fable page, and then looked up again. No. I hadn't imagined it. The handsomest man I had ever laid eyes upon still stood before me, with the second most handsome man at his side.

Of course, Faulke was the handsomest one. Aside from his eyes, I could tell it was him by the small scar that ran through his right eyebrow that I had noticed yesterday in my solar. He also had a heavier build than his cousin Richard. Without his armor, Richard looked almost lean next to Faulke, but I felt certain Richard would make any of my soldiers look lean if they stood next to *him*.

Without conscious effort, my gaze was drawn back to Faulke and I took a quick visual inventory. A sweep of dark hair covered his forehead, and masculine brows offset very blue, very predatory eyes. A short, neatly trimmed beard revealed a square jaw and sharp cheekbones that spoke of Normans in his ancestry. And the mouth was much more appealing without the frame of yesterday's muddy bush of hair. I made a pointed effort to avoid his gaze as I began to note the astonishing changes in him between yesterday and today.

As with most warriors, he wore his hair long so that it could be tied up for additional padding under his chain mail and helmet. Today it was loose and flowed to his shoulders in dark waves, not quite a true black, but very close. The true black could be found in his clothing, complete and unrelieved from his collar to his boots. A form-fitting black leather tunic covered him from shoulders to knees, split at the front and back for riding, and worked in a diamond pattern with silver studs at the corner of each point. Underneath the tunic he wore a long-sleeved shirt and close-fitted pants that were tucked into tall boots, all black, and all of the finest quality and craftsmanship. Even his weapons were encased in black leather and trimmed with silver. The body beneath all of that leather was broad and powerful, but yesterday I had recognized that both men had the builds of warriors.

Still, the effects a bit of grooming had wrought were amazing. Yesterday he was a dirty, scowling barbarian. Today he was a dark and devastating warlord. The cut and color of his clothing was almost an announcement: Here is a dangerous man. As I studied his face, I understood at last why Avalene had tried to warn me about Faulke Segrave's looks. The word "handsome" hardly did him justice. The man practically oozed virility.

A thousand butterflies took flight in my chest, and that strange sensation made me feel light-headed. Shock and horror, I decided. This turn of events was entirely unwelcome.

As I gaped at the magnificent specimen of manhood before me, his mouth curved into the smug expression a man wears when he knows a woman finds him attractive. I made myself look away and pretended to study Richard with equal intensity while I concentrated on gathering my scattered wits.

Richard stood a few paces behind Faulke, equally clean, and just as miraculously transformed, but he could not command my attention the way Faulke did. Women likely found Richard just as appealing, as Avalene had claimed. To me, Richard was a pale copy of his cousin and my gaze strayed again to Faulke. Why look upon the moon when I could stare into the sun?

Although it was no longer a mystery why so many women were willing to marry him, the longer he smirked at me, the easier it was to envision all of the horrible outcomes of this latest surprise. Yes, Faulke Segrave was handsome, but he knew it. Worse yet, he knew that *I* knew it. A plain woman who could not stop gawking at a handsome man was a recipe for disaster. I'd experienced more than my fair share of humiliations in Rheinbaden, and I needed no more.

I purposely cooled my expression and then spoke to him in a clipped tone. "Lord Faulke. I did not expect you this early."

The smug expression faded a little. "My apologies, Princess, if I have arrived at an inconvenient time."

"Your arrival is no more inconvenient now than it would be later," I assured him, "although I appreciate your efforts to make yourself presentable today. I wasn't entirely certain how you would arrive. I hope you don't mind that I arranged for us to meet in the fresh air."

His smirk disappeared. Behind him, Richard made a snorting sound. Without looking over his shoulder, Faulke smacked the back of his fist into Richard's gut and the snort ended in a grunt.

I glanced down at my forgotten wolf page and then handed it over to Gretchen so she could pack it away, although first I had to nudge her shoulder to get her attention. She and Hilda were staring at the Segraves as if they, too, could hardly believe the transformation. Judging by their expressions, they obviously approved. Thank God I had already talked to my ladies about pursuing or being pursued by this godlike creature. I wondered if they would have been so quick to make promises if they had seen this version of Faulke Segrave before they made their pledges.

When Gretchen realized I had noticed the direction of her interest, she lowered her gaze and looked contrite. However, Hilda wore her best "Look at me, aren't I pretty?" smile. That smile disappeared when I cleared my throat, and then she, too, lowered her gaze.

"May I ask what you are working on?" Faulke inquired.

I purposely kept an eye on Gretchen as she placed the page in my writing trunk. I needed a moment to compose myself before I could look at Faulke again and think sensibly. The butterflies had decided to sink from my chest and take up residence in my stomach, and I still felt a little woozy. The truth was slowly sinking in, along with something that felt almost like despair. I would never be able to keep a man who looked like Faulke Segrave faithful, regardless of what I did to his mistresses. All he had to do was smile and women would fall at his feet. My plan was almost laughable in its hopelessness.

"You do not have to tell me," he finally said, his tone stiff.

It took me a moment to recall his question. I turned toward him, and then gestured to a leather-bound volume that lay on the table. "I borrowed a book from my father's library so I could transcribe my own copy."

The storm over his brows cleared to make way for astonishment. "I have never heard of a woman undertaking such a task. Most women cannot even read." He frowned at the pots of ink that were still on the table. "Is there some reason you did not commission the work?"

The deep sound of his voice set the butterflies in my stomach to stirring. Was there any part of him that was *not* designed to make females sigh? Ironically, it seemed he was almost a male version of Hilda, whom I refused to look at. She had better be watching her hands, and not my future husband. I lost the fight and glanced at her. She was still staring at her hands.

Ach, what was wrong with me?

I took a deep breath and slowly released it. If he expected a cow-eyed maid, I was about to disappoint him.

"You have found me out," I said, turning again to Faulke. I widened my eyes and placed one hand over my chest. "I am one of those unnatural females who know how to read and write, and I actually enjoy both pursuits."

My words came out harsher than intended, but that was probably for the best. The people who knew me rarely appreciated my sarcastic stabs at humor, and strangers tended to think I was simply being rude. Faulke's startled look reminded me that we were still nearly strangers.

He started to say something, and then seemed to think better of the idea. Our gazes finally met and held. I refused to look away first, but soon found myself drawn in by the intensity of his eyes. They were such an unusual color of blue, piercing and intense. It was like looking into the depths of the ocean. The longer I stared at him, the more the garden faded away until all I could see clearly were his eyes and face, and I soon felt as if I were staring at him from the end of a long tunnel.

I don't know how long we gawked at each other, but eventually Faulke blinked several times, as if he, too, had been caught in that strange moment out of time, and that brought me to my senses as well. His gaze moved from my face to my shoulders, and then continued to move lower, an insolent inspection that should insult me. I could hardly object when I had just done the same thing to him.

A flutter of awareness went through me and I sat up straighter, wondering if anything about my appearance pleased him. I immediately despised myself for that bit of feminine conceit, and forced my shoulders to relax. I was not the type of woman a man like Faulke Segrave would find attractive. His opinion of my looks meant nothing.

"You would be an unusual royal if you did not know how to read and write," he said at last. "However, I have yet to meet anyone who would copy a manuscript when they have the wealth to commission the work. Most people would find the task too tedious and boring."

His tone was conciliatory, but I was determined to stop the creature inside of me that wanted to smile and simper at this man. "Well, now you have met someone who enjoys being tedious and boring."

He pressed his lips together again.

I felt a twinge of guilt, but tamped it down. Arguing made it easier to avoid the compulsion to stare at him.

By Avalene's accounts, which I now gave full credence, Faulke was rarely the instigator of his affairs at court. At the time, I thought all Englishwomen must suffer from Avalene's mad view of men, but now I understood exactly why they wanted him. As I looked upon this picture of male perfection, a knot of dread tightened inside me and threatened to spill the butterflies from my stomach onto the grass at my feet.

Faulke folded his arms across his chest and I stared at the broad lines of his shoulders. I might have sighed. Not in appreciation of the sight. Oh no. It was resignation. I would see pigs fly before I saw this man be faithful to any woman.

"You are obviously unhappy with our interruption to your day," Faulke said, his voice exactingly polite. "Perhaps we should return at a later time?"

I was tempted to agree. Something was definitely wrong with me. Although Hartman and Faulke looked nothing alike, what the two men had in common were faces that could turn a woman's mind to mush. I just needed to keep my wits about me until the shock of the Segraves' transformation wore off. The cow-eyed staring had to stop.

"My happiness is highly overrated these days," I said. I dipped the rag into a dish of lavender oil, and began to rub the oil into my fingers to remove the ink. The silence lengthened.

"Would you like to take a walk through the gardens?" Faulke asked abruptly.

I blinked once at the abrupt change of topic. "A walk?"

"Aye," he said, "just the two of us. It would be a chance to become better acquainted. Perhaps we could borrow one of the blankets your ladies are sitting upon?"

I looked toward the path that wound through the gardens. We were betrothed. There was nothing scandalous about the request. Perhaps a little time alone would help ease the tension between us. Or, just as likely, increase it tenfold. "Why do we need a blanket?"

"I left my cloak with my groom." He looked at me as if I should understand what that meant.

Baffled, I turned to Hilda and spoke to her in German. *"Lord Faulke wishes to borrow your blanket. We are going for a walk in the gardens."*

"Of course, Princess." Hilda stood up and began to fold the tan wool blanket that had been draped over her stool. Her delicate blond brows drew together. *"Is this some English custom, to walk with a blanket?"*

"Apparently," I said. *"Stay here and do your best to entertain his cousin Richard. Gerhardt will translate for you."*

Hilda and Gretchen exchanged a look.

"What?" I asked.

Gretchen set her needlework aside and then drew her braid over one shoulder. She made quite a production of retying the ribbon that held the plaits in place, an obvious ploy to avoid looking at me. *"He wants to be alone with you and he wants a blanket, perhaps to lie down upon. You are betrothed. Perhaps he has more in mind than just a walk?"*

"Or this could just be some strange English custom," Hilda chimed in, and then she also lowered her gaze. *"But I think Gretchen is right."*

The notion intrigued me. I could barely recall the last time Hartman had wanted to be alone with me for a romantic reason. Even though I could not give Hartman another child, no other man in Rheinbaden would dare seduce the future queen. It was treason. An affair with me was quite literally the kiss of death.

Not that I was particularly alluring to begin with, but the automatic death sentence meant that men did not look at me and think of sex. At least, not in Rheinbaden. But this was England, and I was no longer the future queen. My chaste existence would soon be at an end.

I glanced again at the impossibly handsome man who would become my husband. Lurid images were all too easy to summon in my imagination, but what did Faulke see when he looked at me?

"Is something wrong?" Faulke asked.

Now there was a question I would not answer. I took the blanket from Hilda and handed it to Faulke. "There is a path that winds through the maze to the herb beds. Shall we?"

CHAPTER FOUR

Smitten

GERHARDT STEPPED FORWARD IN AN OBVIOUS move to follow us. I spoke to him in French, for Faulke's benefit. "There is no need to accompany us, Sir Gerhardt. We will be within the gardens. I am certain you will hear me call out, in the unlikely event I need assistance."

Gerhardt frowned at Faulke, but then bowed his head. "As you wish, Princess."

I smoothed my skirts and then set off on the path that led to the herb gardens. My thin kid slippers were adequate for the grassy lawn beneath the trees, but they proved flimsy protection against the crushed shells that formed the garden paths. I stayed in the very center of the path where the shells were ground even finer by foot traffic. Faulke fell into step behind me.

The path wound through the fruit trees and then merged into the maze where thick hedges rose several feet above our heads. The maze was not all that large or challenging, but it gave the gardens the illusion of privacy. We were no longer within sight of my people, although I could still hear the musicians.

"This maze is remarkable," Faulke said. He gestured toward the towering walls of greenery, but his gaze remained fixed on me. He watched me in a measured way that made me aware of every stitch of clothing I wore. Everything felt too tight. "The palace is just as remarkable. Ashland rivals the size of Hawksforth, and yet it is in the midst of London."

"The four wings of the palace enclose the gardens," I said, relieved to talk about something impersonal. "I'm told the grounds encompass six acres."

"You are familiar with the architecture of palace?" he asked.

"Aye, Chiavari's steward gave me a tour when we first arrived." I kept my gaze on the path, finding it easier to ignore his ridiculous handsomeness if I did not look directly at its source. Unfortunately, I could do nothing about the sound of his voice, or the way it seemed to vibrate through my bones.

"Could we slow our pace?" he asked, a few moments later.

I glanced over my shoulder and realized I had forced him to walk a few steps behind me when the path narrowed. I slowed my steps and moved to one side so he could walk next to me again, and then spread my hands. "Is this better?"

"Aye." There was the shadow of a smile around his mouth. An answering warmth in my belly made me wish he was still behind me where I could not see his smiles. "Are you always so . . . intense?" he asked.

"What do you mean?"

"There is little purpose to a leisurely walk, other than to simply enjoy the journey," he answered. "You seem intent upon the destination."

I thought about what he said and realized he was right. "I suppose I *am* the sort of person who focuses on the destination rather than the journey. Everyone in Rheinbaden is industrious, on the whole. If someone is seated, it's often because the task they are performing requires a stool. If someone is walking, it's because they have somewhere to be. Leisurely pursuits are few and far between, even for the nobility. I had forgotten that the English are more indulgent of their idle time."

"That sounds suspiciously like an insult." His eyes crinkled a little at the corners, and I quickly glanced away before I could be swept up again in my strange fascination with his eyes. "And, if you will recall, you are English, too."

My insult was unintentional, but I felt an irrational urge to apologize. Instead I gave a small shrug. "My blood is English, but I have spent little time in this country. The customs of Rheinbaden are more familiar to me than those of England."

I winced when I stepped on the sharp edge of a shell and my weight shifted clumsily to my left foot. He reached out as if to steady me, then seemed to think better of the idea when I ignored his outstretched hand. I kept talking to distract him from my awkwardness.

"My sister, Joan, and I were both born in the Holy Lands," I said. "We were still babes when my parents learned that my grandfather had died and my father was king. My parents began their journey home to claim the throne as soon as they received the news, but my father was still recovering from an attempted assassination. An infidel had managed to get a poisoned knife into his arm at Acre."

"Every Englishman knows the story," he said with a nod.

"Oh."

I was still unaccustomed to people knowing so much about my family, when everything I knew came from tutors and my mother's letters. The woman who sent those letters had never seemed quite real in my mind, and yet I kept each letter and reread them countless times over the years.

"I did not mean to interrupt," Faulke said. "Please continue."

"His recovery and our journey home took almost two years," I went on. "When my parents eventually reached France, they left Joan and me with our grandmother in Ponthieu. By the time affairs at court had settled enough for Joan and I to journey to England, I was betrothed to Hartman."

"I thought you spent more time in England when you were a child," Faulke said, "although I must admit that I knew nothing about you until a day ago."

Aye, the lost child, the one my parents gave away and

forgot about until now. No one in England even remembered that I existed.

"I was six years old when I journeyed to England for the first time," I said. "I left England for Rheinbaden less than two months later."

He stared down at me without comment, his brows lifted, the look in his eyes expectant. I could almost hear him say, *continue.*

I had to draw upon well-exercised memories to even recall the brief weeks I had spent with my parents in England.

"King Rudolph sent representatives to my father to negotiate my betrothal to his son, Hartman," I went on. "The representatives would not sign the contracts until they were certain I was healthy and whole; thus, it was necessary to bring me to England from my grandmother's court in France. Once the papers were signed, my father and King Rudolph had already agreed that I should be raised at the Rheinbaden court. I was to be their queen. It only made sense that I learn the language and customs of the people I would someday rule."

That part of my marriage had actually worked out as planned. However, I was always an ausländer in their eyes, an interloper who would never be fully accepted as one of their own until I produced an heir. When that failed to happen . . . Well, those were the parts of my story that I would never willingly share with anyone in England.

"Of course, everything changed when Hartman died." I spread my hands to indicate our surroundings. "I arrived again in England a little more than a month ago, so in all, I have had just a few months' experience at being an Englishwoman in England."

He studied the path as he walked. The shells made a soft crunching sound under his boots, marking our progress. "Someday I would like to hear more about the years you spent in Rheinbaden."

I could wait a good long time for that day, but nodded as if I agreed. I pretended to watch the path as we walked, but stole sideways glances at him. His body was different than Hartman's, more muscular, broader, and several inches taller. Inappropriate questions started to drift through my head. What does that broad chest look like without a shirt? How many other women know the answer to that question?

Ach.

"You spent so little of your childhood with your parents," he said at last. "I suppose you barely know them."

"None of us were raised in their care," I said. "We were all fostered at young ages to relatives, or we were given to the families of our betrothed to be raised."

"My eldest daughter is nine years old," he said. "My father thinks it past time for her to be fostered, but I find it hard to send her away from Hawksforth at such a young age. I could not imagine sending any of my daughters halfway around the world at the age of six."

Under normal circumstances, I would not question anyone as to how they raised their children. However, it was only natural that I would be curious about Faulke Segrave's daughters. After all, I would soon be their stepmother. How much influence would he allow me to have over his children? "Do all of your daughters still live at Hawksforth?"

"Aye," he said, "but my father sent for them weeks ago, soon after he began negotiations for our betrothal. They arrived in London a few days before me."

I turned toward him before I even realized I had stopped walking. "They are in London?"

"The girls are at our townhouse near Black Friars," he said with a nod. "My father assumed you would want to meet them, once our betrothal became official. Indeed, if the circumstances of our betrothal were different, I would have made the same arrangements."

"They are in London right now?" I could not seem to get beyond that fact.

He nodded again. "Would you like to meet them?"

Yes! Maybe. No? I didn't know for certain. I had assumed the girls were in Wales and I would not meet them for many weeks or even months. Now he was telling me that they were across town, rather than across the country.

The churning in my stomach could be either excitement or terror, or likely a mix of both. I turned and started walking again. Faulke fell into step beside me.

"Tell me about them," I demanded, my thoughts spinning.

He remained silent for a time, and then all he said was, "Claire is nine years old, Jane is six, and Lucy is two."

"Avalene told me that much," I said with an annoyed glance in his direction. We were nearing the end of the maze and I could see a few of the herb beds ahead of us. "However, she knows little else about—ouch!"

The edge of an especially sharp shell cut into the arch of my foot just as I put most of my weight there. The thin kid leather wasn't meant to protect against this type of abuse. I scarcely drew a breath before Faulke had one arm around my waist. His other arm was suddenly in front of me where I braced my hands to steady myself.

"Are you hurt?" he asked.

Embarrassed, I shook my head. Before I could make any objection, he leaned down and then I was abruptly upended. I made a small noise that was as much surprise as protest, but by then he held me securely against his chest.

My first absurd thought was that no one had carried me in their arms since I was a child. The feeling was disorienting, an odd mixture of alarm and comfort. I relaxed a little when it became clear he could handle my weight with no obvious effort. He was so big that he actually made me feel small and dainty. Still, I thought myself immune to this unexpected chivalry until I drew a deep breath.

My second absurd thought was that he smelled wonderful, a mixture of cedar and leather, and some indefinable male scent that made me want to lean closer to him.

I stiffened my neck to resist my urges and looked over his shoulder as he set off toward the herb beds. A tan lump of wool lay on the path behind us. "You dropped the blanket."

"I will retrieve it later," he said. "Is there a bench nearby?"

"Aye." I pointed toward bushy spikes of greenery that were dotted with pale purple flowers. "By the herb gardens, between the rosemary and yarrow."

He carried me to the long stone bench, then he simply stood in front of it, me still in his arms, still feeling foolish.

"You can put me down now," I said, even though I would not object if I had to stay in his arms just a little longer. I had the oddest yearning to lay my head on his shoulder, to nuzzle into his neck. It required a disturbing effort to do neither of those things.

He looked back toward the path where the blanket lay while I admired his profile. "Your gown looks costly. I brought the blanket so you would not soil your skirts on a bench or the grass, if you decided to sit."

Ah, the mystery of the blanket, solved at last. His lack of romantic intentions suited me just fine. My resolve had been wavering, my senses bombarded by his heat and strength and delicious smell, but I could not become another of Faulke Segrave's conquests. Nor could I afford to wonder how he might go about the conquest. Ach! Stop!

"This is an old gown," I assured him, thinking it was past time to stand on my own two feet again. "And the bench looks fairly clean. In any event, I am perfectly able to stand."

"You cut your foot on the shells," he said. "You should not stand on it."

"I think it is just bruised," I admitted. "How did you know?"

He looked down at me and I found myself fascinated

again by his eyes. They shimmered like sapphires in the sunlight, the color so vibrant that I had to concentrate on what he said. "Ladies' slippers are notoriously thin. I am not certain why women even wear them."

"Mine are kid," I said defensively, already applying the worst possible speculations to his knowledge of women's footwear, "and I think it is just a bruise."

"Hm." He set me on my feet, but kept an arm around my waist until he was certain I could balance on my good foot. "Stay here. I will be right back."

He turned and jogged down the path to retrieve the blanket. A moment later he returned and then spread the blanket on the bench.

"Take a seat," he ordered. "Let me look at your foot."

"I am not injured," I insisted, even as my foot throbbed. "Truly, I am fine."

He gave me that look again, a silent, patient look that said he had no intention of doing or saying anything until he got his way. It could not be a good sign that the first trait I found familiar in him was one that annoyed me.

"Oh, very well. Look if you must." I released a little huff of breath as I sat down, and then I lifted my skirts to my ankles and stuck out my injured foot. "There is nothing wrong."

He stared at my foot for a long moment. "You are not wearing stockings."

"I do not like to wear them in the summertime."

He shook his head, and then knelt in front of me. I smothered a gasp when he took hold of my ankle. His big hands were gentle as he removed my slipper, incredibly gentle and incredibly . . . personal. My ladies helped me dress each morning, but there was quite a difference between my ladies' impersonal touches and Faulke's.

Oh, what a delicious difference.

I watched him examine the sole of my slipper, and then he returned his attention to my foot as his fingers stroked along the arch. His grip on my ankle tightened when I tried to jerk my foot away from him.

"Did I hurt you?" He rested one hand on top of my foot, his expression curious.

For some reason, I decided to admit the truth. "I am ticklish."

He looked up and a slow smile transformed his face.

That was all it took. One smile that focused all of that virile male attention on me, and everything logical in my brain melted.

Smitten, smitten, smitten.

That was the word that kept running through my mind, the easiest explanation for an emotion that instantly turned my muscles to warm butter. I wanted to lean toward him and return his smile. How easy it would be.

Instead I sat up straighter and tried to control my racing pulse. No matter how bone-melting his smile, I could not afford to let my guard down around this man. "Why are you smiling?"

"You are always so rigid and dignified," he said, still smiling. "I never imagined you would be ticklish."

"Aye, well, I cannot help it." I frowned at my foot, suspicious now that he was laughing at me. Dignified was an acceptable impression of me, I supposed, but rigid? "Have you finished?"

He gave a nod, and then carefully replaced my slipper. "You were right. Nothing is cut, but a bad bruise is already forming."

He took a seat next to me as I rearranged my skirts. I moved as far as I could toward the end of the bench to put space between us, but he simply moved closer. "Thank you for your care, even though it was unnecessary."

He gave a short bark of laughter. "That is the most insincere thanks I have ever received."

"I told you I was not injured," I said, "but I do appreciate your concern."

His hand was propped on the bench behind me, which made his arm constantly brush against my back and side. His thigh touched mine from hip to knee, but I was teetering so close to the end of the bench that I couldn't avoid the small touches. My body kept alternating between melting warmth and goose flesh. He wasn't even aware of what his nearness was doing to me. Words spilled forth without conscious thought. "'Tis nice to know you will show me the courtesies any lady would expect. I thought you would continue to hold me in the same low esteem you hold my father."

Now he did not look so amused. "Again, that sounds suspiciously like an insult. Two insults, actually."

"Then people must not often speak the truth around you." I pressed my lips together. Who was in charge of my mouth today? Why was I antagonizing him? He studied my face for what felt like an eternity. Now I felt guilty.

"Ach, forgive me," I murmured. "I was rude. My remarks were uncalled for in the face of your kindness."

"All true." That dangerous smile was back, warm, secretive, and yet somehow inviting.

More things began to melt inside me, and my thoughts began to slide away as I recalled what his touch had just felt like on my bare skin. And then I thought about what it had felt like when he carried me, what he had smelled like, what he had—

"Ah, you do know how to smile," he said. Humor colored his words, but his gaze was fixed upon my mouth. "You are too serious, Princess. Tell me, what do you find enjoyable in life?"

"Enjoyable?" I echoed as I made a point to change whatever moon-eyed expression he saw on my face into a scowl. What was wrong with me?

It suddenly occurred that he had been acting very odd since his arrival today. I stared at the scar above his right eyebrow while I tried to discern his true intentions behind all of the smiles and gallantry. "Why are you being so nice to me?"

He gave me a baffled look.

"Yesterday you made it clear that you wanted nothing to do with me or my family, and had only agreed to our marriage under duress. Today you arrive transformed in all ways, from your clothing to your character." I tried not to stare too long at the clothing or the character. "Surely you must admit that I have reason to question your conduct."

"No woman has ever accused me of being too nice," he said with a broad smile that gradually faded when it was not returned. "I must confess that I was not on my best behavior yesterday."

"I am relieved to hear it," I said under my breath.

"Our fathers have been negotiating this marriage for longer than I realized," he said, "and for more reasons than I was aware. It was unfortunate that our first meeting took place before I had a chance to meet privately with my father."

"What magical powers does your father possess to turn yesterday's churl into today's charmer?" Ach. I had said that aloud. I should have just been thankful that he no longer glowered and glared at me. Like he was doing right now.

"Yesterday I tried to envision every possible outcome of the day," he said. "Most scenarios ended with me either dead or imprisoned. Surely you can understand why my mood was not particularly pleasant."

"I was not responsible for anything that happened to you yesterday," I said with a sniff. Nor did I deserve to be blamed, I didn't add. No one cared how I felt about being married off to a stranger. Then again, yesterday Faulke *had* inquired about my feelings on the matter, albeit for selfish reasons.

"The betrothal caught me off guard." He looked away from me. Either he regretted how he had behaved, or there was something of great interest in the hedges. "I assumed you were part of the plot to end my betrothal to Avalene. It did not occur to me until after I left Ashland that you had no hand in yesterday's events." He fell silent again as his gaze moved over me in another one of those disturbingly personal inventories that traveled from my head to my slippers, and then back again. "Our first meeting was so far from ideal that I considered bringing you a gift today, and to beg your forgiveness for whatever insult I caused. And then I realized you already possess riches beyond my imagining, and there is no forgivable excuse for my behavior yesterday."

As apologies went, that wasn't much of one. And a gift did not appear to be forthcoming. "Believe me, you were not what I imagined, either, when I envisioned our first meeting."

He tilted his head to one side, another mannerism that was becoming familiar to me. "Have I managed to insult you again?"

I lifted my shoulders to show how little I cared about his insults, and then I found an interesting cloud to stare at. "Does it matter?"

"It does to me," he said. I watched the cloud drift slowly across the sky until it began to look like a duck. He released a deep sigh. "Where you are concerned, I seem to have a talent for saying the wrong thing."

A twinge of guilt twisted my gut. Despite my runaway imagination, he wasn't flirting with me or trying to seduce me; he was just being nice. And I was being purposely rude in return.

"These are trying times for us both," I admitted.

His lips curved into a wry smile. Ach, something traitorous went on inside me every time that man smiled. Butterflies. I decided I hated them.

Whatever he saw on my face made his smile fade. "How did the king convince you to marry me?"

"A daughter's duty is to obey her father," I answered, almost by habit.

"Yet you are no longer a child," he said, "and you do

not strike me as the meek and mild type. Surely you were given some incentive to marry so far below your station?"

I could not decide if he meant to prod my temper with these frequent reminders that he lacked a noble pedigree, or if he was really that insecure about the differences in our stations. Either way, I supposed it would do no harm to reveal a portion of the truth. "My father says our marriage will avert a war in Wales. He also promised to care for my people, should anything happen to me."

"Your father tends to make threats rather than promises," he said. "Could it be our king is clever enough to make one sound like the other?"

The truth did not require confirmation. My people were safe, only as long as I agreed to my father's plans for my marriage.

"I have answered your question," I reminded him, "but you have yet to answer mine. How did your father convince you to marry me?"

"Much the same as yours," he said. "My father made me realize that our marriage would benefit my people, as much as it would my family. Win or lose, many of our soldiers would die if a war were to break out, and the common folk always pay the highest price when nobles argue. I am not so unreasonable that I would put my people to the sword, if a tolerable alternative exists."

Was his change of heart truly so simplistic? I wondered. "You still haven't told me why you are being so nice."

His mouth flattened. "I would rather begin our marriage as friends instead of adversaries."

Something in my chest gave a painful twist. The death throes of a thousand butterflies, no doubt. He seemed wholly unaware of what his . . . friendliness was doing to me, and it wasn't his fault that I mistook his kindness for something else. He was only trying to make the best of a bad situation. I had plenty of practice in that arena.

"Yesterday you made clear your dislike of my family in general and your distaste of me in particular." I lifted my chin and pretended I didn't care about his opinions of me. "I would rather have honesty between us than a pretense of friendship."

"I do not find you distasteful," he retorted. "Surely you are aware of your beauty. Of your . . ." He shook his head, and made a frustrated gesture with his hand. "Distasteful is the last word I would use to describe you."

The beauty remark was probably incidental, something he told all women, but I couldn't gauge the truthfulness of the rest. Nor could I think of an appropriate response.

"I know few women who are so self-assured," he went on. "You are a queen in all but name. The idea that the king would favor me with such a gift was beyond my imagination. Yesterday I expected to be imprisoned or put to death. Instead . . . You were unexpected."

He waited for me to reply. I had no idea what to say.

"My family could still be ruined," he admitted. "The possibilities plague me, but my father feels certain the king will not interfere unduly in our marriage. That means we are both pawns. How we go forward together from here is the only decision left to us. I am not your enemy, Princess." He watched me very carefully. "Will you give me a chance to be your friend in truth?"

Was this some ploy to win me to his family's side of the political game we played? I didn't know what to think. Or what to say.

"Perhaps we should return to your ladies." The stiffness of his voice jarred me from my thoughts.

"My foot is still throbbing," I said as I flexed the arch of my foot to test the injury. I could probably walk, but I didn't want to risk him picking me up again and sending my senses into another nosedive. "Would you mind if I sat a bit longer?"

A shadow of disappointment crossed his face, but he bowed his head. "I am at your service, Princess."

He put a little more space between us on the bench, and placed his hands on his knees. The wistful look he gave the path that led back to the orchard gave me more to think about. Was he ready to leave because he regretted the things he'd said to me? Were they honest confessions, or all lies? I no longer trusted my ability to discern the truth.

The cynical part of me scoffed at my heart's gooey response to his false flattery. Another part of me longed to believe he found me attractive.

And that was the most astonishing development of this afternoon. A handsome man smiled at me, and my heart became as gullible as it had been when I was a child. I was old enough to know better. My unwelcome attraction to Faulke was ridiculous. His smiles meant nothing. Doubtless he tried to charm all women with that smile. *Smitten*. What foolishness.

"Have you talked to your people yet about our journey to Wales?" he asked, interrupting my tangled thoughts.

I shook my head, thankful for the change of subject. "Not yet."

"I would like to have my cousin Richard work with your steward and the captain of the English guard to make plans for the trip. I know you have relatives along the way who might offer provisions. Could you give your captain a list of those relatives so we can plan accordingly?"

"Aye." My annoyance with my reactions to him disappeared. "There will be a delay of some duration until my English captain is replaced. He died last night."

"The old knight who introduced us yesterday?" he asked. "He did look ill, now that I recall him."

"Sir Roland was poisoned," I said.

Faulke stared at me for a moment in silence, and then he was suddenly on his feet again, towering over me. "What did you say?"

"He was poisoned," I repeated. As I explained everything that had happened that morning, he began to pace back and forth in front of me, asking occasional questions. It never occurred to me that he would have this much interest in Sir Roland's death, although now I wondered what had made me think that way.

"Why did no one send me a message?" he demanded.

"I sent a missive to your townhouse this morning." I lifted my shoulders. "I thought you received it. Chiavari seems to have the situation under control."

"I am your betrothed," he informed me. "Anything that affects you now affects me. I will be informed in person of everything that happens at this palace until we are wed."

There were few people who could issue orders to me. Faulke was not one of them, at least, not yet. If he were not so upset by the news of Sir Roland's death, I would have pointed that fact out to him.

"I do not trust Chiavari as far as I can throw him," he went on. "I find it suspicious that your captain was poisoned in such close proximity to the realm's most notorious poisoner."

"I, ah, I thought that was an unusual coincidence myself," I admitted. "However, it now seems likely that Sir Roland's son-in-law received the poison and inadvertently gave a portion to Sir Roland."

"Perhaps," he allowed. "But what if the situation is reversed? What if Sir Roland encountered the poison here at Ashland, and gave the sweetmeats to his daughter's family? Perhaps Sir Roland found the poisoned sweetmeats before they could be delivered to their intended victim. You."

"Chiavari would not harm me," I said, even though I had asked myself the same questions. "His marriage depends upon my father's continued good graces, and there is some matter he must deal with in Italy that he is counting on my father to support as well."

"You said yourself that you barely know your parents. If you died now, I would be blamed and my life would be forfeit." He gave me a pointed look and spoke very slowly. "If Chiavari is loyal to your father, I have to wonder: Is your father loyal to *you*?"

I made an indignant noise. "My father would not order my death, if that is what you insinuate!"

As the initial surge of outrage faded, I began to question my certainty. My father had lived without me nearly all of my life. I would be gone again from his life within a matter of weeks, my wealth and lands bound in an expensive marriage to a man who played dangerous politics. If I died . . .

A cynical voice whispered in my head that I could actually be worth more to the king dead than I was alive.

"My death so soon after our betrothal would make no sense. The marcher barons would use it as an excuse to stir more trouble among the rebels." I folded my arms across my chest and pretended a confidence I did not feel. "If someone intended to murder me and make you look the culprit, they would wait until we are wed."

"I would be blamed," he said again. "No matter how or when you might die, how long would I live, if the king made certain everyone believed I had murdered his daughter?"

I lifted my chin so it would not quiver. "My father would not order my death."

"I want you to move into my townhouse," he said, as if I hadn't spoken. "I will send for more of our soldiers. Yours will have to do until they arrive."

I raised my brows. Did he truly think my retinue could be contained within a London townhouse? "I cannot leave Ashland Palace until we are married."

"You cannot stay," he insisted.

"Can you house three hundred people in your townhouse?"

He scowled and pressed his lips together in a straight line.

"Then I will move in here," he said at last, nodding as if to agree with himself. "A company of my soldiers as well."

"There is certainly enough room at Ashland for you and your soldiers," I said, "but I doubt Chiavari will allow it. This will remain his palace until he sails for Italy, and he does not want you anywhere near Avalene."

"Aye, you have the right of it," he said with a scowl. He looked thoughtful for a moment, and then I could almost see an idea occur to him. "Chiavari cannot object to an edict from the king. Either your father will agree to my request, or I will have questions about any objections he might make."

The idea of him interrogating my father almost made me smile. Would he really be so foolish? I wasn't certain how I felt about this new protective streak in him. "This is quite a change from how you felt about me a day ago. Yesterday I believe you would have rejoiced had I dropped dead of poison."

"I do not rejoice at anyone's death," he said in a stiff tone. "Yesterday you were a stranger, and I mistakenly thought you were involved in your father's plots. Regardless, you are now my betrothed. I have the legal right and responsibility to keep you safe from every threat, even if that threat comes from your own family."

He sounded as if he meant what he said. Yesterday we

were strangers. Today he was ready to slay dragons for me. No wonder women found him irresistible.

"Do you trust the captain of your Rheinbaden guard?"

"Gerhardt?" I asked. "Of course I trust him. He is sworn to me."

He lifted one dark brow. "Does that vow mean the same in Rheinbaden as it does in England?"

"My people are loyal." I left it at that for the time being. Eventually it would become obvious that most of my people were an assortment of misfits who had lost favor at other courts. Not that Gerhardt numbered among the misfits. He was Gretchen's brother, and my best knight.

"I should return you to your ladies," he said, breaking into my thoughts. "I need to request an audience with your father, and then make arrangements to move into the palace."

The thought of us living under the same roof made the butterflies in my stomach stir back to life. I pushed them down even as I stood up to test how much weight I could put on my foot. "I am ready."

He hesitated and looked as if he wanted to say something more, but in the end he raised his head and stared at the sky. Was he praying? The awkward silence stretched out until he gestured toward my leg. "Can you walk?"

" 'Tis fine," I lied. "I can walk."

He stood next to me and then took my hand and wrapped it around his arm. "Lean on me, if you need to."

I nodded and began to retrace our steps. We walked no more than a dozen steps before he swept me up into his arms again.

"Your foot is not fine," he said, and settled me more securely in his grip.

He was right. The bruise on my foot was worse than I had thought, so I did not object to being carried. However, I enjoyed it as much as I had feared. My heartbeat sped into its silent chant again: *smitten, smitten, smitten.* "Thank you for your assistance."

He looked down at me and a dark lock of hair fell across his forehead. I resisted the urge to push it back into place. Ach, I could get lost in this man's eyes. Instead I averted my gaze and kept my hands to myself. The chant in my head turned into *stupid, stupid, stupid.*

When we came into sight of my people, a small flurry of activity arose. My ladies clamored toward me, my guards stepped forward, and the musicians fell silent. However, I scarcely took note of them when I realized there were two new additions to the company: Mordecai and my father.

CHAPTER FIVE

The King

"WHAT IS HE DOING HERE?" FAULKE WHISPERED
as he lowered my feet to the ground.

His breath was hot against my ear and had a strange
effect on my body, similar to his smiles, but much more
intense, which I had thought impossible until now. I
managed to lift my shoulders in a shrug.

"Why is he carrying you?" Gretchen asked in German.

At the same time Gerhardt demanded, "Are you injured?"

"I am fine." I answered in French, so my father would
understand. "I stepped on a shell and bruised my foot.
'Tis nothing."

Indeed, my small injury was the least of my problems. This was the first time my father had visited me at
Ashland Palace. Sir Roland's death was the most likely

reason. At least, I hoped that was the reason. So far in my life, nothing particularly good had come from any meeting I'd had with my father. I wondered if today would be different.

"Greetings, Daughter," he finally murmured with a brief glance in my direction. He was looking at some of the pages I had worked on earlier, and I studied his bowed head, noting there were only a few threads of silver in his dark auburn hair.

I frowned at the sound of his voice. From the moment we had met upon my return to England, everything about my father had seemed somehow comforting and familiar, even the sound of his voice. The source of these feelings was a mystery. As far as I knew, we had never been familial, and he had never offered me comfort. I thought of King Edward as my liege lord much more often than I thought of him as my father. But something about being in his presence skewed those logical thoughts. He made me feel as if I were a child again, clamoring for a parent's affection.

"Your Highness," I murmured as I gathered my skirts and sank into a low curtsey. "To what do we owe the honor of your company?"

"I suspect you know the reason well enough," he said. At last he set the pages aside. He rose to greet me, and then stepped around the table as I moved forward. He took my shoulders in a fatherly grip and then kissed me on each cheek. His beard tickled my face a little, and I could smell the outdoors on him, trees and meadows, along with a touch of leather. "You look well this day, despite this morning's tragedy."

"I am sorry for the loss of your knight," I said.

"Sir Roland served me well for many years," he said. "He will be sorely missed."

He glanced at Faulke, and then held out his hand. Faulke stepped forward and went to one knee as he kissed the king's ring.

My father was several inches taller than me, but he had always seemed larger than life in my mind. When Faulke rose again, it was a surprise to realize that Faulke was the taller of the two men. The king was known far and wide as "Longshanks," a nickname that referred to his towering height. Now his build looked almost frail next to Faulke's. I had the surprising realization that my father was getting old.

Not that age made him less formidable. He was still the most powerful man in England.

Although I had been a dutiful daughter all my life, some strange instinct made me want to move closer to Faulke, as if he could somehow protect me from the king. What would happen, I wondered, if I repeated Faulke's barely veiled accusation that my father was somehow involved in Sir Roland's death?

It bothered me that Faulke's allegations bore any weight in my mind. He was a near stranger. My father was family. We were tied by blood. Blood ties in a family meant protection.

Faulke was not family, or in any way related to my family. He was to be my partner in a political marriage. He was dangerous, possibly a traitor. It appalled me that I instinctively wanted to turn to him instead of to my own blood. Had I truly learned nothing from my infatuation with Hartman? This infatuation with Segrave was bound to end just as badly.

"Be seated," Edward said as he took his own seat and returned his attention to my manuscript pages.

I took Gretchen's stool on the opposite side of the table from my father, and shifted my weight around as the wooden legs sank a little farther into the soft ground.

"I was on a boar hunt when I received word of Sir Roland's death," Edward said. He was dressed for the hunt in a forest green tunic, heavy boots, and leather leggings. I supposed I should be flattered that he had cut short his hunt to check on me. "Are there any new developments since Chiavari found Sir Roland's daughter and her family?"

"None that I have been made aware of," I said.

Edward nodded and stroked his beard with one hand, from his chin to the middle of his chest. There were only a few strands of silver in his hair, but his beard was almost the opposite, with only a few strands of dark hair among the silver threads. His gaze moved to Faulke. "What are your thoughts on this matter, Segrave?"

"I just learned of the murders," Faulke said. "If I had known what happened, I would have been here this morning. As it is, I am loath to leave my betrothed unattended where a murder was so easily accomplished. By your leave, my liege, I would move myself and a score of my soldiers into the palace to help ensure your daughter's safety."

A twinkle of humor came to my father's eyes. "There are already more than one hundred knights and soldiers here, sworn to keep her safe. Think you a score more will make a difference?"

"They will be *my* soldiers," Faulke said. "I will rest easier if I am at hand and aware of everything that happens in this place."

"Hm. I will think on the matter." Edward glanced at Mordecai, and then his gaze returned to Faulke. "I wondered what your reaction would be to the betrothal. Mordecai tells me that you were not entirely pleased with yesterday's turn of events. I said he must be mistaken. The hand of an English princess in marriage is a gift few men dare to dream will be theirs and even fewer receive." Edward's voice became measured and precise. "Is it possible you find something lacking in the terms of your marriage contracts, or do you find something lacking in my daughter?"

"There is nothing lacking in either, my liege," Faulke said without hesitation. He raked a hand through his hair, looking about as comfortable as a man about to kneel before an axe. "Yesterday we were brought here in chains, with no explanation of what was to happen. Chiavari is not known for his mercy. 'Tis no excuse, but I expected the worst and did not trust that the terms of my new betrothal could be so generous as they sounded. I had no opportunity to speak with my father to learn the full details of the marriage contracts until last evening."

"I expect that conversation was enlightening," Edward said, in a way that made me wonder exactly what was in those contracts. I had read the drafts, but was there something added to the final copies?

Faulke spread his hands before him. "Sire, I never expected to win the hand of a woman so far above my station. I hope you will forgive any perceived lack of enthusiasm on my part. I have already received forgiveness from the princess for my behavior yesterday. I hope you will be as generous in your pardon."

Faulke ended his little speech with a small, lingering bow.

"Is this true?" my father asked me. "Did he apologize to you?"

"He did, my lord." I wondered what would happen if I had said no. There was an undercurrent of animosity between the two men, a reminder that I was the interloper here, a new voice in an old argument. How ironic that I was still an ausländer, even here in England.

"My liege, may I have your permission to move myself and my men into the palace?" Faulke asked.

Edward looked annoyed by Faulke's persistence, but inclined his head. "I see no reason to deny your request."

"Chiavari will object," Faulke said. "He does not want me near Avalene de Forshay."

"Ah, of course." Edward made a dismissive gesture with his hand. "Tell him I have granted your request. He will not object."

"I also intend to participate in the investigation of Sir Roland's death, sire."

"Chiavari feels the brother-in-law is responsible," Edward said. "Do you think differently?"

"I think a murder so close to the princess cannot be examined too thoroughly," Faulke said.

Edward smiled, and it was not a pleasant smile. "You think you know more about this sort of death than Chiavari?"

My breath caught in my throat. According to Avalene, many thought the death of Faulke's last wife was the result of poison. Would he incriminate himself by admitting he knew the art of poisons?

Faulke shook his head. "Sir Roland's death is of less consequence to Chiavari. I will heed his council, but I have more at stake in the outcome of the investigation than he does."

"Indeed you do." Edward spread his hands. "It is settled then. You shall move into Ashland Palace and work with Chiavari to bring Sir Roland's murderer to justice. In the meantime, Isabel, I have selected a new captain of your English guard. Actually, your cousin Aleric of Almain recommended him to me, one of his former household knights who is now a captain in the royal guard. I am told Sir Crispin is keen to assume his new duties."

Aleric was a cousin of mine, once or twice removed. He had been granted the wardship of my estates while I was in Rheinbaden, and I had met with him soon after my return to England. By all accounts, including Aleric's annual reports that were sent to me in Rheinbaden, my estates had prospered during my long absence.

Aleric's father, Richard, had been considered a financial genius, and Aleric had inherited many of his skills. Having now met him myself, I judged his opinions trustworthy. I felt confident that anyone Aleric recommended would be as competent as Sir Roland.

"We shall make Sir Crispin welcome," I murmured.

"Excellent," Edward said. He stood and held out his hand. "Will you walk with me, Daughter?"

"Of course." I took my father's arm. The fabric of his

sleeve was soft and well worn, and I caught the scent of the woods again. "Where do you wish to walk, my lord?"

"To the gates," he said, and then he sent one of his guards ahead to fetch his horse. He glanced down at me. "Duties at court require my attention, but I would have a private word with you first."

We took the path that led to the front gates and I managed to walk without a noticeable limp, although it was painful. When we neared the last of the apple trees, Edward stopped and signaled to his men to continue on ahead of us. He looked me in the eye, a steady gaze I found fascinating, probably because it so closely resembled what I saw in my silvered mirror each morning.

"I would have your true impressions of Segrave," he said. "Do you find him acceptable?"

I'm sure the surprise showed on my face. "Acceptable?"

Was he giving me some sort of choice in this marriage? My mind raced. I scarcely knew Faulke well enough to know if he was "acceptable," but I knew him. Avalene had made sure of my education. There was something to be said for the devil you know. His looks were a mark against him, but I had to admit that it was not such a horrible mark.

As for an alternative to Segrave, I might feel occasional bouts of jealousy about my sister, Joan, and her comfortable life in England, but Joan's husband was even older than our father. I could do much worse than Faulke Segrave.

"He does not seem much like the man described to me by others," I said at last, trying to be honest. "I expected . . . well, I am not certain what I expected. From the little time I've spent with him, he doesn't strike me as the sort of man to stir political unrest or encourage a civil war."

"He has done both," my father assured me. "Trust me, that side of Segrave will reveal itself in time. He will try to win you over to his cause, of that I have little doubt. You must remember where your loyalties lie, Daughter."

"With you, of course," I murmured. It was the right answer, but one that did not feel quite right.

"You can manage the Segraves," he said. "Remind them that they are Englishmen, and they owe all they have to the crown. Encourage Faulke to visit your English estates. Maldon Castle offers a softer life than what he has known at Hawksforth. The less time he spends in Wales, the better."

"I will do what I can."

"You will do what you must," he corrected. He gave me an assessing look as he stroked his beard. "The Segraves are dangerous. Never forget that fact. I have done what I can to limit their powers and make certain they will cause you no harm, but a chained bear will still strike out when given the chance. They will be looking for weak links in their chains."

Did he think I would be a weak link? I squared my shoulders and lifted my chin.

"A king sees through many eyes and listens through many ears," he went on. "The captain of your guard will send me a report each month. I will expect word from you as well in those dispatches."

"I will be happy to add a few lines to your captain's reports," I said, as if I had a choice.

"Excellent, I knew I could count on you." He tilted his head as he looked down at me. "Do not look so somber, my child. I would spare you such a marriage, but your circumstances have tied my hands."

I tried to show no emotion as he delivered the bald truth. He was right. I could expect nothing better. Apparently, neither could Faulke.

"This is what is best for the realm," he went on. "Indeed, your marriage to Segrave could prove even more beneficial to England than your marriage to Rheinbaden."

"Faulke will be furious when he learns the truth," I murmured. "I do not relish thoughts of that day."

"You may do as you wish when that day comes," he said. "You outrank your husband, you have wealth of your own, and an army of soldiers to bar your husband from whichever of your many estates you choose to occupy. But until that day, you must be a wife in all ways so there is no question that the marriage is legitimate." He cleared his throat and looked uncomfortable. "Segrave has a certain reputation with the ladies at court. From all accounts, your marital life will not be unbearable."

Ach, did *everyone* know of Faulke's sexual exploits? I lifted my chin even higher. "I have given you no reason to think I will not do my duty."

"Perhaps not, but I see in you an understandable lack of enthusiasm," he said. "I cannot prevent the problems that will eventually arise in your marriage, but you have my word that you will be allowed to live separate from your husband, if the day comes that you find his company intolerable."

Or, if he found *me* intolerable, was the unspoken finish to that sentence. Still, this was a royal concession I had never dared hope to gain. I should be happy. Instead my sense of dread only deepened. Faulke Segrave did not strike me as the sort of man who would calmly step aside while his wife deserted him. Then again, he might be glad to be rid of me. Hartman had certainly been relieved.

It was hard to believe, but my second marriage was likely to end up much the same as my first. The irony of the situation almost made me want to laugh and cry at the same time. Instead, I pushed those emotions down deep to be brought out and examined later. "I appreciate your support, sire. I would not like to live with an abusive husband."

He frowned at me. "You are allowed to call me Father, you know."

I opened my mouth to reply and then closed it again. What was there to say? It was a name that barely applied. The time I had spent with my parents could be counted in hours. However, he held my future in his hands. It would be foolish to antagonize him. "Forgive me, Father. I intended no offense."

He gave me a thoughtful look. "You are probably unaware of the suffering your mother endured when we were forced to leave you girls with your grandmother."

Apparently my thoughts were more transparent than I intended. I tried harder to affect nonchalance.

"I was not made aware," I admitted, although now I was definitely curious.

He gave a deep sigh. "You should have stayed in England longer, learned more of our customs, and enjoyed more of your childhood before you became a bride."

"My life was not unpleasant," I said. "The people of Rheinbaden were kind to me."

For the most part, I silently amended. My life in Rheinbaden was in the past. It served no purpose to complain of it now. I was more interested in the startling revelations that my parents might have regretted how little affection they afforded me.

"We gave them one of our treasures," he said in a gruff voice. "Our hopes were that your marriage would become as strong as our own. Your child would have been our first grandchild. We were greatly dismayed to learn of his death. Your mother had a mass said for him each year on the anniversary of his death."

"I did not know," I murmured.

"Your mother was sentimental about such things." His expression was distant, as if he were remembering happier times. Then his eyes narrowed. "I fear this marriage will be no easier than your last, Isabel. 'Tis a burden of the royal blood you bear. For the sons and daughters of kings, there is always a political purpose to our unions. Yours is to avert a war and feed the ambitions of the Segraves. They will be so intoxicated with your estates in England that they will be forced to neglect their plots in Wales, at least for the next few years."

I gave him a skeptical look. "Do you truly believe an

earldom and my estates are sufficient motivation to make them step away from their interests in Wales?"

"Child, you have no concept of your wealth." He shook his head. "You might have fewer riches than if you were still the Crown Princess of Rheinbaden, but you were well compensated in your husband's will, and your estates in England have prospered in your absence. Aleric employed many good and steady men at Maldon to oversee your interests. Which reminds me. Aleric offered to bring his stewards to meet with you to review the accounts." He pursed his lips. " 'Twould be a good show of wifely duty if you also invited Faulke to that meeting. You might as well have him there from the start. Act the part of a dutiful wife, and he will take you into his confidence that much sooner. Give him the impression that you are sharing everything with him, and he will have less reason to suspect there are secrets between you."

There was nothing between Faulke and me *but* secrets. Some of his secrets would reveal themselves once we wed. How soon would he learn mine? Secrets and lies—I hated them.

My sigh sounded resigned even to my own ears. There would be no reprieve. I would be wed again. Soon. The little zip of lightning that went through me at the thought of Faulke as my husband was just nerves and dread.

"I must be away," my father said. He placed his hands on my shoulders and then leaned forward to press a kiss to my brow. His lips were warm and firm against my forehead, but his beard tickled my nose and I tried not to squirm away. "Chiavari will keep me informed about the investigation into Sir Roland's death, as will Sir Crispin, once he becomes established here."

He took a step back from me, and I had the strangest impulse to invite him to spend the afternoon with me. I tamped down the wistful urge. "Thank you for your advice, Father. I appreciate the time you took to visit with me today."

He waved off my gratitude as he walked toward his soldiers. Four were already mounted and waited near the gates. He held up one hand when I started to follow. "I can see myself out. Return now to your betrothed."

I gave him a low curtsey. "Farewell, Father."

The name was starting to sound more familiar on my tongue. It stirred an odd sense of nostalgia, a yearning for something I'd never had and never knew I missed.

My thoughts were in turmoil as I watched him mount up and ride away through the gates. My father's care and concern for me had sounded genuine. Then again, he was smart enough to coerce my loyalty with any weapon in his arsenal, including kindness and a fatherly embrace. How much could I really trust him? I muttered a silent curse at Faulke for making me question that trust.

When I turned to make my way back to my company, I stopped in my tracks and forgot all about curses.

Faulke was standing on the path at the end of the maze, obviously waiting for me.

CHAPTER SIX

The Magician

I STRUGGLED TO MAKE SENSE OF HIS PRESENCE, even as I drank in the sight of him. His dark hair and clothing created a pleasing contrast to the bright green foliage of the maze hedges that towered above him. Time seemed to slow, while all the colors of the garden grew more vibrant.

I would illuminate him this way, I thought as I took a moment to enjoy the picture he presented. He looked every inch the noble warlord. And then there was the perfection of his face, the intensity in his eyes. What I saw there made my heart flutter against my chest while some invisible force tried to draw me toward him.

Aye, he was handsome, but that was not what held my attention. There was something else about this man that made him different. Perhaps it was the way he looked at me, as if I were some puzzle he needed to solve. Perhaps it was simply the novelty of knowing we would soon be wed.

I couldn't say how long we stood and stared at each other. It was one of the oddest things that had ever happened to me, and yet these strange staring contests were becoming almost commonplace between us. My pulse slowed. Even my breathing slackened and a malaise settled over me like a warm blanket. I don't think I could have moved if my life depended upon it.

In the midst of all this strangeness, everything felt right. It felt right to look at him. It felt right to be near him. I took a step forward, knowing it would also feel right to touch him.

That step forward is what finally broke the spell. I shook my head to clear away the cobwebs and saw him mirror an almost identical move.

"You followed me?" I asked. I continued to walk toward him, as if it had been my idea all along rather than some strange compulsion.

"I did not eavesdrop," he said defensively. "I could tell your foot was hurting when you left. I thought you might want to lean upon my arm on the walk back."

So much for disguising my limp. I would wave him away and claim I was fine. "I would welcome your assistance."

Ach. Foolish, foolish girl. It was too late to take it back. I kept my gaze on his boots until he came to a stop before me, but then he did not offer his arm. I looked up to find him watching me, studying my face. He looked puzzled.

"Isabel?"

I lowered my gaze and refused to stare cow-eyed at him. Instead I gestured toward the path. "Shall we?"

"Wait." He gave me an uncomfortable look as he raked a hand through his hair. "There is one other question I wanted to ask while we are alone."

"Aye?"

He stared down at me, then made a frustrated noise. "I do not know what comes over me when I am in your company. Truly, I am not this ill at ease with most women."

Yes, I had heard that he was *greatly* at ease with most women. My nails bit into my palms. "Why is that, I wonder?"

"Aside from the fact that you are the king's daughter?" he asked, even as he shook his head.

Yes, I was a royal, but surely he had encountered noblewomen before me? I was no different from them; well, except for my awkwardness around him. *His* awkwardness left me baffled. This should be nothing new to him. He had a wealth of experience, not only with women, but with marriage to strangers. It should not hurt my feelings that he found me so strange that I made him uncomfortable. "What do you wish to ask me, Lord Faulke?"

Again he stared into my eyes so long I wondered if he was trying to read my thoughts. "Will you kiss me?"

I blinked once. "I beg your pardon?"

His mouth twisted into a humorless smile. "Most women do not find me quite so repulsive as you seem to, Princess. If your aversion to me is as strong as it seems . . ."

If he thought I found him repulsive, then I had disguised my emotions far better than I had imagined.

"'Repulsive' is a rather strong word."

"I suspect that is close enough to the emotions you feel in my company." He tilted his head to one side and frowned at me. "My second wife had no wish to wed, not me, not any man. If your feelings are similar, I will do whatever I can to end this betrothal rather than force another woman to the altar. I was told that you and your husband were estranged for many years before his death, but perhaps those reports were mistaken. Do you still mourn him? Or is it just me that you find unappealing?"

I wondered where he got his ideas. And then I wondered about his second marriage to Edith, the woman who wanted to be a nun rather than a wife. It must have been truly horrible, if he was willing to risk the king's wrath to avoid another like it.

"I realize that I am somewhat out of practice, but I seem to recall less arguing in the interludes that lead up to a kiss."

Now it was his turn to blink.

He studied my face, I studied his mouth. It really was a fine mouth. Before I could think better of the idea, I took a step forward, rested my hands on his arms, then leaned up to press my mouth to his.

He stood frozen in my embrace, his lips soft but unyielding. Either he hadn't actually wanted to kiss me, or he'd decided rather quickly that he disliked it.

How humiliating.

I'd had to rise up onto my tiptoes to reach his mouth. In an abrupt move, I settled back onto my heels and drew my hands away from his arms.

"There. I did as you asked—"

He reached out and brushed his thumb against my lower lip, his gaze intent on my mouth. "Do it again."

My cheeks caught fire. Did I do it wrong the first time? While I debated how to do it right, he seemed to grow tired of the delay. His hand went behind my neck to cup my head, and he urged me closer.

"Again," he ordered.

I complied. This time I felt his arms go around me the moment our lips touched, and he drew me closer until our fronts were pressed together and I rested intimately against his body. We both gasped a little at the contact. Being pressed against him was every bit as distracting as being picked up and held in his arms.

The hardness of his body was such a contrast to the softness of his lips that I had to concentrate to get the kiss right this time. Until his mouth opened. And then I lost my ability to concentrate on anything at all.

Kissing was not a foreign concept to me. I had done it often in the first years of my marriage.

Nothing I did with Hartman had prepared me for the intimacies Faulke introduced. The things he did with his tongue reminded me most vividly of the things a man did with his body to a woman in his bed, of the things this man would soon do to my body. No one had ever kissed me this way before. I should be shocked and disgusted by such a lewd invasion. Instead I felt a growing ache low in my belly and I pushed my hips closer to his.

I had always pulled away when Hartman kissed me in earnest. Our mouths never seemed to fit together the way they should. Now I realized that Hartman had been a terrible kisser, whereas Faulke was a master. Although

Faulke's kisses demanded all of my attention, they were not demanding. He lured me closer, made me crave more, and somehow communicated a lifetime of carnal information with his mouth. My arms wrapped around his neck so tightly that I was probably strangling him. I didn't care. Who knew kissing could be this pleasurable? I was greedy and wanted more.

My body shuddered against his and I let myself sink into the sensations, trying to enjoy myself as much as possible before the unpleasant parts would start. I tried to keep my breasts flattened against his chest so he could not easily grab at them, but perhaps my worries were unfounded. He seemed in no rush to hurry things along. His hands lingered on my back and hips as the kiss went on and on. Indeed, his hands kept moving up and down my sides, and then all the way to my legs until he caught one of my knees and lifted it higher. My core pressed against his hip and then I could feel the hard ridge of his sex between my legs. A sound came from his throat that was part groan, part growl. And then in an abrupt movement he pushed me away from him.

I was so astonished by the sudden end to the kisses that I backed up until I felt a stone bench against my legs, and then I half sat, half fell onto the seat. My breath came hard, sounding as if I had just run up a flight of stairs. I could feel my heartbeat in my ears.

What on earth had just happened?

I looked up at Faulke and found him staring back at me. This time there was no anger in his expression. He looked stunned.

That look could mean anything, I told myself. I didn't

know him well enough to judge. Just because he didn't smile and say, *That was the best kiss of my life,* didn't mean there was anything wrong with my kisses or with me. So I had more or less tried to climb inside his mouth. Surely his kisses had the same effect on other women?

He slowly wiped his mouth with the back of his hand.

Well. That was not a ringing endorsement. I felt my shoulders begin to slump until I purposely forced them to square off.

"I was certain you would cringe away from me." He reached toward me as if to test his presumption. When I remained where I was, his fingertips brushed the curve of my cheek and left a tingling flush of heat in their wake. "I thought you would never willingly touch me."

I hadn't imagined I would melt into a puddle simply because a man touched my cheek. I should laugh and make some jest that would dismiss what had just happened between us. He had been stunned because he did not think I would kiss him back, not because he found the experience life altering. Apparently that experience was mine alone. I cleared my throat. "Why would I cringe away from you? You do not frighten me."

"There are many men who cannot make the same claim." He laughed out loud, a deep, masculine sound. "Then again, I suspect you frighten more men than I do."

That was not a compliment, but I was still too astonished by his kisses to take offense. And actually, he did frighten me. More than he knew. If he could weaken my knees with a simple kiss, I could only imagine what would happen if he tried to seduce me in earnest.

Avalene's words echoed in my head: *He has seduced scores of ladies*. Now I had a taste of how it was done.

His smile faded. "Did I just insult you again?"

Aye, you did. "I rarely take offense at the truth."

I put my fingers to my cheek and traced the same path his fingers had taken. It had been almost five years since a man had kissed me, or touched me so intimately. How could I have forgotten so much?

No, I had forgotten nothing. Hartman had never touched me the way Faulke did. I looked down at his hands. They were nicely shaped, the fingers long and slender.

I wanted him to touch me again.

Ach. I needed to be away from him before I did something stupid. Or said something stupider.

"I suppose we should rejoin the others," I said, fixing my gaze on a spot just over his shoulder. I would not look into his eyes again. That way lay disaster.

My whole body tingled. I'd never felt anything like it. I envisioned an afternoon spent with a nice cool compress over my forehead. Just as soon as I could get the Segraves to leave. Surely they wouldn't stay much longer. I wondered what Richard was doing, if he had tried to speak to Gerhardt, or even to my ladies.

"Now?" he asked. Something dark passed through his eyes, gone so quickly I wondered if I had imagined it.

Somehow I managed to sound calm and logical. "My captain is not very talkative, my ladies know little French. They are probably all staring at each other in awkward silence. However, if Mordecai is still with them, he also speaks German. I would rather not speculate on anything he might have to say to anyone."

For a horrible moment, I thought Faulke was going to object, to insist we stay here and . . . Ach, I had no idea what we would do, but if it involved more kissing, I was in serious trouble. I stood up again and barely winced when I put weight on my injured foot. "Are you ready?"

WE WERE BOTH silent on the walk back to the orchard. I kept my gaze firmly on the path . . . except for the times I peeked at him from the corner of my eye.

Not that Faulke paid me any attention. He looked unsettled. Brooding. It was a good look on him, all dark and dangerous. So far today, every single thing made him more appealing to every one of my senses. And then I had fallen into his arms like one of his harlots.

Perhaps I could convince him to grow out his beard again and keep it covered in mud. Not that a bit of mud would ever erase my memory of what he actually looked like beneath it. Or disguise the deliciousness of his smile. Or temper what his voice sounded like when he whispered in my ear. Oh, I was in so much trouble.

Both of our steps slowed when we rounded a curve in the path and found that even more people had arrived. Three more people, to be precise. Two men who wore my father's colors and a lady.

Faulke leaned down and murmured in my ear, "If we keep going for strolls around the gardens, perhaps some of these people will begin to leave us."

The casual remark deserved some sort of pithy response, which might have been possible if his voice hadn't melted most of the bones in my body. I tried a polite smile that disappeared the moment our eyes met. Just like that, we had another one of those disturbing staring contests. It was ridiculous, how easily it happened. The gardens disappeared, our audience ceased to exist, and I could almost feel myself being drawn toward him.

All of it felt familiar. *He* felt familiar. We were barely acquainted, yet I felt as if he was a friend from long ago that I had just rediscovered. We were connected somehow, communicating in a silent exchange on a level I had never experienced before, and had no idea how to interpret. It was unnerving.

I tried to remind myself that everyone could communicate without speaking. A smile or a frown, those were easy enough to interpret. Many times I didn't have to say a word and my ladies could judge my mood. However, this was something entirely different from gauging an emotion. We were exchanging . . . something. Knowledge of some sort. I just wasn't certain what kind of knowledge.

Or maybe it was all in my head.

"Princess?" Gerhardt's voice came from far away.

I watched Faulke do another slow blink at the sound of my name. As easily as it had started, the spell was broken. Everyone had certainly noticed our odd behavior, and yet I was just as certain that no one would remark upon it. Well, with the possible exception of Mordecai, but he had taken my seat at the table and seemed absorbed with the task of leafing through my drawings.

My smile turned brittle as I spoke to Gerhardt in French, just to be polite. "How popular we are today. You must introduce our newest visitors."

The newcomers hastily lowered their gazes when I turned my attention to them. The two men wore spurs, which marked them as knights, and the chests of their bloodred tunics bore the king's device: three golden lions. That would make them my father's knights. The woman stood between the two men. She had brown hair plaited in a simple braid and her face was angular with pale blue-gray eyes, a wide mouth, and lips so red they must have been helped by a rouge pot. Her sky-blue gown was sewn from rich samite, and it emphasized the strange color of her eyes.

Even as I wondered who these people might be, the men bowed and the woman curtseyed as Gerhardt began their introductions. Gerhardt gestured toward the older man first.

"Sir Crispin de Pomeroy, and his wife, Lady Blanche," Gerhardt said, his French precise and efficient. He nodded toward the younger man. "Sir Walter de Gardanne. He is Lady Blanche's brother, and Sir Crispin's second in command. His Highness, King Edward, has appointed Sir Crispin to be the new captain of your English guard."

So, Sir Roland's replacement had already arrived. Gerhardt went on to make my formal introduction to the trio, along with my usual list of titles. They looked suitably impressed. All three kept glancing over my shoulder, and I swore I could feel Faulke's presence behind me, an almost palpable awareness that said he stood a step behind my right shoulder. I kept a close eye on the new arrivals when Gerhardt introduced Faulke, and included his title as my betrothed. None of them looked surprised. Apparently word spread fast at my father's court.

Sir Crispin stepped forward and sank to one knee before me. "I am yours to command, Your Royal Highness."

Not so high these days, I thought. "My crown belonged to my husband, Sir Crispin, and now to his brother. With my husband's death, I am once again a mere princess. Rise, sir."

He arose easily from his knee, a feat Sir Roland had struggled with even when he was in the best of health. Sir Crispin's brown hair bore touches of gray at his temples, and there were a few lines around his hazel-colored eyes, but he was decades younger than his predecessor and looked in his prime. He was not what I expected. The unexpected always makes me uneasy.

Grizzled old Sir Roland had been the ideal captain of my English guard, a veteran of countless campaigns. He knew how to fight, but more important, he knew how to train soldiers and manage troublesome men. Better yet, he was well past his glory days and had been ready to settle into the monotony that goes with an assignment to my guard. Sir Crispin, on the other hand, was no aged soldier in search of a soft bed. He looked to be a knight in his prime, as did his second, the much younger Sir Walter. What paths had led them to my doorstep?

"Tell me your story, Sir Crispin. Who are your people, and what brings you to my service?"

If he was upset by my bluntness, he disguised it.

"I am from Almain," he said. "My older brother, John, commands Lord Aleric's garrisons, and I was John's second for many years. The earl recommended my service to your father, and I had hoped to be considered for this very post when you arrived in England. Instead I received command of a garrison at Windsor Castle, while Sir Roland gained the position at your court."

I remained silent and kept my expression neutral. Silence often bought more answers than direct questions, and Sir Crispin soon fell prey to the tactic.

"I captained the garrisons at Almain only in my brother's absence," he went on, "but I have already proved my skills as a commander in the months I have been at Windsor Castle. I happened to be present at the hunt with your father and Lord Aleric when we learned of Sir Roland's untimely passing. Lord Aleric was kind enough to remind your father that I would welcome the post, and I was honored to accept the appointment."

I supposed a post in my household was preferable to one at Windsor, and worth the effort to obtain it. My father preferred to retreat to Leeds when he was not traveling, or stay at the Tower when he was in London. There was even less opportunity for an ambitious knight in an all but abandoned royal residence than there was in my retinue. I was a step up in Sir Crispin's life, but not a very high step.

"Will you return to Windsor before you begin your duties here?" I asked.

He shook his head. "The three of us were in London with my brother to attend the king's latest hunt with Lord Aleric. My servants are already on their way to

Windsor to gather our belongings and bring them to Ashland. I am ready to assume my duties here, as the king commands."

"My father tells me that Lord Aleric is fond of tourneys and hunts at Almain," I said, "as well as the occasional armed argument with his neighbors. I fear you will find your duties here rather dull by comparison."

"London is rarely a dull place," Crispin murmured. "Nor is Wales."

Faulke made a noise behind me that sounded suspiciously like a snort.

Crispin's gaze slid to Faulke in response to the sound, and a look of pure contempt washed over his face, then just as quickly disappeared. My instincts went on alert.

"Are you familiar with my betrothed, Sir Crispin?"

"We have not met," Crispin admitted, "but I know of him."

He looked over my shoulder and gave a curt nod in Faulke's direction. I would wager any amount of money that what Sir Crispin knew about the Segraves was not positive.

Although they stood behind me where I could not see them, I could almost feel the tension rise in Faulke and Richard. I suspected Crispin would tell me anything and everything he knew, if I gave him leave to speak freely after Faulke left the palace. And that spoke volumes about Sir Crispin's character. If my instincts proved correct, Sir Crispin and I were not destined to be friends.

I turned my attention to the wife and brother-in-law. "What should I know of you and your handsome brother, Lady Blanche?"

The handsome brother stood a little straighter. His sister treated me to a serene smile and spoke for them both. "We are at your service as well, Princess. My brother and I came to Almain when Lord Aleric wed our cousin Lady Francis, now your cousin by marriage. Sir Crispin and I met at Almain and wed a year later. When my husband announced his plan to join the king's service, my brother decided to accompany us. We look forward to joining your household, Princess."

"You are welcome to join my ladies in the afternoons, Lady Blanche." I swept my hand toward Gretchen and Hilda. "We gather in the solar to sew, or here in the gardens when the weather permits."

"You honor me," Blanche murmured, bowing her head.

I suspected Lady Blanche's company could prove interesting. She would have news of Almain and Windsor, if nothing else. I nodded, and then turned to Gerhardt. "I am certain our new captain and his family are anxious to see their quarters."

"I will take you to Sir Bernard," Gerhardt said to Crispin. "He is one of Sir Roland's knights, now yours. He will show you to your quarters."

"Excellent." I clasped my hands together and pretended enthusiasm. "Sir Bernard will see you settled. I look forward to your company at the evening meal."

Sir Crispin looked confused, likely wondering how he had been dismissed without actually being dismissed. The men bowed and Lady Blanche gave me a low curtsey, and then the trio followed Gerhardt from the gardens.

I glanced over my shoulder and met Faulke's gaze, but for only an instant. There was a silly sense of relief that he was not watching Blanche's retreat. Indeed, he looked at me so intently that I doubted he'd even noticed the other woman's departure. A tendril of warmth began to unfurl in my stomach.

I hastily lowered my gaze. The staring contests we'd had were bad enough. If simply touching him set my thoughts to wandering, what sort of blathering idiot would I turn into if we looked into each other's eyes again?

"I must return to my townhouse and prepare for my move to Ashland," he said. "We will be forty in all, twenty of my soldiers, eight knights, four squires, my three daughters, their three servants, Richard and myself. I trust your steward or Chiavari's steward will prepare quarters for our arrival tomorrow."

I tried to think of an appropriate response to that astonishing list. Before I could make any reply, he lifted my hand for a perfunctory kiss. "Good day to you, Princess."

CHAPTER SEVEN

The Wedding

Dante and Avalene were married the next morning.

Apparently the idea of Faulke Segrave living under the same roof as Avalene was all the incentive Chiavari needed to spur him into action. He and Avalene were already betrothed. The king provided a written request to the church to dispense with the reading of the banns. All they needed was a priest's blessing to finalize their marriage. Chiavari found a bishop.

From the looks exchanged between the two men, and the obvious fear on the holy man's face, Chiavari knew something interesting about the bishop. That, or he'd threatened some dire consequence if the bishop refused to perform the ceremony. Either way, Chiavari got his wish and the two were wed in a small ceremony in Ashland's chapel with less than a score of witnesses present, which included Avalene's father.

I intended to enjoy all the delights of the feast I had purchased, particularly a washtub-sized boat made entirely of sugar that held hundreds of prettily colored almond comfits.

Faulke had sent word this morning that he and his men would not arrive at Ashland until late afternoon, and his daughters would not take up residence until he had time to see to their quarters personally. That meant there were still a few hours before I had to face him again, and a few days to think through my first meeting with his daughters.

In the meantime, everyone at the feast looked cheerful. The hall was bedecked with sweet-smelling flowers and garlands, the rushes were sprinkled with fresh herbs, and my musicians filled the hall with lively songs. Avalene sat next to me with Dante to her left, then his knights, Oliver and Armand, to his left. Avalene's father, Baron Weston, sat to my right, then Gerhardt, and finally Sir Crispin.

I had toyed with the idea of allowing Lady Blanche a seat next to her husband, but decided against it in the end. There would be other occasions when she would be seated above the salt. Her rank hardly justified special seating at this affair, so I had placed Lady Blanche and her brother after Gretchen and Hilda at the next lower table.

Lady Blanche's expression as she watched her husband converse with Gerhardt looked sour with envy. Just then she caught me looking her way, and suddenly she was all sweet smiles.

I needed to keep an eye on that one.

A sudden screech drew my attention to a buxom serving wench who held an enormous pitcher of ale. As I watched, a dwarf jester poked her backside with his mock scepter, which resulted in another screech. The bells on the jester's hat and shoes chimed merrily as he danced around her in his rolling gait. In solid colors, his clothing would have been considered finely made, but everything he wore was deliberately sewn into a riotous motley pattern. His hat was a mock crown, stuffed with wool to make the points stand upright. Without the hat, I don't think the top of his head would have reached much past the serving woman's waist.

"How did you convince Muckle Muck to entertain at this feast?" Baron Weston asked from my right. "He is quite famous throughout Wales."

I had to think a moment to connect the name with the dwarf. "Reginald found him. Ashland's steward," I clarified. "Apparently Muck's former master passed away, and the new lord turned him out. He is in London seeking a new post, or so I am told. Reginald tells me we were quite fortunate to get him on such short notice."

"His former master was Robert Wrockwardine," Weston confirmed as he leaned a little closer. "Wrockwardine was a friend of mine, a Welsh marcher lord long loyal to the English crown. I have heard that the heir is not as fond of Muckle Muck as his father had been. If you have no objections, I would like to offer Muck a place in my household before I leave the feast."

"You have my permission, of course." I looked back toward the scene of Muck's foolery.

The wench with the empty pitcher was now seated on the lap of a doused soldier, her head thrown back in a hearty laugh while the soldier's hand casually crept beneath her arm to cup one of her breasts. There was a moment in every feast when a celebration could shift from merry yet respectful to downright ribald. I had a feeling we were at that threshold.

Chiavari seemed to have the same thought. He stood and made a short speech thanking me for their feast before sweeping Avalene into his arms and taking their leave, amid cheers from the drunken soldiers.

I turned my attention back to Avalene's father, who nodded toward the door that Chiavari and Avalene had just passed through.

"Your first wife was Welsh, was she not?" I asked him.

"Aye, she was a cousin to Llewellyn, the last Prince of Wales." He gave me a frank look. "Surely you are aware that her lineage is the reason Faulke Segrave wanted Avalene for his bride?"

"Oh, most definitely," I said. "I am curious why you would sign a betrothal agreement with Faulke, when you must have known my father would never agree to the match. Tell me, how did Faulke convince you of his suit?"

Weston had little liking for the blunt question, that much was clear. Anything he said to me could be easily repeated to my father, or to Faulke. He studied his hands for a time in silence. "The Segraves' allies surround me," he said at last. "My lands are rich, and my neighbors would need little convincing to join a siege, if the Segraves imagined some slight on my part."

"Ah, covetous neighbors," I said in a sympathetic tone. "I am familiar with such a plague."

"The king could not intervene in an argument among so many of his barons," Weston went on. "Not without the risk of turning his vassals' swords toward the crown. There is also the fact that the king's army is well occupied in the north these days with the Scottish situation. My castles would eventually fall, and my neighbors would absorb my lands into their own."

"So a marriage meant Faulke would stand with you against the other marcher lords?" I asked.

Weston frowned. "My neighbors would not have turned upon me in the first place, unless they were already aligned with the Segraves' cause. All they lacked was an excuse."

"The Segraves' cause?" I echoed.

He picked up his goblet and scowled at the empty cup. I signaled to one of the pages, and the boy hurried forward with a pitcher to refill the goblet. It was a delaying tactic, but I was patient. Weston took a long drink of wine before he continued.

"Your father should be the one to tell you these things," he said. "The king, or one of his advisers. And your betrothed, of course."

My father had spoken in generalities about the Segraves, and I could not imagine Faulke sitting down with me for any sort of lengthy discussion about treason. So far, Avalene had proved the most valuable source of information. Surely her father would have even more insight.

"My father's time is precious," I argued, "and I feel certain he would consider you an expert in the matter of Welsh politics. Will *you* act as my adviser, Baron Weston?"

Weston used his dagger to prod at the contents of his trencher. A few pheasant bones remained that he had already picked clean. The longer he poked at the greasy mess, the more obvious it became that this was another delaying tactic to decide what, if anything, to tell me.

Finally, he leaned toward me and spoke in a low voice. "I do not know the knight next to me, but I am familiar with the new captain of your guard. This is not the place to discuss such matters."

So, Baron Weston had something of interest to tell me. I wasn't about to let this opportunity pass. I leaned forward and caught Gerhardt's attention, and then spoke to him in German. *"Baron Weston would like a private word with me. Perhaps you could make a round to ensure our people are well fed and their cups full. My new English captain should do the same."*

"As you wish," Gerhardt said with a slight bow of his head. He passed the message along to Sir Crispin.

Soon Baron Weston, my ladies, and I were the only ones left at the head table.

I gave him an expectant look. "Do not worry, my ladies speak only a few words of French."

Weston nodded, and then looked over his shoulder as if someone might be behind us. He leaned closer and spoke in a low voice. "Muck was the fool at Cherleton for years until Lord Robert died, and I knew both men well. There are rumors that his son Landon intends to throw in his lot with the Segraves. Indeed, I heard gossip that Landon had sent Muck to London to find his way into one of the courts loyal to the king where he could act as a spy. That is why I found it interesting that Muck found himself in your hire, with a petition to join your household."

"You think Muck is here to spy upon me?"

"You are new to England and will want to fill your court with more Englishmen, now that you have returned home," he went on. " 'Tis the perfect opportunity for both your father's enemies and Faulke's to plant spies in your midst. I suspect your gates will soon flood with distant relatives, soldiers, servants, and entertainers of all sorts who hope for a place in your court. There will be spies among their numbers, and Muck is unlikely to be the first."

"I appreciate the information, and I will refuse Muck's petition to my household, if you want him." I wondered how many of my English servants and soldiers were already spying upon me. I would speak with Gerhardt, tell him to be on his guard and to watch for anyone suspicious. Spies were a way of life for me, but I did not intend to make their jobs easy. Stupid spies could be molded to fit my own purposes. Clever spies were dangerous.

When it came to political machinations in England, I was woefully ignorant of everyone and everything. It had been almost refreshing to be free of the political gamesmanship that had dominated my life in Rheinbaden. Now I realized that I had been living an illusion. Politics had been at work all along, and I had best reawaken to that fact.

Weston's loyalty to my father would color his opinions, but he had information I needed. "Tell me more about these marcher lords."

AN HOUR LATER, I had a much better understanding of the political climate in the marches.

According to Weston, two marcher lords were definitely aligned with the Segraves, and five were of questionable allegiance if war broke out. Landon Wrockwardine was now a sixth questionable lord, a man likely to back whomever he thought would emerge the victor. Interestingly enough, my cousin Aleric was among the questionable numbers. I found that extremely interesting, given that he was one of my father's favorites, as well as the fact that one of his men was now the captain of my English guard.

I would not put it beyond Aleric to place a spy in my court, but murder was a bit extreme to accomplish it, even for my family. So far, I had nothing more than Weston's word that my cousin Aleric might be doing . . . something. Indeed, I had no idea what grudges Weston might hold against Landon Wrockwardine or Aleric of Almain that might have colored his opinions. The implied accusations might warrant a message to my father, but now I knew to be careful of any messages I sent through Sir Crispin.

Weston took his leave of the feast, and I asked Sir

Crispin to escort the baron and his men to the gates. That gave me a chance to invite Gerhardt to the head table for a quiet conversation with him and my ladies about Sir Crispin.

"Keep a close eye on all three," I told them in German. *"I do not trust that their assignment here is a coincidence. One or all of them could be spies for my cousin Aleric."*

It sounded silly when I said it aloud, but I was still suspicious. Aleric's involvement with Landon's conspirators was too coincidental.

Hilda made a face when I told her to request French lessons from Lady Blanche. Gretchen spoke up to stoically predict that Lady Blanche would try to seduce Faulke at the first opportunity.

"She is a harlot," Gretchen said with a sniff of superiority. *"They are at Ashland less than a day and already she has tried to work her wiles upon my brother. He rebuffed her advances, of course."*

I looked at Gerhardt. He lifted one shoulder as if to say, *What else could I do?*

It was no secret that Gerhardt appreciated a pretty woman as well as the next man, but the handful of women he had pursued were timid types; bold women seemed to hold no appeal. Gerhardt was no woman's prey.

Hilda had learned that lesson the hard way when she first came to my court. I don't know exactly what happened between the two, but Gerhardt was always overly cordial in Hilda's presence, while Hilda studiously ignored him. Given that Blanche now seemed cut from the same cloth as Hilda, I could safely assume that Gerhardt's virtue would remain intact. However, I had no idea what type of women Faulke preferred.

If Blanche were here to spy upon us, becoming Faulke's mistress would be her first order of business. Yet there was one important benefit to outranking my future husband, I decided. If Blanche planned to become Faulke's bedmate and confidant, I would make certain of Sir Crispin's transfer to a place far worse than his last assignment at Windsor. His wife and brother-in-law would be forced to go with him, of course.

"French is not so difficult to learn," I told Hilda. "Should you happen to befriend Lady Blanche's brother, Sir Walter, I would be very interested in anything you could discover about Lady Blanche and Sir Crispin. Lady Blanche will, of course, be welcomed to keep our company in the afternoons."

My attention was drawn to the far end of the hall when Reginald's staff rang out again, three metallic thumps against the flagstones. The doors were thrown open and at least a score of men stood there, all wearing the Segraves' bloodred dragon on the chests of their black tabards. The butterflies took flight in my stomach.

Faulke and Richard stood next to Reginald. Today they wore knee-length tunics, more formal than those their men wore. Reginald announced them to the hall even as Faulke and Richard walked purposely toward the head table.

The closer they came to me, the faster my heart began to beat. Richard wore his hair in a topknot. Faulke again wore his hair unbound, but there were waves that indicated his had also been in a topknot until very recently. I wondered if they had come from the practice field. And then I wondered what Faulke would look like in battle, even in a mock battle. Fearsome, I was sure. More butterflies took flight.

The noises in the great hall dwindled to whispers as everyone turned to get a look at my future husband. A startled shriek drew some gazes toward the back of the hall, where Muck emerged from a cluster of serving women, his expression just as innocent as the one he'd worn earlier in the day.

Muck's diversion seemed to break the spell that had held everyone silent, and conversations started up again. Faulke and Richard finally reached the head table and halted before me, and then both gave a proper bow.

"Greetings, Princess," Faulke said as he straightened. "There are rumors in London that a wedding took place this morning at Ashland. My guess is that Chiavari learned of my intent to move into the palace."

Faulke looked . . . bemused. He also looked as striking as he had in his court finery, although today's garments were not quite as costly. Black was definitely his color, one that complemented his hair and made his blue eyes look even bluer. There was something about his beard. It made him look dark and dangerous, and at the same time, very virile. I wondered if he was aware of the effect.

Even after Baron Weston's revelations, the fluttering in my chest was an unwelcome reminder that my heart was being stubbornly susceptible to this man. It wasn't just the fact that he would be my husband. I was attracted to him in ways I had never been attracted to another. Hartman had made my heart flutter because of his regal bearing and noble chivalry, a girl's infatuation with her hero. Faulke made my heart beat in a more animalistic rhythm, something that felt like lust. It was a novel emotion in my life. I willed the butterflies to settle.

"Aye, this would be their wedding feast." My voice sounded higher and sharper than I intended. "Dante and Avalene retired more than an hour past, but there is still plenty of food and drink to be had. Baron Weston and his men also departed not long ago. There should be seats available. Of course, you and Richard are welcome to join me at the high table."

"I appreciate your hospitality," Faulke murmured.

"Sir Crispin," I called out. The knight had joined his wife and brother-in-law at the lower table after Lord Weston's departure. He stood now and bowed to me. "Perhaps you could make certain Lord Faulke's men find ample room at the tables?"

"Aye, Princess." Crispin bowed again, and then walked toward the middle of the hall, tapping several shoulders as he went. The English soldiers began to regroup, filling in the empty places left by Baron Weston's men, and soon two of the tables stood empty. Faulke motioned to his men, and they filed into their seats. I sat down again, but Gerhardt remained standing.

"*I will make certain the Segraves' servants find the quarters we assigned to them,*" he said, still speaking in German. "*And I will see that their animals are stabled.*"

I nodded once and he was gone. Meanwhile, Faulke and Richard had made their way around the end of the table. I was surprised when Richard took the seat next to Gretchen that Gerhardt had just vacated. Soon he was even attempting a conversation with Gretchen, using many hand motions. Faulke sat in Avalene's chair next to me. I was flanked by Segraves.

The servers took their cues and brought fresh trenchers for the newcomers, and then large platters that someone in the kitchens had heaped with the jumbled leftovers of each course.

"What was that?" Faulke asked. He pointed to the remnants of the sugar subtlety with the point of his dagger, and then speared a generous portion of ham. The massive sugar boat had been placed on the table in front of Dante and Avalene at the start of the feast, but now it stood in ruins, its masts gone, all of its sides broken away. Only a few dozen almond comfits remained, colorful confetti scattered among the ship's ruins.

"A boat. Actually, it was a ship," I said. "It was to signify their journey to Italy. There were Venetian and English banners in its masts."

"I am sorry I missed it," he said. "I suspect it was rather spectacular in its original form."

His fingers brushed over chunks of sandy sugar that littered the dark wood of the tabletop. Breaking apart a sugar sculpture was always a messy affair, but well worth it. Sugar was a rare treat, even for me, and Dante had generously decreed that each guest receive a portion of their sugar boat.

I watched Faulke draw an S in the sugar sand, and then he licked the tip of his finger.

He made a sound deep in his throat and closed his

eyes as he savored the treat, his expression one of almost carnal delight. "I cannot remember the last time I had a taste of sugar."

I watched, transfixed. I could not remember the last time I had enjoyed watching someone eat it. I would hand feed him every remaining grain of the sugar boat, if he would keep making those interesting sounds.

Ach, I was becoming a woman of loose morals. Just a few moments in this man's company filled my head with lurid ideas. What was it Faulke Segrave possessed that made me lose control of my thoughts so quickly?

He was obviously enticing to look at, but there was something more. It was not any single characteristic on its own, but how all those qualities came together in this one man. Faulke Segrave possessed some indefinable magic that I found irresistible. Of course, I was far from alone in my susceptibility to his charms. The recollection of Avalene's tales about his exploits with women at the royal court cooled my blood, but not as much as I would have liked.

"So. Chiavari obtained a special license," he said as he turned his attention to the food on his trencher and cut another piece of ham. He speared the meat on the end of his dagger, and then stared at the pink cube as if it were something of great interest. "When I heard that news, I sent word to your father and requested his assistance to obtain a special license for our own marriage. He has agreed with my reasoning."

I choked on the sip of wine I had just taken. All of the air suddenly left my chest. Faulke put the ham in his mouth and began to chew, watching me try to catch my breath. The noise of the crowd became a faint buzzing in my ears as I stared at Faulke.

Until this precise moment, my marriage was a future prospect, one not long in the making, but far enough away to seem not quite real, at least, not yet. I would have almost a month to accustom myself to marriage, weeks to acquaint myself with the man I was to marry, and time to come to terms with my fate. With a special license, Faulke could marry me today.

Chiavari had just proved how quickly a marriage could be accomplished. Faulke wanted a hasty wedding. There was nothing my father would like more. Dread doused the butterflies.

Faulke's tone was deceptively casual. "You do not look pleased by this news."

Parts of my conversation with Baron Weston replayed in my mind. For the first time in my memory, I said the first thing that came into my head. "Do you intend to murder me, too?"

CHAPTER EIGHT

Ancient History

FOR A LONG MOMENT, FAULKE LOOKED FROZEN in place. Because I did not so much as breathe, I probably looked much the same. I nearly jumped out of my skin when he grabbed my arm. He was on his feet a moment later and I actually cowered when he leaned over me.

"Come with me right now," he hissed in my ear.

His fingers wrapped around my arm in such a tight grip that I could either obey or be dragged away. I chose to obey, and even tried to look dignified as I matched his long strides. Everyone had fallen silent, even the musicians. I refused to look over my shoulder to gauge their reactions to this startling turn of events. No, I had to keep moving forward and pretend that I wanted to leave.

Faulke's grip was tight enough on my arm that it was sure to leave bruises. I had forgotten what it was like to fear a man. It was an unpleasant reminder of things I had tried hard to forget, bruises and cuts and days of waiting in my chamber for the swelling to recede.

Those were the sorts of useless thoughts that filled my head as we marched through the maze of hallways. When we reached the doors to my solar, Faulke propelled me into the room, then turned around to face me.

"Can we at least leave the door open?" I hated the quaver in my voice, hated asking for something that I would have ordered without a thought at any other time.

He didn't answer. Instead he dropped the thick board into place that barred the doors from the inside, ensuring that no one on the outside would be able to enter.

It took everything in me to maintain the shell of my composure. He was still the handsome man I had mooned over just yesterday—ach—just minutes ago. Now I realized how little I actually knew him. Was he a violent man?

Not that I thought he intended to murder me at this precise moment. At least, I didn't think that was his intention. Still, I did not want to test the bounds of his anger when help was on the wrong side of a very thick door. Why had I prodded him with such a stupid question in the first place?

I examined my surroundings with new eyes. There was only one entrance to the solar from the palace, and he had just barred those doors. There was nowhere to run.

My gaze went to the tall mullioned windows. The grounds of the garden were at least twenty feet below the openings, but suddenly that distance didn't seem so far. Perhaps that was an option, if the situation turned desperate.

And then an obvious thought clicked into my brain. There was a bar on my bedchamber door as well. If I could escape to my bedchamber and barricade the door against Faulke, perhaps that would buy enough time for his anger to cool or a rescue to arrive.

Faulke still stood before the barred solar doors with his arms crossed over his chest. For a long time, we simply stared at each other. I lowered my gaze to his boots and began to back away toward the door to my bedchamber.

Unfortunately, it only took him a few strides to cover the distance between us. He took my arm, this time in a less forceful grip, and led me to the wooden armchair near the fireplace. The ashes at the edge of the hearth stirred and a tendril of smoke curled upward, evidence of the lingering embers from this morning's fire. I wished it still blazed. I felt chilled to the bone.

"Sit," he ordered.

I sat.

"Ask me again," he demanded, his words clipped and precise.

Before I could answer, I heard Gerhardt's voice call out to me, muffled by the stout oak doors.

"Prinzessin!"

I looked toward the barred doors, and then I looked at Faulke. His gaze was on my arm, where I was trying to rub away the sting from his grip. I saw a brief flicker of regret in his eyes, and then he took a step backward.

The doors were rattled, followed by entirely predictable pounding and demands to open the doors. *"Öffnen sie die türen!"*

The bone-chilling fear began to melt away. My people would never let anything happen to me, even at the hands of my soon-to-be husband.

"Order them to stand down," Faulke said, his expression hard again. "Do it now."

I thought that over for half a second, and then slowly shook my head.

"I do not intend you any harm. Truly," he added when I rubbed my arm again. "If you do not tell them to stand down, the only blood that will be shed today will be from your soldiers and mine."

A great thud at the doors added an exclamation point to his words. It was the sound of someone's shoulders ramming the doors. They would eventually break them down. I wondered what would happen then. In Rheinbaden, Faulke would be dead before the last man came through the doors. Here, in England, he was my betrothed. He already had the legal rights he would enjoy as my husband. Perhaps that would be enough to stay Gerhardt's hand.

Perhaps not.

"I have no plan to hurt you," he bit out. "There are many ridiculous stories about the deaths of my previous wives; I am not ignorant of them. Did you think I would discuss the lurid details of my marriages in the great hall, in the midst of a feast, where anyone could overhear?"

Was that really what this abduction was all about? I had just discussed equally lurid topics with Weston in those same circumstances. Although, now that I thought about it, the head table had been deserted at the time, and I had made certain our voices did not carry.

Another series of thuds distracted me from my thoughts, but the doors still held. I would have to praise Gerhardt about how well the bar and braces had performed under actual use. Not that he would be pleased.

"Tell them to stand down, Isabel. All I want is a private word with my betrothed."

Well, now he sounded almost reasonable.

I was the king's daughter. Everyone knew we were here together. If he meant to strike me, surely he would have done it by now. Besides, I wanted to hear what he wished to say to me in private.

I stood up and we stared at each other for another long moment, and then he stepped aside to let me pass. The thuds were rhythmic now: *thud* . . . pause; *thud* . . . pause; and then a longer pause, and then they would repeat. I stood in front of the doors and yelled, *"Halt!"*

The thuds stopped immediately. Faulke was at my side an instant later, and then a step in front of me, a protective stance that I had seen often enough from my own guards. This insane man intended to keep me behind him while opening the doors himself.

I laid my hand upon his shoulder. He turned to give me a questioning look, and my voice sounded almost steady. "Remove the bar, but let me open the doors."

He pursed his lips and seemed to mull over the idea, then finally nodded. It was good to know he could be reasoned with in a tense situation. He lifted the bar from its brackets and then stepped to one side, but I noticed he held the bar over one shoulder like a club. His caution was warranted.

"I am going to open the doors now," I said in my loudest voice, and then repeated the words in German. "Stay back."

Before I could think better of the idea, I pulled the doors open, but only as wide as my body.

More than a score of men crowded the hallway, and I was certain there were even more around the corners, beyond my sight. Some wore my colors, others my father's colors, and others still wore the Segrave standard.

"Let us in, Princess," Gerhardt ground out. His right hand rested on his sword. A drawn sword would be very bad in this situation.

My gaze moved over the other men in the hallway. All of them looked ready for a fight. The longer I looked, the more my mantle of sovereignty settled back into place. I straightened my spine. "There has been a misunderstanding. My betrothed wished for a few private words, and he acted rashly in his haste to speak with me. I am here willingly. Return to your duties, all of you."

I closed the doors before anyone could argue, although I turned my head and placed my ear on the crack between the doors for a moment to make certain no one tested my order. If I had any sense at all, I would fling the doors open again and surround myself with guards.

On the other hand, I did not want Faulke to think he could cow me whenever he got angry, or think that I would need a score of soldiers to rescue me. I needed to handle him on my own. I would start this marriage on equal footing.

"I did not—"

Faulke fell silent when I spun toward him and held my finger to my lips in a quieting gesture. He still looked angry, but my mind was made up. I walked toward the windows, and then motioned for him to follow me through the antechamber where Gretchen and Hilda slept, and then into my bedchamber. He hesitated just long enough to replace the bar on the solar doors, and then he followed me.

Once we were inside my bedchamber, I left the door ajar. I don't know why that opened door soothed my nerves, but it did.

Faulke looked just as apprehensive about being in a confined space with me. He no longer looked angry; he looked . . . dumbfounded. His gaze traveled everywhere, and then seemed to settle on the bed.

I had brought my own bed from Rheinbaden, of course, a massive four-poster made of walnut from the Black Forest. The canopy and curtains were made of pink and white cloth sewn into wide stripes with gold thread. A padded quilt of the same pink and white fabric covered the bed, and the bolsters were trimmed in white ermine fur. Smooth linen sheets lay beneath the quilt, and a thick down mattress completed the cozy nest. Altogether, it was my most impressive piece of furniture. I gave Faulke a few moments to take it in.

My frayed nerves began to settle amid the familiar surroundings. I moved to the deep-set windows and took a seat on the padded cushions, and then motioned him to sit. Faulke continued his visual inspection of the room, obviously ill at ease, but he finally took a seat opposite me on the edge of my bed.

"They will be listening at the door to the solar," I explained. I held up my palms to indicate our surroundings. "You said you wanted our conversation to remain private. Here, no one will overhear what we say."

"You are not afraid to be alone with a murderer?" he asked, his words close to a challenge.

"My death here would mean your own," I answered. Oddly enough, I felt calm. The usual riot of emotions his presence set off in me were quiet now. It still hurt to look at him, he was that handsome, but I was beginning to see the man behind the attractive face. A man who might not be my enemy. "I assume you have not lived this long by making a habit of rash decisions."

He stared at me for a long moment, and then shook his head. "I forgot who you are, *what* you are. It will take time before I grow accustomed to . . . Nay, 'tis unlikely I will ever grow accustomed to the gulf between us."

The thought occurred that he might be as angry with himself as he was with me. And then I wondered "what" he thought I was, although I was fairly certain I knew the meaning of "who." He had dragged an English princess from a room filled with the king's soldiers, in front of my own Rheinbaden soldiers. It was stupid of me to have allowed it, and even stupider to think I could disguise my abduction. Surely he had known there would be consequences to his actions.

"You will always outrank me," he said, easily reading my thoughts. He set his jaw, and in that moment, I realized my rank was a bitter pill for him to swallow. He nodded toward my arm, where I could still feel the imprint of his fingers. "Forgive me, Princess. I never meant to hurt you."

"I accept your apology." My arm hurt, my heart still beat too fast, and the knot of tension in my stomach remained. I folded my hands together in my lap to hide their tremors. "You wanted to tell me about your previous marriages?"

He looked as if he wanted to say something more about how we got here. His gaze went to the door, then to me, and then back to the door again. He took a deep breath and braced his hands on his knees. "I would ask that you never question me in public about the deaths of my previous wives. Ask me anything you like in private, but I do not want you to raise any more speculation over those deaths than already exists."

Even I could admit that a wedding feast was an inappropriate venue for my question. His announcement about the special license had thrown me out of sorts. Actually, I had been out of sorts since I had met him. "You are right, of course. I should not have said something so provoking in front of others. I apologize."

He looked surprised, and then nodded to accept my apology. He raked a hand through his hair that left it mussed, and I bit down on my lower lip to keep myself from walking over to comb my fingers through his hair to straighten it.

"We are private now," I said. "Will you tell me the truth of your involvement in your wives' deaths?"

"Aye, you deserve the full truth," he replied. "On the day we met, I told you that I did not murder my wives. I did not murder them, but there is a possibility that at least one of them *was* murdered."

"Avalene already told me how your wives died," I said when it became obvious he was awaiting my reaction. I ticked off the list. "Childbirth, a fall, tainted food. You are either a very unlucky man, or one who is fortunate to still have his head."

" 'Tis my luck that is lacking," he retorted. "The idea that I could kill a woman . . . To have most people believe the worst of me. It is a hard charge for a man to live with."

"With three dead wives in less than ten years, 'tis a near certainty that at least one of the deaths was unnatural," I pointed out, trying to keep my voice reasonable. "You said yourself that you are aware of the gossip."

"Aye," he answered, his voice bitter. "They say I am responsible for the deaths of all three, but even a baron's son is not above the law."

"So you have some sort of alibis?" I asked.

"I was by Jeanne's side when she died of childbed fever," he said in a quieter tone. "Jeanne struggled throughout her pregnancy, the delivery was difficult, and then she grew weaker each day after the babe was born. Her death was clearly due to complications of childbirth.

"I was in London when Edith fell to her death, and then I was at your father's court at Caernarfon Castle when I received word that Alice had succumbed to dysentery. I was nowhere near my last two wives when they died."

I dismissed the first death because Avalene had told me that his marriage to Jeanne of Wentworth had been a love match, and a mother's death during childbirth was not unusual. Faulke's absence only meant he did not have a direct hand in the deaths of his last two wives, but he could have ordered them done.

"People remark that you have been uncommonly fortunate in the wealth your brides brought to your marriages," I said. "Wealth that remains in the hands of the Segraves."

"My father arranged all of my marriages," he replied, "and he has an undeniable talent for it. Jeanne was a noblewoman with wealth of her own that will pass to our daughter, Claire."

"Your last two wives were commoners, as well as wealthy heiresses," I pointed out. "Will their wealth also pass to their daughters?"

"In part," he admitted. "All of my wives' families were wealthy and powerful in their own rights, and my family's wealth increased with each bride. I will not apologize for making sensible marriages."

"If your wives' families are as influential as you claim, surely they demanded some sort of justice when their daughters died?"

"The king himself ordered a full inquest after the deaths of Edith and Alice," he said. "Roger Bigod presided over the inquests."

"Earl of Norfolk and Marshall of England," I murmured. "I am told he is well respected by my father and his court."

"Aye, 'tis true. I was actually grateful to be judged innocent by a man with more to gain if I were found guilty," he said. "However, there is still plenty of speculation about my guilt. No one came forward to say they witnessed Edith being pushed from the tower, or saw someone put poison in Alice's food. At the same time, no one could say that they saw Edith slip and fall, and no one else died from the same food that Alice ate. Their families remain convinced that I am behind their deaths."

"Accusing someone of murder and proving that guilt are two separate things," I said. Had he gotten away with murder, or was he unfairly accused?

A muscle twitched in his jaw. "I cannot be proved guilty, because what little evidence exists points to my innocence. The lack of evidence also means I cannot prove myself innocent beyond any doubt."

I stated the obvious. "So everyone can believe what they will about your marriages, and people are ever ready to believe the worst."

He tilted his head. "If my wives had been poor orphans, everyone would have looked upon me with pity when they died and cursed the Fates. Because they were wealthy, everyone looks at me with suspicion and waits until my back is turned to accuse me of crimes I did not commit."

"Surely you cannot blame them for being suspicious," I said. When Avalene first told me the rumors, they had seemed salacious gossip. Now was the reality. I was about to marry a man who murdered women, or one who stood unjustly accused of their murders. There was no sure proof either way. I would have to decide for myself.

"There are times when even I wonder at the manners of their passing," he said. "Their deaths were untimely, but my responsibilities to marry well and produce an heir did not change. These are concepts you are familiar with, Princess. I have three daughters who need a brother to ensure their futures, should something happen to me before I can arrange their marriages."

That last comment made a tendril of guilt wrap around the knot in my stomach. He needed an heir, and he would not get one from me.

"Normally, the opinions of others do not concern me," he said, "not until the gossip begins to affect my family. I was negotiating a betrothal contract for my eldest daughter, Claire, when Alice died. If Claire marries well, her husband can take care of Claire and her sisters, if I should die before my time without a male heir. However, Kenric of Remmington broke off negotiations within a fortnight of Alice's death, claiming his son was still too young for him to make such an important commitment."

"The Warlord?" I blinked once in astonishment. "Kenric of Remmington is . . . He is—"

Faulke made a cutting motion with his hand. " 'Tis an open secret in England that Kenric of Remmington is your half brother. Apparently he was your father's only youthful indiscretion, a liaison with a baron's daughter made shortly before he met and wed your mother, but one that had lasting consequences. I knew the circumstances of Remmington's birth long before I approached him about a possible marriage between our children."

Kenric of Remmington. I had first heard of him at my father's court, and learned of our blood ties soon after. Remmington had proved his mettle in the Holy Lands, as well as in the last outbreak of war in Wales. Indeed, he was feared by his enemies as well as by many who considered him a friend. If Claire wed into that family, Remmington could prove a powerful ally for the Segraves, but one who would never turn traitor against the crown. At least, I did not think Remmington would turn against our father. On the other hand, my family's history was littered with brutal betrayals between fathers and sons.

Another thought gave me pause. "Did you agree to our marriage to improve your daughter's chances of marrying a Remmington?"

"That possibility was not on my mind when Chiavari dragged me to this palace to break my betrothal to Avalene de Forshay." He shook his head and frowned. "My daughters' futures were very much on my mind later that day, when I spoke to my father about our marriage. Right now, the cloud of suspicion that hangs over me also extends to my children. 'Bad blood,' I've heard whispered."

Aye, I could well imagine. Everyone knows that murder and madness runs in the blood. Who would want their son wed to the daughter of a murderer, a trait that could easily pass to their offspring? That would take strong incentive, indeed. Say, the incentive of making a match with a newly made earl's daughter, whose stepmother is an English princess.

"So our marriage will be the leverage you need to renegotiate your daughters' futures."

It wasn't a question, but he answered anyway. "Aye. Claire's betrothal is my first priority, once we are wed.

Remmington's son is my first choice, but there are others who will do."

I supposed he was wise to strike while the iron was hot. There would be few offers once the English realized our marriage meant Faulke would eventually lose everything, and there would be no offers at all if I, too, suffered an untimely death.

"Which of your wives do you think was murdered?" I asked, becoming more certain that he did not have a hand in the outcome.

He looked startled by the abrupt change in direction, and then his expression turned thoughtful. "Edith. More than a few of my people think she was somehow lured to the parapets, and then pushed over the side. She did not like heights, and few think she would have gone to the wall willingly."

I cleared my throat. "There are rumors that Edith was so opposed to performing her wifely duties that she might have committed suicide."

Faulke stared at me in silence.

"What is it?" I asked.

"Your frankness," he said. "I suppose Avalene de Forshay has been filling your head with tales about me?"

"Many people whisper in my ear." I lifted my shoulders. "You will likely hear rumors about me as well. I am simply asking if this rumor about Edith is true."

"Edith was far too religious to commit the mortal sin of suicide," Faulke said firmly. "Indeed, she was religious to the point of fanaticism. She even petitioned me for permission to enter a nunnery."

My face must have showed my astonishment. His tone turned defensive.

"The request is rare, but not unheard of among nobles," he said. "The church will allow husbands or wives to leave their marriage, if they have the calling."

"Edith had no right to ask," I sputtered. "Noble marriages are binding agreements, and the terms of the contract must be fulfilled before the arrangement can be concluded. Neither party can remarry while the other lives. I have never heard of a noblewoman daring to ask for such a boon before she gave her husband at least an heir and a spare."

"Edith's parents coerced her into the marriage," he said. "Throughout the entirety of our marriage, she was single-minded in her goal to become a nun."

I made a sound of impatience. "If Edith were so averse to being a wife, she should have opposed her family and refused to wed anyone except Christ."

He gave me another odd look.

"What did I say now?" I demanded.

He simply shook his head. "Edith did not have your strength of character."

I studied the man sitting on my bed and tried to decide what Edith had found so objectionable in her marriage. "She rose from a merchant's daughter to become a baron's wife and the mother of his child, the lady of a substantial keep with servants of her own. What more could she have hoped to find within a nunnery?"

"God," he said simply.

"Sometimes I do not understand people," I muttered.

Not that the way Edith lived her life mattered anymore. It was her death that concerned me.

"So Edith's death was unlikely to be a suicide," I said, "and just as unlikely to be an accident, yet there were no witnesses to say what actually happened. What about Alice?"

He rubbed the back of his neck and scowled at the floor. "Most of the time I believe her death was an unfortunate case of spoiled food. However, the symptoms described to me could as easily describe a deliberate poisoning."

"And here, too, no one saw anything amiss that could point toward foul play?"

He shook his head, his expression grim.

"Why are you telling me this?" I asked. "These are speculations you need never share, and I would be none the wiser that you had ever entertained such thoughts."

"You will be my wife." He gave me a direct look. "That has proven to be a dangerous occupation."

I was surprised he would make such an admission, but he was not done with his revelations.

"Most days I set aside my misgivings and tell myself I am seeing crimes where none were committed. Other days, I wonder at the inconsistencies and odd coincidences." He leaned forward to let his arms rest on the tops of his legs and loosely clasped his hands together. "The odds of any intentional harm befalling you should be small. Between your soldiers, the English guards, and my own men, you have a small army who are sworn to safeguard your welfare. However, my last two wives died under suspicious circumstances, and I know that I was not their murderer. An assassin may be in my household even now, awaiting my next wife's arrival."

An icy finger of dread went down my neck. Now I was certain I wanted to remain in London.

"There is also the fact that my marital history opens paths to new villains. I have enemies who would welcome the opportunity to murder you, if they knew the king would never learn their identity. Your father would need no proof of my guilt beyond the fact of your death to order me beheaded. Your murder would mean my own death sentence, as well as the ruination of my family. You will—" He pressed his lips together. "That is, I would *ask* you to take sensible precautions."

Aye, everything he was, everything he possessed, now depended upon my life. Of course he wanted me healthy. Apparently my thoughts were reflected in my expression.

"My concerns about the deaths of Edith and Alice are reasonable," he said. "I would make the same request if our marriage contract did not contain its more unusual requirements."

"I'm sure you would." Silently, I wondered.

"You will be my wife," he said in a deeper voice. "You will be a part of my family, the mother of my daughters . . . and hopefully the mother of our own children. I have always done my best to protect my family, and the mantle of my protection now includes you."

The reminder of the heirs I would never bear tempered my mood. Ach. Would I ever hear the word "children" and not feel a wave of guilt? As for his protection,

I had no need of it. However, my inclusion in his family touched me more than I cared to admit.

"I have no intention of being foolish," I said with less heat than I had intended.

He smiled a little at that. "Foolishness is the last thing I would expect of you, Princess."

Again I felt the sting of a backhanded compliment. I decided to sting back. "Then we are in agreement that a fourth dead wife would benefit neither of us?"

"Aye, none I hold dear will benefit from your demise," he said in a grim voice.

I turned my head to look through the diamond-shaped panes of glass and into the gardens. The sky was as gray and dreary as my thoughts. Murder, lies, treason. How could there be room for any happiness in our future?

"I did not want to burden you with these worries," Faulke said at last, breaking into my thoughts. "But the ink is scarce dry on our betrothal, and already one of your men lies dead of poisoning. Then your question in the great hall . . ."

My gaze went back to him and I realized that somehow I was beginning to believe he was innocent. However, there was a cynical voice inside my head that wondered if I would be so willing to believe the same story from a man who appealed less to the eye. And yet, there was more to Faulke Segrave than a handsome face and strong sword arm, something that had pulled at me from the very start.

"I know my reputation," he said. "I know there is nothing I can do or say to prove my innocence. 'Tis a wasted effort to even try. People believe what they will, no matter the truth."

That was a sentiment I agreed with wholeheartedly.

"I am not convinced of your innocence," I said honestly. "But I am beginning to believe in its possibility. That means I must accept that you suffered an unusual number of losses in a short number of years, or someone has little liking for the women you marry."

"That is one way to put it," he said dryly. His brow smoothed just a little. I think it was relief that I might actually believe him.

"So you would have me believe there is someone in your household who does not care for your brides, or someone was sent there to assassinate them, and you have enemies who would like to see me in particular die in such a way that you can be blamed for my death. Is that the gist of what you wanted to tell me?"

Those few traces of softness left his face. "Aye, that is the gist of things."

I studied the toes of my slippers. My father had known these same facts. Say what he might about regrets over my childhood, his actions spoke louder than words. When it came to royal politics, I was simply a type of currency, a fact I would do well to remember. The only person in the world I could truly trust was myself.

"I can only speculate about the future based upon events of the past," he said. "All I can say with certainty is that my enemies will be your enemies, and yours will be mine."

"My enemies might be more numerous than you think," I retorted.

He lifted one shoulder. "I could make the same claim."

"It seems we have that in common," I mused. "One can only wonder how many new enemies we will create once our vows are read. How do you think your people in Wales will react when they learn your new wife will bring a small army of the king's soldiers into their midst?"

"My lands in Wales are on the edges of the frontier, often on the edge of lawlessness, when the native Welsh become restless," he said. "Most will be grateful for the extra swords, but there is no doubt they will be wary. I suppose you will need time as well, to accustom yourself to the change in your circumstances."

"My circumstances?" I echoed.

"You have come down a step in the world, Princess. A very large step," he said as his gaze moved purposefully around my bedchamber, and then he held up his empty hands. "I am no prince. I cannot give you a crown and a kingdom, or lands and jewels, or rarities I cannot even imagine. But you are to be my wife and you will live where I live. You will learn soon enough just how different your life will be as Lady of Hawksforth."

"I am much more than the Lady of Hawksforth," I reminded him.

"First and foremost, you will be my wife," he countered, "and Hawksforth is my family's seat."

I wondered at his attachment to the place. "Surely you are aware that my estate at Maldon offers ample comforts? And the moment we wed, Maldon will become your new family seat."

"I will visit Maldon," he conceded, "but Hawksforth will be our home."

Whatever he saw in my expression made him frown.

"You will be easier to protect at Hawksforth," he said, apparently rightly thinking that I wanted an explanation. "I know little of Maldon and its people, and even less about its defenses. We will not live there until I am certain it is safe."

I raised my brows at that last edict. And then I lowered them when I realized he would have that right as my husband, to decide where I could and could not live. At least, until my father intervened. Ach, I could spend years in Wales, a virtual prisoner at Hawksforth. Now *there* was something unpleasant to look forward to. Unless . . .

"All three of your wives died at Hawksforth," I pointed out.

"I do not forget that fact," he said. "However, if one or more of their deaths were intentional, there are three likely culprits. It could be someone I know well, a Segrave who would stand to gain something when I remarried. Or the culprit could be one of my enemies who would have something to gain if I were hung for their crime. A Segrave would have no reason to kill you, and every reason to ensure your safety. My enemies are another matter. They have ample reasons to plot your death. However, this time I am aware of the threat they pose. You will be even more protected than my other wives, surrounded by servants and men I trust, as well as the soldiers in your father's hire. And your own people, of course."

"It sounds as if you intend to make me a prisoner."

"I intend to make you safe." He sounded stubborn on the point.

"You said there were three possible culprits: a Segrave or one of your enemies." I held up one finger, and then a second as I listed the suspects, and then I wagged my third finger. "The third possible culprit. Who do you suspect?"

He found something interesting to look at through the windows behind me. He hesitated as though considering a chess move, and his voice turned quiet. "Dante Chiavari."

CHAPTER NINE

Magnetic Forces

WHAT A RIDICULOUS CLAIM. CHIAVARI HAD nothing to gain from murdering Faulke's wives. I stared at him until the pieces fell into place.

"You think my *father* ordered Chiavari to murder your wives?" I sputtered.

He hesitated a moment, then lifted his shoulders in a shrug. "The idea has crossed my mind. More than once, after Alice died."

"Why would my father order their deaths? Any of their deaths?" I shook my head. "That makes no sense."

"Your father has little liking for my family," he said. "I now live under a cloud of suspicion because of my wives' deaths. It has made me a near outcast. Honorable families refuse to betroth their daughters to me, or my daughters to their sons. Baron Weston was given little choice in the matter, but Weston was so desperate to keep Avalene from me that he enlisted the king's help to break our betrothal." He gave me an assessing look. "Frankly, I am still amazed that you are part of that bargain. I have become a cynical man, Isabel. The terms of our marriage contracts make me wonder if the king somehow knows you will not enjoy a long life."

I took a deep breath and forced my voice to sound calm. "You think my father would conspire to murder me?"

"I no longer know what to expect from your father," he said carefully. "Although I do not think even he would sacrifice one of his children's lives for political gain. If this marriage is intended to be an olive branch, I am willing to accept it. I have been completely honest with you about the dangers you will face as my wife. If there is some problem with your health or well-being that you know about, you would be well served to tell me now."

I forced myself to look him straight in the eye. "There is no problem with my health or well-being. Indeed, I will probably outlive you, unless one of your enemies or my father murders me first."

He had the grace to break eye contact and look at the floor, in what I assumed was a moment of guilt. I supposed that made him a better person than me. Just because I told the truth did not mean I told the whole truth. Yes, I was healthy. And barren. Faulke would learn soon enough of my family's natural ability to turn a phrase to our favor.

It also occurred to me that he had professed his innocence in the deaths of his wives, but he had never claimed to be innocent of treason. Not that I expected him to claim anything but unwavering loyalty to the king. Anything less could mean his head. Still, it was something to think about.

"Surely I would be safest right here in London, here at Ashland Palace," I argued, "at least until you are comfortable with Maldon's defenses. Chiavari will be gone soon enough. I am surrounded by men I trust, and I am certain my father would allow us to stay at Ashland as long as we wish."

"We will live at Hawksforth," he said, unmoved.

Not if I could help it. Three of his wives had died at Hawksforth. I did not intend to be the fourth.

"I did not want to trouble you with my worries," he said in a sincere tone, "but your question at the feast convinced me that we needed to have this discussion."

"I know my father has encouraged you to spend time at my English estates," I said. "Do you intend to ignore the king's 'suggestions'?"

"He cannot object to my actions, if your safety is my first concern." The corners of his mouth turned downward. "I will make your life with me as comfortable as possible. In time, I think we will find our marriage tolerable."

It was my turn to frown. "Is there something about me now that you find *in*tolerable?"

He put up his hands, as if beseeching the heavens. "I did not intend to insult you again!"

"You do have a talent for it," I said. "You are fortunate that I have thicker skin than most."

"Indeed, I am thankful," he agreed, just before his expression turned anxious. "Not that I think your skin is thick. It is quite lovely. The loveliest. Exquisite, even."

We stared across the room at each other. To my amazement, his lips began to curve into a slow smile. Just as amazing, I felt my face reflect the same expression.

Aside from whatever strange force was at work between us, I had always been a good judge of character. Hartman was the exception, but I could excuse that poor reasoning to the folly of youth.

Yes, Faulke had a quick temper, but so did I. It was a Plantagenet family trait. His temper could be reasoned with. Mine, not always. He was the kind of man who would give his life to protect his family, and I would soon be his wife. Given the provisions of our marriage contract, I would always be as safe with him as I would be with my own people.

The dangers were undeniable, and the secrets between us only increased those dangers. Our journey together would probably end badly, but whenever I was in his presence, there was an unshakable feeling that we were meant to be together . . . no matter how long our union might last.

The more I stared into his eyes, the more my thoughts about him began to drift into dangerous territory. Yes, he had frightened me, and yet some irrational part of me wanted him to comfort me as well.

The irony of that feeling was less worrisome than it should be.

"What are you thinking about when you look at me that way?"

"Nothing," I blurted out, far too quickly. In other words, nothing I wanted to tell him.

"You feel it, too, don't you?" he asked.

"Feel what?" Ach, I sounded like a simpleton.

He opened his mouth to say something, and then closed it again, his expression troubled. "I cannot explain it."

I was not about to try. His brows drew together and I could almost see his mind at work on the puzzle.

"An alchemist once visited Hawksforth," he said at last. "He showed me sets of lodestone magnets and explained how they worked. Are you familiar with magnets?"

Magnets? He was going to tell me a story about magnets? I lifted my shoulders. "They are not uncommon in Rheinbaden."

He nodded, and then continued. "The alchemist showed me how one end of a magnet would attract another magnet with twice the power." He held up his index fingers and pointed them at each other, and then tapped his fingers together. "Next he turned the ends around so they would repel each other and make it nearly impossible for the two ends to touch." He folded his fingers down and bounced the knuckles toward each other in the air without touching. "I could feel the invisible power contained within the magnets when I worked them together. We even made a game of using one magnet to push another across a table."

"I have played a similar game," I said, remembering the strange, invisible force that surrounded the dark chunks of metal.

"The power that draws and repels the magnets is a mystery," he said, "but that invisible energy is the closest I have felt to the force that is at work between you and me."

It startled me to realize he was right. An unseen force almost hummed in the air around us, sometimes repelling us, keeping us a set distance apart, other times turning us toward one another and drawing us together with a power outside our own will. I could feel it, sense it. And yet, I could not give it a name.

Our gazes held while I thought about what he'd said. Everything he'd said. I was a good and experienced judge of liars. Unless he was an unrivaled actor, he had been telling me the truth about his wives' deaths, about his strange attraction to me. And I was resisting him with the last resolve left in me.

What would it be like to stop resisting? Even now, my hands were clenched along the edge of the window seat and my feet were braced against the floor, my mind's subconscious resistance to the invisible force that drew me toward him.

"We will be good together," he said slowly. He did not move, but I could feel his words move over me like a caress. "Do you want me, Isabel?"

I blinked once. "What did you say?"

He stood up and walked toward me. I stood up as well, because I did not want him to tower over me. He did not stop until his boots brushed against my skirts. His voice sounded deeper, rougher.

"Suddenly I am having trouble concentrating on anything beyond the fact that we are alone in your bedchamber, and my rights as your betrothed." He stroked the side of my cheek with one finger, the look in his blue eyes intent. "Do you want me, Isabel?"

This time I blinked twice. That was the only response I could muster. That question could mean so many different things. Regardless, if I said no, he would surely recognize the lie.

He didn't wait for my answer. The butterflies in my stomach took flight when he bent his head to kiss me, a soft, undemanding kiss that quickly deepened. His arms went around me and I melted against him, sensations I was almost beginning to expect began to bombard my senses. Just like that, my calm, rational state of mind departed.

My arms went around his neck and his hands skimmed over them, as if to assure himself that they were properly placed, and then they slid down my sides, over my waist, then my hips, and then he pressed me into his body. At the same time, his tongue swept into my mouth and a mewling sound came from my throat, a sound I wasn't even aware I could make. My heart seemed to slow down and yet speed up at the same time, the beats so strong and deliberate that I could feel them against my ribs.

He tilted his head as though he wanted to taste me from every angle, savor each touch, and yet he crushed me to him as though I might try to pull away. I *should* try to pull away . . . for some reason I could no longer recall. He overwhelmed my senses.

During all of that emotional upheaval, my thoughts kept whirling back to magnets. I held on to him as if the magnetic force were a part of me. My skin wanted to cling to every part of his body. I don't think I could have peeled myself away from him if I had tried. Even the air felt charged with the energy that drew us together.

Soon our breath came in harsh gasps and I swore I could hear both our hearts beating while our hands moved over each other with rough urgency. Despite the randomness of his caresses, I knew that he was memorizing my shape with his touch, knew it because I was making the same survey of his body, recording all the details in my greedy mind to be reviewed again later. The curve of his massive shoulders, the ridge down the center of his back, the height that meant I had to raise my hand to stroke his chest. And the heat of his body. It was amazing. I wanted every measure.

He continued to do remarkable things to my mouth. The first time he had kissed me this way I had been unprepared, overwhelmed. It was still overwhelming, but now I wanted to participate. When I stroked my tongue against his, he responded with a low growl, his arms sliding completely around me as he claimed my mouth. His hand moved up to the nape of my neck and he wrapped his hand around my braid to hold me in place while he explored my mouth.

Soon the fabric and leather between us felt cumbersome and unnatural. I wanted to feel his skin, the source of all that heat. He stirred emotions that had lain dormant for longer than I could remember.

No, they were not remembered feelings. I had never felt this way in Hartman's arms. This was new territory. A new awakening.

A sound of some sort penetrated my senses enough for a tendril of sanity to blow across my fevered mind.

Royals were not ruled by animal passions. And yet, here I was, ready and willing. My bed was just a few paces away.

That thought stirred a vague sense of panic. What was happening to me? He made me feel helpless in his arms. I did not like feeling helpless. At least, I did not like it until today. Now I wanted to somehow give myself over to his care, which was ridiculous. I took care of myself. But how nice it would be to lay my head upon his shoulder and simply luxuriate in the decadence of being held in his arms, of being treated like a woman rather than a princess.

My thoughts were so muddled with lust I could barely think straight. I shook my head, trying to clear the cobwebs. Something very strange was happening here.

Faulke trailed a line of kisses along the side of my neck, and then lifted his head to look down at me. "Where did you go?"

"I am right here," I said, purposely misunderstanding him.

The undisguised lust in his eyes fueled my panic. No one had ever looked at me that way.

Faulke stood straighter, but he did not let go of me. His hands went to my hips and he held me in place as he pressed his hips against mine, not crudely, but as if he could not help himself. The proof of his desire was unmistakable. He gave a sigh that somehow sounded both frustrated and satisfied. "We are betrothed, Isabel. There is no sin in what we do."

"I know that." But I still turned my head away when he tried to kiss me again.

"Is it . . ." He cleared his throat as he straightened. "Are you thinking about your . . . about Prince Hartman?"

Well, I hadn't been. Now I tried to imagine Hartman in this situation. We would not be talking; of that I was certain. He came to my bedchamber at night, climbed into my bed, poked and prodded, grunted and sweated, and then left within the hour, often without saying a word. It was a horrible memory that I quickly pushed away.

Hartman had never been driven by lust when he was in my company. The few kisses we had shared shortly before and soon after our marriage were almost as chaste as those exchanged between close relatives. Indeed, I was beginning to wonder if Hartman had viewed me as more of a sister than a wife.

The answer no longer mattered. What mattered was that Faulke Segrave already treated me more like a wife than Hartman ever had, and we weren't even married, at least not yet. It was hard to recall the fact that I did not want him to treat me like a wife or a lover. That I did not want him to care for me. Ach. What if I began to care for *him*?

And those ridiculous thoughts proved just how much his kisses had scrambled my brains. That, along with my next question.

"Are you thinking about your other wives?"

He shook his head and gave a gruff laugh. "Princess, a man would be a fool to think of another woman in your presence. You occupy all of my thoughts."

Well. That was nice. No. *No*. Not nice. Thoughts led

to questions. He could not learn my secrets until our marriage was unbreakable, and we still needed the blessing of a priest and the church. I frowned at my hands when I realized they still clung to his shoulders.

"We are betrothed," he repeated again, his gaze fastened on my mouth.

His lips captured mine in another kiss before I could protest, but the sounds I began to make were definitely not a protest. This kiss was more demanding than the others, more dominant. One hand gripped the back of my head to hold me in place, while the other hand slid down my back and then pushed my hips against the bulge of his erection between us. His hand moved lower and he caught one of my knees, lifting my leg to the side of his hip. The position made the press of his erection even more intimate against me. I could barely breathe.

For several long, selfish moments, I let myself think of nothing but the feelings he unleashed in me, feelings I had never experienced. The more he kissed and caressed me, the more I thought it might be all right to allow myself this new experience, to let him seduce me for a while longer.

That thought lasted until he moved us closer to the bed and began to tug me down toward the mattress. I suddenly froze inside.

That wave of ice was all I needed to bring me back to my senses. "Stop!"

His arms were wrapped around me like iron bands and I pressed my forehead to his chest, afraid to say anything, but I could not stop the shivers that made me tremble like a leaf.

His hands went to my shoulders and he set me apart from him. I could feel his gaze on me, intent, studying everything about my odd reaction. That made me even more afraid. He was so close to the secret I had kept from everyone except Hartman. I could hardly breathe.

"Did I do something wrong?" he asked, puzzled.

I shook my head, trying to get ahold of my fear. I stared at his chest for what seemed an eternity, and concentrated on slowing my panicked breaths. Finally, he released a long sigh.

"I did not intend for this to happen," he said, sounding more pleased than regretful. He tilted my chin up to meet his heated gaze. "The idea of being allowed into your bedchamber before our wedding did not occur to me. However, I have given plenty of thought as to what we would do here, when we were finally alone."

What he had in mind seemed fairly obvious. I shook my head.

"You are a royal princess," he muttered. "The consummation of our wedding should be preceded by a religious ceremony, a sumptuous feast, and too much wine."

"Aye," I agreed, perhaps a little too eagerly, now that I sensed a reprieve.

He moved away from me almost imperceptibly. "You deserve more than a hurried coupling while scores of soldiers debate whether they should ignore your orders and break down the doors to murder me."

"Aye, there is that." Relief washed through me.

I jumped a little when he took my hand and held it to his cheek. Without conscious intent, my fingers stroked the side of his face. His skin felt sandy, like the grains of the sugar boat. I had forgotten what a man felt like, the differences in the texture of their skin, their strength, their sheer size. My gaze went back to his mouth. I might have licked my lips.

"We cannot do this," he said in a tight voice. He turned his head and pressed a kiss to the center of my palm, and then captured both my hands and held them at my sides. " 'Tis not right."

I wondered if he was trying to convince me, or himself. Whatever he saw in my face made him sigh, a restless sound that shuddered toward the end of it. He was trying hard to do what he thought was right. He was an honorable man. The voice of reason said to step away from his embrace, and that voice was getting louder. I made my hands slide away from him. My own sigh was none too steady when I took a step backward.

"You should not have taken me from the feast."

"Aye, 'twas a mistake. But this was not." He walked to the door, pushed it open, and then turned toward me again. "My soldiers will be growing anxious. We should return to the great hall."

"That would be best," I agreed. I wanted to sit down and think about everything that had just happened. My whole body hummed with frustration, and yet we were already addressing each other as polite strangers rather than almost lovers. The magnets had turned again and we were back to pushing each other away. I motioned toward the door. "I suppose you will want to get settled into your new quarters."

He looked as if he wanted to say something more, but in the end he simply stepped aside to let me pass into the solar. We walked straight to the doors that led to the hallway. This time he stood in front of the doors when he opened them, protecting me again, I surmised. A moment later, I was glad of his precaution.

As soon as he opened the door, a body fell into the solar and landed at his feet.

"What in God's name is going on here?" Faulke demanded.

The man on the floor wasn't dead, judging by his grunt of pain. His clothing marked him a Segrave man. Indeed, a line of soldiers in black tunics stood with their backs to us, swords drawn. Richard appeared between two of the Segrave men and pushed his way into the solar.

"The Rheinbaden soldiers intended to break open the doors," Richard accused, jabbing his thumb in the direction of the hallway. "Their captain led the effort. Stephen shoved Sir Gerhardt aside and got stuck for his trouble. The wound is not serious, but the—"

"Gerhardt!" I called out. There was some sort of commotion on the other side of the wall of Segrave men. I turned to Faulke. "Tell your men to let my captain pass."

"Let him through," Faulke ordered without hesitation.

The Segrave men slowly backed into the solar, their swords held before them, and then they stood where Richard directed, behind Faulke. The wounded man got a hand up and managed to stand, his face tight with pain. My Rheinbaden soldiers advanced just as slowly, their swords drawn as well, all pointed toward the Segraves. They took up a line on my side of the room behind Gerhardt, whose expression betrayed none of his feelings. The English soldiers stayed in the hallway, although Sir Crispin and Sir Walter now stood in the doorway, also armed with swords, their gazes darting between the Segrave soldiers and the Rheinbaden soldiers. Every soldier I could see bristled with weapons and suspicion.

Gerhardt bowed low to me, a sure sign that he had done something I would not like.

"Tell me what happened," I demanded in German.

Gerhardt straightened from his bow, and then he looked me square in the eye, another sign that he was about to tell me something I did not want to hear. *"I became concerned some time ago when we heard nothing from within the solar. We knocked on the door, but there was no response."*

I could imagine his reaction to that situation. *"So you decided to break down the doors?"*

Gerhardt shook his head. *"There is enough of a space between the doors that I could slip a misericord between the gap to work the bar free. A man came at me from behind. My blade was in his shoulder before I realized he did not have a weapon drawn against me. It would seem the fool thought he could simply push me away from my post."*

I eyed the misericord that was sheathed on Gerhardt's sword belt. The blade was so thin that it probably didn't do much damage, but I was surprised the wounded soldier wasn't making more of a fuss.

"I told everyone that I wished to have a private con-

versation with my betrothed," I reminded him. *"Everyone should have heeded my words and returned to their duties."*

"You are *my duty,"* he said, as if I should know as much . . . which I did. *"This man is not your husband, yet he dragged you from the great hall and then locked you in the solar. Would you have me abandon my post under those circumstances?"*

I could not find fault in his actions. Gerhardt had acted in my best interests. It was an unfortunate misunderstanding. One that could still turn deadly, if someone said a wrong word.

"No, you were right to remain," I admitted. *"But Lord Faulke is my betrothed. We must all tread carefully where he is concerned."*

Gerhardt scowled.

"Did the Segrave men provoke you in any other way?" I asked.

"They did nothing else threatening," he said, *"although they made lewd comments when there was no response to my initial knocks."*

Which no doubt fanned the flames of Gerhardt's anger over his inability to control the situation. I pressed my lips together, lips still swollen from Faulke's kisses. I could well imagine the sorts of speculation going on among all of the men, but Faulke's soldiers knew him best. They would know if he made a habit of seducing ladies when he was alone with them. If they knew just how easily Faulke had seduced me, I would likely be the talk of the barracks . . . and still might be.

Just then Faulke turned his hand over and curled his

fingers, motioning me toward him. I moved a few steps forward without thinking, and then he closed the distance between us before I quite knew what had happened.

Faulke leaned down to whisper in my ear, "Present a united front."

The feel of his lips as they brushed against my skin and the intimacy of his breath in my ear sent a wave of shivers through my body. My thoughts were muddled even more when I felt his hand come to rest on my waist, and I struggled to keep myself from leaning into him.

"Stephen's injury was the result of an accident," Faulke said to all of the men, and then his gaze came to rest on Gerhardt. "An accident that will not be repeated."

I set my jaw and tried my best to concentrate on what he was saying. Thoughts skipped through my head too fast to catch, and most involved recollections of Faulke's most recent kisses.

"We are of three houses, three lands, and more than three languages," Faulke said. "If we are to exist together in peace, we must learn more about each other, our customs and ways, as well as our languages. Sirs Richard, Gerhardt, and Crispin will devise a plan to integrate their men into each other's companies, and then present the plan to the princess and me for approval." He then turned to me. "Do you agree with this course of action, Isabel?"

It was one of the few times he had used my given name, and I suspected it was not an accident. He was announcing that we were already on intimate terms, already united. I would be foolish to argue with him, especially since Faulke's plan was brilliant. I should have thought of it myself.

I gave him a demure smile. "'Tis as if you read my mind, Faulke."

That ignited more than a few whispers among the men. We stood united, and they knew it. I took a moment to savor the feeling.

Hartman had rarely agreed with me on anything, and we constantly bickered and quarreled. How odd to have Faulke purposely take my side. It was an utterly foreign concept to me, but I immediately saw its advantages. I just did not expect the accompanying emotions.

If Faulke reached down at that moment to hold my hand, I would let him. I wanted to lay my head on his shoulder and smile up at him. Ach, if this kept up, the man would turn me into a simpering maid in no time. There were valid reasons to let him take the lead in this matter, but I could still stand on my own two feet.

"Return to the feast," I ordered the men. "There is still food and ale aplenty. Enjoy what is left of this day. Gerhardt, send for Bruna to tend Faulke's injured soldier. You will stay here, in the event that Bruna needs someone to translate her words to Stephen."

It was a demeaning duty for Gerhardt, but one he'd earned. He was lucky his carelessness had not started an all-out battle.

The English soldiers began to file away, but the Segraves and my men remained where they were, still tensed for action as they faced each other across the room. I leaned up to whisper in Faulke's ear.

"My men will not leave me here with so many of your soldiers."

He gave an imperceptible nod, and then said, "Richard, stay with Stephen and Gerhardt." He turned toward his men and gestured toward the door. "The rest of you, return to the feast, as the princess ordered."

There it was again, that warm feeling that fogged my senses, simply because he had supported me in front of his men and mine.

"Have Stephen taken to our barracks when his wounds are tended," Faulke told Richard when the last soldier left the solar.

"Aye, my lord." Richard held a wad of fabric against the injured man's shoulder, but he spared a glance toward Gerhardt. It was not a friendly expression.

I simply gave Gerhardt a pointed look, and he responded with a short nod. He knew what I expected of him.

"I would like another word with you in private," Faulke said as he nodded toward the door that led to my bedchamber.

I could not help but hesitate. A word in private is what caused all of this trouble in the first place. On the other hand, surely it would cause no more. At my nod, he led me to the window seat in my bedchamber, although this time I chose to remain standing. He closed the door and I waited for him to say something, but he remained quiet, his gaze fixed upon the floor, his expression thoughtful.

"Who officiated Chiavari's wedding?"

"Bishop Winchelsey," I answered, wondering why he cared.

He blinked once. "The Bishop of Canterbury?"

"Aye."

"And the wedding mass took place in Ashland's chapel?" Faulke asked.

This time I hesitated. There was a purpose to his questions, one I would probably not like. "Aye."

He mulled that over for a time. "Chiavari's betrothal to Avalene was made official on the same day as ours. There is no reason we cannot be wed on the morrow, or the day after, at the very latest."

"Tomorrow?"

My horrified tone made him frown. He spread his hands in a gesture that conveyed curiosity rather than anger. "The longer we wait to unite our houses, the more excuses these soldiers will find to fight among themselves, and the harder it will be to protect you."

"I don't see how our marriage will change anything among our soldiers."

"Your own captain drew his weapon against one of my men," he said with a sound of exasperation. "What would your reaction be if Richard had skewered one of your soldiers?"

"If Richard had attacked one of my men, I doubt that Richard would still be alive," I said honestly. "Gerhardt rarely hesitates when he encounters a threat, which is the whole reason your man was injured." I looked up at him with dawning awareness. "Do you want Gerhardt punished for his actions?"

"I would have shown him the back of my hand at the

very least," Faulke confirmed. "A captain should not act with so little thought to consequences. But he is not my man, at least, not until we wed."

"What do you mean?" I asked.

He tilted his head a little and studied my face. "I will expect Gerhardt to swear his fealty to me on our wedding day, as my men will swear their fealty to you. The English knights and their soldiers are sworn to your father. However, your men and mine will unite under one banner."

"You must be jesting." The words were out of my mouth before I could consider them.

Faulke shook his head. "Our soldiers and servants are separate now, but they cannot remain that way."

"Why not?" Did he intend to take my people away from me? Isolate me among servants and soldiers who spoke only Welsh gibberish? My hands curled into fists at my sides. I would not allow it.

"You will never return to Rheinbaden," he said in a more cautious tone. "To keep them separated now is to simply delay the inevitable. Your people will live out their lives in England and Wales. Their children will grow up here and marry into English and Welsh families." He folded his arms across his chest and looked down at me. "Our peoples need to unite, sooner rather than later."

The idea of losing my people among Faulke's had never occurred to me. Why it had never occurred was a mystery. I should have anticipated this outcome, just as Faulke had.

Our households would only be united for as long as it

took Faulke to realize the full impact of the king's deception. But I had not considered how little time it might take for my people to form friendships and intermarry. We could be with the Segraves for months, perhaps as long as a year or more. What if some of my soldiers and servants formed family ties with Faulke's people and decided to stay with the Segraves? It was a question I had never considered.

"There are other benefits to a hasty wedding," Faulke went on. "Once we are wed, our soldiers will have no right nor reason to object to us spending time together in private. My measures to ensure your safety will also be made easier after our marriage. Surely you have no cause to disagree with my reasoning?"

I had ample cause to disagree. Sadly, they were not excuses I could share. I'd gone from weeks to anticipate my marriage to hours.

To be fair, I had already considered the possibility that our wedding would be hastily arranged. What caused the most concern was the unwelcome realization that the structure of my household would also undergo a change when we wed; perhaps not much, and not right away, but it would change.

However, I could not argue with Faulke's reasoning. His arguments were valid. It was my turn to scowl.

"My father intends to give us a wedding feast," I said. "Even the king cannot accomplish a royal feast in one day."

"I am no foreign prince to be lauded and celebrated," Faulke pointed out. "There is no need for the usual pomp. The feast to celebrate our marriage can take place in the days or weeks after the ceremony, whenever your father wishes. The marriage itself is most important, and you know that your father will agree with my reasons for hurrying the ceremony."

My father would agree wholeheartedly. No doubt he would have a jolly laugh at Faulke's unwitting impatience to close the trap. And I was trapped just as securely as Faulke. I wanted to warn him. My nails dug painfully into my palms.

"You are right, of course. There is no reason to delay the ceremony, and many reasons to hasten it."

"Good. I will make arrangements on the morrow," he said with obvious satisfaction.

I looked at my slippers, my head weighed down with equal measures of guilt, fear, and frustration. Sometimes it was easy to forget how much Faulke would someday hate me. This was not one of those times.

"I will do my best to make certain you are happy in our marriage," he said, a note of hesitation in his voice. "My name and the gossip about my family precedes me in England, but I will not allow anyone to slander your name, simply because you married me."

Ach, he only made me feel worse. He truly believed that he was marrying up in the world, and I was marrying down. The guilt twisted in my gut. I was about to do or say something very foolish; I could feel the truth clawing its way to the surface.

I pressed my lips together even as I wondered at the strange compulsion. The truth was a foreign commodity among most royals. We dealt best in lies and intrigues, and I was my father's daughter. However, I was not a complete villain. I told Faulke as much of the truth as I could allow.

"I will be honored to call myself your wife, and I will do whatever I can to make certain you are happy in our marriage." I did not add, *for as long as you want me.* God only knew how much time we would have together to play at a happy marriage. I had best enjoy this fantastical interlude while it lasted. The fact that I also enjoyed the physical aspects of his attentions was worrisome. What else would I find to like about this man before he was gone?

Faulke lifted my hand and pressed a soft kiss to the inside of my wrist, never taking his gaze from mine. "You continue to surprise me, Princess."

The gesture was so sweet that I wanted to melt at his feet. My voice was little more than a whisper. "I want to be a good wife to you, Faulke."

My goals from now on, I decided, were to tuck away whatever guilt I felt into a nice, dark corner, and simply live for the moment. I leaned up to press a kiss to his cheek, but he turned his head at the last moment and expertly captured my mouth beneath his.

Oh, how I loved his kisses. He tasted like nothing I could describe or even imagine words to describe, something unique and his own that made me fist my hands in his tunic and move closer.

His kisses demanded all of my attention, and yet I still had room to revel in the fact that this handsome, dangerous, and impossibly likable man was mine. For now.

Eventually he lifted his head and pressed a lingering kiss to my forehead.

I couldn't contain a wistful sigh. "I wish moments like this could last forever."

He made a sound deep in his chest that I took for agreement, and then he took a step back to hold me firmly at arm's length. His mouth curved into a contented smile. "I cannot be alone with you any longer. There will be more appropriate moments within a day or two. Right now, we should return to the solar before anyone else gets injured."

Kisses were apparently off the agenda. I tucked away my guilt, and then gave a short nod. "Very well."

CHAPTER TEN

Childish Things

THE NEXT MORNING, WORD CAME THAT MY FA-
ther had agreed to petition the church about the banns.
He had provided Faulke's messengers with the necessary
letters for the clergy, but he also insisted that Bishop
Winchelsey perform the ceremony. Unfortunately, the
bishop had left London right after Dante and Avalene's
nuptials, but he would return to town again in two days.

Although part of me was glad for the extra days, it
was just more time to fret about Faulke's reaction when
he realized I was not good at the more intimate aspects
of wifely duties. It shouldn't matter; noble marriages
were about duty, not lust. Sadly, I knew enough about
men to know that it would matter to Faulke. I wondered
if he would compare my lack of enthusiasm to his second wife, Edith, the religious fanatic.

Each hour we spent apart, I vacillated between dread at the thought of seeing him again, and unbearable excitement at the same prospect. I hadn't thought about what the days would be like between the time we met and married because it had never occurred to me that I would actually like the man or enjoy his company. The last thing I had expected was to become hopelessly infatuated with him. Faulke made everything seem so easy, as if we could truly be happy together.

"Do you plan to wear pearls?" Avalene asked, interrupting my dark thoughts.

I nodded absently, then picked up the ropes of pearl necklaces that I had draped on top of a pink gown. Faulke had left to discuss our upcoming wedding mass with his father, so I was left to my own devices for the afternoon. Avalene had volunteered to help me pick out an outfit for the ceremony, and I had unpacked nearly every trunk in my chambers to display the choices. However, there was only one obvious choice.

"What would you wear with this outfit?" I asked Avalene. "The white kid slippers or the pink ones?"

Avalene looked at the beautiful garments I had worn the day I met Faulke. She looked disappointed. As she turned to poke through a trunk filled with shoes and slippers, I smoothed the skirts of one of the gowns and tried to pretend her answer did not matter.

"None of these," she said.

I let the pearls slip through my fingers and back onto the bed. The beads clicked in a rhythmic patter, a shimmering white waterfall worth a king's ransom. "What is wrong with my garments?"

"There is nothing wrong," Avalene said as she straightened from her search. "This finery announces to the world that you are a wealthy German princess."

"Well, of course," I agreed. "That is the reason they were created."

"Hm." She turned her back to me again.

"Royals should not look like commoners, or even other nobles," I said.

"Mm-hm." Avalene wandered over to the garment trunks and began to rummage through their remaining contents. "You say the ceremony is to be a small affair, without the attendance of your father or court dignitaries?"

"Aye, my father refuses to attend masses, even wedding masses." I gave a sigh of impatience. "Just tell me what is wrong with my choices."

"Perhaps the gown for your ceremony need not be quite so fine," she said in a tentative tone.

"Why not?" I said. "Granted, the mantle with Rheinbaden eagles on the shoulders might be a bit much, but every woman should wear her finest garments on her wedding day."

Avalene nodded, as if she agreed with me, then gave me a guileless look. "How would you feel if Lord Faulke came to your wedding in the livery of his last wife's house?"

"His last wife was a peasant," I snapped, incensed at the thought of such an insult. "I doubt her family has a crest, much less colors."

"Aye, but let's say for the sake of argument that they did," Avalene insisted. "Or, think of his first wife, Jeanne.

Jeanne's family colors are blue and gold, with a falcon for a device. What if Lord Faulke dressed in blue and gold from head to foot with a falcon emblazoned on his chest? How would that make you feel?"

At least as angry as just the thought of it made me feel. I would want to rip the clothes off his back, and not for any lustful reasons. I could not tolerate the idea of another woman's mark upon him, even though I knew that three other women once had a claim to him that was just as valid as my own. They were in his past and needed to stay there. I looked at the sea of white and pink in my chamber, and realized the point Avalene was trying to make.

"A gown in the Segraves' colors might find more favor in Faulke's eyes than a gown that will surely remind him of your prince," Avalene said, still digging through one of the trunks. "I am certain I saw you in black garments the other day. Black is one of the Segraves' colors."

I nudged her out of the way and pulled out a wool surcoat. "Several of my gowns and surcoats were dyed black to disguise ink stains, but nothing went to the dye vat that is so fine as my court clothing."

Avalene picked up the skirt of the surcoat and held up the embroidered hem. The original scroll design on the hem had been done in pure silver thread and accented with flowers embroidered in pink. Now the surcoat and its pink embroidery thread were dyed coal black. However, the silver metal threads stood out in an interesting design and made the garment worth keeping.

"Your definition of 'fine' means something entirely different from what the word means to most people,"

Avalene said. "Any of your cast-off gowns are finer than anything I own." She caught her lip between her teeth. "Well, that is no longer true. Dante has been very generous. But still, your cast-off gowns are quite fine."

"I cannot wear all black to my wedding ceremony," I said. "Even Faulke would find that dreary. I have several white shifts. I will wear one of those under this black surcoat."

"Dante is having gowns made for me," Avalene said. "His family's colors are red and gold. The Segrave colors are black and red."

I had no idea what she was about.

"I could lend you one of my new gowns for your wedding ceremony," she went on, now in earnest. "You can wear it under this black surcoat. Several red gowns have been patterned but remain uncut. I am an excellent seamstress, as are your ladies. By the time of the ceremony, I am certain we can have you in a gown fit for royalty. Good English royalty."

Avalene's enthusiasm was infectious. I smiled at her. "It would be nice to have new colors to wear."

She looked very pleased with herself. "Let's go find your wedding gown."

CONSTRUCTION ON THE new gown was well under way by late that afternoon. Blanche, Gretchen, Hilda, and Avalene had set up their stools and embroidery hoops in the center of the solar where the light from the windows was best. The seams were quickly sewn, fittings were made, and they were already at work on embellishments. Having no sewing talent whatsoever, I brought out my writing trunk and continued to work on my book of fables.

"My embroidery thread is red," Blanche said in French to my ladies, her voice far too loud. She held up her needle and motioned with her hands. "Needle. Embroidery thread. The *color* is *red*."

While Blanche's attention was on Gretchen, Hilda rolled her eyes.

"My ladies are German, not deaf," I chided Blanche. "There is no need to shout at them."

"Aye, my lady," Blanche murmured, and then her eyes rounded. "I mean, Princess!"

Normally I did not stand on ceremony with my people, and they referred to me as their lady almost as often as they referred to me as their princess. I made a vow then and there to stop correcting the ausländers. It was good for the newcomers to have a reminder of my rank.

"English cow" a young voice muttered in Italian from under the table.

"When one insults the servant, one insults the mistress," I said in the same language as I nudged Rami with my foot. "And do not forget that Italian is spoken by many people in this palace."

Rami's head popped up on the other side of the table. Chiavari's page had dark hair and the olive complexion of many Italians, but I knew from Avalene that the boy was Arabic. Chiavari had saved the child's life, and Rami had sworn himself to Chiavari's service out of gratitude . . . regardless of Chiavari's feelings on the matter. These days, Rami was often assigned to attend Avalene.

I watched him cram the last bite of a pear into his mouth before he tossed the core into the ashes of the fireplace. An apple appeared next in his hand, and he polished it on one of his sleeves as he met my gaze with a bold, dark-eyed look.

"My apologies, Princess," Rami said, with a courtly bow. "I meant no insult. This woman is new to your court. You cannot be held accountable for her ignorance."

He took a bite of the apple and waited in silence for my response. I eyed the apple, then returned his stare. The boy was incorrigible.

Soon after Chiavari's arrival at Ashland, I learned that Rami's clothes were a veritable pantry. They contained an astonishing variety of foods that he managed to steal from the kitchens or dining tables. Not that he had to steal the food; it would be given to him gladly, but that point seemed lost on the boy. It no longer startled me when a small hand would suddenly appear from under a table to snatch away something edible. He was always hiding under a table, or crouched in a corner, or tucked away in the shadows, gnawing on some treat or another. I had told Avalene that she should keep the boy better fed, but I had since learned that no amount of food could satisfy him. If quantity of consumption was any indication, Rami would be ten feet tall when he grew up.

I gave him a smile that bared my teeth. "Since you cannot behave in a manner that reflects well upon your mistress, you can reflect upon the errors of your ways while you go fetch Reginald the steward to meet with me here in the solar. Tell him that I wish to plan the meal that will follow my nuptials."

Rami bowed flawlessly, and then he was gone.

I didn't look up from my work when the solar door opened again, assuming it was Rami returning from his errand.

"Princess?"

Just the sound of his voice made me smile. Then I looked up at him, and the smile froze on my face. Faulke stood before me, looking just as delicious as ever, but he was not alone. In addition to Richard and a half dozen of their soldiers, there were three women, clearly servants, and three children. I immediately knew the children's identities. One of the servants held a red-haired toddler with green eyes who sucked her thumb: Lucy. A dark-haired girl clutched a stuffed doll and tried to hide behind her maid's skirts: Jane. A taller girl with her father's dark hair and blue eyes stood with her feet braced apart, hands on her hips, glaring at me with a defiant gleam in her eyes: Claire.

Faulke gave me a polite bow, and then came around the table to lift my hand for another indecent kiss on the inside of my wrist. I glanced at the girls as he did it, embarrassed that they might know what he was doing.

"Greetings, Princess," Faulke murmured, his tone formal. His hands went out to encompass the children and servants. "I would make my children known to you: Claire, Jane, and Lucy."

On the outside, I kept my face a careful mask of indifference as I studied each child. On the inside, someone kept squealing, *Oh my God, they're here!* If I had known they were coming this afternoon, I would have worn a better gown. My soldiers would be wearing their best. My ladies would be wearing their best. I would have practiced something to say to them. What would I say to them? *Oh my God, they're here!*

"I am pleased to meet you," I said to the girls. "Someone will find you a bench so you may sit, and then we will get to know one another." I signaled Gerhardt with a meaningful nod of my head, and he sent two of my soldiers to retrieve the bench. "In the meantime, let me introduce my ladies."

The soldiers returned with two benches by the time the four women were introduced. Faulke finally took his seat beside me when the two older girls were seated with their maids standing behind them. Lucy's maid held the toddler on her lap and sat next to Jane.

I spoke to the girls, but gave Faulke a sideways look so he would know that I was talking to him. "This is such a surprise. I did not expect to meet you girls today."

"I thought to surprise you," Faulke told me. "It was a surprise to the girls as well."

"Well, I am surprised." I leaned closer and whispered so only he would hear. "Do they know about our wedding?"

"Aye, they are well aware of who you are."

I glanced at the girls again. Lucy was playing with the strings on her maid's bonnet, Jane seemed more fascinated by her doll than by anyone else in the room, and Claire was staring daggers at me. Lucy was too young to carry on a conversation, and Claire looked like she would be a challenge, so I decided to start in the middle.

"Have you named your doll, Mistress Jane?" I asked.

Startled, Jane glanced up at me, and then seemed too frightened to look away. "Aye, m-my lady—Princess."

Claire reached out to clasp her sister's hand, which seemed to calm Jane. That small show of comfort made me think there was hope for Claire.

I kept my voice low and even. "Would you share her name with me?"

"M-Mistress Buttons." Jane moved closer to her sister.

"Mistress Buttons's friends are very pretty," I said honestly. Faulke's oldest girls were exceptionally handsome, and Lucy was cute in a babyish sort of fashion. Having had a description of Lucy's mother from Avalene, and looking at Claire's and Jane's obvious likeness to their father, Lucy certainly did not favor her mother, or her supposed father. Faulke had claimed Lucy, but she was in no way his.

I stole a glance at him. Most men would have kept Lucy separate from her sisters. From what I had heard, Faulke treated Lucy no differently than Jane or Claire. I'm not sure why that bit of charity warmed my heart, but it did. Perhaps because I had once been an unwanted child, and no one had fought to keep me. No matter what the gossips said about him, I knew that deep down, Faulke was a good man.

I looked back at Jane. "Is this Mistress Buttons's first trip to the city?"

"Aye, my—Princess. None of us have been to London before." She glanced at Faulke. "Except my father, of course. He goes to court to meet with the king."

"And what does Mistress Buttons think of London so far?"

Jane clutched the doll tighter. "'Tis very big. And smelly. And the streets are dirty."

Lucy made an odd baby sound and then yelled, "Cup!"

The maid holding her tried unsuccessfully to shush the girl.

"Cup!" Lucy yelled again, pointing to a goblet sitting next to Hilda. She made a few more noises, and then continued to yell. "Cup, cup, cup!"

"Forgive me," the maid shouted over Lucy, who was now sobbing and wailing *'cup'* every now and again. "I will take the girl to the kitchens, if someone will show me the way."

Faulke nodded to one of his soldiers, who hurried to escort the maid and screaming child from the solar. We all listened to the fading sobs as if transfixed.

"Pardon the girl," Faulke said with a chagrined expression. "She is obviously very young and does not yet know how to conduct herself in adult company."

I waved my hand in a casual dismissal. "And what of you, Lady Claire?" I asked her. "How do you find London?"

"I am *Mistress* Claire." She sat up straighter and remembered to glare. "And I hate London. I want to go home."

"You are aware that your father will assume my titles when we wed? He will become an earl," I reminded her. "That will make you a lady, and a step-granddaughter of the king. I would advise you to become accustomed to the responsibilities of that title."

Claire's expression turned mutinous, and she muttered something unintelligible. She poked the toe of her slipper at a corner of a rush mat near her foot. "I still don't like London. 'Tis dirty and smelly."

"Parts of the city are both," I agreed, "but it can be a fascinating place. We shall visit Westminster before you leave, and walk the London Bridge to watch the boats on the Thames. Perhaps we could also introduce you to my father and tour the Tower, although I daresay he will leave London soon. Troubles in the north, I hear."

Claire's eyes widened. "You would introduce us to the king? At court?"

"Not at court," I clarified, recalling Lucy's screeches. "I would request a private audience, but the king is a very busy man. I can make no guarantee that he will have time for us before he leaves."

"But you will try?" Claire persisted.

"Claire," Faulke said in a warning tone, drawing out her name.

I tilted my head and made her wait for my answer. "Aye. I will try."

Claire had the grace to blush. "Thank you, Princess."

"Have you been to any of the guild streets yet?" I asked.

Claire gave her father an uncertain look. "Guild streets?"

"Aye, the streets where guilds sell their wares," I explained. "Baker's Lane is a particular favorite of mine. You can find any pastry you ever desired there, and some you never knew existed." I gave her an exaggerated examination. "You will all need new gowns, now that you will be ladies. We could visit Weavers Lane to pick out fabric, and then go on to Mercers Street for belts and headbands, and the cordwainers for slippers."

Claire looked again at her father. "Could we do that, Papa?"

"We will make a day of it," Faulke said, spreading his hands to encompass Jane and her maid. "I suspect we could even find a new stuffed friend for Mistress Buttons."

It was Jane's turn for her eyes to widen. She looked at her father. "Mistress Buttons would like to have a new friend, Papa."

"'Tis decided then," Faulke announced. "We shall soon spend an entire day shopping in the city, but the princess and I have business at court we must attend to first. No nagging your maids in the meantime or we won't go at all. Am I clear?"

"Yes, Papa," both girls answered in unison.

"Excellent." He nodded toward Richard. "Now you must go with Cousin Richard to see your new quarters. Your new mother and I have plans we must discuss. I will rejoin you in time to walk you to the great hall for dinner."

The girls were less enthusiastic about the prospect of leaving their father. They bobbed awkward curtseys, their faces masks of exaggerated misery. Not that I cared about their pouts. I was too distracted, still thrown off balance by Faulke's reference to me as their mother. I was a mother now. *A mother!*

"I should not have surprised you," Faulke said when the children were gone.

"Everything worked out," I said, thinking about the shops I wanted to take them to.

"What is your impression of my girls?"

"They are lovely," I said honestly. "Will you really accompany us on a shopping excursion around the city?"

"I had planned just such an outing, but hadn't gotten around to telling them about it," he said. His eyes were very blue, and he rested his hand on top of mine on my thigh. His thumb began to brush a pattern against my skin. "We can go tomorrow, if you would like."

I nodded an agreement, even though I scarcely heard him. I was too distracted by the feel of his hand against mine, the leisurely pattern he traced on my skin. Was he even aware that he was doing it?

He took my hand in his and stood, pulling me up with him. "Come. Let's take a walk in the gardens."

CHAPTER ELEVEN

Changes

AT FIRST I THOUGHT THE GARDEN WALK WAS simply an excuse to find a private place to kiss. Instead we talked. We walked and talked for hours. Conversation flowed and the world outside the garden ceased to exist.

He told me more about his childhood, how he and Richard had constantly competed, and the time they had joined forces to trick the stable master into thinking all of the hounds had escaped. The two boys sounded like they were a handful. Several times he started to laugh before he could tell me what he was laughing about, which made me laugh, which made him laugh even harder. He spoke with such affection for his family and his people that I became even more certain that he would never purposely harm anyone in his care.

Somewhere on that journey to nowhere, the butterflies in my stomach stopped fluttering for the most dangerously handsome man in existence, and began to take wing for Faulke Segrave, the man.

Fortunately, he only told me of happy memories, so my dreamy smile was probably appropriate most of the time. Other times, my smile would fade of its own accord when his eyes would glaze over in the midst of recalling some adventure, especially when his now-absent mother was involved. I knew somehow that those were not happy memories, and I found myself wanting to somehow comfort him.

I was not a comforting type of woman, but with Faulke, I wanted to make him forget the unpleasant memories. Whenever he looked somber, I changed the subject, usually by telling him about one of my childhood adventures with Gretchen. We were not nearly as adventurous as Faulke and Richard, but we played our share of pranks on our maids and on the other children at court. The stories reminded me that not all or even most of my time in Rheinbaden had been unpleasant. I had many good memories of my years there.

We looked at each other as we talked. Really looked. His gaze moved over my face, returned to my eyes, took in my hair, moved lower to the neckline of my gown, and then returned to my face to start the journey all over again. I felt as if he was cataloguing each of my features and expressions, because I was doing the same in return. The few small flaws I inventoried didn't surprise me.

There was the scar through his eyebrow, of course, but that only made him look more dangerous. That eyebrow was also a little higher than the other. His hair could use a good trim. Sometimes he made a sound when he laughed that was just as ridiculous as my donkey bray when I laughed too hard. I almost cherished those small flaws, because they made me realize I was no longer blinded by the façade of perfection. Yes, he was handsome, but he was also funny, frustrating, bossy, and intelligent. Most of all, he was mine. And I wanted to keep him.

I thought about all the women in his past, all of the obstacles in our future, and realized these moments of happiness with him would be fleeting. I felt equal measures of gratitude and anger toward my father for putting Faulke in my life. I felt guilty for deceiving him, but at the same time, I enjoyed my time with him so much that I could not bring myself to ruin things between us. I wished that we could go on forever as these two people in the garden, that we could live a long and happy life at Ashland Palace. Sometimes I could forget, but deep down I knew that another heartbreaking lesson lurked just around the corner.

"What is that look for?"

His voice seemed to come from very far away. I blinked once to clear my thoughts, and realized I had been staring at him in silence. I looked around at the greenery where we sat near a bed of yarrow, and realized I had stared at him long enough for it to be strange, even between us. It wasn't one of our odd staring-contest stares, but had instead been an unseeing gaze that took my thoughts to dark places.

"Will you make me a promise?" I asked, the hesitancy in my voice revealing my uncertainty.

Wariness replaced his earlier unguarded expression. "This sounds serious. What must I promise?"

"You have a reputation at court with the women there," I began, watching his face harden. "I don't want to know them."

He tilted his head to look down at me, his expression guarded and neutral. "I'm not certain I understand your meaning."

"Your women," I said, waving a dismissive hand as if they meant little to me. Just the thought of them made my hands want to ball into fists. "I do not want to be introduced to them, I don't want to speak with them by accident if I don't know who they are, and I don't want any of them under the same roof where I sleep."

"Isabel, those women are in my past." He reached for my hands and gently squeezed them until the fingers un-clenched, then he held them between us. He waited until I looked up at him, then he stroked one finger along my cheek. "I spoke the truth the other day."

"Hm?" I tried to hold on to the conversation, but that small touch unbalanced me.

"When I said that I could think of no other woman but you." He gave me a slow smile and I forgot what we were talking about. "You are the only woman I want, Isabel. 'Tis a blessing we are betrothed, for I would want you even if I couldn't have you."

His head dipped down and his lips captured mine for a sweet kiss that made me want to take his shirt off. I felt suddenly aggressive, unsatisfied by the chaste kiss. I moved closer to press against him, but he lifted his head.

"What about you?"

I blinked once. "What about me?"

"Surely you had men pursue you in Rheinbaden? Men who caught your eye."

"Nay, never," I answered absently as I stared at his mouth and wondered how I could get him to kiss me again.

He put his hands on my shoulders in a firm but gentle grip when I tried to lean toward him. "You and Hartman were separated for many years," he said. "I find it hard to believe that no man ever pressed his suit with you."

"None did." I frowned, remembering. "Well, one set his men upon me and there was a lot of bloodshed as a result. No one tried again, after that."

I tried to lean into him again, but his muscles suddenly felt like marble. His hands were firm on my shoulders and he held me away until I looked up at him. His eyes narrowed.

"Who set his men on you?"

I cleared my throat and leaned back, trying to judge his sudden anger. It looked contained, but simmering.

"His name is Leopold von Tyrol, the cousin of Hartman's favorite mistress, Maria. Leopold was a great favorite in the tournaments, but there were always rumors about his cruelty. He and his men stopped at Grunental on their way home from a tourney, and asked to be granted hospitality. I had no good excuse to bar him from the castle, although I wanted to."

"He tried to seduce you?" Faulke's voice was close to a growl.

"I knew better than to provide an opportunity," I said. "He has a reputation for preying upon women, so I dismissed all of my female servants and ladies, and had only men serve in the great hall that evening. I had expected some sort of argument about the insult to his honor. His unusually proper behavior made me wary."

Faulke's jaw looked as if it were made from granite. I stopped talking, trying to decide how to tell him what happened next. His voice was firm. "Finish the story."

"Perhaps it would be best if I tell you the version related to me by one of my spies." I looked unseeing at a spot over his shoulder and tapped my chin, remembering. "In those days, I had spies everywhere in Rheinbaden, including a knight in the von Tyrol household. My spy there did not yet realize what had happened at Grunental, but he overheard every word of Leopold's report to his father when he returned home.

"By his own words, Leopold went to Grunental with the express purpose of compromising my honor. His cousin Maria wanted to marry Hartman, and she believed that would happen if Hartman became a widower, and the von Tyrols would have closer ties to the crown if they helped make that happen.

"In Rheinbaden as here in England, a crown princess or a queen is put to death for treason if she is caught in bed with a man who is not her husband. However, the man caught with me would be executed as well. Leopold was not stupid enough to sacrifice his own life for his cousin's schemes. Instead he recruited two disreputable knights to his company, men whose taste for rape might have surpassed his own."

"What did Leopold do to you?" Faulke asked. I glanced up and realized he was not merely angry. There was murder in his eyes.

"I am getting to that part," I said. "But I should tell you now that I was not physically hurt in any way."

He raised his brows. "Continue."

"Aye, well, Leopold had convinced the two knights that he could shield them from any consequences of their actions. That night, Leopold made sure the two knights drank more than the rest, and stoked their fury by questioning my right to deny them the comforts of a few comely women."

Faulke stood and began to pace, but he motioned for me to keep talking.

"Someone needed to teach me a lesson, and of course they encouraged Leopold to be that man. But he said the lesson would come better from a knight, rather than a nobleman near my rank. He had coached his own men to agree with him, but to raise concerns about losing their heads. Then one of Leopold's knights argued that I would never let it be known that I had been bedded by lowly knights. It would be a right and fitting lesson.

"Leopold had his own spies, and he knew that I did not post guards at my door at night, and only my two ladies slept in my chambers. Gretchen was at court with Gerhardt to attend their brother's wedding, so they expected only Lady Hilda and me to be there. The two knights would enter my rooms and subdue Hilda while they took their turns with me. Leopold and his men would stand guard in the hallway.

"In reality, Leopold waited until the two knights entered my apartment, and then they left for the great hall to rouse some of my soldiers. They claimed that the two knights had been drunk and talked about accosting me, and now they were missing and Leopold feared the worst. He took the soldiers back to my apartment where Leopold had already planned to slay the two knights immediately for being in my quarters. He wanted my soldiers as well as his own knights to stand as witnesses to my crime of allowing myself to be raped.

"What Leopold didn't count on was my complete distrust of his reasons for being at Grunental in the first place, and his strange behavior at dinner. I had the most vulnerable women moved into my apartments that night and more men set inside to guard the doors. The two knights and one of my men were already dead by the time Leopold arrived. Of course, he disavowed any knowledge of his two knights' intents. He even pretended to take offense that I would dare question him." I ended my story with a shrug. "Leopold's quarters were put under guard for the remainder of the night, and they left in the morning."

"What did your husband do?" The tone of Faulke's voice told me what he would have done.

"The information I gained from my spy was only hearsay," I said, "and the word of a spy would hold no weight in my husband's court."

"Did you tell your prince or King Rudolph what happened? What *really* happened?"

"I knew better than to cause trouble within their court. Especially when I had no proof." The anger I had felt at the injustice of that episode had faded long ago, but I could feel it begin to rise again. "The von Tyrols apologized to the king and to Hartman, they paid the weregild for my knight who was slain in the fight, and that was the end of it. Leopold never came to Grunental again, but Gerhardt was furious when he learned what had happened. Leopold is the reason there are now bars on all of my doors."

Faulke was still pacing. Silent. I could almost feel the waves of anger radiate from him.

"It was a long time ago," I said quietly, sorry that I had upset him with the story, and knowing I had one more that would make him even angrier. "It was a lifetime ago, actually. I was still wed to Hartman, you were wed to someone else, and you didn't even know I existed. There was nothing you could have done then or now to change what happened."

"Do not humor me," he ordered.

I folded my hands in my lap and pressed my lips together.

He came to a stop in front of me and put his thumb beneath my chin. "And do not give me that silent look of yours that says you are still humoring me."

That made me smile. He blew out a frustrated breath, then pulled me to my feet and kissed me. My mouth opened in surprise and he deepened the kiss. His arms swept around me, lifting me to my toes. There was urgency and possession in his kiss, and the heat coming from him was incredible, scorching me. His tongue touched mine, and I forgot all about Leopold and Grunental.

"I would have killed him," he said at last as his lips skimmed down from the curve of my ear to my throat. "You are mine now, Isabel. No man will threaten you and live to apologize for it."

His undisguised possessiveness sent a streak of heat through me. "Even if that man is a king?"

An unreadable expression crossed his face. "Has your father made a threat against you?"

"Nay!" I touched my fingers to his cheek. "I don't know why I asked that question. I cannot think straight when you kiss me."

In an instant, the light in his eyes changed from anger to a smoldering fire. He covered my hand with his to trap it against his cheek. His gaze dropped to my lips, and then dipped lower. The gown I wore was cut no lower than my others, but he took a deep breath that shuddered on the way out. The sound made me shiver with awareness of the effect I had on him. The heat in his eyes warmed feminine places inside me.

"And I cannot think straight when I hear about dangers to your life before we met." He moved my hand to his lips and gently kissed the backs of my fingers. "I know you are accustomed to dealing with troubles on your own, but you can lean on me now. Whatever troubles you, tell me, and I will do whatever I can to make it trouble you no more."

My chest felt tight, and there was a suspicious stinging in my eyes. I laid my head on his shoulder and hid my face against his neck, just in case tears started to leak out. My voice was a little breathless. "I think that's the nicest thing anyone has ever said to me."

I felt him stiffen, as if he were angry again. I began to look up, but he pressed my head back to his shoulder and then his arms went around me. My bones wanted to melt into him, the pull between us magnetic again. The dangerous impulse to give him what he wanted rose up within me, an almost overwhelming need to tell him all of my troubles, and then see if he still wanted me. I was no longer so sure of the answer. Not when his solid strength surrounded me, making me feel safe and protected. I hadn't felt that way for a very long time.

He took a step backward and I actually tried to cling to him, but he gathered my wrists in his hands and held me at arm's length. His gaze went to the rows of windows that overlooked this section of the grounds, then returned to give me one of those hungry looks that turned my insides to warm butter. "These gardens are deceptively public, and I am distracted by intentions that should remain private. We need to rejoin the others."

I nodded reluctantly, then made no objection when he took my hand and led me back toward the great hall.

WE TOOK FAULKE'S daughters shopping the next morning. Despite my nerves, I was determined to create an experience so special that we would all look back on this day with smiles and fond memories. Even Lucy participated at first, when I insisted she should attend, but I regretted my insistence about an hour later when Faulke sent the wailing toddler back to Ashland with her maid and two of our soldiers. Apparently, a two-year-old did not make an ideal shopping companion. Lucy's defection left me undaunted. She wouldn't remember the day anyway, and now I had more time to concentrate on winning over Claire and Jane.

Although Claire had begun the day with the same terse responses and dagger glares for me, she became friendlier as the day went on, despite her obvious intent to remain cold and aloof. She was still guarded, but I managed to make her smile on occasion, and once she even squealed when I allowed her to order a pair of ermine-trimmed slippers. Jane was her usual quiet self, but I discovered she liked to shop nearly as much as her sister. The girls' maids were silent spectators.

It was a good thing Faulke insisted on having so many soldiers accompany us. They made handy receptacles for all the goods we purchased, and dutifully hauled packages from one vendor to the next, most notably fabrics to seamstresses. Both girls were amazed that they would have two new gowns made up for them by strangers within as many days.

After shopping, we stuffed ourselves with pastries, and then walked to London Bridge. There we visited more stalls with trinkets for sale, watched the river traffic as boats and barges and rafts of all sorts competed for space on the Thames, and occasionally spied ocean-going ships with full masts that made the other watercraft look like children's toys.

Despite the distraction of the girls, Faulke found a way to keep me constantly off balance, like when he reached out to move a stray tendril of hair from my face, or when he made a habit of placing his arm around my waist when we talked to a merchant, or when he brushed a few stray crumbs from my chin when we ate our pastries. I loved when he looked at me. There might have been some staring contests involved.

It was one of the most perfect days of my life.

CHAPTER TWELVE

Another Wedding

MY SECOND WEDDING WAS EVERYTHING MY
first was not. The first had taken place in a cathedral
with hundreds in attendance. No more than two score
attended my second. There were also hundreds of white
doves released at the end of the first ceremony, and bells
in every church had pealed to let everyone in the city
know that their crown prince was wed. Someone belched
at the end of my second ceremony, and then several people were overcome with fits of giggles.

Even I smiled at the incongruity, and decided I liked
laughter much better than the rigid propriety that had
marked my first ceremony. The day itself was not half as
stressful as I anticipated. Avalene had been right about
the red and black gown. The look in Faulke's eyes when
he realized I had dressed in his colors made all the prod-

ding and fittings and last-minute adjustments to my garments worthwhile. Indeed, each look Faulke and I exchanged made the day worthwhile, and I tried to imprint every image in my memory, to recall for all time.

Aside from the belch and laughter, the ceremony was already beginning to blur in my mind. The small feast in the great hall that followed our wedding was another round of toasts and smiles and well wishes that sent my emotions careening among happiness, anticipation, and panic.

By the time Faulke took my arm and made our excuses to depart, I was tempted to gather my skirts and bolt in the other direction. To where, I had no idea, but something would come to me. Anything was better than what was coming.

Just as I gathered my skirts to flee, Faulke stopped and put his hands on my shoulders to steady me. We were alone in one of the dimly lit passageways that led to my solar, but the concern in his eyes was clear to see.

"What is wrong with you?" he asked.

"N-nothing."

He gave me a wry look. "You have been shaking like a leaf for the past hour. 'Tis why we left the feast so early. Others were beginning to notice."

We left early? The feast had seemed endless, but now I could only recall a few of the dozens of dishes I had arranged to be served. This problem I could solve. "I will send word to Reginald, and have him send several courses to the solar for our evening meal."

"I do not care about the food," he said with a trace of humor.

"But there is a sugar boat with almond comfits! Those were ordered especially for you. They had better not serve them if we are not present."

He framed my face in his hands, and his lips curved into a smile. "I love that you remembered my fondness for sugar, but you are the only sweet I need today."

His head descended, his lips captured mine in a kiss, and I waited for the magic that would make me forget all of my fears and worries. He lifted his head almost immediately, and I made a small mewl of distress. His hands still held my face, and I closed my eyes when his thumb brushed across my mouth. If there was magic, I could not find it in the waves of panic and dread that washed over me. Again I felt as if I were drowning, but this time in a very, very bad way.

"Isabel, your heart is racing so fast that I can see it beat against your chest. Tell me what is wrong."

My heart chose that moment to sink to the floor, along with my hopes. I could continue to pretend ignorance and let him discover for himself what was wrong with me, or I could confess. I glanced in each direction toward the darkened ends of the passageway, where anyone might overhear. "I will tell you, but not here."

His gaze held mine for a long moment, and then he gave a short nod of agreement.

The walk to my solar had never seemed so short. We were in my bedchamber all too quickly, with the doors barred from the inside and guards posted outside. It was our wedding night. This time no one would disturb us.

Faulke motioned me to the window seat, and then sat beside me. He lifted my hand and pressed a kiss to my fingers, the gesture so tender that my eyes were suddenly blurry.

"I am your husband now," he said in a quiet voice, although I detected a trace of wariness. "You can tell me anything, Isabel."

Ach, if only that were true. This wasn't even supposed to be the big secret that the king insisted I keep at all costs. What I had to tell him, only Hartman knew. And Gretchen had only guessed at it. "I am about to disappoint you."

"How so?" he finally asked when I could not find the words to elaborate.

No matter how long and hard I had thought about this moment, there was no possible way to escape it without humiliating myself. "I am not like most women."

"I am well aware of that fact."

It took me a moment to realize we were not talking about the same thing. "Oh. No. That is not what I meant. What I meant is . . . I do not respond to men the way most women do."

He gave me an astonished look, and then he began to laugh. Then his expression sobered and his mouth flattened to a straight line. "Do you respond to women?"

"What? No."

He gave a huff of relief, but he still looked confused. "Then I do not understand what you are trying to tell me."

"Ach, must I spell it out for you?" If his baffled expression was any indication, the answer was yes. Why did he not understand? "I cannot please a man in bed."

He gave a short bark of laughter, then visibly struggled to hide his grin. He brushed his fingers along my cheek to lessen the sting of his inappropriate humor, and his eyes darkened a shade. "You have never been to bed with me."

Goodness. He did not lack in confidence. Not that it would change anything. I bowed my head and stared at the floor. If he laughed at me again, I honestly didn't know if I would get angry, or break down and cry. "I had hoped it would be different with you, but I recognize the signs anytime we kiss for too long. I do not . . . respond the way I am supposed to."

"How do you respond?" he asked.

"My blood turns to ice and I start to shake, as I did in the great hall. My husband said that it was impossible for a frigid woman to please a man."

"*I* am your husband now," he repeated with an edge of anger to his voice, "and I have never said such a thing."

"Hartman said it was impossible," I clarified, with my gaze fixed on the floor. Anger I could deal with, and I braced myself for it the longer Faulke remained silent. There was little doubt in my mind that his second wife, Edith, had suffered from a similar affliction, and his magical kisses had not cured her, either.

Finally, he lifted my hand and kissed my fingers. The action was so unexpected that my gaze flew to his face. He cradled my chin in his hand. "How many men have you been with, Isabel?"

"Just my husband, of course!" Now I was indignant. Before I could get righteous about my anger, he pressed his thumb against my lips.

"I am your husband now," he reminded me again, with

an edge of exasperation, "and frigid women do not respond to men the way you respond to me."

"They don't?"

He ignored that question. "What do you think about when I kiss you?"

"Colors," I replied without thinking, "and magnets. But then I start to feel cold when it becomes obvious you want to bed me."

He thought that over for a while. "What did Hartman do before . . . that is, what happened before . . ."

My cheeks burned. I knew what he was trying to ask. "He sent a servant to let my ladies know he would visit my chamber that night."

Faulke simply stared at me, clearly astonished.

I lifted my chin. "My husband—" I immediately rethought my words when his eyes narrowed. "Hartman was considerate. He tried to keep our encounters as brief as possible, since we both found them distasteful."

Faulke released a sigh that sounded an equal measure of anger and frustration, and then he leaned forward to rest his elbows on his knees and clasped his hands together before him. Well, now he knew. His disappointment was understandable. What man would be happy to know his wife could not please him? On his wedding night? Poor Faulke. He was such a carnal creature, and yet he'd had the misfortune to wed not one, but two women who were frigid. Half of his wives. That had to be some sort of record. Eventually he would find out that I was barren as well.

There was enough pity rolling around my stomach for both of us. Instead of some Welsh barbarian, I found myself wed to a handsome, charming man who would soon hate me. The Fates had not been kind to either of us.

I cleared my throat. "I will try very hard to think about your kisses when we are in bed together."

He held up one hand without looking at me. "Give me a few moments."

He returned to his contemplation of the floor, and I returned to contemplating a very bleak future. Finally, I could stand the silence no longer. "What are you thinking?"

"I am thinking about how old you were at your first wedding," he said, still without looking at me.

"I was a woman," I told him, "fully blossomed, and already as tall as some men."

"You were a child of twelve," he said, "and likely no more than thirteen when you delivered a babe with great difficulty. I have witnessed difficult births. They are nothing a child should see, much less be a part of."

"But I was not a child," I argued.

He turned his head to look at me, and then glanced at the top of my head. "Were you as tall as you are now when you wed?"

"Nay," I admitted, "I outgrew most of my gowns in the first two years of my marriage."

"Children become taller," he said. "Adults do not."

What that had to do with our situation, I could not piece together. Now that I thought about it, my wedding to Hartman did seem like a long time ago, and I seemed like a very different person in those days, young and naive. But I had been a woman, of that I was sure.

A muscle in Faulke's jaw kept moving, as if he were

grinding his teeth. Likely steeling himself for the night ahead. I steeled my nerves as well. "Should I . . . should I get into bed now?"

"No."

Well, that was a relief. But I had no doubt it was only a reprieve. Too much depended upon this marriage for Faulke to let it go unconsummated for even a night, even with the news I had just given him. I was anxious to get it over with.

"Hartman came to my bed countless times," I told him. "I am ready to do my duty. It might be unpleasant, but I know it won't kill me. It doesn't even last that long. If we start now, we might finish in time to send one of the guards to fetch the sugar boat before it's served."

His head turned in my direction, but he remained bent over with his elbows on his knees and his hands clasped before him. The incredulous look he gave me made my lips press together of their own accord.

My gaze went to the bed and then bounced to the window. The sun was bright and high in the sky. It would be hours before evening, and even more before dawn.

Gretchen once said that she used to rub Engel's neck and shoulders when he was upset, and that always put him in a better mood. I didn't want to think about what Hilda would do. I'd also heard women say that special food and drinks could cool a man's anger. Despite that look, I would definitely ensure that the sugar boat was delivered to the solar at some point, along with a generous portion of wine.

In the meantime, the hours stretched before us. Aside from the bedding, which would not end well, I would have to spend the entire night with a man who was angry, frustrated, and unsatisfied. Unless . . . no. He would surely spend the night here to avoid any questions about the marriage being consummated.

"This night has taken a far different turn than what I had planned," he said at last, startling me from my own thoughts. He straightened slightly to look into my eyes. "Despite your claims otherwise, you were a child when you married Hartman. To make matters worse, he did a very poor job of . . . 'Tis little wonder you developed an aversion to sex." He took my hands in his and made a pointed effort to look me straight in the eye. "Believe me, Isabel, you are not frigid."

After all this thinking time, he had fixated on what he could not change, determined that I was somehow mistaken. I pulled my hands from his and released a frustrated sigh.

His eyes narrowed. "Listen to what I have to say, Isabel. You have been with one man. I have been with more women than I care to admit, although right now, I am glad of my experience. You have almost none, and the experience you do have needs to be forgotten." He shook his head. "You were wed before you were old enough to know what being a wife meant." He put his fingertips on my lips when I started to argue. "Do not tell me I am wrong. You are an amazing woman in many ways, but in this, you are amazingly ignorant."

"Do you think me some dolt who does not know how sex is supposed to work? Not all of my knowledge comes from Hartman. I have overheard people talk about their experiences in bed. I know other women like sex. I am not stupid."

"I did not call you stupid." He smiled at my expression, which made me angrier. He gave my hand a gentle squeeze. "Ignorance is a lack of knowledge, not a lack of intelligence. As for that lack of knowledge, I intend to be a better teacher than your first. What we do together as man and wife will bear little resemblance to the relationship you had with your prince."

He was no longer smiling, and his voice held a definite edge. Had Hartman's lack of sexual prowess truly been the reason our physical relationship was so horrible? I shook my head. That couldn't be right. Hartman had mistresses who adored him, who vied to be his favorite. The problem had to be with me.

"We are going to do the same thing," I argued.

"No," he countered. "You and Hartman performed a duty that you both found unpleasant. I am going to teach you how to enjoy sex, and then I am going to teach you how to please me as well."

I searched his face and found only sincerity and confidence.

If anyone could accomplish such a miracle, surely it was the man before me. "I am listening."

"First, you need to stop referring to sex as a duty," he said, softening the order by rubbing his thumbs across my knuckles. "You are a princess, born and bred, but you must leave the princess at the door to our bedchamber. Within these walls, you are my wife. Here you must learn to be a wife who submits to her husband in all ways, who obeys him without question." He lifted my hand and turned it over to press a kiss to my wrist. "I need your trust in this, Isabel. No matter how you feel about our marriage outside these walls, when we are alone, you must learn to trust me without hesitation and without question. I promise you, the rewards will be worth your efforts."

He sounded so sure of himself. I didn't know how what he had planned could be all that different from having sex with Hartman, although there was no question that he had far more experience than me when it came to sexual partners.

My pride was already in tatters. Really, I had nothing left to lose if I tried to follow his lead. "What would I have to do?"

His lips curved into a satisfied smile, and he gave my hand an approving squeeze. "Kiss me."

Surely it could not be that simple? I leaned away from him to study his expression, looking for the trap.

"You must obey without question," he reminded me, and then he tapped one finger against the corner of his mouth. "Kiss me, Isabel."

I tried not to think as I leaned forward and pressed my lips to his, but the proximity of the bed was impossible to ignore. His lips moved tenderly over mine and his arm encircled my waist. He took my hand and held it to his cheek, encouraging me to explore the warmth of his skin and the fascinating textures: the rough sand of dark stubble along his jaw, the smooth silk of his hair when I wrapped my arm around his neck.

His tongue traced the seam of my lips and I opened for him. The sensual assault on my mouth made my heart race, but not all of the emotions sweeping through me were pleasant ones. There was fear as well, along with a little dread, but I could barely concentrate on them while his mouth explored mine so intimately. Just as I began to think too much about the bed just a few feet from us, he pulled away.

"That was very good," he said in a low voice. "I will want you to kiss me often when we are alone. Do you enjoy kissing me?"

The answer seemed fairly obvious, but I nodded anyway.

He tilted his head toward me and cupped his ear with one hand. "I could not hear your answer."

I made a little huff of annoyance. "I like kissing you."

"Good." He reached out to touch my lower lip with his thumb. "Tell me exactly what you felt when I put my tongue in your mouth."

My eyes widened and his hand went to the back of my neck to hold me in place when I tried to lean away, shocked by his boldness.

"You will obey me without question," he reminded me. "I want to know what thoughts went through your head, and how every part of your body felt when you parted your lips and let my tongue into your mouth."

My face burned, and I could feel the blush spread down my chest, but I did as he demanded. "It reminded me of the sex act, when a man thrusts himself inside a woman, but it was pleasurable."

"How was it pleasurable?" he asked, his gaze fixed on my mouth. "Tell me your body's reaction in detail."

I didn't think it was possible, but the heat of my blush

seemed to rise several degrees. I lowered my lashes. "There was a feeling of butterflies in my stomach, and all of my muscles seemed to clench, especially those lowest in my belly."

"Very good. That is what I hoped you would say." He pressed a soft kiss to my lips, and I felt an absurd flutter of happiness that I had pleased him. Rather than kiss me again, he took my hand and drew me to my feet so we stood facing each other. "We will both be more comfortable without all of these formal wedding clothes. Remove my belt and surcoat."

Obey without question. Do not think, just obey. I bit my lip and studied his belt. My pulse accelerated, but I reached for the buckle. "I have never helped a man disrobe."

"You must remove the weapons first," he instructed.

He wasn't wearing a sword, but I unsheathed the knife he had used at the feast, and then the ornate silver-handled dagger, and set them on the trunk that held my shoes. He reached around his back and produced a deadly sharp misericord that he handed to me hilt-first, and then I set all of the weapons aside. I struggled a bit with the buckle, but it finally came free.

The sleeveless surcoat was fitted like a vest to his waist, then flared out and reached well below his knees, made mostly of black leather trimmed with silver. I managed to get the garment off his shoulders, but had to go behind his back to tug it down his arms. He just stood there, patient, but entirely unhelpful. The garment felt as heavy as a saddle. I tossed it onto the trunk with his belt and weapons.

He gave a short huff of laughter. "My squire will never fear for his post when he sees how you handle my garments. Try not to tangle the laces when you remove my tunic. Just loosen the laces enough that it can slip over my head."

He lifted his arms and clasped his hands behind his head to reveal the leather laces at his sides. The tunic took much longer than I anticipated, likely because it was the first time I had ever done such a job. It felt intimate to touch him so much, even so impersonally. At last he leaned forward so I could tug the garment over his head, and then he stood before me in a black shirt and leather pants. Lud, men wore as many garments as women. My gaze came to rest on the laces at the front of his pants, and the clearly visible bulge beneath the laces.

"I like this gown." His fingers traced a line down my neck to the tops of my breasts, and then he drew a line across my breasts, on the skin exposed just above the scarlet fabric.

Hilda had been in charge of sewing the bodice, and it was indecently low. She claimed there was no better time than a wedding for a woman to flaunt her assets, and mine were on full display. I suddenly felt naked.

"You are trembling, Isabel." He took my hands and placed them high on his chest, flattening my palms against him with his own. "You need to kiss me again."

I rose up on my tiptoes to obey, but I was shaking so badly I had to wrap my arms around his neck and lean against him to steady myself.

"Shh," he whispered against my lips. His arms went around my waist to hold me safe. "I will not hurt you, sweetheart. You need to trust that I can make your body ready for mine."

He sounded so certain. I was far from it. I didn't even know what he was talking about, making my body ready for his. My body was ready to leap out the window. I just wanted to get this over with.

Still, he seemed to have a plan, and I was willing to go along with it. I lifted my lips to his and pressed a kiss there. He took over almost immediately, molding his mouth to mine, his hands sliding possessively over the curves of my back and waist and hips.

The kiss seemed to go on forever, possessive, but undemanding. The trembling inside me began to subside, but I still felt weak and shaky when he finally lifted his head. I thought he would say something, but he just cradled my head against his shoulder and rested his chin on the top of my head.

"Hush, now," he murmured. His hands stroked along my back and shoulders, petting and calming me.

To my mortification, I realized my eyes were wet and I was making little sounds of distress. "I'm s-sorry. I don't know what's wrong with me."

"I do," he said quietly. When I went stiff in his arms, he gave my hips a squeeze. "And, no, you're still not frigid."

"Am I like your second wife, Edith?" I wanted to take the question back as soon as I asked it, but curiosity won out. "Is that how you know what is wrong with me?"

"You are nothing like Edith," he admonished, as if the notion had never occurred to him. "Your . . . reactions to me have an entirely different cause."

I had leaned back to watch his expressions as he made those pronouncements. "If you know what is wrong, you must fix it."

His lips curved upward, and the corners of his eyes crinkled. "I am trying."

"You will try harder."

"You are too demanding, Princess." He tapped his finger against my lips, and he looked so handsome doing it that I had a hard time objecting. "This will not work until you let my sweet, obedient wife back into that clever mind of yours. You can be the princess when we are in public, but when we are in private, you must be my wife in the most traditional sense of the word. As your husband, I am your lord and master, and you are pledged to serve and obey me without question."

There was that "lord and master" nonsense again. If he thought he could turn me into a servant to do his every bidding, he had another think coming.

Then again, if acting like a servant would help cure my failings, then perhaps I should not dismiss the notion out of hand. I would only be the servant-wife in private. No one else would ever know that a royal princess had so thoroughly debased herself, and I would deny it to the last breath if he ever dared tell anyone.

I gave him a bobbed curtsey. "How may I serve you, master?"

He studied my face. "You can say that again and mean it."

Was he serious? I wiped away the last of my silly tears.

"I am waiting."

"This is ridiculous," I muttered.

"This is what you asked for," he countered. "You want to know the secrets of enjoyable sex, and I promise that you will receive as much pleasure as you will give to me. You have my word that I will do nothing to purposely frighten you, and I will never hurt you. I vowed to honor and cherish my wife, and I take those vows seriously. In every way possible. Now, say it again."

Ach. I had to become his slave. And mean it. I gave him a subservient curtsey, and bowed my head. This time I kept my tone respectful. "How may I serve you, master?"

"Better," he said, "but not perfect. You need more practice. Each time we find ourselves alone together, you will ask me that question."

I kept my expression carefully blank. He had promised not to hurt me. It was not such a terrible concession. "Aye, my lord. It shall be done."

He gave me an approving smile. "You are going to remove some of your garments."

My eyes widened and my pulse began to race. This part was familiar.

Faulke held up one hand. "Not all of them. Not yet, at least."

"Do you . . . do you want me to put on my night garments?"

He released a deep sigh and looked up at the ceiling. "Did you ever see your prince naked?"

My lip curled, I couldn't help it. "Of course not. We are not animals."

Faulke muttered something under his breath. Something that sounded unflattering to Hartman. "We are going to be naked, Isabel. Men and women actually enjoy being naked together, skin to skin. It excites me to think of you naked before me. Indeed, I have imagined it in great detail for the past fortnight. Have you never imagined me without clothing?"

I pressed my lips together.

He shook his head. "You will obey me, wife. Answer my question."

"I have wondered what you would look like on the practice field," I confessed, "without your shirt."

"Was it pleasurable, the thought of seeing me without my shirt?" he asked.

Mortified, I could only nod.

"Take off my shirt."

Well, I should have expected that order. I frowned and began to work at the laces, doing my best to take as long as possible, trying to decide if I was excited or frightened to see what he looked like beneath the shirt. He finally made a sound of impatience and pulled the garment over his head.

My eyes widened, and he seemed to take up even more of the chamber than he did before. His skin looked so smooth, and yet his arms and chest were corded with muscles. He let me stare my fill. He even turned in a small circle so I could see him from all sides, and all sides were equally impressive.

"While you gawk at me," he said, his mouth turned up in a grin, "take off your surcoat."

It was rather pleasant to look at him as I shrugged out of the sleeveless garment and let it fall to the floor. I tried not to think about what it meant to take off my surcoat. It hadn't occurred to me that he would want me to disrobe in front of him. All of the laces on my garments were in places I could reach, but only so I could change into the rather risqué night rail by myself while he enjoyed a goblet of wine by himself in the solar. It didn't occur to me that he would want to watch me undress.

"I can see your ladies will continue to play an important role in the upkeep of your wardrobe," he said with a nod at my discarded surcoat. He crooked his finger. "Come here."

I did as he ordered, hardly able to breathe as he removed my belt, and then the gold link girdle that clung to my hips. He stood so close, and there was just so much of him. The heat I could feel coming from his body was not imagined this time. I was close enough to feel it.

What might have been my imagination was that he seemed to touch me more than necessary when he untied the laces of my sleeves and slid them down to bare my arms. He lifted my arms and had me clasp my hands behind my head in a stance that mimicked his when I had unlaced his tunic, and then he definitely took longer than my ladies ever had to unlace the sides of my gown.

The trembling started again when I stood before him dressed only in my chemise. The garment was nearly transparent. Already I felt naked. How much worse would it be when I was actually naked? Another shiver went through me. His bare chest no longer seemed so fascinating, and I was no longer excited. My hands were actually shaking.

"Isabel—"

"This always happens! It makes me look like a coward, but I am not afraid. I am not afraid of you. I am not afraid of anything." To prove it, I wrapped my arms around his bare waist, and pressed myself against his naked chest, with my cheek resting on his shoulder. "*Please,* just get it over with."

CHAPTER THIRTEEN

Lovers

BOTH OUR BODIES WENT STIFF AT THE INITIAL contact, but he was the first to recover. He smoothed his hands down my shoulders and bared arms, and then his hands came to rest on my hips. He tried to separate us, but I clung to him like my body had been turned into a magnet.

"Did you just hear my promise that I would not hurt you?" he murmured. "The marriage must be consummated, but I will not begin it by raping my wife on our wedding night." His hand moved up and down my back in a soothing motion. "We can take our time."

"'Tis not rape," I protested. "I am ready and willing to do my duty."

His voice darkened. "You will not refer to sex with me as your duty."

I nodded against his chest. "I want to have sex with you. Right now, please."

There was a moment of silence, and then a huff of laughter. "Isabel, you turn my world upside down. One moment you are as shy as a virgin, the next you are as bold as a pirate."

"Sex is not a mystery to me," I told him. "Just because I am not good at it does not mean I know nothing about what happens between most men and women."

"Actually, that is reassuring." He rubbed my back again. "I suspect we will not consummate our marriage until many hours from now."

"Hours?" I didn't mean to sound horrified, it just happened. I rested my forehead on his chest and released a shaky sigh, resigned to hours of this torture. "W-what should I do n-now?"

"Nothing," he murmured. His arms wrapped around my waist and he pulled me closer. "Just let me hold you while you remind yourself that you can trust me."

My body gradually relaxed the longer he held me. The odd feelings of safety and security that I'd always felt in his arms returned and proved an effective cure. Eventually. My tears dried, the trembling subsided. I rubbed my cheek against his shoulder and then I reluctantly lifted my head. I had barely looked up when he gave me another order. "Kiss me."

I blinked once, and then obeyed. As usual, I became enthusiastic when he deepened the kiss, and then panicked when it deepened too far. That kiss ended much the same as the first, except the trembling was not as bad, and there were fewer tears.

I lost count of the number of times we repeated that routine. He would order me to kiss him, I would get excited again, I would begin to fall apart, and then he would stop and simply hold me. It was nearly dark outside my windows when I began to anticipate being held and petted afterward, and each kiss became a little more erotic, each touch a little more sensual.

My heart still beat too fast when the kisses went on too long, but I no longer felt the suffocating sense of panic. Faulke had accustomed me to being in his arms half naked, and to touching his bare skin as much as he touched mine. When he just held me, he actually made me feel safe.

He became bolder, his hands stroking my hips, and then my breasts. When he touched my breasts through the thin fabric of my chemise, I felt as if he had touched me with lightning. My hips pressed against his, and I heard myself moan. He took my hand and pressed it against the front of his pants.

"This is what you do to me, Isabel. You can arouse my body just by looking at me." He pressed my hand more firmly against the warm, tight leather. "The feel of your hands on me gives me pleasure. Does it please you to touch me?"

I gave a distracted nod. His hand was on my breast, kneading, playing, sending fire streaking through me. He leaned down to kiss me again, and then his lips moved along my jaw, down my neck. He pushed my chemise off one shoulder until I felt the fabric slide away to expose my breast. His lips moved along the swell of my breast, and then brushed over my nipple once, twice, and then a gentle nip that made my knees tremble . . . perhaps in a good way. I didn't have time to analyze the feeling before he began to suckle. My whole body felt as if it had caught fire. I fisted my hands in his hair as one of his arms wrapped around my waist to hold me in place while his hands and mouth taught me about pleasure. I made odd little sounds in the back of my throat when his fingers pinched on one side while his teeth bit down gently on the other, but it wasn't exactly painful, and I had no control over the noises I made. I would have been embarrassed by the sounds, but he seemed to enjoy them. He laved away the small stings with his tongue, which made me want to bite him, or encourage him to bite me again. It felt good. It felt deliciously wicked.

The fact that all men seemed fascinated by women's breasts was common knowledge, and even Hartman had shown some interest in the early days of our marriage, so I wasn't surprised by Faulke's preoccupation with mine. Each tug of his mouth made my loins clench, and I could feel a slick warmth between my legs that had never been there before.

Faulke finally lifted his head to look down at me, and then he wrapped his arms around me in another one of those comforting hugs. "Tell me how I made you feel when I was touching you."

"It felt as if I had touched lightning." It was starting to feel almost natural to be held in his arms, and to tell him things I would never admit to another soul. "My breasts ached, and sometimes it was almost painful, but that only made me ache in more places."

"Tell me where," he said, his voice suddenly hoarse.

"Between my legs," I admitted. "I feel warm and wet there."

This time it was his body that was wracked by a shudder. "Take off my pants. I want you to see what you do to my body."

He would be naked. He wanted me to look at him when he was naked. I felt my own shudder, but I resolved to continue to play the part of obedient wife.

The laces at the front of his pants were impossibly tight. I fumbled with them so long that he finally made a sound of impatience and reached over to the trunk that held his weapons to grab a dagger. A moment later, the laces were cut away and the front of his pants gaped open. He gave an obvious sigh of relief. It must have been painful to keep that much hard, swollen flesh contained within the tight leather.

I had managed a few glances at Hartman's sex in the past, but it had always looked pale and half limp. Framed by black leather, Faulke's erection stood rigid against his belly, long and thick, and darker than the skin of his stomach. It twitched every once in a while as I studied him, and twitched harder when I licked my upper lip. When I bit my lower lip, his hand wrapped around his shaft to give himself a slow stroke. I don't know why, but it was the most erotic thing I had ever seen.

"Do you see that drop of liquid?" he asked as he rubbed his thumb near a pearly bead at the tip of his cock. He stroked himself again when I nodded, and the pearl began to slide down his shaft. "That is my body weeping for yours. It wants to be inside of you. Some call these milky drops warriors milk, and it is a well-known aphrodisiac for women. It gives a woman power over a man. Sexual power."

I gave him a dubious look, but he was staring at my mouth. My gaze dropped again to his sex, and I just knew what he would order next. Sometimes it was good to be wrong.

"One day you will kiss me there," he said, holding himself toward me in a shameless offering.

I took a deep breath and imagined my lips pressed to the tip of his sex. I wondered what he would taste like. I might have licked my lips.

Faulke groaned and pulled my hand to his shaft, and then he encouraged me without words to explore. His skin was impossibly hot beneath my fingertips, and yet impossibly soft. I could not take my eyes from his sex, the way it throbbed almost constantly, as if it had a pulse of its own.

He gave a sharp tug on my braid and I looked up at his face. His thumbs rubbed into my shoulders harder than I think he realized, his gaze fastened on my mouth, and then he leaned forward to lick the seam of my lips before his mouth closed over mine in a rough kiss, his tongue thrusting into my mouth in the same rhythm his hips thrust against my belly. His urgency began to overwhelm me and I began to tremble again.

Before panic could take hold, his head dropped to my shoulder and he wrapped me in his arms while he took deep breaths. I calmed almost immediately, knowing he would give me the time I needed to soothe my fears.

I could admit it now, the fear that seized me whenever Hartman had announced his intention to bed me. Hartman had always bedded me in the midst of those bouts of fear. Now I knew there could be pleasure as well. A great deal of pleasure. Faulke would not plow into my rigid body just to do his duty and consummate our marriage. He wanted me soft and willing. Unlike Hartman, he knew how to make me soft and willing.

Faulke's mouth closed over the pulse on my neck and he suckled a little until he ended the kiss with a gentle bite. I liked that, a lot. There was a growing list in my mind of things to ask him to do again in the future.

"I am imagining your mouth on me," he growled. "The pleasure you will give me. We'll have to try that. Soon."

His bawdy words took a moment to register, and then they reignited the warmth in my own loins. A newfound sense of feminine power rippled through me, along with a sensual craving for him. I felt on edge and aroused. My body ached for his.

"I want to please you, master." My submissive words actually made him shudder again. Playing the part of the obedient wife added to my power over him. The discovery made me smile. Feminine wiles might be more intriguing than I had ever imagined.

"Finish undressing me," he said, his voice hoarse.

This time I obeyed without hesitation. The sight of his body no longer intimidated me, and I even purposely trailed my fingers across his shaft and hips as I set about my task. I knelt down to remove his slouch boots, and then I rose up on my knees before him to work the pants down his hips. His sex was directly in front of me, and I heard him suck in his breath when I leaned closer to push the backs of his pants down his legs. The size and shape of him fascinated me, his male body strangely foreign to me, and yet I wanted to know everything about him, the taste and feel of every part of his sex, how to please him. Even his scent aroused me. It seemed natural to rub my face against him like a kitten, so I did it before I could overthink my actions. His shaft was scorching hot against my cheek, and his reaction was somehow satisfying. He groaned and pulled me to my feet.

"Your boldness amazes me," he said as he cupped my buttocks and pressed me against his arousal. He smiled down at me. "Kiss me again, Isabel."

Of course I obeyed. He took control almost immediately, his kisses overpowering, smoldering, burning a trail to my shoulder as his hand tugged at the ribbon that laced my chemise. He used both hands to pull the gathered neckline apart until he could slide it down my shoulders.

My arms were trapped at my sides, my hands fisted, unable to touch him, which made me feel like some sort of pagan sacrifice. It was erotic and sensual, and yet I was starting to tremble like a leaf. It seemed impossible that I could be aroused and panicked at the same time, but I was. Faulke was so attuned to my body that he recognized the change in me immediately. He began to trail kisses upward across my chest, then my neck and cheek, and then a lingering kiss to my forehead before he tucked my head against his shoulders and wrapped his arms around me.

I buried my face against his neck and took deep breaths while he soothed and petted me, murmuring low, comforting words, nonsense about my boldness and bravery.

The words were sweetly spoken, but far from the truth. I was such a coward. But the refuge he offered was irresistible. My heartbeat and breathing began to slow as I relaxed in his arms. His patience was amazing. He acted as if it would not bother him to spend the rest of his life in these endless rounds of arousal, panic, and comforting. However, I knew he had a very specific goal in mind, and it seemed he had a will of iron to reach that goal.

"I'm going to finish taking off your chemise," he said without moving. My body stiffened. "Hush. I am just going to hold you afterward, exactly as I am holding you right now. And that chemise is so thin that it can hardly be called a garment. It does not hide much."

I felt him tug at the fabric, and then the garment pooled around my feet. Just as my breath began to come in gasps, his arms wrapped around me and I burrowed into the comforting safety of his embrace. I could feel his shaft burn against my bare belly like a brand, but he just held me as he had promised, his hand smoothing up and down the line of my back, calming me as he had at least a score of times already. The trembling began to subside again.

"The spells are not lasting as long," he said, his hands still moving in soothing motions. "You are doing better than I had hoped. You are very brave, Isabel."

Spells. That was a good word for what happened to me, for the unreasonable fear that assailed me. His patience humbled me. "I am a coward."

His hand cupped the back of my head and he pressed me closer. "You are a lion, a Plantagenet lion. Do not doubt me."

"Forgive me," I said, meaning to sound flippant and failing.

"Who are you asking to forgive you?" he said. It took me a minute to figure out what he meant.

"Forgive me, master," I said.

Despite my trembling, I managed to smile against his shoulder when his sex swelled against me. I liked the physical proofs of his attraction to me. It was a balm for all the years that Hartman had hurt me while he made me feel unwanted and undesirable.

There was no possible doubt that Faulke wanted me physically, and his tenderness showed that he also cared for me in some measure. He handled me as if I were some sort of breakable treasure. Come to think of it, I was broken. Faulke was fixing me.

Everything was so new and different with him that I knew—at least, I hoped—that sex with him would be just as new and different, rather than the endurance of discomfort and shame that I had come to expect. Already he made me feel proud of the way his body responded to me, and I had never known that I could react to a man the way I did to Faulke. The emotions were all so new and raw that I had trouble sorting them out in my head, but then the "spells" would strike and my whole body would shut down. Except for the shaking.

The way he held and comforted me through each of the spells made me feel humbled and treasured at the same time. And the edge of arousal never quite left me.

I knew he would continue his assault on my senses as soon as I recovered. Each time the trembling subsided, I began to anticipate what would happen next.

"I am going to step back and look at your body," he warned, "and I know the sight of you is going to arouse me even more. Indeed, I suspect we will soon move to the bed, although I will stop and hold you whenever you have another spell. Even though I might not act like I want to stop, do exactly as I say."

I nodded against his shoulder, even as he began to move away from me. He would stop if I started to shake again. I closed my eyes and clenched my fists at my sides, willing myself to remain as still as possible.

"Look at me," he ordered. "See what the sight of your beautiful body does to me."

I opened my eyes. In all honesty, his body looked much the same as it had before. He was still rampantly aroused, and his sex jerked against his belly as I looked at him.

"Get into bed and lie on top of the quilts." His voice was a little hoarse. He held up one hand when I turned to walk away from him. "Walk slowly. I want to watch you."

I slowed my pace, but I could not slow my pulse. This was it. We were finally going to have sex, and prove once and for all if I were capable of enjoying it. I lay down on the bed and stared at the sea of white stars sewn into the pink fabric of the canopy above me. Faulke would not hurt me. He had promised.

I felt the mattress give, and then Faulke was beside me. He gathered me into his arms again.

"Shh," he murmured as he tucked my head against his shoulder. "You are a brave, beautiful woman, Isabel. You should never be afraid of anything we do together."

I heard the ring of truth in his voice. He believed what he was saying. My mind knew it, but it still took time for the tremors to subside and my body to grow calm again. The soothing motions of his hands became more sensual. He turned me so that I lay on my back again while he stayed on his side, his head propped on one hand to look down at me.

"You have the most intriguing curves," he said. His fingers skimmed one side of my breast, then my waist, and then my hip. They trailed down to my knee, and then made the return trip again. He touched my lips with the pads of his fingers, and then dragged them over my chin, along my neck and down the center of my chest. "Your body was made for me, my beautiful lioness. Every time you become aroused, your body is trying to tell you that even greater pleasures await."

He leaned down to kiss me, his lips feather light as they brushed across mine, his touch tender as his hand cupped my breast. My hands fisted in the quilt when he licked a sensual line down to my belly button, and then flicked his tongue into the indentation until my hips lifted off the bed.

He put one hand on my hip to hold me in place and sat up beside me. His gaze never left mine as he swung one leg over mine, and then he straddled my hips. His weight rested on the back of his heels, and the position spread his legs apart to fully expose his sex to me. He captured my hands and pressed my palms to the tops of his thighs.

"No touching," he said in a strained voice. "I am just going to sit here for a while and look at you. I want you to be comfortable being naked in front of me, because I will always want you to be naked in our bed."

I knew a blush stained my cheeks, and probably my chest as well, but I felt no sense of shyness, no maidenly urge to cover myself from his sight. He was the only man who had expressed any interest or pleasure in seeing me naked. I was proud of the fact that the sight of my body could arouse him. My palms smoothed along his thighs and I shifted restlessly beneath him. He drew a deep, shuddering breath.

"No moving. You will keep your hands on my thighs until I tell you otherwise." His hands encircled my waist, and then he pushed his hands upward until his thumbs were just beneath my breasts, his big hands spread out to span my ribs. "Just the sight of you arouses me so much . . . I need to distract myself."

His hands moved upward to cup my breasts. My hips bucked up and my breath caught in my throat. He shifted his position to rest more of his weight on me, pinning my hips to the mattress until their rhythmic thrusts met an unmovable wall of resistance and I was forced to be motionless. Only then did his hands continue their carnal assault, pulling, tugging, twisting.

"Does that feel good, Isabel?"

I managed to nod.

"I could not hear your answer," he prompted.

"Aye, it feels good," I gasped.

"Then open your eyes and look at me, know who it is that gives you pleasure."

I opened my eyes and forced myself to look into his eyes.

"Are you wet for me, Isabel?"

I could feel the slick heat between my legs, even on the insides of my thighs. "Aye . . . master."

His groan was low and sensual. "You must prove it to me, or I will find out for myself."

My wrists were suddenly pinned to the mattress above my head, and his body was stretched out on top of mine. He held both wrists with one hand while the other trailed down my body. His knees moved between mine, holding my legs open. He began to pet me, and then his fingers parted me, and he discovered for himself how much I was aroused.

"Do you want me?" he asked as he thrust one finger inside me.

"Yes," I managed.

"Yes, what?" he demanded, cocking his head slightly as if to better hear my answer.

"Yes, master." I could barely comprehend his words, but I would say anything at that point if he would just do something. Anything. I needed him. He needed to do something to ease the terrible ache and longing and pleasure and pressure.

I thought he would hold me again until I calmed down, and I groaned in frustration when he shifted his weight. My breath caught in my throat when he thrust into me with one powerful stroke. My entire body rose off the bed to meet him. This time I was the one who made incoherent animal noises, growly sounds I hadn't even realized were possible. He held himself perfectly still, buried deep within me, and I could feel every pulsing sensation of our bodies as we adjusted to each other. Incredibly, I could feel him swell inside of me.

He released a harsh noise, and then he thrust once and held himself still above me.

"Do you still want me?" he said.

I lifted my hips.

"Answer me," he said in a harsh voice as his hips pinned me to the bed.

I tried to thrust my hips upward again. "Aye, I want you, master."

"Open your eyes. Watch what you do to me."

I met his gaze and he began to thrust with slow strokes that inflamed my already sensitized sheath. Something was building inside me, anticipation and pleasure, something that felt right and yet something so unfamiliar that it frightened me.

He watched the emotions play across my face and somehow knew just when I started to panic. "Let go, my love. I'll keep you safe."

His words set off a wave of explosions that made me see stars. I thought I was dying. I thought I was fully alive for the first time ever. My body began to milk his in waves. I was just aware enough that I could see the effect on him. It looked painful, and yet I didn't care. My body didn't care, it just kept rhythmically clamping down on him as reason gradually returned.

His gaze had never left mine throughout that adventure, and his lips twisted into a grin of smug satisfaction, erased when an especially strong ripple went through my body and pulled on his, in the aftermath of whatever had just happened. He propped himself up on one elbow and his hand gripped the back of my neck, while his other hand pinned my hip to the mattress as he thrust into my body. And then he pulled himself all of the way out, and then thrust into me again so hard that I would have been pushed into the headboard if he hadn't been holding me in place. The friction on all of my sensitized nerves almost sent me over the edge again. It was . . . amazing.

His gaze locked with mine, a glimpse of male satisfaction in his eyes when he watched my reaction to his thrusts, or when I made a sound that particularly pleased him.

Soon I began to crave it, being pinned and helpless to do anything but receive him, to submit to his complete domination.

The last time he buried himself completely he did not withdraw, but instead pushed against me harder, as if he could somehow get deeper within my body. With one last stroke, he threw his head back and actually roared, a lion announcing to every other male in the forest that he had claimed his mate.

The feel of Faulke coming inside me defied description. The sensation of his hot seed spurting against my womb set off another explosion inside of me, and I could feel my body suckle his to draw out every last drop from his loins. I couldn't catch my breath, or control what my body was doing to his in any way. His forehead dropped to mine, and then he collapsed on top of me. My arms were tucked beneath his, wrapped around as much of his chest as I could hold. My legs encircled his waist, and I locked my ankles together, some instinctive drive that told me to hold him to me, inside me where he belonged. We were magnets again.

I reveled in the feel of his dead weight on top of me, the waves that continued to roll through my body and his in the aftermath of pleasure, and then began to gradually diminish. I had never experienced anything like it, and I wanted to commit each feeling to memory so I could recall every moment of this experience in the future. And then it became difficult to breathe.

I began to take short little breaths, panting almost, to get just enough air into my lungs to keep from fainting. He finally stirred and shifted just enough to nuzzle my neck, his beard leaving a satisfying burn in its wake. It stung enough that I knew it would leave a mark, and I was glad. I wanted everyone to know he had marked me, that he had claimed me. He had awakened a lioness inside of me, and I wanted my mate in every primitive way possible. Shockingly erotic images drifted through my head; shocking because they were all things we had just talked about or done, things I had never considered, and, in some cases, had never known were possible.

It had been six years since I last had sex, almost one fourth of my lifetime. But I had never had the kind of sex we just experienced. Every muscle in my body felt either soothed or sore or overly sensitive, and all in a good way. I never wanted to leave our bed. I never wanted him to leave my body. He rolled onto his back to take his weight off me, but he pulled me with him to stay sheathed within me. I lay sprawled across him like well-fed puppy. A sudden wave of exhaustion washed over me and I tried to stifle a yawn.

"Go to sleep now," he murmured in my ear.

Being a properly submissive wife, I obeyed.

CHAPTER FOURTEEN

Uncharted Waters

TWO DAYS LATER, WE STILL HADN'T LEFT THE
sanctuary of my apartments. Faulke had managed to
keep everyone at bay, except the servants who brought
food, water, and an occasional bath. We had already
broken our fast this morning, and his hunger had been
satiated in every possible way. He continued to pick
through some of the leftover food while watching me
bathe before the fireplace in the solar. Seated in my armchair with his leg crossed at the knee, he looked every
inch the lord of the manor. He even had a lecherous look
in his eyes as he watched me.

It was these quiet times together that I liked best,
when we talked about things that were inconsequential
and important at the same time, stories from our pasts
about the people, places, and things that had been im-

portant to us, funny or poignant stories about people we had known, and I quizzed him endlessly about his daughters. I could not wait to make them a bigger part of my life. It was a glorious time. I treasured each moment, because I knew these idyllic moments out of time could not last.

I knew that in my mind, but my heart and body pretended that we would stay in this cocoon of carnal delights for the rest of our lives. My life had changed completely, and I was in no great hurry to return to ugly realities.

"I want you to bathe me tomorrow," he announced. His gaze followed the cloth as I drew it down my arm and then back up again. The movement was brisk and efficient, but his eyes said he was getting aroused just by watching me bathe. I slowed my movements to let him savor the moment.

"Perhaps this evening," he said. I lifted one foot in the air, above the waterline, and washed my leg with long, slow strokes. "Nay, when you are done with your bath."

The thought of bathing him, of touching every inch of him, was more erotic than it should be at this point. My body was sore from the unaccustomed workouts, and there were bite marks and bruises in the most intimate places. I looked down at one of the marks on my breast, and, once again, my lips curved into a satisfied smile. I don't know why his marks made me smile, but every time I looked at them I felt an equal measure of satisfaction and arousal. He had marked me. I was his.

Still, I was grateful that they were not yet put on full display to others. My ladies would be scandalized. Well,

Gretchen would be shocked. Hilda would probably offer her congratulations. They would see the marks eventually, but for now, I liked keeping every part of our time together private.

"Wash your leg again."

I raised my brows at the tone of his voice, but he just raised his brows in answer. The agreement we had come to our first night had undergone a few slight modifications the past two days. I still required some extra care between the kissing parts and the actual beddings, but we both realized early on that it worked best if he was in charge. His promise remained, that he would defer to me when we were in front of others, but when we were alone, I was his to command.

I lifted my leg out of the water again and repeated the slow strokes. He licked his lips. He actually licked his lips. I felt like the most powerful woman on the planet. I might have giggled.

"You will not laugh at your master." He frowned at me, and then his frown deepened. "Unless I am making a jest. Then you can . . ."

His voice drifted away as I put my leg straight up, and slowly drew the cloth down. "You were saying?"

"I didn't realize I had marked your thigh." He nodded toward the limb I still had in the air, and then made a gesture that encompassed all of me. "Did I hurt you, kitten?"

Faulke had started to call me that ridiculous nickname when he decided the sounds I made during lovemaking were more kittenish than lionlike. I felt another one of those secretive smiles curve my lips. "Did I complain?"

A rap at the door made us both frown. Faulke tightened the tie to his robe as he went to the door to investigate. No one would disturb us unless it was an emergency. Faulke had a short conversation with the guards, then closed the door and returned to the table. He carried a scroll that bore my father's seal, which he broke before spreading the parchment across the table. I glanced toward the door that led to the hallway to make certain it was barred again, and then I got out of the bath to dry off and put on my own robe while he began to read the message.

I crossed the room to resume my seat at the table across from him rather than read the message over his shoulder. He glanced up briefly, and kept reading. He didn't look happy.

I folded my hands in my lap and waited.

"Your father wants my word, in writing, before witnesses, that the marriage is true," he said at last.

"That is not unexpected news," I said, wondering why that would make him scowl.

"There is more," he said, and the tone of his voice said that this would be the bad news. "Your former father-in-law, King Rudolph, is dead."

"God rest his soul," I said automatically as I crossed myself. "I had heard he was ill before I left Rheinbaden, but I didn't realize it was so serious. Do they suspect foul play?"

"Nay," Faulke said, "but there is no specific mention of how he died."

I nodded, and then realized that his frown was still

just as fierce. In fact, he almost looked apprehensive. "What is it?"

"An ambassador from Rheinbaden will dock in London within the next few days. They sent a messenger ahead of their party with a petition and to request an audience with your father. King Edward wants you at court when the ambassador arrives."

"And?" I prompted when he pressed his lips together and looked angry.

"There is no easy way to tell you." He smoothed out the end of the parchment and began to read again. "Albert, the new king, intends to recall all of your people to Rheinbaden. Soldiers and servants alike are required to return on the ambassador's ship. You, of course, are exempt from that edict, and any females who may have already wed Englishmen. If any of your male soldiers or servants have taken English brides, they are to accompany them to Rheinbaden, or be left behind."

I sat in stunned silence. Gretchen, Hilda, Gerhardt . . . My people, everyone I knew and who knew me, taken away with the stroke of a pen half a world away. "W-why?"

"The message doesn't say." He shook his head.

"Albert," I whispered. "He doesn't like me. I was told he objected to me taking so many of his father's subjects to England, but I never thought he would recall them all."

"King Edward wants us both to deliver the witnessed testimony of our marriage to the Tower by the watch change this afternoon," he went on, almost apologetically. "Your father wants to meet with you before he grants an audience to Count Otto."

The name sent an icy finger of dread down my spine. I looked at my husband as realization washed over me. I would not have Faulke for much longer, either.

"Isabel?" He gave me a sharp look. "What did I say?"

I shook my head. "Albert sent Otto of Tyrol. Otto despises me, and he is . . . unpleasant."

I didn't add that Otto was also Maria's uncle, which made him a granduncle of Hartman's children by her, and their legal ward after Hartman's death. And now Otto was in England. I could almost feel the trap closing over me.

"Otto of Tyrol." Faulke narrowed his eyes. "Didn't you say the man who tried to attack you was from Tyrol?"

"He is Leopold's father," I admitted, and then shook my head. "Count Otto has never physically hurt me, but even before Leopold came to Grunental, he wanted my marriage to Hartman annulled and me sent back to England."

As Faulke stared at me, I could see the anger build as thoughts went through his mind. His voice was tight. "Why would King Albert send him here, knowing there is bad blood between you?"

"I . . . I am not well liked in Rheinbaden."

"Hm." His gaze never left my face as he rubbed his chin. "What are you not telling me?"

Ach. He knew me too well already.

Soon there would be no secrets between us. Otto would find some way to ruin everything. Perhaps that was his reason for coming to England.

I could tell Faulke about Maria, here, while we were alone, or in public, before the king. Waiting until we were with the king was the wrong choice. I knew that, but I didn't want to destroy the illusion.

Not now. Not so soon.

I looked at him and got lost in his eyes. It was the last time he would look at me this way. When I admitted this last secret, Faulke would despise me. I would truly be a stranger in a strange land. Realization began to dawn that I would soon be abandoned. Again.

Whatever he saw in my face alarmed him. "What is it, my love?"

Everything inside of me stilled.

It was simply a lover's endearment, I told myself, one that he had used with increasing frequency in the past few days. Likely he called all of his women "my love." Still, it made a thousand butterflies take flight in my stomach.

What I felt for Faulke was unlike anything I had ever felt for anyone or anything. Ever. It was as if all of my love and passion had lain dormant inside me, just waiting for this moment and this man to set it free.

The intimacies we had shared were amazing. Embarrassing, at first, but Faulke had a way of making everything we did feel normal and natural. Well, normal and natural for things that felt amazing. He made me feel as if we had been created for each other's pleasure. I had never felt so treasured in my life.

Those feelings made it ridiculously easy to convince myself of dangerous notions, and to pretend that this marriage was something it was not. Every time he opened his arms to me, I pretended that Faulke Segrave was the love of my life. The way he looked at me, the things he said, his patience and kindness, all contributed to the illusion that this was real, that he cared for me, that at last someone loved me.

But I was no longer a naive child, foolish enough to think he felt anything close to what I deceived myself into thinking we both felt.

He got up and moved around the table, then pulled me up to wrap his arms around me. It reminded me of all the hours he had already spent just holding me, waiting for my bouts of panic to subside.

"Tell me what is wrong with you," he demanded.

"N-nothing." The denial would have been more convincing without the little sob in the middle.

He took my chin in his hand and waited until I met his gaze. The longer we stared at each other, the more my eyes filled with tears. He began to look alarmed. "Tell me what is wrong and I will fix it."

Ach. He was breaking my heart. I threw my arms around his neck and clung to him as I began to cry in earnest, great wracking, uncontrollable sobs that came from somewhere deep inside me that I didn't know existed. But I knew what was wrong. I clung to him as if I could keep us both safe from my secrets, simply by holding on to him.

When the sobs slowed down, he tried to comfort me.

"Hush, my love. Stop crying."

His words only made me cry harder. "S-stop calling me that."

"Calling you what?" he asked, his expression baffled.

"Your love," I whispered. "There is no need to humor me."

"Isabel—" Whatever he saw on my face made him press his lips together, likely the tears. I could almost see his mind working as he stared down at me. "I have never been good at coming up with words of my own," he said, "spoken in just the right way at just the right time."

"I . . . see."

"I want you to keep that in mind when I tell you that I use endearments only when I mean them." He watched me carefully as what he said sank in. I might have looked suspicious. "We both have admitted that the other was not what we expected when we met. You are so much more than what I imagined. You are my love as well as my wife. I want to slay dragons for you."

"Don't say that," I whispered.

"Why not?" he asked, sounding genuinely puzzled. "I can tell you are starting to feel the same about me."

Starting?

"Men watch you constantly, and women, too," he went on when I remained silent. "You think it is because you are their princess and the most important person in their world. Sometimes that is true, but there are other times when women watch you because they want to emulate your grace and poise, they envy your ability to command any man and take command of any situation. They want to be like you, but you were born to be a queen, and they will never be more than your handmaidens."

That was ridiculous. Women did not envy me.

The suspicion in my mind must have shown in my eyes. He shook his head, denying my doubt. "Men watch you because you are a force of nature, as beautiful as you are unique. You give them all cool looks of disdain that only make them try harder to please you. One soft look from you would bring a man to his knees. You brought *me* to my knees, when I vowed this would be no more than a marriage of convenience."

It wouldn't make a difference, but I had to know before he knew the truth about me. I blurted out my question before I lost my nerve. "Did I please you?"

"Did I complain?" he asked with a smile, throwing my earlier words back at me. "Other men might suspect there is a sensual lioness beneath your tame exterior, but no other man will taste your fire, my love. No other man will know what it is to burn in your arms. The beautiful lioness is all mine."

He lifted my hands and put them behind his neck, and then ran his hands down my arms, making me shiver. His eyes were dark sapphires as he looked deep into mine.

"I began to fall in love with you that first day in the garden," he said. "However, I didn't realize I was already in love until you gave yourself to me after our wedding, body and soul, every part of yourself into my keeping."

Ach! I was going to cry again. I blinked several times to chase the hateful tears away, while I tried to absorb everything he had just said. Naturally, my first instinct was to think he was lying. He had to be lying. No one loved me.

The longer I looked into his eyes, the more I suspected it was the truth. He thought I was special. And beautiful.

He was so wrong. This was part of God's punishment for my lies. He gave me a man so perfect it hurt my heart just to look at him, and then He blinded him to my imperfections.

It was about to end. I would become a victim of my own deceits. It was wrong to let him love me, but no one ever had before. My mind could hardly grasp the possibility. I wanted to enjoy the feelings, just for a moment.

"Let me slay your dragons, Isabel." He brushed his thumb across my lips. "Tell me what is wrong."

I was going straight to hell.

The space between us was not enough. I took a step backward, and he let me. He thought our marriage was too good to be true, and he was right. It was. All of the fantasies I had built up around us were a myth. I had to destroy his trust in me and admit that I was never worthy of it in the first place.

The truth would crush every tender feeling he had for me. The marriage was consummated, and he could not escape it. I had to watch his love turn to hatred now, before either of us fell any deeper into my web of lies.

"There is something I must tell you."

He looked down at me with concern, but remained silent.

This was the moment I had dreaded from the day we met. Faulke was the first person to ever think he might love me. I could not hug that knowledge to me for even a day before I destroyed the illusion.

"Count Otto has a niece," I said at last, and I suddenly knew exactly what to say, and how I would tell him. The words began to pour out of me. "She was Hartman's mistress for at least a year before our marriage, and they continued the affair after we were wed."

He stepped away from me, his gaze wary, that of a man who suspects he is about to be betrayed somehow. I wanted to keep my arms around his neck, to do anything that would hold him to me. It was too late. I took another step backward. The most unlovable woman in the world. There should be a crown for that title.

"As you said yourself," I went on, "I was still a child at the time of my first marriage, my head filled with chivalric notions of true love. I was blissfully ignorant of the affair. Maria was wed to an old man at the time, and I actually pitied Maria that she didn't have a handsome young husband like mine."

My eyes tracked Faulke as he took a step backward as well.

"When . . . when I delivered my child, Hartman and I were both seriously ill with the mumps. Many people at court died that year, including my babe and Maria's husband. Still, Hartman and I had a duty to produce an heir for Rheinbaden. Our duty." I gave a humorless laugh. "It all seemed so important at the time, when so many children had perished during the plague. I did not object when Hartman came to my bed less than a month later, but something in my body had not yet healed."

His face descended into a scowl of epic proportions. Did he already suspect? I took a steadying breath and tried to hurry through this part of the story without thinking about my emotions at the time. "There was a lot of blood. Hartman was disgusted by the mess I made of us both. He gave me a few months to recover from my injuries, but that's when the spells that you witnessed began, whenever Hartman sent word that he intended to visit my bed."

Faulke had gone very still. There was no emotion at all in his face now, but his gaze went to the floor, as if he couldn't bear to look at me. Whatever I had expected from him, this awful silence wasn't it.

"At first, the strange attacks baffled Hartman," I went on. "He knew something was wrong and left me alone, but eventually he said we could wait no longer and we would both have to suffer through the ordeal to fulfill our duty to Rheinbaden. I agreed, of course, but Hartman could no longer disguise how repulsive he found me, and that only seemed to make the spells worse. And then I learned that Maria was pregnant again.

"The affair between Maria and Hartman had never stopped. Maria had given birth after her husband's death, just a few months after the birth of my child, except her son lived. She birthed three more children over the next few years. All four are Hartman's bastards."

I watched Faulke closely, expecting pity, and then anger. He continued to stare at the floor as if he found something of great interest there. And then I noticed his whitened knuckles, how his hands clenched and unclenched at his sides, as if he wanted to both strangle and hit someone at the same time. I knew who that someone would be and I took a prudent step backward.

"The physicians think something happened to me during the birth," I said, just babbling now to fill in the growing silence. "I think it was afterward, the first time Hartman came to my bed and made me bleed. I think he broke something inside of me. I never felt the same again."

Ach. Faulke's face looked like it was made of stone. His hands were the only parts of him that weren't unnaturally still, and their reflexive movement worried me. Finally, I could stand the silence no longer.

"I didn't know if my body could even respond to a man until now. You fixed that part of me." I reached toward him as I whispered the only thing that gave me hope. "Isn't it possible you fixed all of me?"

His voice was low with warning. "Do not touch me."

My hand dropped to my side. Hope fell beneath my feet.

At last he looked up. I had already seen him angry, the day I asked if he intended to murder me. I would not dare give voice to that question right now. The Faulke I knew was barely recognizable in the face of the man who glared at me. I almost wished he would stare at the floor again. What I saw in his eyes was an enraged beast. His lips barely moved when he spoke. "Finish your story."

"I—I did not want to deceive you," I said. "My father gave me no choice. I am very sorry I did not tell you everything before we wed. I—I hope you can find it in your heart to someday forgive me."

The longer he stared at me, the more his face began to change. The fire in his eyes slowly faded into . . . confusion? "That's all you have to say?"

That wasn't enough? No, of course it wasn't. I clasped my hands together in front of me. "My feelings for you are real. They were never part of any deception. Whatever you think of me now, I swear to you, I am truly sorry."

The silence stretched between us. He seemed to be waiting for something more, but I wasn't sure what to do or say. It would not take much for him to see begging and pleading. Not that I thought they would buy his forgiveness. I only wished I knew if anything would.

"We are done," Faulke said at last. His eyes narrowed as he made a cutting motion with his hand. I watched in stunned silence as he turned on his heel and walked toward the door.

"The king has summoned us both," I reminded him, even as the finality of his words cut through me. "He will expect us both to appear. I cannot predict how he will interpret your absence."

I hadn't meant it as a threat, but my words certainly sounded like one. He glanced over his shoulder at me. The anger in his eyes was hot enough to burn through my tattered heart. "You dare to—"

He pressed his lips together. His whole body radiated anger. A noise came from his chest that sounded like a deep growl, and then he left me without another word.

CHAPTER FIFTEEN

Revelations

GRETCHEN AND HILDA ARRIVED IN MY BED-
chamber an hour later to find me dry eyed and seemingly calm. I hadn't cried at all while I waited for them. I
was too cold and numb inside to feel anything. Not that
the numbness had quieted my memory. I had plenty
of time to reflect on what had just happened. The more
I thought it through, and the more I thought about
Faulke's reaction, the more something seemed off. He'd
been angry, that much was evident when he shouted at
me, but he hadn't asked many questions. Then he'd simply left.

"You sent for us, Princess?" Hilda asked as I stared
out the window.

I nodded and fiddled with the tie to my robe, wondering what to tell them.

"Gerhardt is in the solar," Hilda went on. "Lord Faulke found him in the great hall and said that you are to be made ready for an audience with the king this afternoon. He also had Gerhardt and Sir Crispin sign as witnesses to Lord Faulke's word that your marriage was consummated. Is the summons why he looks so angry?"

I shook my head, unwilling and probably unable to explain without breaking into tears. "We received news that a messenger arrived from Rheinbaden. King Rudolph has died, and Albert is now king."

"God bless the king," they both murmured as they made the sign of the cross.

I gave them a few moments to absorb the news before I continued. "Lord Faulke and I have been summoned to the Tower. We are to appear at the gates no later than the afternoon changing of the guard."

"King Edward wants to discuss the news from Rheinbaden?" Hilda guessed.

I gave her a nod. "Count Otto leads the contingent from Rheinbaden that should arrive within a few days, and my father will grant him an audience. He wants Faulke and me at that audience as well."

"What is that foul creature doing in England?" Hilda demanded.

"He is here to make trouble," Gretchen predicted.

I released a long sigh and wished I could be more like Hilda. "Count Otto has caused trouble already."

Hilda and Gretchen exchanged a look. Hilda guessed the truth. "You told Lord Faulke about Lady Maria?"

I could only nod.

"That is why he was so angry." It wasn't a question, but I nodded to confirm Hilda's suspicion.

"Will the Segraves leave us now?" Gretchen asked, her face suddenly stricken. I gave her a sharp look. "Forgive me, Princess. I did not mean to distress you further. It's just that . . . Well, it's Richard . . ."

It was impossible for anyone to distress me further, but it was still possible to surprise me. "Richard Segrave?"

Gretchen nodded, even as her face turned bright pink. She lowered her head and murmured, "He has been very attentive since the Segraves first arrived. He is . . . interested in me."

I looked at Hilda, who seemed to find something of great interest on the ceiling. Whatever had happened between Gretchen and Richard, Hilda knew about it.

"Are you interested in him?" My tone was sharper than I had intended, but she gave me a miserable nod. I stared at her, shocked. After all of these years spent mourning Engel, Gretchen had finally found another man she might come to love.

And I had ruined it for her already.

Gretchen twisted her hands in her skirts, her eyes very blue with unshed tears. "I tried to resist him, truly, my lady."

"This romance happened the few times you were together? With others in attendance?" I demanded.

"We were alone sometimes," Gretchen said. "Although we were most often with others, such as in the gardens or at the wedding feasts."

"My romance with Faulke was rushed," I said, "and

that was a betrothal, sanctioned by the king. How did Richard manage to win your affections so quickly?"

Hilda still wouldn't meet my gaze. Gretchen looked embarrassed. "Richard is very . . . persuasive when he wants something, and he has decided he wants me."

"Aye, I know just how persuasive the Segraves can be." I rubbed my forehead, wondering if I should have anticipated this development. Regardless, it seemed an almost welcome distraction from my own worries. "How do you even communicate? Does he speak German?"

"Nay," Gretchen admitted, "but I speak and understand more French than I've let on. We . . . manage."

I thought of Albert's edict. "Has he spoken of marriage?"

"Aye, we have sworn to each other," she admitted.

That news made even Hilda's eyes widen, and her attention turned from the ceiling as she joined me in staring at Gretchen. If it was true, Gretchen and Richard had handfasted, a union that was as legal and binding as any rites performed before a priest. I hadn't thought she could astonish me further. "What would make you do such a thing?"

"I have decided I want him, too." Gretchen lifted her chin. "Richard intends to speak with Gerhardt when the time is right," Gretchen continued, and then her breath caught on a small sob. "At least, that was his intent, to wait a few weeks after your wedding to negotiate our betrothal. Now . . . now I don't know what he will do."

Gretchen lowered her head and began to cry. I could not bring myself to feel sorry for her. I was still too numb. Perhaps I would find some sympathy for Gretchen's situation tomorrow or the next day, but today I had used up all my pity on myself. "Did Lord Faulke return to the solar with Gerhardt?"

"No, Princess," Hilda answered, with a small frown for Gretchen. "Reginald is in the solar. He told us that Lord Faulke went to gather his men and he intended to ride out for his father's townhouse."

"Oh." He had left me already. I wondered if he would dare to defy the king's summons and refuse to go to the Tower. I almost hoped he would. I was not yet ready to face him again. "Send Reginald for Lord Dante. Tell him to send my apologies for disturbing Chiavari, but it is urgent that I speak with him."

Hilda curtseyed and left to deliver the message. That left me with a softly sobbing Gretchen.

"I don't know if there is any possibility of salvaging your relationship with Richard Segrave," I told her truthfully, which only made her cry harder. "I can do nothing about it until I return from the Tower, and even then I have no idea what will happen with my own marriage, much less yours. I suspect Faulke will soon return to Wales, and I will not be going with him."

Gretchen looked stricken. "I would have to go to Wales by myself?"

"I have my doubts that Gerhardt would approve the match," I said, deciding to keep the news of Rheinbaden to myself for now. "Even if there were none of these problems between Faulke and myself, I have no doubt he will forbid the union if it means you must strike off on your own with a man he barely knows. However, you are a grown woman. You do not need your brother's permis-

sion to follow the man you handfasted. If Richard asks
you to go to Wales with him, prepare yourself to make a
difficult choice: your family and everyone familiar to
you, or your new husband."

Gretchen lifted her chin and dabbed away the last of
her delicate tears with the sleeve of her gown. Her nose
wasn't even red. "If Richard still wants me, I will choose
happiness."

Hilda returned and I tried to dismiss Gretchen's distress. I would deal with her troubles later. There were
other problems that were more pressing at the moment.

"Help me sort through my wardrobe and jewels," I
told both women. "I do not want to appear before the
king or my husband as a Rheinbaden princess."

Hilda pushed up her sleeves and Gretchen dried the
last of her tears, and then we began opening trunks.

The remainder of the day was a blur of numbness
amid a flurry of activity. I sent Chiavari to the Tower,
trusting that he or Mordecai would know someone who
could open my mother's wardrobe. She had been tall like
me, and I had little doubt there would be something
among her clothing that would make me look suitably
English. I just hoped my father would not mind me bor-
rowing her clothes.

After my bath, Chiavari returned with two trunks
filled with garments to choose from and a chest of jewels, claiming Mordecai had foreseen the situation, and
had already obtained the king's permission for me to
borrow my mother's things. For once, I was glad of Mordecai's strangeness. My ladies spent the rest of the day

making certain I looked just as regal as the queen who had once worn my borrowed garments.

Wide slashed sleeves trailed to the ground, lined with scarlet samite that was embroidered with so many gold lions that the red fabric was hardly visible. White ermine encircled the neckline and edged the sides of the surcoat to the floor, which was also embroidered in gold thread with dozens of Plantagenet lions the size of my fist. A gold belt as wide as my palm went around my waist, on top of the surcoat, and its ends reached nearly to the floor, with eight gold castles on each strap.

Chiavari told me the three-towered castles represented each child my mother bore, sixteen in all, each added to her belt at our births. The castles were the devices of her father and my grandfather, the King of Castile.

Altogether, my outfit was even gaudier than my Rheinbaden court attire. It was perfect for the effect I intended. I was a princess of England, and the descendant of powerful kings. Count Otto and his liege, King Albert, no longer held sway over me.

Faulke had still not returned to Ashland when it was time to leave, so I departed for the Tower without him. I was accompanied by six Rheinbaden soldiers, six of my father's soldiers, Crispin and Blanche, Gerhardt, Gretchen, and Hilda. The soldiers were there to keep foolish thoughts from the heads of any would-be thieves we might encounter on the streets. I was wearing a fortune in gold and jewels, and it had taken the concerted efforts of two men to hoist me into the saddle. I had to pay close attention to keeping my balance on the horse during the journey, lest the weight of my finery topple me off my mount and land me in the gutter.

My soldiers and horses made it as far as the ward nearest the postern gates that led to my father's apartments. The soldiers would await our return and keep the horses ready. My two knights and three ladies made it to the hallway outside the king's apartments, where benches lined the walls for attendants to await their master or mistress while they were received by the king. A servant allowed me alone inside the apartments, into what was probably once my mother's solar. The servant showed me to a seat at the long table, and then disappeared through a smaller doorway that led to my parents' bedchamber.

I had been here before, when I first returned to England, but I had never been left alone until now. The solitude gave me a chance to absorb my surroundings.

The age-darkened beams of wood on the ceiling matched the color of the planks on the floor. Tall windows overlooked the greenery of an outer ward. The unglazed windows were framed by heavy wall hangings that hung from poles above the windows with brass rings sewn into the tapestries that let them slide over the windows at night or during the winter. A large, scarred table that looked as old as the ceiling beams stood in the center of the room, with long benches at each side, and a massive wooden armchair at the end closest to the brazier. The chair would also afford the best view of the ward. There was no question whom that seat belonged to.

A cold meal had been laid out on the table and the servant had said to help myself to whatever I wanted.

There was fruit, hard-boiled eggs, sliced meats, fresh bread and cheeses. Everything was cleverly arranged to please the eye, but none of it appealed to me. I took a seat in front of the fruit platter and contemplated the best way to explain Faulke's absence without getting him into trouble.

It was my fault that I had waited to tell him my secret, but my original hope was not to tell him at all, to let him discover the truth on his own at some point in the far future. Now I wondered how I had ever thought that a viable plan. Months or years of keeping such a secret would have been unbearable. This day was inevitable. I just wished it hadn't happened so soon. Indeed, I wished I had never been put in this situation to begin with. If I had never known Faulke, I would never know what it felt like to lose him.

My father might be the only man in England who could convince Faulke that I truly had no choice but to go along with the deception. Not that I thought it would earn his forgiveness, but perhaps Faulke would realize that not everything in our short marriage had been a lie. I did not deceive him about my feelings for him. Those were very real. They still were.

The door to the hallway opened and Mordecai entered the solar, followed by Faulke. My breath caught in my throat. I had eyes only for my husband. My gaze greedily soaked in the sight of him, as if I hadn't seen him in weeks instead of mere hours.

He had dressed for court as well, in his black garments with the understated silver trim. He needed little ornamentation to let others know he was a powerful and dangerous man. It was in his bearing, in his very bones. Ach, I loved his bones. My heart yearned for his touch. I could feel it aching in my chest.

His face was carved from stone. He met my gaze for a brief moment and I tumbled headfirst into those blue depths. His eyes lowered to take in my English garments, and then he made a point of looking away from me. I felt as if he had slapped me.

Mordecai's arrival seemed to be some sort of signal. The door to the king's bedchamber opened again, and my father finally emerged. The servants who followed behind him were dismissed with a wave of his hand, and the men bowed their way out of the apartments. I dropped into a curtsey when my father turned his attention in my direction, at the same time Mordecai and Faulke bowed to their king. Mordecai's bow was respectful. Faulke's bordered on insolence. My curtsey was made awkward by the weight of my garments.

Edward looked from Faulke to me, and then raised his brows, the question clear in his eyes. I gave a small nod.

"Ah, yes, I assumed these unexpected visitors from Rheinbaden would bring other matters to light." He turned to Faulke. "I was told that you were accompanied to the Tower this morning by your father rather than your wife, just a few days since your marriage. I am also told that your father requests an audience."

It wasn't a question, and Faulke remained silent.

"Is your marriage consummated?" he asked Faulke.

A muscle in Faulke's jaw worked several times before

he handed the king a sealed parchment and answered, "Aye."

"Then I have no business with your father. My servants have already told him that he is dismissed."

"Your pardon, my liege. My father wishes to renegotiate parts of my betrothal contract, now that new information has come to our notice."

"The marriage is done," the king said. "The contract is sealed. There will be no revisions."

"I ask only that certain provisions be added for my daughters' betrothals," Faulke said.

I held my breath, aware of my father's temper, knowing it could be set off by Faulke brashly continuing his plea to the king.

"I am listening," Edward said, sounding more curious than angry.

"My youngest, Lucy, is all but settled on Baron Tenby's heir, Albert," Faulke said. "However, my eldest daughter, Claire, and my middle child, Jane, are still unclaimed. Claire is the granddaughter of the Earl of Wentworth, and she is of an age with your son, Edward. Perhaps—"

"The future King of England will not wed an earl's granddaughter." Edward stroked his beard as he gave Faulke a speculative look. "But you knew that already. Do you have more appropriate grooms already picked for your daughters?"

"I do, Your Highness," Faulke said after a brief pause. He gave my father a deep and, this time, respectful bow. "I have tried to negotiate a match between Claire and Remmington's heir, but Remmington will not commit. If you gave your official blessing to the match, I feel certain we could draw up the betrothal papers to both our satisfaction. As for Jane, she is a substantial heiress through her mother. Gilbert de Clare's nephew, Henry, is of a suitable age, and also an heir to a barony. Jane's wealth would suit Henry's needs, and his titles would suit mine."

"You would consider these betrothals appropriate compensation for your own betrothal contracts and the new information that has, how did you say it? Come to notice?" Edward asked.

Faulke gave me a sideways look, and then returned his attention to my father. "If the contracts are drawn up favorably to my daughters, and the grooms are the ones I mentioned or similar substitutes, then aye, betrothal contracts for Claire and Jane would be acceptable and I would ask for no more addenda."

"You will not contest your marriage or any of its terms?" Edward asked.

Faulke gave me a look I could not interpret. "Nay. The marriage will stand uncontested."

"Very good. Mordecai, see to it that the betrothals are arranged." He motioned to the benches. "All of you, be seated. Mordecai, read Count Otto's petition to us."

My heart sank. My father had no intention of explaining anything to Faulke about my unwilling role in our marriage. The bargain was made, the contracts sealed, and now we were all obliged to live with the consequences.

Despite my husband's feelings toward me, or lack thereof, I felt a silly surge of relief. I had known my father would never consider an annulment, but there had been that small sliver of doubt that I had not voiced, even to myself. Now I knew for certain that Faulke was tied to me for the remainder of our lives. That thought should not make me feel better, but somehow it did. He would always be mine. Whether he wanted me or not.

It was not much, as far as consolation went, but it was all I had at the moment. The rest of our lives could be a very long time. He already told me that he needed my connections. Perhaps he could learn to forgive me.

My father took his chair, I sat next to him, and Mordecai took the seat next to mine. Faulke sat across from us, as far from my father and me as possible.

My mood dimmed.

Mordecai began to recite the contents of the missive from a parchment that had appeared from one of his sleeves. My gaze went again to Faulke, drawn to him like a magnet. I noticed one of my marks on his neck, just above his collar. I thought of my ladies' reaction that afternoon when Hilda and Gretchen had dressed me, when they realized that Faulke's marks were all over me, too.

After an embarrassing silence, Hilda said that a man who had so clearly staked his claim on a woman would not be satisfied with a few short nights in her bed, and she predicted that he would have new marks on me within a fortnight. I hadn't believed her optimism then, and, looking at the icy gaze Faulke kept trained on my father, I didn't believe it now.

The mention of Leopold's name brought my attention back to Mordecai, who was naming everyone in

Count Otto's envoy from Rheinbaden who would attend him at King Edward's court. I felt my blood run cold.

"A squire by the name of Hartman von Tyrol is also listed," Mordecai said, giving me a pointed look. They had brought my husband's bastard to my father's court. "The count has requested a private audience with you first, Princess, before he meets with your father. Do you have any notion why he would request such a meeting?"

"Unless Otto has greatly changed since the last time I saw him, he intends to blackmail me into supporting whatever his mission in England might be." I frowned, seeming to recall Mordecai saying something about the petition from King Albert seeking my father's support for something. Ach. I needed to pay less attention to Faulke, and more to the events unfolding before me. "Given the list of men who accompany him, I doubt his goals are anything I would care to sponsor."

"Tell us what you know about each of these Rheinbaden men," my father said, "anything at all that might be useful to know before we meet them."

I began with Count Otto's six attendants and their relation to King Albert. All were minor noblemen, some good, some bad, all ambitious. And then I told them an abbreviated version of what I had told Faulke the night before about Otto, but I left out Leopold's visit to Grunental several months before Hartman's death.

"His squire is his niece Maria's eldest child. 'Tis a well-known secret in Rheinbaden that all of Maria's children were fathered by my first husband," I said in conclusion, really for Faulke's benefit, since my father and Mordecai already knew the boy's identity. Despite young Hartman's age, I would assume he was my enemy. Faulke had once made it clear that he wanted to know the names of all my enemies. My health and longevity would matter to him now more than ever. "I do not know the child, but I am certain he loves me no more than his mother does."

"So he has brought the boy here to taunt you," Edward surmised, with a glance at Faulke. "Or to threaten you with secrets that are already exposed."

"That is a reasonable assumption," I agreed, staring down so I wouldn't have to see the anger in Faulke's eyes. In addition to remaining quiet about the reasons I was coerced into my marriage, it would seem my father had no intention of outright admitting his knowledge of Maria and her children. In his role as king, I could understand his reasoning. As my father, he had betrayed me.

"Tell him the rest," Faulke bit out.

"I have said everything of importance."

Faulke's level tone didn't change. "Liar."

"Have a care, Lord Faulke." Mordecai inclined his head as he spoke and gave Faulke a look that demanded obedience. Faulke scowled at him in return.

"By your leave, Your Highness," Faulke said to my father, with exaggerated politeness, "my wife left out a very important part of the story about Leopold and his father that will clearly illustrate the characters of the men King Albert has sent to you as his representatives."

At the king's nod, Faulke repeated every word of the story I had told him about Leopold's visit to Grunental, and how Leopold had tried to compromise my honor.

By the end of the story, my father's hands were fisted on the table.

"You should have told me about this plot, Isabel." The anger in his voice was as clear as the note of censure. "Was King Albert aware of the incident at Grunental?"

I lifted my chin. "Everyone at court was aware of what happened, and speculated on what didn't. The rumor began to circulate that I had invited Leopold's knights to my apartments. Of course, no one knew who had started the rumors, but the culprit appeared obvious to me."

I jumped when my father's fist smashed down onto the table, and I had my first taste of the quick, explosive anger he was known for. I thought I caught the trace of a smile on Faulke's face, but when I turned to look at him, he was staring at the king with no expression at all.

"These men dare to set foot in England?" Edward rose to his feet and pointed toward the door as he glared at Mordecai. "Send for my guards! When their ship docks, take every one of them to the dungeons. Put the screws to each, until one of them confesses their crimes against my daughter."

"Sire," Mordecai began, holding his palms up in supplication, "they are ambassadors, representatives of the rightful King of Rheinbaden."

"I don't care if they are representatives of Jesus Christ himself," my father raged. "I want them arrested."

"Aye, that can be easily done," Mordecai said.

My father was angry on my behalf! I couldn't help but smile.

Mordecai held out his hands in supplication. "Arrests cannot be so easily undone. There will be consequences, my lord, far beyond the offense to our allies in Rheinbaden. We have ambassadors in other courts even now, negotiating with rulers who might rather see them on a spit. What sort of example would it set for future negotiations with our allies and enemies alike?"

"I don't care." My father sat back down, still fuming, but I could tell from the tone of his voice that he did care, and his anger was fading. His next words were an equal mixture of bluster and frustration. "What good is it to be king, if my hands are forever tied by wretched diplomats?"

"There are other ways to bring justice to criminals."

Something in Mordecai's tone made a chill go down my back. I knew without being told that Dante Chiavari was one of those ways, and I felt certain Mordecai had other methods at his disposal that were just as deadly.

"Aye, there are," my father agreed, with a remarkable improvement in his mood. I could almost see the anger fade into something craftier.

I wondered if I had just witnessed a warrant for someone's death, Leopold's for certain, and perhaps his father's as well. No, I was reading too much into that brief exchange.

"Is there any possibility that King Albert does not realize these men are your enemies?" Edward asked me as he reached for a boiled egg.

"None, sire."

"When they arrive for an audience, show Count Otto

and his contingent to my small receiving chamber," he told Mordecai. "Assemble six of my most trusted knights to stand as guards. None others are to attend me. I would have the smallest audience possible, when we learn Count Otto's real objectives here."

He sounded calm and sure of himself again. If I hadn't just experienced my father's anger, I would have denied it could have happened.

"Count Otto and his son are my daughter's enemies, and are therefore no friends of your king," he told Faulke, his tone still matter-of-fact. "These men are foreigners one and all, loyal to a king with uncertain allegiances to England. You will set aside any differences you have with me, or with your wife, and stand as a faithful servant to the crown while these men are in England."

"I am your true and loyal subject, sire." The two men exchanged a long look.

"Bring your sword and weapons upon your return here," Edward said at last, with a nod to Faulke's empty scabbard. "Isabel will stand to my right. You will stand a pace behind her. The new English captain, Sir Crispin, will stand to my left, and then Isabel's Rheinbaden captain. I want them to know that we welcome her people, but Isabel now stands with me, with England." He gestured toward me. "Just in case her garments fail to remind them that she is first and foremost a daughter of England."

The longer he looked at me, the more I felt it necessary to say something. "Thank you for allowing me the use of my mother's garments and jewels, Father. If you have no objections, I will wear these garments to the audience with Count Otto."

"Aye, Mordecai informed me that you did not want to wear Rheinbaden's colors," he said, "and you were unlikely to have appropriate garments made up in your husband's colors so soon after your marriage."

From the corner of my eye, I saw Faulke's head swivel toward me.

"'Tis just as well," Edward continued. "The Castile devices and the Plantagenet Lions make a more obvious statement than the Segrave dragon. You will have ample opportunity to wear your husband's device, once Count Otto returns to Rheinbaden. In the meantime, your mother would be pleased to see her garments put to good service."

My fingertips again traced over the castle I had claimed as my own on her belt. It was somehow reassuring.

"The Rheinbaden envoys will be shown to the small receiving chamber when they arrive," Mordecai said. "The knights you requested await your pleasure, sire."

"Excellent," Edward said as he drew his knife and sliced his egg into quarters. He waved the tip of the blade toward the doorway. "Escort my daughter and her people to their horses."

"Aye, my lord."

It was a dismissal. Faulke bowed and I curtseyed, and then Faulke offered his arm to escort me from the chamber. I just stared at his arm without moving.

"For this purpose we are united," he said under his breath as he placed my hand on his arm. The warmth of him gave me goose flesh, but I knew our nearness had no effect on him. His arm was as stiff as a board, and he walked as far from me as possible.

My heart leaped in my chest when Faulke leaned down to whisper in my ear.

"Do not think I have forgiven you."

CHAPTER SIXTEEN

Secrets and Lies

MUCH TO MY SURPRISE, FAULKE ACCOMPANIED
me back to Ashland. The sun was beginning to set. I
wondered if he would brave the dark streets of London
to go to his townhouse tonight, or if he intended to stay
at Ashland. We didn't have a chance to speak privately
after we left my father's quarters, so I had no idea what
thoughts were running through his head. My imagination provided plenty of possibilities.

"We will eat in the great hall tonight," Faulke told Reginald, who greeted us at Ashland's stables. He watched
two of my Rheinbaden soldiers help me off my horse.
Haul me down, more like. His expression flattened when
one of the soldiers kept hold of my waist too long and
I had to brush his hands away. He turned to Gretchen
and Hilda. "See to your lady. Get her out of those ridicu-

lous garments and into something more suitable for the
evening meal."

I bristled at hearing my court garments called ridiculous.

"He is still angry," Hilda whispered as she straightened my train. "Do not take to heart anything a man
says in anger. You look wonderful in your mother's jewels."

"Thank you, Hilda," I said. I turned to say something
biting to Faulke about his taste in fashion, but he was
already striding toward the great hall with Richard close
on his heels. Richard, I noticed, turned for one yearning
glance at Gretchen, but Faulke didn't turn to look at me.

"You should allow Hilda to pick your garments tonight," Gretchen said in a speculative voice. She took a
firm hold of my elbow. "Come, Princess, we have just
enough time to get you changed before dinner."

TWO HOURS LATER, I felt like one of the pastries that
were put on display each morning in the baker's shop.
The gown Hilda had chosen for me was my most revealing, made of a soft charcoal-gray cashmere that clung to
me like a second skin. The neckline of the gown, what
there was of it, was cut below my breasts. It was a common style in the Alps, almost prim when worn over a
proper chemise. The chemise I wore tonight displayed
the tops of my breasts and was so sheer it was practically transparent.

The sleeves were the only conservative part of the
gown, although that very feature made the gown more

risqué. They were as tightly fitted as the gown. Even the skirt clung to my hips, leaving little to the imagination as to what was beneath the gown.

I had waited in vain for the surcoat. Gretchen and Hilda both assured me that a surcoat was unnecessary and the gown was perfectly appropriate when paired with a floor-length silver veil, held in place by a headband of seed pearls.

I knew they lied the moment I walked into the great hall and everyone fell silent. It wasn't that they had been gossiping about my newly married state, or the roaring sounds Faulke had made in my bedchamber for three days and nights, or even the fight between Faulke and me that the whole palace probably knew about by this point. No, everyone stopped talking and stared at me because they had never before seen quite so much of me. The silver veil that Gretchen and Hilda had cooed over only served as a frame for my nakedness.

I almost turned around and marched right back to my solar. All that stopped me was the look on Faulke's face. The mixture of stunned disbelief and male pleasure was quite satisfying. I walked over to my place next to him at the head table as if I always arrived naked to the great hall.

By the time he had me seated, a dark frown had replaced the heat in his eyes, and he was no longer looking at my gown. He was busy scowling at other men in the room who were looking at *me*.

"Do you intend to remain in residence at Ashland?" I asked when I could no longer contain my curiosity.

That got his attention. He finally looked at me again, his gaze traveling from head to foot, and then back up. "Who dressed you?"

"Gretchen and Hilda," I answered. My mouth flattened. "You said to dress in something more suitable for the evening meal. We assumed that meant fewer jewels."

"Aye, but I did not mean fewer clothes." His gaze seemed fixated on my breasts. I wondered if some of his marks showed through the sheer fabric of my chemise. I knew the marks on my neck were clearly visible. He muttered under his breath, "Your ladies are punishing me."

"You haven't answered my question," I reminded him when he continued to stare in silence at my breasts.

"We are married," he said, finally looking up into my eyes. "Of course I will live with my wife."

Of course? I wondered if some miracle had occurred and he had decided to forgive me after all. His eyes glittered when I said, "I was under the impression that you did not want to be in my company."

"I don't like being lied to," he replied.

"Neither do I," I retorted. I thought about the concessions he had won from my father, how prepared he had been to state them. I blurted out what had occurred to me on the ride back to Ashland. "You knew. Somehow, you knew."

"I know more than even your father, it would seem." He looked around the great hall. Dante and Avalene had wisely decided to have their evening meal in their solar, but there were others at and near our table who could overhear our conversation if they tried. "There are things we need to discuss tonight in private. Right now, I missed the midday meal and I'm famished. Let me eat, and then we will retire for the night. I have questions of my own that require answers."

His scowl didn't intimidate me. It made me sad, yes, but he would have to do much more than scowl to make me cower. The worst was done. He knew my secrets.

I looked down at my trencher and tried to be glad that he didn't seem inclined to take out his anger at me with his fists. Not that he seemed all that angry anymore. Then I began to wonder what he meant, that he knew more than my father.

Richard had been seated next to Faulke for the dinner. Faulke found plenty of reasons to speak with his cousin throughout the meal, and none to speak with me. I turned my attention to Gerhardt instead, who had been seated to my right. Gretchen was next to him, and then Hilda. Now that I knew Gretchen's dilemma, it amazed me that Gerhardt didn't see how often Richard and Gretchen exchanged looks.

All of my people had been informed of King Rudolph's death and the new king Albert's edict, Gerhardt informed me. Surprisingly, Gerhardt wasn't pleased with the news. He was a second son, with no lands to return to, but he was a well-respected knight with many connections at court. Even in King Albert's new court, he was still related to the royal family. I couldn't think of any reason he wouldn't prosper under the new king. If I didn't know better, I would say he was afraid of Count Otto. Or of King Albert. It was very strange, but he remained elusive when I tried to question him on the matter.

"'Tis time," Faulke said, interrupting my musings about Gerhardt.

The words sent a shock through my system, as it suddenly occurred to me that he might not only plan to stay at Ashland tonight, he might also be planning to stay in my bed. And planning everything that went along with staying in my bed.

No, he would not want me that way anymore. I could not give him children. There was no point to pretending anymore. He could have any woman he wanted, and I no longer qualified for that list.

I looked at Faulke and found him watching me already, his expression sober. I tried to swallow, and found my throat suddenly tight. "Do I need my ladies?"

"Not unless you want them privy to our conversation."

Did I? My brain worked frantically. If I brought them along, perhaps he would keep his anger contained. Not that his anger had been all that volatile, considering what I'd told him. My ladies' job in the evening was to prepare me for bed. I didn't want to put any ideas in his head. I turned and then leaned around Gerhardt to speak to Gretchen and Hilda in German.

"Lord Faulke wishes to have a private discussion. Give us at least an hour before you retire."

Gretchen nodded. Hilda smirked. But both remained in their seats when I stood. I turned again to Faulke. "I am ready."

That was a complete lie. I wasn't ready for anything

that involved private time with my husband, but I pretended rather well. At least, I thought I did. My hands were shaking by the time we reached the solar. Faulke ordered the guards to take their post outside the doors. We were alone.

"Stop panicking," he said as he poured two goblets of wine from an ewer that had been set on the table. He jerked his head in the direction of my chair. "Take your seat. I only want to talk."

Of course. I glanced down at the wanton display of my breasts and suddenly felt ridiculous in my revealing gown. He only wanted to talk. He would probably leave at the end of our conversation, which would likely be the end of our marriage, in the traditional sense. I wondered if I would ever see his girls again.

"Isabel?"

I looked up at him and realized I was still standing.

He gestured again toward my chair. "Have a seat."

Why was he so calm?

"Tell me," I said as I settled onto my chair. "What do you know that my father and I don't?"

He wasted no time getting to the point. "That Countess Maria had a lover for many years, a lover other than Hartman."

He set a goblet of wine in front of me and I frowned at it, uncertain what that had to do with anything, and then it all came together in my mind. "Her children . . . they might not be Hartman's?"

"'Tis unlikely that any but her first child are from your prince, the one named for him."

Faulke handed me a goblet and I took a deep gulp as

I absorbed the news. Maria's younger children might not be Hartman's, the ones born after we both had the mumps.

My skin felt as if I had just stepped too close to a fire. It tingled everywhere. "How do you know this?"

For the first time, he looked ill at ease. "My father sent spies to Rheinbaden a month after your prince died. He knew you would be returned to England when your mourning period was over. My wife, Alice, had already died. My father knew that just the possibility of a marriage to Avalene de Forshay would provide the king with more incentive to agree to a match between you and me. He wasn't sure it would happen, so he didn't tell me anything about his efforts to arrange this marriage until after we were betrothed."

"I had spies at Maria's house. Why did they not tell me?"

"Are you certain your spies were loyal?"

My retort was automatic. "Of course my—"

I stopped midsentence. Spies were not known for their honesty. Their very profession required lies. And they were Rheinbadeners. For a secret that big, their loyalty would lie with their prince.

"Hartman had died by the time my father sent spies to Rheinbaden," Faulke said. "'Tis often easier to find out secrets about a dead man than a live one."

I gave an absent nod. That made sense. Maria had made enemies, people who would turn on her when she was no longer the favorite mistress of the crown prince. "Are you certain?"

Faulke nodded. "Maria had a lover, but Hartman had

many over the years. Given their numbers, Hartman should have fathered several bastards, but Maria was the only one to make that claim."

How could I have been so blind? The question sobered me. "What did your spies learn about me?"

He folded his arms across his chest. "That you were loyal. To your people, to your family, to your faithless husband."

I took another sip of the wine and remained silent, my brain trying hard to process all of this new information and its implications. Everything I had believed for the past ten years could be wrong.

"You knew all of this going into our marriage," I said. "That there was a possibility I could provide the children required to secure your lands and titles."

He shrugged, unrepentant. "The only real probability was that Hartman could not father a child. In all likelihood, the disease left you sterile as well."

I looked up at him as a different question suddenly occurred. "Who is rumored to have fathered Maria's children?"

He didn't answer me right away, and instead took a moment to refill my goblet. "Maria's children all favor Hartman. All of the royals, even the cousins, have icy blond hair and eyes a distinct shade of pale blue. Maria had been giving birth almost every year until you moved your court. That turned attention to the men within your court. It didn't take long to get a name."

I sipped at my wine. There was only one man in my company who was related to Hartman, who looked very much like his cousin. "Gerhardt."

Faulke nodded.

I slammed my goblet onto the table and went to the doorway before Faulke realized my intent. I removed the bar and threw open the doors.

"Send for Sir Gerhardt," I ordered one of the soldiers. "Tell him I need to speak with him immediately."

Faulke closed the doors after I gave the order and led me back to the table. He put the goblet of wine in my hands.

"Think carefully how you intend to accuse him," Faulke warned.

I gulped the wine and tried to take his advice to heart. I wasn't sure of anything. This could all be speculation. I ran through Faulke's accusations, examined them from every angle, and came to the same conclusions. A knock at the door announced Gerhardt's arrival.

For the first time, I looked at Gerhardt and saw Hartman. In addition to the hair and eye color, the similarities were there in the same lean, angular build, his height, even some of his mannerisms, such as the way he narrowed his eyes at me right now.

"Princess? You called for me?" He stood in the middle of the room, looking uncertain.

"Speak French," I told him. " 'Tis rude to speak before my husband in a language he cannot understand."

His gaze went to Faulke, and then returned to me. "What can I do for you, Princess?"

"Tell me why you do not wish to return to Rheinbaden."

Gerhardt glanced between Faulke and me. "King Albert is no longer your brother-in-law, and he is not your liege lord. As your sworn man, I am not obliged to answer his summons; only a summons from *your* liege lord would compel me to abandon my post."

I drummed my fingers against the tabletop. "Now tell me the real reasons."

Gerhardt shifted restlessly and toyed with the hilt of his dagger. Faulke came to stand beside me, where he would be in a better position to protect me. It hadn't occurred to me until that moment that I might need protection from my protector.

"The princess has discovered your role in Countess Maria's deception," Faulke said. "She would like an explanation."

Gerhardt tried to hide his reaction, but it was too late. His eyes widened, and I knew the truth in that moment. He was guilty. He had lied to me for years, or allowed the lie that had shaped much of my adult life.

"Gerhardt?" I asked. My tone demanded an explanation.

"You were never supposed to know," Gerhardt said grimly. "No one was supposed to know, although I knew it would not remain secret once Hartman died."

"That was the reason you were so anxious to leave Rheinbaden," I said.

Gerhardt raked a hand through his hair. Hair the same shade as Hartman's. "Otto knows the truth, and Albert suspected, but they could do nothing about it while Hartman lived."

"Did Hartman know?" I asked.

Gerhardt nodded. "I had been . . . intimate with Countess Maria before she caught Hartman's eye. I stepped aside for the prince, of course. Then almost a year after you lost your babe, Hartman made it clear that he wanted me to return to Maria's bed. He said that as long as I kept the affair secret, I should enjoy her company with his blessing."

"While Hartman continued to see her?" I said, trying to keep the disgust from my voice.

"Aye," Gerhardt admitted. "We both knew the truth. Hartman didn't want anyone to think the disease had left him any less a man, but it had. None of his other mistresses bore him children, only Maria. And I was the father of all but her oldest son, Hartman, named for the prince."

A small muscle ticked along his jaw as he awaited my response.

"You could have told me," I said quietly. All the years of deception. The years of feeling less than. Had Hartman truly hated me so much?

"Hartman swore me to secrecy," he said. "He was family. I swore my allegiance to his service when I first became a knight, and the knowledge of Maria's children would have changed nothing for you."

He was wrong. The entire country had blamed me for the lack of an heir. There would have been no heir, regardless, but Hartman could have shared the blame. My head was spinning, not only from the wine, but from all the lies.

"I hoped you would never learn the truth," Gerhardt admitted, staring at me in earnest, silently begging my forgiveness. "If a miracle occurs and you bear this man a child, it will be God's will and cause for celebration."

I did not feel like celebrating right now. I couldn't even allow myself to think about that possibility. "Did Gretchen know?"

"Of course not," Gerhardt said. "She would have told you the moment she found out."

At least one of my people was loyal. I took another drink of wine as I considered what to do with my new-found knowledge. Gerhardt had truly been like an older brother. I had entrusted all of us to his care. He had charge of the soldiers, the head servants reported to him, every cog in the wheel that was my household had a place fitted for him.

"Forgive me, Princess. I never meant for you to be hurt."

I couldn't even look at him. All the years I had blamed myself, the mistresses I had put up with because I thought myself less of a woman and Hartman still a whole man. Years. And Gerhardt wanted my forgiveness?

"Can I at least know who betrayed me?" he asked. "How did you discover the truth, all the way in England?"

"A dead master's servant is easily bought," Faulke said when I remained silent. "Maria's servants also confirmed the tale, when confronted with the truth and a bag of silver."

I had wondered how the Segraves managed what I could not, and uncovered a secret that had remained hidden even from my father. Keeping secrets from the king, even in faraway Rheinbaden, was no easy feat.

"Princess, please," Gerhardt entreated. "I am still

your man, I have no more secrets, and my loyalty will remain with you until I die."

Pretty words, spoken too late. When I sent Gerhardt away, my household would be in shambles. If Count Otto had his way, all of my people would soon be leaving for Rheinbaden, which meant my household would be in shambles regardless. And then there was that journey to Wales that Faulke was keen to make. Would my father force me to go with Faulke? My imagination simply shut down when I tried to envision that journey. I took another drink of wine.

"Leave us," Faulke ordered while I was still lost in my musings. "The princess will let you know your fate on the morrow. Tonight she has other matters to contemplate."

It was an unwelcome reminder that I still had Faulke's anger to somehow appease.

"Princess, please—" Gerhardt tried again.

"Leave." The dark undertone in Faulke's voice made the hairs on the back of my neck rise. Gerhardt wisely decided to retreat.

I gulped the last of my wine and pretended not to notice his exit. Except it wasn't the last of my wine. My goblet was full. Again. I wondered how often Faulke had refilled it. Not that it mattered. Gerhardt was gone. My secrets were out. I could afford to let myself be drunk. It made me care less what Faulke thought of me. I stared down at my watery reflection in the goblet, fascinated by the way my breath made little waves on the surface.

"So, you played my father and me for fools," I said,

feeling dangerously bold. I lifted my glass to salute him. "Congratulations. Well done."

Faulke eyed my goblet, then picked up his own before he sat down next to me. His expression was unreadable. "Your father had the same goal. He wanted us wed before I learned that Maria had children, supposedly Hartman's children, while you remained childless all these years."

"Hah. The laugh is on my father. He might end up with a very expensive grandchild out of me after all!" Judging by the look on Faulke's face, my smile might have been a bit maniacal. I took another swallow of wine, and admitted to myself that I was more than a little drunk.

"We thought you were aware of Maria's deception," he went on, watching me carefully. "You have lived for years under the same roof as the man who fathered the children your husband claimed were his own bastards, and that man's sister is your closest friend. I have known from the start that there was a possibility you could give me a child. If you thought the possibility existed but had no way of proving it short of committing adultery, I would have forgiven your silence on the matter."

I stared at his mouth and tried to understand the words he was saying. I loved his mouth. I loved the way his lips moved, the way he rubbed his mouth when he was frustrated. I loved the way his mouth softened when he said my name.

"Isabel, are you listening to me?"

"Aye." I shook my head.

He frowned. "How much wine have you had?"

"Not enough," I said before I took another swallow. "This is very good. I'll have to ask Reginald to serve this wine every night."

He took my goblet and put it back on the table when I would have taken another sip. I frowned up at him.

"You and your father tried to deceive me," he said. His gaze hardened, grew distant. "It's not my fault if you were caught in the web of your lies."

"No, it's not," I agreed. I tilted my head to one side. "You had already planned what you intended to say to the king about your daughters' betrothals."

It wasn't a question, but he nodded anyway. "I intended to wait a year after our marriage before I approached your father. If you didn't quicken with child, I would ask for the concessions. When I realized you and your father were unaware of Hartman's deception, I decided to ask for the betrothals to be arranged while he still might be feeling some measure of guilt about his intent to deceive me."

"You weren't deceived though." I heard a giggle, and realized it came from me. Faulke's expression was still stormy. I cleared my throat and tried to be serious. "Why did you even agree to our marriage? After you spoke with your father, you even seemed happy about it. Was that a lie, too? Everyone is lying to me these days, or not telling me things I should know. 'Tis frustrating."

"You were lying, too," he reminded me. "At least, you thought you were lying."

"Oh, aye, the joke is on me." I slapped my hands against my chest. "I was lying about a lie I didn't know about. I think." I shook my head and tried to clear it. "How did that go again?"

He took the goblet out of my hand again and put it out of my reach on the table.

"I'm thirsty."

All four of his eyes narrowed. "Somehow I doubt that."

I propped my elbows on the table, put my chin in my hands, and pouted at the unreachable goblet. "I don't care that you don't like me. Why do you even want to stay married to me? I probably can't have your children anyway, so you might as well give up on me now, rather than next year or the year after."

"Stop it."

"Stop what?" I dragged my gaze from the goblet and was soon drowning in a sapphire sea. I loved his eyes so much, almost as much as his mouth. His eyes were so . . . so . . .

"Stop feeling sorry for yourself."

I sat up straighter in my chair and tried to look offended. "I have never felt sorry for myself a day in my life. Well, I might have felt sorry for myself for an hour or two here and there, but it doesn't accomplish anything. I'd rather not care. I tried not to care for you."

His mouth tilted up in a wry smile. Or maybe my head tilted. "Do you care for me then, Isabel?"

Ach, I loved the shape of his mouth when he said my name. He caught my hand just before my fingertips touched his lips. To my delight, he turned my hand over and kissed my wrist. I think I shivered. "That feels delicious."

His eyes turned a darker shade of blue. "Do you like it when I touch you?"

"I like almond comfits," I said, deciding to list everything I found delicious. "And I like that wine. Remind me to ask Reginald to get more for dinner each night. Mm. Delicious."

"You're drunk."

I saw no reason to argue. "You are, too?"

For some reason, he smiled. "No. I shouldn't have refilled your goblet so often, but I thought you needed fortification for Gerhardt's news."

"Fortification, aye." I gave my abandoned goblet a baleful look. "Everyone knew but me."

He shook his head. "Very few knew until Hartman died. You were never meant to know. If Hartman had lived, it would probably still be a secret."

"You're right!" That sounded too loud. I cleared my throat and tried to moderate my tone. "I would still be stupid."

That wasn't right, but I couldn't think of the right thing to say, and it suddenly felt too complicated to think about it anymore.

"This might be the time to tell you the rest."

"There's more?" I rubbed the space between my eyes. "Are there other children?"

"Nay, it's about the same children," he said. "Actually, it's about Hartman's only child."

"Hartman the Younger?" I asked.

Faulke nodded. "Hartman was granted an audience with the pope. He had planned a trip to Rome only a week after his death."

I frowned at him, unable to think why the pope would want to see Hartman. At least, not before he inherited the throne.

"He was negotiating an annulment, Isabel. The preliminaries were done, if the papers our spy saw were genuine. Your marriage would have been annulled within the year."

I blinked once and stared down at the table. There was a knot in the wood right in front of me. I used my fingertip to trace the whorl. "He wanted to marry Maria."

"Aye, he planned to marry Maria and adopt her children. Hartman's natural son would have become his heir. Hartman's brother, Albert, would surely contest the line of succession, but that was the plan."

If an annulment had happened, I would have been sent back to England in shame. That was a sobering thought. "Why are you telling me this?"

"Maria's uncle is obviously your enemy, and he is likely here in part to look for revenge. They have already demanded that your people return to Rheinbaden. You need to prepare yourself for every other possibility."

"I don't want to see them," I admitted. I shuddered a little. "I definitely don't want to be left alone with any of them."

He put his hand on mine to stop me tracing the knot of wood with my fingertip. It was instantly distracting.

"I am your husband now, Isabel. I will be at your side throughout this visit from Count Otto. Do not go anywhere without me while they are in town. Promise me."

I nodded solemnly. "I promise me."

He smiled. "I will remind you of this conversation tomorrow."

"Promise you won't leave me alone with them."

His smile faded. "Perhaps you will not need a reminder after all."

"Why didn't you ask my father for an annulment? Why did you even marry me in the first place?" I rubbed my hands across my eyes and tried to concentrate. "You knew before we married that we are unlikely to have children. Why would you risk everything for such a slim possibility?"

He leaned back in his chair and studied the knot of wood on the table. He took so long to answer that I had mostly forgotten my question.

"Two dead wives at my age was suspicious," he said. "At three, I became notorious. We could restore our family honor with the might of the Plantagenet name and its wealth behind us. My daughters could marry into good families. And we would still have more wealth than any bride had brought to our family. Wealth buys influence."

He gave me a meaningful look that was lost on my hazy brain.

"My father, Anselm, is now the sheriff of Maldon," he went on. "Your brother, the future king of England, lives in Langley, a short distance from Maldon. My father plans to make his presence known to Giles of Oudenarde, who is charged with the management of your brother's household.

"I predict that he and my father will become fast friends, and my father will become a familiar figure in your brother's life. Now that our families are connected through marriage, my father's presence will not only be tolerated but likely encouraged. Then there is the fact that your father is not a young man, and the lines of his subjects' inheritances can be changed on a king's whims. Or on a future king's whims."

He leaned back and took a long drink from his goblet. His continued silence finally penetrated my senses and I realized the story had ended.

"So, your father hopes my brother will change the terms of our marriage when my father dies?"

"My father views this opportunity as his calling and duty to England, to take a hand in the education of our next king," he said. "There is no one better suited to teach a prince the rigors of knighthood, as well as the skills he will need to become a leader. My father's skills will be more useful to the future king than Giles of Oudenarde's knowledge of how to balance household ledgers. If that relationship also benefits my family, all the better."

"I see." And I did, sort of.

"Without you," Faulke continued, "my reputation is such that no one would willingly tie their daughter to me. My infamy has spread to my daughters, and I could not secure adequate husbands for them, either. Our marriage has already changed my family's situation for the better."

And I was just a pawn in a game Faulke played with my father. However, the only blame I could lay at Faulke's door was his claim to be falling in love with me. That was cruel.

"Our marriage was your best course of action." I released a little sigh, feeling sorry for myself again. "You will want to try for an heir, I suppose."

Faulke just lifted his brows and stared at me. Either I had shocked him, or he had not yet considered the awkwardness of our future intimacies. As in, there would be no more intimate moments. Those had all been lies. We would be back to doing a duty.

I tried not to think about how horrible that would be, knowing I was once again nothing but a brood mare. At least with Hartman I hadn't known it could have been so much more than an unpleasant duty. I began to feel slightly nauseous.

Faulke cleared his throat. "What do you plan to do about your captain?"

For a moment, I had forgotten all about Gerhardt. It was an unwelcome reminder that Faulke was not my only problem.

"Gerhardt was a member of my family." I rested my chin on my hands, depressed again. "He was like a brother to me. A brother with a very pointy sword and a strong arm to swing it."

"You have my pointy sword now," he reminded me, "but do not be so quick to dismiss Gerhardt. His loyalties were divided. In the end, he tried to take the road that would cause you the least trouble."

My head was beginning to ache just thinking about the days to come. Gerhardt. Gretchen and Richard. Count Otto and his odious son, Leopold. Faulke. Mostly Faulke. How was I supposed to act, now that he knew the truth? I had played out this moment so often in my head. He wasn't reacting in any of the ways I had anticipated.

Maybe if I put my head down on the table for a few minutes and rested, my thoughts would clear.

"Let's get you to bed."

That announcement woke me up. I sat up straight and the panic must have shown in my expression.

"You had too much to drink, Isabel." He stood and snagged my wrist to drag me up as well. "A good night's sleep will do you good."

I looked toward the door, wondering if he planned to sleep in his own quarters tonight. "I'll send for my ladies."

"I can manage to get you into bed." He glanced down at the gray cashmere and his gaze seemed glued to my chest. "You are hardly dressed as it is. From now on, I don't want you to wear this for anyone but me. Unless you want bloodshed. Walter de Gardanne stared at your breasts so much I was ready to blind him."

The thought was fleeting that my gown might have been the reason for his foul mood at dinner. That thought was gone as I suddenly had to concentrate on standing up without falling over. Ach. "I am drunk!"

There was a rumbly sound in Faulke's chest, but I was clinging to his chest at the time and didn't dare look up to see if he was smiling. A smile probably would have made me mad. Why, I wasn't sure.

"You are very drunk," Faulke confirmed, steering me toward my bedchamber.

The floor had suddenly taken on a life of its own, tilting and dipping as much as the ship we'd taken from Calais to London.

"Something is wrong," I gasped, almost tripping us both. "The floor is moving!"

"I would imagine it is," he agreed.

He steered us into my bedchamber and I collapsed onto the bed. There was some tugging and pulling, and then I drifted into the sweet oblivion of sleep.

CHAPTER SEVENTEEN

Trust

THE BIRDS WOKE ME THE NEXT MORNING. CHIRP, chirp, chirp, sing, sing, sing. It was maddening. I pulled the goose-down pillow over my head and wished that someone would shoo the birds away from my window. *"Mein kopf, mach, dass es aufhört!"*

They didn't stop. I burrowed deeper under the covers and tried to fall back asleep.

"Isabel?"

My breath stilled in my lungs. Faulke. He was in bed with me. I didn't remember how we got there. I quickly checked beneath the covers. Ach! "I'm naked!"

There was no response to that announcement. I pulled the covers to my chin, scrunched my eyes closed, and wished I could shut my brain off as easily. Memories of the previous day come pouring back in. My confession.

The audience with my father. The strained meal with Faulke. Bits and pieces of our conversation in my solar. Gerhardt's deception with Maria and Hartman. Wine. A lot of it.

I needed to go back to sleep.

I tried to even my breathing, praying I could catch the elusive slip of sleep that hovered at the back of my consciousness. Between the stupidly happy birds and the stupidly unhappy spike in my head, sleep was now impossible. My eyes popped back open and I spied my robe at the foot of the bed. If I could just keep the sheet in place for modesty, I could quickly snag my robe and cover myself, and then find someplace dark and quiet to curl up and die. After a drink of water. If I breathed through my mouth, I was certain dust would come out.

Bolstered by my plan, I pinned the sheet to my sides and sat up, then tried to grab my robe. The spike in my head turned into a sword, so intensely painful that my whole body rebelled, especially my stomach. I half stumbled, half fell from the mattress and grabbed the chamber pot beneath the bed. Thank God it was clean.

I soon had a used chamber pot in my hands.

It was disgusting. It looked like everything in my stomach had bled a strange shade of pink and red. And it reeked. Wine. Ach. I would never drink another drop of it.

Finally, someone handed me a damp cloth and I gratefully wiped my mouth. I was disgusting. Mm. Someone was rubbing my back. It felt comforting.

"Oh God." The words slipped out before I could stop them. Faulke was behind me. He had held my hair back while I was sick. He gave me the wet cloth to clean my face afterward. He was rubbing my back even now.

I was stark naked. Puking.

I glared at the floor when it didn't open up and swallow me. Humiliation soaked through me, the wave so strong it almost brought on another bout of heaves.

"Are you done?"

"I—I don't know."

I felt him move away from me, and then the robe was draped across my shoulders. Stupid robe, you are too late, I thought as I managed to get my arms through the sleeves. Still it was nice to be covered. Faulke produced a cup of water next, from where, I didn't know. I was too grateful to care. I took several gulps of the water before he took it away. I was about to protest, but instead I leaned over the chamber pot and was sick again. So much for the water.

The next time he handed me a cup, I took a much more careful sip, and swished it around in my mouth before spitting it out into the chamber pot.

I glanced up at him for the first time, fully expecting to see disgust. His look of genuine concern surprised me. I soaked it in for a moment until another thought occurred. Oh, right. He would be hung if I died.

He had watched my face while I processed those thoughts, and seemed to read my mind. His mouth flattened. "How much do you remember of last night?"

"All of it." I looked toward the ceiling and scowled. "Most of it. Well, maybe not most of it. I don't remember going to bed. I think someone tried to poison me."

His expression softened. He thought I was joking. "So you remember Gerhardt?"

I nodded as I covered and pushed the disgusting chamber pot back under the bed. I looked toward the outer room where Hilda and Gretchen slept.

"We are alone," he said in answer to my silent question.

I sat gingerly on the edge of the bed and wondered how to apologize. For the deception, for getting drunk, for this morning's mess. My whole world had changed in the space of a day, and my entire life was falling apart. The mattress sagged when he sat next to me.

"Gerhardt was right about one thing," he said. "He is sworn to you, as are all of your knights and ladies, even your servants, and your father is once again your king. You are sworn to England. That means Albert cannot force your people to leave with Count Otto. They can stay with you, unless your father agrees with Albert's 'request.'"

I hadn't thought through the situation that far, not last night and definitely not this morning. My people might not leave after all. I would be happy about this development when I felt better. "Each volunteered to accompany me to England, certain it was for their lifetime. I made a promise that I would always take care of them."

"I will help you keep that promise," he said.

I looked into his eyes and tried to find the lie, but saw only honesty. Everything he said seemed wrong. He was supposed to hate me. He was supposed to send me away or allow me to go away on my own.

"What happened since my confession yesterday?" I

asked. I didn't have to feign confusion. "Why are you being nice to me again?"

"You are my wife," Faulke said, as if that explained everything. His brows drew together and the corners of his mouth turned downward. "I will not give you up, Isabel. God willing, we will have a long life together."

God hadn't willed much pleasantness my way so far. I didn't trust Him to start now. "Yesterday you could barely stand to look at me."

"I was angry." His voice lowered and turned darker. "Do you have any idea what it was like to listen to what that bastard had done to you? I couldn't help but picture it in my head. You were a helpless child who had just given birth to his child, and he raped you less than a month later. When you told me about the blood, I wanted to peel the skin from his bones. I wanted to—"

He pressed his lips together and stopped talking. His hands were once again white-knuckled and flexing into fists. I was too astonished by what he'd just said to break the tense silence. He took a deep breath and slowly released it. Then another.

"I wanted to kill him," he said at last. "Instead I had to keep reminding myself that I could not kill a dead man, that he could never, ever touch you again."

"You wouldn't let me touch you," I reminded him.

He looked puzzled for a moment, and then his expression began to clear. "The things you said were making me crazy. I could not be certain my anger would not hurt you, not after the marks I left on your arms the day I dragged you here from the great hall."

Hope bloomed in my chest. "Then if you aren't mad at me—"

"I didn't say that," he interrupted. "If you had thought there was a possibility that you could fulfill the terms of our marriage contract, no matter how slim that possibility, I was ready to forgive you for the part you played in your father's schemes. Instead you purposely conspired to ruin my family."

In other words, I thought I had knowingly betrayed him. He shook his head and the disappointment in his eyes crushed me.

"Yesterday I was angry. I am still angry," he said, although he didn't seem any more upset now than he had the night before. "I'm angry with your father for his deceptions, and angry with you for going along with his plan. But anger changes little, except my trust in you."

"You just pointed out that I am sworn to England," I said, "and my first duty is to the king. I had no choice."

"Perhaps not," he said, "but I am your husband now, and your duty is to me. I will not tolerate another betrayal. If there are any more secrets between us, now would be the time to confess."

"There is nothing more," I murmured. I was free at last of those burdens. However, I was no longer so certain what that freedom meant for my marriage "You know everything now. You can leave with a clear conscience."

"We are in this marriage together, Isabel. I reminded you last night that our vows are binding," he warned. "I have no intention of letting you go."

My muddled brain struggled to recall that conversation, to make sense of what he was saying. Nothing came to mind.

"Last night you kept asking if I intended to keep you. You spoke of yourself as if you were some stray pup I found on the road." His voice hardened. "Now you look anywhere but at me, as if you cannot wait to be away from me."

That wasn't true. Was it? I stopped looking at the door, and then stared down at my hands. No one had ever wanted to keep me. Not for any reason I found agreeable. "I am sorry if I gave you that impression. It was not my intent."

His fingers tilted my chin up until I looked at him. "Tell me what is on your mind."

My gaze slid to the door again without my permission. I would give almost anything to avoid this conversation. "I . . . I'm not feeling very well."

I glanced at his face just long enough to see skepticism, and then resignation. "I should not have allowed you to drink so much wine last night."

"I am responsible for my own actions," I said. "No one forced me to drink, and I am old enough to know my tolerance."

"You were distracted," he said. "I took advantage of your distraction to serve more than you would normally imbibe. For that, I am sorry."

I gave a small wave to dismiss his apology. It didn't excuse my behavior, but it explained a few things. I always drank in moderation. An unguarded tongue could be a fatal flaw, and there had always been too many eyes and ears watching my every move to make such a foolish mistake. I closed my eyes and prayed that I had not said anything profoundly stupid.

"You still seem uncertain on one point," he said, interrupting my morose thoughts. "I intend to keep you."

That made me look him in the eye. "Why?"

Whatever he saw in my expression made his gaze soften. He took my hand in his and his thumb began to rub a circular pattern against my pulse point. I don't think he was even aware of doing it. He took a deep breath and slowly released it. "Do you remember Chiavari's feast, when you asked if I intended to murder you, too?"

"I—I recall."

"You had heard the rumors," he said. "I knew you thought me guilty. Yet after I told you my side of the story, you believed me. I could see it in your eyes. Every day since then, you maintained your belief in me. You gave me a measure of your trust, and I treasured that gift."

I wasn't sure where this story was going, but my head hurt so much that I almost didn't care. "You are . . . welcome?"

"It's not just your wealth or the titles and lands your father gave me," he said. "It's you, Isabel. You were made for me, I know it."

And once more, he left me speechless. I looked down at our joined hands and wondered how he could say those things to a woman who had just vomited into a bucket. How he could say those things to *me*?

"Come. I will call for a bath and your ladies." He stood and pulled me up with him. "I can tell you really do feel ill. Perhaps you should take a nap after your bath to help speed your recovery."

I wobbled to my feet, and then stood there dumbly. I wanted to crawl back into bed, but I felt too awful to even lie down. Perhaps a bath would refresh me. Hopefully it would refresh my brain as well. Very little of what Faulke said made sense.

I lifted my chin and tried to look dignified. "If you would send for my ladies, I would like that bath now."

I WAS MOSTLY myself again by early afternoon. At the very least, I didn't wish for death any longer. Surprisingly, Avalene provided the cure. She swore that a goblet of ale would have my color back in no time. I thought her insane, but forced a goblet down when Hilda also insisted it would work. They were both right, and I felt remarkably better by the time the vessel was empty, although there was an alarming moment before the first sip when the smell hit my abused senses and I thought I would need a chamber pot again.

"Gretchen, I need to speak with your brother in private. Please send for him."

Gretchen gave me a questioning look before she curtseyed. "Aye, Princess."

So, Gerhardt had not yet told his sister. He must be suffering. Good. I wanted him to suffer, to get just a small taste of the misery I had lived with for years. But Gerhardt had been right. Knowing for certain that Hartman could not father a child did not mean I could carry one. The knowledge had changed everything, and yet nothing.

Gerhardt looked miserable when he finally arrived at the solar. His blond hair looked dull and disheveled, his jaw set. There were dark circles under his eyes. I doubted he had slept much the night before.

"What do you have to say for yourself?" I asked when we were finally alone.

"I beg your forgiveness, Princess." His words were stiff and formal. After a visible struggle with himself, he pressed his lips together and remained silent.

"What will happen if you return to Rheinbaden?"

"Nothing good." Apparently I hit on the right question. He released the breath he had been holding. "King Albert suspects the younger children are not Hartman's, and Count Otto knows for certain. Servants might gossip, but I would be believed. Maria received a handsome settlement upon Prince Hartman's death, and a guaranteed place at court for young Hartman. Otto would not want that jeopardized."

"So you fear your life could be in danger?"

"Count Otto would not mourn if some tragedy were to befall me on the journey to Rheinbaden." He spread his hands. "If you dismiss me, I will not willingly return there."

No, I supposed not. Like me, Gerhardt had known his life in Rheinbaden had ended the day we received word of Hartman's death. Unlike me, Gerhardt could make his own way in the world. A good captain could always find work at almost any keep or court, in any country.

"I thought of you as a brother," I told him. "Your silence betrayed me."

He hung his head. "Aye, Princess."

"Count Otto blames me that his niece did not become queen and his great-nephew did not become the king," I said. "Albert should thank me, but somehow Otto has convinced him to work against me. I plan to fight for my people, for their right to choose if they want to return to Rheinbaden or stay with me." Faulke's words from that morning echoed through my memory. "I need someone loyal by my side, but you have damaged my trust. It will take time for you to regain that trust."

Gerhardt fell to his knees. They buckled, and he actually fell. "I swear by all that's holy I am loyal to you, Princess. Tell me what I must do to prove myself. Name any task, send me on any mission, and I will do as you ask."

I tapped my lower lip and pretended to consider my options. "Swear that you will never withhold a secret from me again."

"I so swear." His head raised up and, for the first time, he looked hopeful.

Faulke's declaration that he didn't intend to let me go meant I was bound for Wales at some point. We would all do well to learn the language. "You will learn Welsh, if you can. I cannot understand a word of that Welsh gibberish, but all of us should at least try."

"I am learning already," he said. "I have memorized the greetings and a few short phrases."

"You will swear your allegiance again to my husband, and this time you will mean it."

That one made him swallow. "Aye, Princess."

"You set an example for the others, Gerhardt. The Segraves are my family now. I will live with them for the rest of my life. We all need to become Segraves." I wasn't entirely certain that Faulke wouldn't change his mind, but that was my problem to deal with. My people needed to become a part of this land, no matter where we lived.

"People will think I was born in Wales," he said.

"Well, I don't know if *that* is necessary," I countered, "but you will make a special effort to become friends with Richard Segrave, or at least treat him as your equal. He is Faulke's captain, and worthy of your respect. No more deliberate slights or insults."

"*Richard* Segrave?" Gerhardt tilted his head to one side. "I can treat him with respect, but is there some reason you would have me cultivate a friendship?"

"Aye," I muttered. "But I would have your word before I tell you why."

"I will befriend him," he said without hesitation. "You have my word."

"You will accept Richard as your brother-in-law," I blurted out, "when he makes the request."

"*What?*"

"Richard and Gretchen have handfasted," I said, hurrying on. "I don't know if they've told Faulke yet. Gretchen just told me. She fears you will object."

"Of course I will object," Gerhardt exploded. "She knows nothing of the man. I know little enough. He has a reputation with women. He's an ausländer!"

"Those are my terms," I said in a quiet voice, wishing he would lower his. "Do you accept them?"

He thought about defying me, I could see it in his eyes. At last he released a long sigh. "I accept your terms, Princess."

"Good." I allowed myself a small smile. "There is no need for Gretchen to know of our bargain about Richard, or of your involvement with Maria. She will not hear about either from me. If you want to tell her, that is your decision."

"Thank you. I will tell her . . . perhaps when she tells me about Richard." There was a glint in his eye when he placed his hand on his chest and gave me a deep bow. "My life is yours, Princess."

"Keep it strong and safe for me," I replied, almost from habit. Except that few had sworn their lives to me. "I want to trust you again, Gerhardt. Please do not make me regret this decision."

"I will swear to your husband, but you will always have my first allegiance," he said. "My first loyalty is to you."

I gave him a small nod. "That is all we need to say on the matter for now."

He bowed once, and the matter was done.

"HOW ARE YOU feeling, truly?" Faulke asked.

I put one hand to my forehead. "Better than I expected."

We were in the solar again, this time with my ladies, Richard, and a few soldiers. Faulke took the seat next to me and filled his goblet from the ewer on the table. He gave the goblet a suspicious sniff. "What is this?"

"Apple cider," I replied, unable to contain a small shudder. "Stronger drink is off the table for now."

He smiled in understanding. "Do you feel up to a walk?"

I shook my head.

"Very well," he said, leaning back in his chair. After that, we spoke more of his daughters, their life at Hawksforth, and how it would change once I was there. He spoke as if there had never been any question that we would remain together.

The more he talked about the future, the more uncomfortable I became. I blamed the aftereffects of the wine for my edgy restlessness, but in my heart I knew its source sat next to me. My heart shouldn't try to fly from my chest each time he touched me, but it did. Every time I looked at him, I thought of the intimate things he had done to my body in the days after our wedding, some in this very room.

"Are you all right?" he asked at one point.

His fingers were doing that annoyingly delicious tracing thing on my hand again. He looked only mildly interested in my answer, so I just nodded. As he turned to Richard to discuss some matters, my gaze moved to my ladies, who were practicing French. I wasn't paying them much attention, but it helped to look at something other than my perfectly polite husband.

The hours slowly disappeared with the sun. I tried to take Faulke's lead, to pretend we were nothing more than amiable partners. Keeping up the pretense was exhausting. By the time the evening meal was cleared away, I could no longer contain my yawns. Part of me hoped he would depart for his own quarters so I could finally collapse into bed. Another part of me wanted to delay his departure, although why I wanted to prolong the torture of sitting next to him was beyond me. I just knew that I would miss him when he left for the night. I would probably start crying.

"Take your leave, all of you." He was staring into my eyes when he spoke, and I felt a moment of panic. Did he mean me, too? He snagged my wrist and held me in place when I went to rise. "Your lady and I wish to be alone for the night."

Well, *that* cleared things up for everyone. Hilda gave me a sly look and actually elbowed Blanche in the ribs when the other woman loitered. Hoops were abandoned, guards made one last sweep of the room. Within minutes, we were alone.

Faulke refilled our goblets with cider. "Are things settled between us after last night?"

"What do you mean?" My heart began to beat faster.

"Richard tells me you have forgiven Gerhardt," he said. He picked up my hand and turned it over to kiss my wrist. There was a subtle lift of his lips. "He also says that Gerhardt announced his intention to become Richard's friend."

I tried to concentrate on what he was saying, and not what his lips felt like when he smiled against my skin. I looked at the table and strung the words together in my head. Gerhardt was so literal. Of course he would announce his plan to Richard to become his friend. In his mind, that would be the most logical step toward accomplishing his goal.

"Did you have something to do with Gerhardt's change of heart about us?"

"I told him that he must pledge you his loyalty, and that anyone who wants to stay in my service should plan to learn your language and become part of your household. Become Segraves." I looked to where our hands were still joined. "I also told him that Richard intends to become Gerhardt's brother-in-law. Has . . . has Richard spoken to you about Gretchen?"

Faulke nodded. "He told me his intentions before they handfasted."

"I didn't keep that a secret from you on purpose." I squeezed his hand to emphasize my sincerity. "When you asked if I were keeping anything else secret, I simply hadn't thought of it at the time. Truly, it was an oversight."

Sapphire eyes met mine, and I felt myself falling into a deep blue sea. "All right."

All right? I leaned away from him a little and studied his expression. He looked . . . hungry. Or maybe I was just seeing what I wanted to see. I couldn't stand the suspense anymore.

"You said this morning that you intend to keep me." My voice sounded like an accusation. Now I wasn't entirely sure what he had said, since I had felt quite ill at the time. "You will not change your mind?"

Faulke shook his head. He turned his chair to face mine and took both my hands in his. "When we leave London, we leave together."

I nodded, suddenly more appreciative of Gerhardt's misery this afternoon when I had called him into the solar. I had thought for the past hours about what I wanted to say. The whole of my confession came out almost as quickly as the wine had this morning.

"I had no choice," I said. "My father insisted that I might still have children, if God willed it, so I wouldn't really be lying. But Hartman's children with Maria convinced me I was wrong, that it would be unfair to trap you in a childless marriage. Then I would think of the war that might result if we didn't wed, of all the soldiers lying dead on battlefields, fathers and husbands and brothers, and the families that would starve without them, fields of charred crops, fortresses in ruins. My father promised I could move to one of my other estates when you learned the truth and turned me out or became violent."

His mouth flattened at the last part. "You planned to leave me?"

"Of course," I said. "You would despise me. What reason would you have to keep me, other than to make my life a misery? I even hoped you might agree to let me go peacefully."

"So, my reaction yesterday was not what you expected?"

"You ordered me not to touch you," I reminded him. "*That* was expected. What followed was not. It never occurred to me that you had known more of the truth than me all along, that you would gamble so much on just the possibility of a child. I didn't consider your alternatives, that your reputation would prevent you from finding another bride, that my father would continue to tax you until you were beggars."

His mouth curved downward. "You are not the only one who anticipated the wrong reaction."

"What do you mean?" I tilted my head, and then was sorry when a wave of dizziness struck. Stupid wine.

"As your husband, everything you own is now mine, to do with as I wish, all but the entailed lands and titles. I told you that I intend to plunder your wealth, and my father is plotting to wrest your land and titles from the next king to keep them in our hands. You didn't seem very upset by those facts."

"People have used me all of my life," I said with a shrug. "My parents, Hartman's parents, Hartman, even my own people. It was never me they wanted, but what I represented. I knew going into this marriage that my wealth and connections were the main lures for you, along with the titles and estates." I recalled his father's plan to ingratiate himself with my brother. "I also understand your father's intention to become one of my brother's favorites. We are royals. People use us. I would expect no less of you."

His eyebrows slammed down, but he had no argument for the truth.

"Why should I be angry?" I asked. "I would do the same, if I were you. Indeed, I had expected no less on that score, although I did not anticipate the plan to gain my brother's favor." I thought about that plan. My father did not have the time to guide my young brother or mold him into a king. Anselm Segrave had many skills and connections that would serve my brother well over the years. A closer relationship between our families would mean the future king would have closer ties to all of the barons in the Welsh marches. That could only prove useful to my brother in the future. "Perhaps we could visit Maldon before we go to Wales, and introduce your father to my brother during that visit? The rest will be up to your father, of course."

He shook his head, but not to disagree. "I never know what to expect from you."

"What do you mean?"

He growled deep in his throat. "I told you the truth; my father intends to use your brother. Why would you help that to happen?"

"Does your father intend to be a false friend to my brother?"

"Of course not. He intends to help the boy, in any way he can. No man in England could provide the future king with a better military education than my father. He is a brilliant strategist."

"Why would I deny my brother that opportunity?" I shrugged again. "When I agree with your goals, I will help you. If it is within my means to do so."

He picked up his goblet and contemplated the contents for a long time. "This marriage is not anything I imagined it would be."

My heart sped up a little, wondering what he had imagined. Someone prettier, I supposed. Probably a more biddable wife, one who didn't break his trust before they were even wed. Well, that was too bad. We were stuck with each other, and I couldn't find it in myself to be sorry.

This marriage wasn't anything I had envisioned, either. Faulke had accepted me, even knowing the chance of an heir was unlikely. He seemed to value my opinion. He had been kind to me. My heart still did crazy things around him. I had expected none of that.

The days after our wedding . . . it was impossible not to think about them. A whole new world had opened for me, if only for a few days. I didn't know how we would move forward, how much of our time alone had been a pretense on his part, just to ensure that none could ever question the validity of our marriage. I was almost afraid to find out. Happy endings had never been my specialty.

I folded my hands in my lap and stared down at them as I muttered, "I am not sorry we wed."

"You are mine now, Isabel." His big hands cupped my face and he waited until I looked up at him. "Only death will take you from me."

His claims calmed my nerves, but I wanted more. I wanted him to *make* me his again, to leave physical marks of his claims on my body. Ach. He had made me a harlot.

"What must I say to make you believe me?" he whispered as he searched my face. When I leaned toward him, he didn't wait for an answer. His lips found mine and he kissed me, gentle at first, and then his tongue explored the seam of my lips and I opened to him. Then his mouth claimed mine, demanding my own hungry response.

He held my head in place, but I ran my hands down the front of his tunic, wishing it would disappear. His hands left my face to capture my wrists and hold them away. His forehead dropped to mine.

"You said your father's soldiers would help you leave

me," he said. His voice was rough, his breath ragged. His grip on my wrists tightened. "Did you intend to leave me by force?"

"What? No." I tried to lean away but he held me in place. "I asked for that provision in case you turned violent when I didn't give you an heir. I had no idea who you were. I did not want to live with a man who could beat me whenever he wished."

"I would never hurt you," Faulke murmured. His breath shuddered across my face, and then he used his hold on my wrists to pull me to my feet. He tugged my hands around his waist as his lips found mine for a kiss that sealed his promise.

I thought he'd never kiss me like this again, and I still didn't quite trust that it wasn't some fevered dream. Good or bad, I'd known my future husband would loom large in my life. I'd expected the worst. I couldn't let it go. "You were supposed to hate me."

The depths of his eyes turned stormy. He stared down at my mouth and his finger traced the outline of my lips. "I didn't want to care for you, but no one has ever felt so right in my arms." Those arms went around me, and I luxuriated in the feel of his hands on me. They clasped my buttocks and he lifted me against him. My skirts were wide enough that I managed to wrap my legs around him, grinding my hips into him, because even being that close wasn't close enough. I pressed kisses along the column of his neck. There was no longer any doubt. He still wanted me. "Mm. Everything about you feels so right, and yet you still drive me crazy."

His head fell back and my mouth explored the strong

column of his throat until my tongue darted out, and then he groaned and dropped his head to my shoulder.

"We were fated, kitten." His whiskers rasped against my neck and I wanted to rub against him with my whole body. "I felt it the first moment we met. You did, too."

"Aye." I leaned back in his arms, and it was his turn to trail shiver-worthy kisses from my ear to my shoulder, and then his lips went lower to trace the sensitive skin above my bodice. He cupped my breast and rubbed the nipple through my gown, sending sparks of lightning through my body. I had to admit, the mewls that came from me would do a kitten proud.

I felt a rocking motion and realized he was carrying me into our bedchamber. He lifted me a little and then dumped me unceremoniously onto the bed. His knee landed between mine, his weight on my skirt trapping me in place.

"I can't get enough of you." His hands began to unlace my gown and then he growled in frustration. "It was torture to lie beside you last night and not take you."

"That probably would have ended badly," I said, thinking about the chamber pot.

I felt movement and realized he was unlacing his pants. A moment later, my skirt was pulled up to my waist and his weight covered me. I felt the hot tip of him press against me. Nothing had ever felt so wicked, being almost fully clothed, feeling him press into the most intimate part of me. I made some more kitten noises, and then chanted his name when he finally seated himself within me, buried himself deep. He made a rumbling sound in his chest, then lifted himself to rest his weight on his arms.

"I want to stay with you like this always."

I began to smile.

"You feel like home to me, kitten."

I began to cry.

This time the tears weren't embarrassing. No sobs, no runny nose, just the slow trickle of tears from the corners of my eyes. He leaned down and licked away one of the tears, and my body clenched around his. His forehead dropped to my shoulder and he released a shuddering breath. "Don't ever leave me. I need you. All of you. The haughty princess. The innocent girl. The sexy kitten. You are everything I never knew I needed."

Ach! "I am in love with you!"

My eyes widened when I realized I had said that aloud, and also because he swelled inside me at the same time I said it, and then he pulled back and buried himself deeper than I had imagined was possible.

"Oh!"

"Say it again."

I bit my lower lip. He pulled out until just his tip rested against me, and then he tugged on the loosened laces of my gown until one breast popped free. He licked and bit a path to the hardened nipple, and then made my hips thrash against him when his mouth closed around me, but he had me pinned and he stayed just beyond where I wanted him.

"Say it again," he repeated, his voice slightly muffled by my breast.

I knew I was being manipulated. Then again, I wasn't

certain I minded. He claimed my mouth again, his kisses deep and greedy, fierce and possessive. His hands were all over me, tugging at my clothes in frustration. I got the feeling he wanted to touch me everywhere at once, and for that he wanted me entirely naked. I wanted him naked, too, but settled for slipping my hands under his tunic and stroking his back.

His mouth scorched a trail to my neck. He lifted himself again to work on freeing my other breast. His lips curved upward when he accomplished his task. My toes curled when his mouth closed over the newly exposed nipple, and I realized my slippers were still on. More mewling ensued, but he still held himself away from me.

"Please," I whispered, growing frantic.

"You are breaking your promise," he said between bites and licks to soothe the bites.

I stilled at the accusation. "What promise?"

"You agreed to do everything I said when we are alone together, to follow every command without question."

I looked up into his eyes and allowed myself to relax as much as was possible under the circumstances. There was a trace of humor in his eyes.

"Kitten?"

Ach, I loved his name for me. My hips rose against him again, and once again he pulled away from me. I frowned my frustration.

"Do you love me?" he repeated.

Of course I did. I stared into his blue eyes and realized a part of me already lived inside of him. He was right; he was everything my heart never knew it wanted. I would be devastated if he ever turned against me, if he ever left me. I had been relieved when Hartman ordered me to leave him. I wondered if I would even survive if Faulke ever issued a similar order.

" 'Tis more," I whispered.

"More than what?" he asked.

I lifted my hand to his cheek, gazing into a deep blue sea that I wanted to explore for the rest of my life. "More than love."

We held each other's gazes for a heartbeat, and then his mouth and body lowered to mine at the same time. He took me tenderly, possessively, his hands gentle, yet he held me tightly enough to leave bruises. He claimed me all over again.

I was fully naked by the time I was drowsily thinking about just how satisfying a husband I had. Sleep was just a breath away as I thought of wicked ways to wake him the next morning. My eyes popped open and I sat up.

"No spells!"

"Hm?" His voice was gravelly and sleepy.

"Not one," I said, more as a revelation to myself. I nudged his shoulder and repeated my astonishing news. "I didn't have a spell this time."

His eyes cracked open. "Blow out the candle and lie back down. I want to hold you."

I opened my mouth to argue, but then remembered I had to obey him here. After I did as he requested, I had to admit that being held by him, surrounded by his heat and strength, felt right.

"I knew they would pass."

"The panic spells?" I asked.

I felt him nod, even as his arms tightened, surrounding me in his strength and warmth. "It shows that you trust me. In your heart."

I smiled and burrowed deeper into his hold. He was right.

CHAPTER EIGHTEEN

Diplomacy

It took three days for the Rheinbaden envoys to arrive in London, along with a summons from my father to meet him at the Tower the next day. We had returned from another shopping expedition less than an hour ago, and I was in the solar with Faulke's girls—my girls—reading aloud to them from *Aesop's Fables*. Lucy was already asleep on my shoulder. Jane played quietly near the fireplace with Mistress Buttons and her new friend, Princess Peacock. Claire sat like a proper lady behind an oversized embroidery hoop, purchased just that day with a myriad of other baubles. Avalene sat beside her, showing the girl an intricate pattern and the proper way to accomplish it in floss. Hilda and Blanche had their heads together, gossiping about something salacious. Richard and Gretchen made cow eyes at each other while he helped her rearrange a box of threads.

Faulke had found a horse market on our expedition, and had returned there with two of his men to inquire about additional mounts for our journey to Wales, so it was left to me to read and answer my father's message. It was short and to the point:

> *Count Otto has arrived. Present yourselves at my chambers in the Tower at Sext tomorrow.*

I was almost glad the meeting with Count Otto was at hand. The hours I had spent speculating over the fate of my people had driven me half mad. Tomorrow we would have the answers.

I nodded to Lucy's maid to take the sleeping toddler, then turned to Hilda, speaking quietly to her in German. *"Would you lay out the garments and jewels I wore to meet with my father?"*

My father had already approved of the outfit. I wanted him to know I valued his opinion.

Jane and Claire stayed with us for the rest of the afternoon, and I had my first taste of what daily life would be like with my new family. They clearly adored their father, and I think they were starting to like me, too. I was happy in their company. It was a strange emotion, happiness. It had eluded me for so many years that I was afraid to put too much stock in it. There were many forces working against us. What made me even more afraid was my decision to trust that any of this would last.

*   *   *

THE NEXT DAY was a blur of preparations, and all too soon we found ourselves standing uncomfortably in the small chamber where my father held more intimate audiences that were not open to all of the court. Mordecai had arranged us like dolls around the dais where my father's empty chair was placed. The dais ensured that he would tower over us all, even when seated.

Even so, I stood directly to my father's right. Faulke stood behind me, with Richard next to him. Gretchen and Hilda stood a little farther back. Crispin was on the other side of the dais, and then Gerhardt, Walter, and Mordecai. A dozen of the king's guards lined the wall behind us all.

"Small" was a relative term, when it applied to a king. The small chamber was twice as large as my solar. Each wall was covered from floor to ceiling with tapestries that formed the entire scene of a hunt within a dark forest. If there were any windows in the chamber, the tapestries covered them completely. Tall candelabras were the only source of light, and scores of beeswax candles lit even the corners of the room.

A knock was followed by a shifting in the tapestries as another royal guard appeared, pulled aside the tapestries to reveal a previously unseen door, and then allowed a half dozen men to enter. My gaze went to Count Otto, and I found him staring back at me. He looked slightly surprised, as if he had found me greatly changed. Regardless, he looked much the same.

Otto was a burly man, with hair so blond that he appeared to have no eyebrows or lashes, which made his ice-blue eyes even more startling. Leopold also had his father's eyes, but darker blond hair and a still slender build. His mouth curved into a smirk when I looked at him, so I made certain to keep my gaze moving. Maria's son stood behind them, the image of his father, down to the look of disgust he gave me.

I made a quicker inventory of the other four men and found them little changed from when I had known them at Rheinbaden. All of the envoys wore their finest court clothing in the colors of their houses: blues and reds and golds. Only young Hartman wore the pink and white colors of Rheinbaden's royal family. I wondered if that had been Otto's idea, or Leopold's.

"I had hoped—" Otto began.

"Count Otto, you will forgive us," Mordecai interrupted, all smiles and kindness. "The king is delayed on an urgent matter. You should have been told that His Highness does not allow his subjects to speak in his audience chamber until he is present, which I'm certain will be any moment. Our apologies if you were not given that information."

Otto looked disgruntled, but he pressed his lips together. I could tell from his expression that he'd been told of that quirk of my father's, but had somehow thought the rule did not apply to him. Actually, it didn't; he could speak as much as he wanted. We just wouldn't respond. And as far as I knew, the king's only pressing business was his midday meal.

The moments that Mordecai had optimistically suggested dragged on until I could see a noticeable difference in the height of the candles.

Those who knew the king were accustomed to silently waiting long, uncomfortable hours for an audience. It put some on edge, built up their dread or anticipation of the actual meeting as their nerves began to prey upon them. People unaccustomed to audiences with the king would often become agitated and out of sorts, even ill-tempered. You did not want to be any of those things in my father's presence, which was the entire reason he did it.

The tactic seemed to be working especially well on the Rheinbaden envoys. These were men bred on order and efficiency. They began to murmur among themselves. I could almost feel their nerves begin to fray. Even Gerhardt shifted restlessly.

Knowing Leopold would only smirk and preen if I looked at him, I kept my gaze on Otto, making certain he saw me staring at him every time he glanced in my direction. I hoped it unnerved him.

The king finally arrived with his knights, three fanned out on each side of his chair, and all stood a pace behind us. Mordecai made the formal introductions, and there was no surprise on any of the Rheinbaden envoy's faces when he listed Faulke's new titles and my own as his countess. He left out any reference to my former titles in Rheinbaden. I was Faulke's wife now. Rheinbaden was in my past.

Their faces remained carefully blank, so either they had been busy gathering the most recent information about me, or they were all good at concealing their reactions. Otto stepped forward and bowed low to the king.

"Greetings, Your Royal Highness," he began. "My esteemed sovereign, King Albert, sends his warm regards to his father's dear friend and our faithful ally to the west, and I bring word of our good king's intentions to continue that friendship well into the future."

Otto waited for some reaction from my father, and shifted nervously when he got none.

"It was with heavy hearts that we sent news ahead of great King Rudolph's passing," he went on. "King Albert insisted that I appear in person to our good English friends, and to our former princess, whom he was certain would be distressed by the passing of the man she has regarded as a father for so many years, claimed so soon after the passing of her husband. King Albert bid me offer his condolences, and confirm that Princess Isabel has everything she needs to make tolerable the transition to her new life in England."

His words skated very close to marginalizing my own father's place in my life, which, true or not, was hardly diplomatic. My fingers traced the outline of a castle on my mother's belt and I began to relax.

"I assume you were distressed by the news of King Rudolph's passing," my father said to me, "but you seem to have your grief in hand. Tell me, Daughter, is there anything I have not provided that would make your life in England more tolerable?"

I watched Otto press his lips together, too late, as he realized the implications of his words and their insult.

"King Rudolph was a beloved king in Rheinbaden,

and I mourn his passing. I will always have warm memories of my time in his lands," I said. "But there are few women who would not envy my new life in England, Father. I need nothing more."

That was a lie. What more I wanted was to never see Count Otto and his entourage again in my lifetime.

"King Albert will be comforted to know his brother's widow is in good hands," Otto said, his gaze flicking over my shoulder in Faulke's direction.

It was a sly insult. I was now Faulke's wife, and should no longer be referred to as Hartman's widow. What did he hope to gain by antagonizing Faulke?

"What other news from Rheinbaden?" Edward asked.

Otto visibly relaxed, and I knew this part of his speech he had practiced well. "King Albert would like to renew the close ties between our two kingdoms. His heir, Prince Frederick, is a healthy boy of twelve years, the very image of my nephew here, young Hartman.

"Your youngest daughter, Princess Elizabeth, is of a like age," Otto continued. He spread his hands, as if in apology. "Although Princess Isabel's union with Prince Hartman did not prove as long and fruitful as we had all hoped, King Albert feels certain a marriage between Princess Elizabeth and Prince Frederick will result in a more favorable outcome."

I looked at Young Hartman. Perhaps the boy was not brought here as part of some blackmail plot after all. Still, a lump of dread formed in my throat as I realized my father might actually consider the match. King Edward's disputes with the French king were ongoing, so an alliance with Rheinbaden on France's eastern border would still make sense. The crimes Leopold's men had committed would not stand in his way, if it meant he could keep the French forces divided.

"King Albert offers the same terms as the previous union of our kingdoms, made under his father's rule," Otto said, looking confident again.

I glanced at my father to gauge his reaction, but his face remained impassive. He had been at war with someone the whole of my life. The war in Wales was done for now with the Welsh subdued, but now he had to deal with his own marcher barons' demands and threats of uprisings. The war on the Scottish border continued, as did the war with the French over his ancestral lands in Normandy. His resources were thin. An influx of Rheinbaden gold and the strength of their army on the eastern border of France would surely tempt him.

"I will need to give the matter of a betrothal more thought," Edward said. "Is there anything else?"

"Aye, Your Highness." Otto cleared his throat and tugged at his collar, clearly uncomfortable. "If I found Princess Isabel in good health and company, King Albert decreed that her people return with us to Rheinbaden. Times are uncertain in the Germanic kingdoms. The king will have need of his soldiers in the months and years that lie ahead."

Silence greeted that announcement.

My gaze went to Leopold. I wanted to slap the smirk off his face. His father looked just as satisfied with himself. I assumed that this was part of their revenge upon me, my punishment for failing to allow Leopold's men to rape me, and then let myself be executed for adultery.

"Of course, we would be willing to allow our people in England to attend Princess Elizabeth in her household, should she become betrothed to our prince," Otto continued, his expression sly now. "They were, after all, intended to serve the Crown Princess of Rheinbaden rather than the dowager, and Princess Elizabeth will likely have questions about her new homeland that Princess Isabel's servants can answer."

The knife of dread went a little deeper into my heart. Otto's arguments were sound, and I had not considered the lure of a new alliance between our countries. My people could be lost to me through my sister.

"Sire, if I may?" Faulke asked. At the king's nod he continued. "My wife has grown attached to her people, and they wish to remain at her side. Isabel was very young when she went to Rheinbaden. Princess Elizabeth is old enough to have her own staff, servants that I am sure she would wish to accompany her to Rheinbaden, should a betrothal be forthcoming. Is Rheinbaden so poor that they cannot provide servants for Princess Elizabeth without taking them from my wife? Or man their garrisons without the handful of soldiers and knights who have sworn themselves to her service?"

My father waved his hand in Count Otto's direction. "Well? Is this the sort of penury Princess Isabel was subjected to in Rheinbaden? Should I expect more of the same if I send Princess Elizabeth to your court?"

"Nay, of course not, Your Highness." Otto did an admirable job of backtracking. "King Albert simply thought that Princess Isabel might no longer appreciate the reminders of her life in Rheinbaden. He made the offer as a courtesy, nothing more. If the princess wishes to keep our people in England, King Albert has no objection."

My entire being felt lit from the inside out. I wanted to kiss Faulke right there in front of everyone. I would thank him in other ways when we were alone tonight.

My father cleared his throat, interrupting some very lewd thoughts, and I tried not to look as guilty as I felt. "Do you wish your people to return to Rheinbaden?"

"No, Father."

"Then 'tis settled. Isabel's people will remain in England. You have given me much more to reflect upon regarding Elizabeth." My father rose to his feet, and everyone in the room stood a little straighter. "I will need at least a night to give the matter its proper consideration. In the meanwhile, I bid you and your attendants my leave to enjoy the pleasures of the city."

Otto's smile was near beatific. He was almost as certain as I was that my sister would return to Rheinbaden with them. Everyone was happy.

"Sire, there is that one other matter," Mordecai reminded my father.

"Ah, yes," Edward said as he settled back into his chair. Mordecai stepped up to the dais to whisper something in the king's ear. Edward nodded several times, and then waved him away. He fixed his gaze on Otto. "I have been made aware of a disturbing incident that took place when your son and his knights were granted the hospitality of Grunental Castle when my daughter was in residence there."

"The incident was several years ago," Otto said smoothly, obviously prepared to address the issue. "The men involved were new to my son's service and their true natures were unknown until then. They are dead now, slain by the princess's own knights. We have paid the weregild for her knight's death. King Rudolph and Prince Hartman both accepted our apologies."

"True," Edward said, his gaze narrowing on Leopold, "but no apologies or explanations were made to me. Furthermore, there were rumors that followed the incident that could have proved dangerous to my daughter, rumors caused by the actions of your son's knights. Indeed, the actions of these knights could have resulted in my daughter's death, had she been less vigilant of her reputation. When a lord is given guest rights within a keep, he is held responsible for the actions of anyone in his company, most especially when those actions threaten the life and safety of their future queen. Your son should have been drawn and quartered to make an example of him, and to ensure that none others made such a poor choice of companions when they visited your crown princess and a daughter of England."

"My son was forgiven by our king and crown prince," Otto said again. "Our laws are different in Rheinbaden, and the matter is settled."

"Ah, but we are not in Rheinbaden, are we?" Edward said, a new slyness in his tone.

"We are ambassadors," Otto sputtered, "representatives of King Albert."

"*You* are King Albert's representative, Count Otto, not your attendants." Edward stroked his beard. "Your king asks me to send another royal princess to Rheinbaden, when crimes against the first daughter I entrusted to your king's care go unpunished. On the other hand, you have delivered the criminal to our shores and he stands before me. It would seem that King Albert has made it possible for me to sit in judgment of the crimes against my daughter after all, whether by accident or intent."

There was stunned silence as Otto gaped at the king, his mouth working ineffectually, as if he were a beached fish.

"Leopold was forgiven," Otto insisted, "and you have no authority over my son!"

Edward's voice was silky smooth. "Do I not?"

Otto retreated a step. All of the Rheinbaden men eyed my father's knights, who were well armed. Faulke took a step forward, positioning himself to protect me. Count Otto's unarmed men moved closer together.

"Your Highness," Otto tried again, this time in a subservient voice. "We travel under the protection of our sovereign's flag. The incident that you speak of happened years ago. If you or Princess Isabel hold some ill will toward my son over the affair, I was not made aware of it. I will be happy to offer reparations to make this right, sire."

My opinion of his diplomatic skills fell even lower. Really, what had Albert been thinking to send Otto here? I had learned everything I could about my father before I returned to England. Otto had obviously not done the same. He had just left himself vulnerable to any sort of vengeance that King Edward decided was appropriate. And he was about to learn exactly why everyone tread carefully around my father.

"Perhaps we could temper our justice in this case," Edward mused, "given the length of time that has elapsed since the crime took place, and the strain your son's execution might place on our negotiations."

Otto looked shaken, but also visibly relieved. Foolish, foolish man.

"Trial by combat will decide the matter," Edward decreed, as if he were deciding which horse to ride that day. "Aye, the outcome will decide the matter of your son's guilt or innocence. I assume he is skilled with a sword?"

"Aye," Otto said, still not realizing that his answer was an agreement to wager his son's life.

Edward settled more comfortably in his chair. "My daughter's champion will, of course, be her husband."

I felt the blood drain from my head. Foolish, foolish me. Leopold might make a habit of preying upon women and the weak, but he was feared in combat. I could not say how many tourneys he had won, but his losses were rare.

Avalene had never spoken a word about Faulke's prowess in battle. I had heard much more about his skills in the bedchamber than I had about his skills with a sword or lance. The only conclusion I could draw was that he did not possess those skills.

The king would certainly be aware of Faulke's skills, or lack thereof. Yet my husband could scarcely refuse, when my father named him my champion. I felt a horrifying suspicion that my father had just ordered Faulke's death.

And then the larger picture of what was really happening unfolded in my mind.

Leopold had actually committed a crime against me, according to English law. If my father let that crime go unpunished, others in Rheinbaden might feel free to jeopardize Elizabeth's safety, if she wed Prince Frederick. Edward needed to make an example of Leopold.

Faulke's death now, nobly defending his wife's honor, would mean that all of the Segraves' holdings would be mine, and eventually belong to the crown. And the marcher barons could not argue with a man's right to defend his wife's honor.

I considered myself ruthless with my enemies, but even I could barely comprehend the layers of my father's deceptions. Faulke had played his part, and now my father had but one last use for him: to send a message to King Albert that Edward would not tolerate any threats to his daughters. It did not seem to bother him that Faulke would likely die in the process of sending that message.

Having finally put all the pieces together, I still knew better than to even whisper a protest. There would be consequences. Given my father's uncertain tempers, the consequences would likely be beyond my ability to undo. I needed time to think, to plan, to outmaneuver.

"The trial will take place today," Edward said. "Here and now."

"*What?*" Otto and I both said in unison.

"All parties are present, there is no reason to delay." The king nodded toward two of his knights. "My men will supply you with appropriate arms, and then you will return here anon and the trial will proceed."

I glanced at Leopold and my stomach roiled at what I

saw. His expression left little doubt that he looked forward to killing my husband.

"Father, I—" I was interrupted by Faulke's hand on my shoulder in an almost painful grip, and Count Otto's objection.

"Sire, I must protest." He looked from his son to Faulke. "This is . . . King Albert will be very upset if my son kills one of your earls. 'Tis not a promising start to our negotiations. We have no wish to upset you, Your Highness. Let us pay the princess a weregild, whatever reparation you feel is appropriate."

"I have named my price." My father motioned to two of his men. "Prepare them."

That was the end of the discussion. Both men left, both seeming eager, Faulke with a steel jaw, Leopold with an ever-present smirk.

In my father's defense, perhaps Edward thought Leopold would not want to jeopardize the betrothal negotiations by killing Faulke, but I knew that Leopold would fight to his last breath to win, regardless of any consequences. I did not want Faulke anywhere near Leopold when they were both armed. And I was powerless to stop it.

"He is better than you think," Richard murmured behind me, so quietly only I could hear. "The king knows this."

My heart fluttered. Of course, Richard would think Faulke invincible. Or perhaps I could be a widow again before the day was out. I refused to consider it. Refused.

"Shouldn't we do this on a tourney field?" Count

Otto asked. "There are preparations that should take place, squires to prepare the knights and tend their battle armor, and there should be horses."

I silently agreed with him. There should be more. Mostly, more time to prepare.

Leopold was deadly in tournaments. Faulke had actually fought on the Welsh frontier. Surely that counted for something? However, even if Faulke presented himself well, accidents happened. He could be killed by a lucky strike.

I wondered what the punishment would be if I threw up in front of everyone. My stomach was as tight as a knot.

The two men returned. Both had shed their tunics and much of their court finery, and both looked of a similar height. Faulke wore all black, and his stance said he was ready for battle. It was like watching a panther turned loose among house cats. The finely tooled belt was gone, replaced by a heavier one that held a short sword and an assortment of knives. Leopold also had a short sword and knives strapped to his side so they would be evenly matched with regard to weapons. My hands balled at my sides.

"Prepare yourselves," the king ordered, wasting little time on the niceties. "Leopold von Tyrol, you stand accused of endangering the life of your future queen and a princess of England. Faulke Segrave, you stand for your wife's honor. The first man to draw blood will be declared the winner."

"Oh, thank God." I didn't realize I spoke those words aloud until my father gave me a disapproving look. It was just such a relief to realize he didn't intend for the contest to end in a death. Not today, anyway. Faulke had a chance to come out of this ridiculousness alive, but I still didn't trust Leopold.

My father's knights stood closer to their liege and to us as the men squared off against each other. The Rheinbaden envoys found places along the far wall so the center of the room was empty, except for the two combatants. Each man circled, sizing up the other, and then Leopold struck out with a lightning-fast blow that Faulke easily deflected. Faulke's guard was up now and his eyes narrowed on his opponent.

He allowed Leopold to strike out a half dozen times, nearly giving me heart failure each time. But Leopold's sword never came close to Faulke. The distinctive ring of metal against metal was deafening in the chamber, and each metallic ring made me flinch in fear, sliding my gaze over Faulke after each blow. I longed to run my hands over him to check for damage.

"He's learning his opponent," Richard said in a low murmur, leaning close to my ear so we wouldn't be overheard. "Leopold is showing his impatience. He will begin to tire from those swings. Faulke will find an opening. He is looking for a place to draw blood without killing him."

Richard's words calmed me a little. I viewed the fight through new eyes, and realized that Faulke expended little effort deflecting each blow, while Leopold put his whole body into each swing. Leopold was not looking for an opening to draw blood; each of his swings would have crippled or killed Faulke if they had managed to connect with flesh. But each blow left Leopold vulnerable. Indeed, he left an opening each time he swung, but I couldn't fathom why Faulke didn't take advantage of those openings.

Another blow came down from Leopold's sword, slashing hard, but he changed direction at the very last minute. My breath stalled in my throat when there was no metallic clang, replaced by the sound of fabric ripping.

Somehow Faulke had anticipated Leopold's move. He stood unscathed, while Leopold cradled his sword arm, a long, jagged tear in his sleeve. Blood gushed from a deep wound to Leopold's biceps. Faulke turned to face the king and held his sword up to salute his liege lord.

"It is done," Edward announced as he got to his feet. He glared at Leopold. "You are judged guilty, Leopold von Tyrol. Take him into the crown's custody."

The two knights my father had signaled stepped forward, swords in hand.

"That was a lucky blow!" Leopold protested. "He barely scratched me!"

"Sire, you cannot do this!" Otto said at the same time.

Leopold foolishly decided to continue his protests by holding the knights at bay with his sword. The king's two knights stopped their progress, warily eying Leopold's weapon. Before I even saw him move, Faulke had stepped in from Leopold's side. He knocked Leopold's sword from his grip and the weapon clattered to the floor several feet away. He made it look easy. And then he twisted his blade around and blood appeared on Leopold's left sleeve, this cut even deeper than the first, but in exactly the same spot as the cut on his right arm. The knights ignored Leopold's screams of pain and protest. They quickly stepped forward and fully disarmed him, and then dragged him from the chamber, still yelling his innocence.

Faulke resheathed his sword, bowed again to the king, and then came to stand in front of me, his back to Count Otto. He lifted my hand for another of his indecent kisses on my wrist that I was beginning to expect, and then he looked up and winked at me. It was done so quickly that I hardly had time to register what he'd done. He had winked! As if this were all a big joke to him. As if he had not just taken a year off my life from fear! I glared at him as he walked to my side, nudging Richard out of the way.

"Where is my son being taken?" Otto demanded, taking a threatening step forward.

"He will be our guest in the dungeons until your departure," Edward said. "The sooner we conclude our negotiations, the sooner your son will be released, and you and your men will be free to leave England."

The king gave Mordecai a meaningful look, and then he left the chamber.

"Count Otto, give me the name of the inn where you will be staying," Mordecai said. "We will send word when the king will grant your next audience."

Otto glanced at the tapestries that concealed the door that the king had exited through, and then he looked at the tapestries behind him, where Leopold's wails could barely be heard in a distant corridor. His mouth was a thin, angry line.

"You realize I will tell King Albert of this . . . this . . . treatment," Otto said with a glare for Faulke.

"Your son grievously insulted my wife; he was judged guilty by right of combat." Faulke's tone was mild, but there was a note of steel in his voice. "Your king was aware that Princess Isabel would not rejoice to see your son or nephew here, yet you were allowed to bring them anyway. If I were you, I would question the reasons why, rather than complain about the justice of another king. Men have been drawn and quartered for lesser crimes in England."

Count Otto opened his mouth to argue, and then abruptly closed it again. His gaze flickered from me to young Hartman, whose fists were balled at his sides, and then back to Faulke. From his expression, Otto had already asked himself those questions. "We shall await your king's summons."

We remained where we were until the Rheinbaden envoy had left. Faulke glanced toward Mordecai. "I would prefer that my wife not be subjected to their company again."

"Oh, right, you have not heard." Mordecai shook his head with a patently false look of befuddlement. "Your father leaves for the north tomorrow morning. Scottish troubles again. I doubt he will return to London before snowfall."

Faulke exchanged a glance with me. I shrugged, indicating that I had been unaware of my father's plan, and

then stopped midshrug. Count Otto would also be unaware of my father's plans. Leopold could spend months
in the dungeons, awaiting my father's return. I might
have smiled. Faulke might have shared that smile when
he saw it.

CHAPTER NINETEEN

The English Princess

DINNER THAT NIGHT IN THE GREAT HALL WAS more like a feast. Even Chiavari and Avalene joined us.

At the beginning of the meal, I reassured my soldiers and servants that everyone could stay in my service, or return to Rheinbaden with Count Otto and his envoys if they didn't want to continue on with me to Wales. It was another unknown land for them to consider, wilder by far than England, but more civilized than we had been led to believe. Throughout the meal, most of my people came up to tell me that they would gladly stay.

Everyone milled about between courses, repeating the tale of Faulke's challenge in the king's court to anyone who hadn't heard the story yet, and to many who had. Leopold became more villainous and bloody with each telling. Faulke, well, it was harder to make him more of a hero in my eyes than he actually had been, but many tried.

To my surprise, Hilda and Gerhardt were seated together, their heads bent in conversation each time I glanced their way. What did those two adversaries have to discuss?

I didn't worry about it for long. Fear and suspicions were no longer my constant companions. Happiness wanted to burst from every pore in my body.

Faulke served me the best portions from his trencher, while his other hand did indecent things under the table. He whispered suggestions in my ear that made me turn red and look forward to the end of the meal, until the musicians struck up a round and he grabbed my hand to dance. He was a good dancer, of course. All the ladies danced, even Hilda and Gerhardt. It had been so long since I had danced with anyone that I was breathless and laughing when we returned to the table. I took a long drink of the cider I had requested, thinking my exertions must have made the cider taste strange. I pushed it away and sat down to enjoy the next course.

Looking around the hall, I finally felt as if I had come home. English, Welsh, and German voices filled the air, but the sound was hearty and festive. Faces that weren't outright smiling at least looked happy or satisfied. Faulke was right. This was the life I never knew I wanted.

"He bled like a stuck pig," Richard told Dante again. "A quarter hour was all it took. Not even a quarter hour. My saddle was still warm when we returned to Ashland!"

That was the third time Richard had told Chiavari

and his knights the tale of how Faulke had bested Leopold. I meant to tease Richard about his exaggeration, but my throat felt suddenly tight and I couldn't seem to catch my breath. Those dances were more taxing than I realized. I started to take another sip of cider, and then remembered it hadn't tasted good. I put the goblet down just as I began to wheeze.

"What is wrong with you?" Faulke demanded. Whatever he saw on my face made his grow pale. His arm went around my waist and he lifted me to my feet, feet I couldn't feel for some reason. "Good God, Isabel! What is wrong?"

I meant to answer him, but my lips were numb. I pressed my finger around my mouth and felt nothing. Then I rubbed my hand across my face. I was beginning to feel numb all over.

There was a clatter when Faulke swept his arm across the table in front of us, and pushed all the dishes aside.

"What are you doing?" I said with some difficulty.

Faulke lifted me into his arms, and then I was lying on the table.

"Stay still, don't move," Chiavari ordered. He stood next to Faulke and leaned toward me. For a crazy moment, I thought he intended to kiss me, right there in front of everyone. Instead he sniffed my breath, and then raised up enough to look into my eyes. It was weirdly impersonal, the way he stared at me. "Her pupils are too large."

"This is—" I stopped talking, my voice only a harsh whisper. What was wrong with me?

The odd thought went through my head that, laid out

on the head table, I must look like a suckling pig that had just been served. Everything was suddenly brighter. Too bright. There were halos around each of the high windows where the late afternoon sunlight streamed in. It was as if I suddenly had super sight.

If my eyes were working too well, my ears weren't working well enough. There was a lot of noise in the great hall, but it sounded muffled, as if I were underwater. It took a moment to realize the commotion was over me. The only voice I could hear clearly was Faulke's, and he sounded frantic.

"I know she's been poisoned! Do something about it, Chiavari!" His blue eyes were nearly black with rage and fear, and I wanted to take his sword and run through the creature who made him feel that way.

I had missed part of the conversation. Faulke held my hand in a tight grip and I realized with a start that my hand was numb. I turned my head and saw Gerhardt holding Hilda, while Richard had his arm around Gretchen as they all stared at me with similar expressions of dread and fear. Avalene stood to one side with Chiavari's knights, Oliver and Armand. Rami was insistently tugging on her skirts. When I looked out over the great hall, everyone had stopped eating and drinking to stare at what was happening at the head table. Every expression looked serious, and many hands were clasped together, their lips moving in prayer. Maybe this wasn't so ridiculous after all.

My stomach began to hurt.

Poison. I tried to understand it. Someone had poisoned me. Someone wanted to take me away from Faulke.

The truth finally penetrated my numbed senses, and I'm sure there was horror on my face when I looked back up at him. There was terror on his.

"Don't you die, Isabel. Don't you dare die!" He leaned over me and I saw a strange radiance outline him. Was this the magnetic force we had discussed so often? I watched as the colors around him radiated dark, angry red streaks with occasional eruptions of lemon yellow.

"Not a halo," I rasped, reaching up to touch his cheek. How I loved the rough feel of his stubble, loved to feel it against my skin. "Something is wrong."

"Chiavari has gone for an antidote," he told me, his tone urgent. "Hold on, Isabel."

I heard voices all around me chanting Latin prayers. Who was praying? Who would poison me? Count Otto, or one of his men from Rheinbaden? No, it had to be someone in the great hall, perhaps one of my own Rheinbaden people in Otto's hire as a spy. How ironic if I died, and never even knew who killed me.

I looked into Faulke's eyes and let myself get lost in the turbulent blue depths. This time I didn't try to stop the staring contest, but embraced it. I felt as if I was looking beyond his eyes straight into his soul, a soul that loved me. I wondered idly if he saw the same thing in me. It felt intimate, but I no longer cared about the crowd of people watching us. I kept my gaze locked with Faulke's as my heartbeat slowed and my breathing became marginally easier.

Someone shook me and I realized I had closed my eyes.

Chiavari was back. He handed a goblet to Faulke. "Make her drink this. All of it."

Someone propped me up and a goblet was held to my lips. Something vile trickled into my mouth and I tried to close it. That same someone who propped me up had their hand on my jaw, forcing my mouth to stay open.

"Drink it, Isabel!" Faulke commanded. "You were poisoned. For your life, drink it all."

It was horrible. And black. No cure should be oily black. It looked and tasted evil. Faulke's panic-stricken expression cleared some of the fog. If I wanted to live, I had to drink the sludge. And I wanted to live. For the first time in my life, I had someone to live for, someone I would not leave without a fight.

Faulke had never made a declaration of love, but I saw it in his eyes whenever we were alone together. He looked at me the way Dante looked at Avalene, the way Richard looked at Gretchen, and, strangely enough, the way Gerhardt had looked at Hilda tonight. I was glad I had confessed my love to him, as embarrassing as it had been at the time. I wanted to say it again, but the horrible cure was being forced into me.

I barely had the last of it down before I started to retch. Faulke held me over the side of the table as everything I had to eat and drink at the feast ended up on the floor. It was worse than the wine. I closed my eyes so I wouldn't have to look at it, and silently apologized to the poor servants who would be stuck cleaning up the mess.

"I'm cold."

Faulke's already pale face lost all its color. "You said

this was the cure!" he bellowed over his shoulder. "'Tis killing her!"

"The poison needs to get out of her body as quickly as possible," I heard Dante answer, and then a hand was placed on my forehead. "'Tis obviously a fast poison, but I am not certain what was given to her. Purging is the first part of the cure, and then charcoal tea. I don't know how much she ingested. We will not know until morning if the cure will work."

Something shattered, and then I heard Faulke roar. Not one of his roars from our bedchamber, but an ear-splitting shout of rage. Something else broke. I was too tired to open my eyes and look, too exhausted from retching to care. Someone was stroking my hair. Gretchen. She was crying. The sounds in the great hall faded again, and I closed my eyes.

I WOKE UP choking. Avalene was seated on my bed, trying to force a concoction down my throat that was only marginally less offensive than the first cure. A tea of some sort, I recalled Chiavari saying. I knew without looking that the strong arms around me belonged to Faulke. He was holding my mouth open but my bodice felt sopping wet. I wondered if there was more tea on me than in me.

Avalene suddenly leaned back and I watched her eyes widen. "She is awake!"

"Isabel, thank God!" I was jostled a bit, and then Faulke was in front of me, staring into my eyes. He lifted both of my hands, carefully turning them over to make certain his lips touched every spot. His eyes never left mine, as if he were afraid I would close them again. His big hands moved over my face, brushing from the center toward the sides while his lips moved in some silent incantation.

"Are you casting a spell over me?" I rasped.

His hands stopped their repetitive petting, and he gave me a sober look. "I was saying a prayer of thanks."

"I—I can feel my hands again," I said.

"You couldn't feel your hands?"

"Aye, my hands and feet were numb. I couldn't hear right, either." I frowned, recollecting the halo that wasn't a halo. "My lips are still numb."

"Here," he said as he reached behind him and Avalene handed him the goblet. "You must drink this. As much as you can."

I managed a few small sips.

"More," he encouraged, tilting the goblet up.

I took another sip and then pushed the revolting stuff away. "I will be sick again."

"That is not a bad thing." He made me take another swallow. "I would rather watch you puke than stop breathing again. Isabel, I nearly lost you."

Really? I had been that close? I looked around and realized I was in my bedchamber, in my own bed. My hands and feet were still a little numb after all, I decided as I flexed my fingers and toes. Even that small effort felt monumental, and my eyelids were fighting a serious battle to stay open.

It suddenly struck me that my eyes might never have

opened again, that I might never have looked upon Faulke again.

I looked at the window and saw the faint glow of dawn. "How long have I been here?"

"The entire night," Faulke said. "You would not even rouse to drink."

"Your cider was poisoned," Chiavari said on the other side of me. He nodded at Faulke, who looked more haggard than I had ever seen him. "You have been unconscious since he carried you here from the great hall."

Even as weak as I felt, with the memory of the first cure still too fresh in my mind, I knew I owed Chiavari my life. "Thank you for saving me."

"You are welcome, Princess." He smiled down at me, but there was still an edge of worry in his eyes. He turned to Faulke. "Have her drink the tea that Avalene brewed. Make her drink as much as she can. The poison is still not out of her."

Faulke nodded, his gaze never leaving my face. "She will recover?"

"Aye." Dante rubbed his jaw. "I will check on her again after . . . after I make certain Armand does not do too much damage."

A terrible light came into Faulke's eyes, but he gave Dante a tight nod.

"Armand broke something?" I asked, remembering the loud sounds of something breaking in the great hall the night before.

Faulke shook his head.

Avalene cleared her throat. "Armand is . . . interrogating the poisoner. Dante will make certain Armand does not get too enthusiastic before we can obtain answers."

"You know who did this?" I asked them both.

"Aye." Faulke's voice promised death. I actually shivered. "But not the reasons you were poisoned. That silence will not last long once I—"

He looked down at the goblet, his grip so tight the knuckles were white. "All that matters is that you drink this tea. I will not leave you until I know for certain you are better and there is no more of that vile poison in your body."

A noise at the doorway caught my attention. Gretchen and Hilda stood there, watching me, tired smiles of relief on both their faces. For some reason, their expressions made me realize they had not expected to see me again. Not alive anyway. I really had almost died. I began to quietly cry.

Avalene hesitated, looked at Faulke, and then said, "I will leave you alone."

She wasn't even out the door before Faulke had his arms around me, lifting me carefully to hold me while I cried. The tears didn't last very long. They might have been tears of joy that I was still alive. I had thought to call Gretchen and Hilda into the room, but was glad I didn't. I still felt weak as a kitten, but my emotions were getting a workout. My tears fell all over Faulke's chest, but he didn't protest. Instead he held and rocked me and murmured nonsense as the fear and fright poured out of me.

When the last of my tears were dry, Faulke tried to ply me with more tea.

"Wait, first tell me the name of the poisoner," I said. "Was it a servant? How was it done? How were they caught?"

Faulke held the cup away, his look foreboding. "Someone did see. Sort of. You had drunk from one jug of cider all night without incident, and no one else who drank from the jug was ill. The poison had to be put in your cup while we were dancing. That is the only time no one was at the head table to see it happen. No one, that is, except Rami. He was beneath the table during the dances, and recognized the garments of the only person who approached our place at the table while we were dancing. As soon as you fell ill, he told Avalene. If not for his spying, it would have taken much longer to find the culprit."

I remembered Rami tugging on Avalene's gown. I would never again complain about the boy sneaking around.

"Who was it?"

CHAPTER TWENTY

Torture

I**T TOOK ANOTHER DAY BEFORE** I **COULD WALK TO** the solar without stopping to rest, but then my recovery progressed at a rapid pace. On the third day, I could take it no more.

"Help!"

"What are you doing?" Faulke asked.

"Help!" I called out again.

Hilda and Gretchen were in my doorway in an instant.

"Princess?" they asked in unison.

"Make him stop," I pleaded, waving an ungracious hand in Faulke's direction. "I cannot drink any more of that foul tea. I am cured. Convince him!"

Their heads swiveled toward Faulke, who didn't turn

his head at all. He glared at me. "Just drink this last cup-ful, and then I will ask Chiavari if we can stop."

I glared right back at him. "You said that about the last cup."

"I mean it this time. You have my word."

Unmoved, I gave an exasperated sigh. "You said that last time, too."

"I would not lie to you," he said, sounding affronted. "I did ask Chiavari. He said it was better to be too cautious than too quick to stop the treatment."

I narrowed my eyes. "How did you ask him?"

"What do you mean?"

"Did you ask, 'Can she stop drinking tea that tastes like a latrine?' or did you say, 'She is being unreasonable. Tell me why she should continue the treatment.'"

"I did not say that," he muttered. His expression said it was something close to those words. "You are not well yet."

"Ah, do you need us to remain?" Gretchen asked in German, just in case.

I waved them away. I looked at Faulke and struggled to keep my tone reasonable. "The only reason I am weak is because I have been lying in bed for almost four days. The poison is gone now. Truly. Please let me stop drinking that foul concoction and start eating real food. I am starving. You are starving me to death. I am weak from lack of food!"

So I might have turned a bit unreasonable.

"Fine," he said between clenched teeth. "Chiavari said you could stop drinking the tea today, but he did not say when. I suppose now is as good a time as any. I will have food brought to the solar."

I bit my lower lip and looked toward the door. "I would like to see the prisoners."

"No."

FAULKE INSISTED I eat first, but at last he gave in to my demand after a long discussion that might have sounded like an argument to everyone else in the solar. So far, the prisoners would not confess, to admit who had sent them and why. A confession was the only way to hold the person who was ultimately behind the plot responsible, and we did not have that person in custody. I finally convinced Faulke that I might succeed where they had failed.

Ashland Palace didn't have a dungeon. The securest place to keep a prisoner was in the treasury, which I found ironic, keeping the worst people with the best goods, but it was the only set of rooms with heavy locks.

Chiavari, Armand, and Oliver were already with the prisoners. Gerhardt and Richard insisted on accompanying us to the treasury. I was glad of the torches they carried when we made our way through the dark, narrow tunnel that led to the vaulted room. Faulke already had his hands full since he insisted upon carrying me the entire way. I was secretly thankful, for I still tired too easily, but I asked him to put me down when the tunnel widened again into a guardroom. Two guards stood before a thick wooden door that was heavily banded with iron straps.

I heard someone inside scream.

The sound was muffled, here in the bowels of Ashland with a thick door between us and the person screaming, but it was obvious that someone was being tortured. I struggled not to shiver, but I did not struggle with sympathy. One of these people intended to murder me, and Faulke would have likely paid the price for that murder. They were my foulest enemies. They, and the man who had ordered my death.

Faulke's hand came to rest on my waist, warm and reassuring in this place of dark misery. "You do not have to do this, Isabel. Someone will confess his name, eventually. Chiavari knows what he is doing."

"I am fine," I assured him, still staring at the door. It was eerily quiet. I gave the guards a nod, and one of them opened the door for me.

The first thing that hit me was the smell. Blood and urine and fear. It was not a good combination. I took shallow breaths through my mouth to accustom myself to the noxious odor. A quick glance at the prisoners made me look away just as quickly. I steadied my nerves by looking at everything that had been in the room before it had been turned into a torture chamber.

The treasury room was lined with shelves on one long wall, most of which held boxes of expensive spices and salt. The top shelves were crammed with gold and silver plates, goblets, candlesticks, and an assortment of jewel-encrusted treasures that sparkled in the torchlight. Trunks were stacked at the narrower end of the room, and I knew they contained everything from bolts of expensive fabrics to books to sacks of coins.

All of the trunks had been moved away from the wall opposite the shelves. Chiavari and his men stepped back to make room for us, and I forced my gaze to continue with its inventory. Three sets of manacles and chains had been bolted into the wall. The chains were drawn tight so the prisoners' arms were stretched high above their heads with their feet barely touching the floor. When they passed out, they would hang by their wrists, which would only cause more pain that would eventually wake them. It was a hellish cycle. Torture treated no one kindly. The prisoners themselves were barely recognizable. I finally allowed myself to look at their faces.

The three unfortunate creatures returned my stare, something akin to hope in their eyes, as if I could save them. My gaze moved to the woman, recognizable only by her hair and what was left of her clothing.

"Mercy, please," Lady Blanche managed.

I stared at Blanche, my face purposely wiped of emotion. There wasn't an inch of her that didn't look bloodied or battered. I tried to remember the color of her garments at the feast and realized she still wore the same blue gown, now ripped in places and almost black with crusted blood.

The gown had been a very distinctive shade of blue, almost sapphire. No one else at the feast had worn a gown of a similar color, and Rami was certain she had lingered at the head table while we were dancing. More poison had been found in her chamber, and she had already admitted under torture that she was the one who poisoned me.

I looked at her hands and realized someone had removed two of her fingers. It was obvious they had bled until she was probably weak from blood loss, but they were sealed now to prevent the loss of too much.

My gaze flickered over the other two prisoners. Her brother, Sir Walter, was no longer handsome, and never would be again. A low moan escaped his battered mouth each time he exhaled. Sir Crispin's chin had dropped to his chest while I was inspecting his wife, and he hung limply from his wrists.

"Mercy, please," Blanche said again in a hoarse voice, drawing my attention back to her.

Three days of torture had reduced her to this pathetic state. What would she look like in three more?

"My husband wants to kill you slowly," I told her, coming to stand in front of her but far enough away that the mess that accompanied three days of being chained to a wall and tortured didn't come near me. "I don't know how good he is at it, but I'm certain he would be willing to listen to advice from Chiavari about how to make it last and be more painful.

"You will be punished until you confess everything," I went on. "Including the name of the man who ordered you to kill me. Think hard about what you have already endured at their hands, and then think about what Faulke will do. He wants you to suffer as you intended for him to suffer, for his family and all of his people to suffer. That's quite a lot of suffering, Blanche. Do you think you can tolerate that much torture?"

I could almost see the hope of a swift death fade from her eyes.

"Chiavari is here to make certain your questioning is painful but not fatal," I told her. "He understands all aspects of how to bring about death. Fast or slow. Which will be your choice, Blanche?"

She shook her head as her chin sunk to her chest.

"One of you poisoned Sir Roland and his family. Aleric of Almain was with my father when Sir Roland died, ready to offer up Sir Crispin's name again. Did you think no one would find that a strange coincidence?"

Actually, the coincidence might have gone unremarked, or it would have been only speculation at best, without Rami as an eyewitness to my poisoning. I would still be dead. Faulke would likely be dead. And these three would have probably gotten away with murder.

"They did not know," Blanche muttered, her head still hanging down. "My brother and husband are innocent."

I shook my head, even though she could not see. "They are accomplices, Blanche. Sir Roland would not have accepted a gift from a woman he did not know, even the wife of a fellow soldier. Crispin or Walter gave him the poisoned sweetmeats, and Sir Roland shared it with his poor family. Four people are dead. Your brother might be innocent of that crime, but he was close to the both of you. If he remained ignorant of the plots, he did so on purpose. That also makes him an accomplice and just as guilty."

Walter began to make sounds that I eventually realized were sobs. His innocence was possible but not probable. If no one confessed to the Roland murders or explained Aleric's part in this plot, Walter would be judged by the company he kept.

"Were you Aleric's lover?" I asked. "Is that how he set you on such a bloody path? Or were you and your husband promised riches and power?"

Blanche remained silent, her head still bowed, but I could tell she was listening to me.

"Do you see Aleric in this room? Do you think he has enough power in this country to rescue you from your fate?"

Her head tilted a little to one side and she started to look up at me, but then caught herself and put her chin back down. That telling gesture made me wonder.

"It should be obvious by now that no one is coming to your rescue. Whatever Aleric has promised you is not true. If his plot succeeded, he would not allow three people to live who had murdered one of the king's children, accomplices who knew he was behind the plot. There is only one way to ensure that none of you would repeat the tale, or try to blackmail him." I gave an exasperated sigh. "You would be as dead as me, had you succeeded."

Faulke put his hand on my shoulder when I took a step forward, but I shook my head slightly and his hand dropped away. Blanche was no longer a danger to me.

"The most you can hope for is a quick death," I assured her. "That is your best hope. The alternative is unending torture until you confess to what you could tell us right now. My father is outraged by this plot, and he has given us leave to judge and execute you all. You have already been found guilty. The king did not say how quickly we had to execute you, and I did not lie about Chiavari. He knows how to keep a person painfully alive. Whatever my husband does to you, Chiavari will make sure it is not fatal, and he will undo just enough damage so my husband can torture you again and again. Your suffering will be unending."

I looked up and down the row of prisoners, making certain they saw the resolve in my eyes.

"I will confess!" Walter shouted, between sobs. His voice was remarkably clear.

"No!" Blanche cried out. "We are dead either way. Do not betray him."

"Be silent," Faulke hissed at Blanche.

At the same time, I saw Richard go to the door and motion the two guards inside. The more witnesses to a confession, the better.

Blanche's voice had been shrill enough that Crispin stirred awake. He turned his head to look down the wall toward his brother-in-law, but his eyes were dull and lifeless. I wondered how much of Sir Crispin was actually left in there.

"You were his lover, not me," Walter spat to Blanche. He actually spat. The spray was bloody. I took a few steps backward. "Crispin came up with the idea of poisoning Roland. We met Roland at a public house that he often visited where he met with his daughter's husband, and we befriended him with the tale that we had also competed for his post. The sweetmeats were a gift of congratulations from the losers."

Oliver approached Walter as soon as the young man stopped talking. He gave Oliver a resigned look, but

Oliver had nothing more deadly than a cup of water in his hand. He held it to Walter's lips and the young man drank greedily. So greedily that I wondered when the prisoners last had anything to drink. It was a strange thought. Caring. I had once cared for these creatures . . . to a certain extent. I pushed those emotions away. If they could endure torture, I could endure hearing their confessions.

"Continue," Faulke bit out.

Walter gave a weary nod, but his voice was not as strong. He had given up. "You were right. The earl promised us lands of our own and powerful positions at Almain if we killed the princess after the wedding, and made certain no one could trace the murder back to him. He was the one who suggested poison, whenever the time was right. Aleric said that everyone would suspect the Segraves." He shook his head, his expression hopeless. "I knew his promises were too good to be true. I knew it, but Crispin and my sister were certain they were clever enough to accomplish the deed."

"What reasons did he give you for the plot?" Faulke asked.

Walter's gaze went to Faulke. His voice had enough heat that I knew Walter believed everything he said. "Aleric said you were a traitor, that the king wanted you dead but could not find enough evidence to order your execution. Aleric was aware of the betrothal negotiations from the start. King Edward wanted his council on the terms, since Aleric had managed all the princess's properties when she was in Rheinbaden. The king wanted to know their exact worth. Aleric showed him a false set of records."

Walter hesitated, at last wondering if he had said too much.

" 'Tis all right, boy," Oliver said in a soft voice. "This is the king's own daughter. He would never condone her murder, under any circumstances. You are bearing witness against the true traitor. Go to the grave with a clear conscience, son. God will forgive you."

I wondered if that was true. Not that it mattered. Walter would die either way. He had simply chosen the time of his passing. These were his last words.

I swayed a little, and Faulke's arm was instantly around me. It was a relief to lean against him. I was still weaker than I realized from the poison, and hearing how my cousin plotted to murder me was taking its toll. Knowing these three people would soon die as a result seemed surreal, a dream, but I knew it was horribly real.

Faulke leaned down to whisper in my ear. "Do you wish to leave?"

I shook my head. I would listen to everything Walter had to say. Oliver continued to coax the young man, speaking to him as if they were friends.

"Aleric has been collecting more than his share of the princess's wealth over the years," Walter said at last. "No one expected that she would ever return to England. The records were carefully falsified so that her eventual heir would have no questions. There would likely be a new king on the throne by that time, one who did not know that the estates were worth far more than Aleric reported each year. And then Prince Hartman died. Soon after, Aleric was called to court to produce copies of his records for Maldon and all of Princess Isabel's estates. That was when he decided to act."

Walter's voice was growing hoarse, and Oliver brought him another drink of water. The look of gratitude in Walter's eyes chafed at me, that he could be grateful to one of his torturers for something so simple. Poor Walter. I wondered how he had been so misled. His soul was surely black before this business began, but there was sin and darkness in every man's soul. No one had to act on that darkness. Walter's downfall was his willingness to be led astray.

I tried to harden my heart again, but the amount of torture that had taken place in this room was starting to affect me, to seep through my defenses. I didn't need my imagination to wonder what these three had already endured. The evidence was before me. I prayed that Walter finished his confession soon, or the meal Faulke had insisted I eat would be on the floor.

Dante summarized what Walter had just told them. "So the princess was to die to conceal Aleric's embezzlement."

Walter nodded.

"What else?" Chiavari asked with a subtle glance in Faulke's direction. Faulke's nod was just as subtle.

"N—nothing," Walter whispered. "That is the whole of it."

What happened next was so fast that I would have missed it if I had blinked. A knife appeared in Chiavari's hand and a red smile appeared on Walter's neck. The young knight never saw it coming.

I gave a little gasp of alarm and Faulke pulled me to his side to tuck me beneath the shelter of his arm. I couldn't keep my horrified gaze from Walter. Chiavari held one hand in a tight hold on Walter's neck to stop the spray of blood. The other hand was curved around the young knight's head in an almost fatherly grip as Walter's head fell to Chiavari's shoulder. Walter jerked and thrashed a little in the throes of death, but he was already weakened by three days of being chained and tortured. His body didn't put up much of a fight. Chiavari made comforting hushing noises as Walter began to twitch less and less, and then finally slumped over, dead.

Chiavari was covered with blood when he stepped away from the dead man. Armand handed him a cloth and Chiavari cleaned himself as best he could. His face was completely expressionless, even when he turned toward Faulke.

"Crispin knows something more," he said, nodding toward the now-conscious knight who had not seemed to react at all to Walter's death. "I could see it in his eyes when the boy spoke. If Crispin knows, his wife likely knows as well."

I glanced up at Faulke. Whatever he saw in my expression convinced him that I could not put on a hard face for the prisoners again. I was done interrogating them. The room reeked of blood and death.

"Why do you dislike me so much?" Faulke asked almost conversationally as he turned toward Crispin to await an answer.

The heat in Crispin's eyes was just a flicker, but it was there.

"Do you really wish your wife to suffer for your secrets?" Faulke asked. "We will start again on her torture, if you do not answer."

"She is Aleric's whore, not mine," Crispin croaked. "He gave me Blanche to keep her close at hand. Do what you will with her."

I looked to Blanche, and then back at Crispin. He had been a household knight, and Blanche had been a well-born mistress to his lord. The arrangement was common enough. Crispin's reward for the marriage was likely a handsome dowry and recommendation to my father's service, to elevate Crispin from his brother's shadow. And to involve him in this plot. I doubted Crispin took much convincing.

What bothered me most about today's revelations was that I had briefly met Aleric at court and I thought him trustworthy. He was a powerful earl in the west. He had the king's ear. He was family. My judgment of him had been entirely wrong, based mostly upon the fact that he was family, I realized. Now I wondered at my stupidity, considering how many of my ancestors had conspired against one another.

It was easy to lean on Faulke, but I was not a coward. I steeled my spine to address Crispin and stood on my own. "You grew up at Almain. You have known Aleric your whole life. Your loyalty is commendable, but you must know that Aleric is already a dead man." I nodded toward the other men in the room, including the English guards. "The king will hear them testify to Walter's confession. To conspire against me in my absence was to conspire against the crown. I hold lands and wealth in England through the grace of my father. Aleric was given the job of managing those estates, for fair payment in return. Instead he stole from me, which meant he stole from the crown. And then to plot my murder?"

"No one will lift a hand against my lord," Crispin said with some difficulty. "Aleric's father was the king's own brother, his grandfather was our king. The barons will stand with Lord Aleric. He has more sway in England than you and your traitorous husband, or that foreigner and his men."

That last was said with a glance at Chiavari. Apparently, Crispin was unaware of Chiavari's true identity.

"Aleric will never face a trial," I agreed, "but he will not enjoy a long life. My father has other ways of punishing proven treachery."

Crispin stared at me until comprehension dawned in his eyes.

"The king's assassin," Crispin breathed. A dreadful look of understanding crossed his face. Amazingly, he had no idea that he was in the same room with my father's notorious hired killer. Chiavari was retired now, but I was certain that Mordecai had already found another to put in Chiavari's place. There was always another.

"Aleric and his supporters would certainly dismiss the word of those he considers beneath him," I said as I gestured to the other men in the room. "But my father will listen to the truth and deal with treachery accordingly. I doubt Aleric will outlive you by more than a fortnight. So tell me," I tried again. "Why do you and your lord hate my husband so much?"

Surprisingly, Crispin answered. "Promise me mercy, and I will tell you all of it."

Apparently he finally believed my claim that Aleric was a dead man. I was fairly sure it was the truth.

I looked up at Faulke. To promise Crispin mercy was to deny Faulke his revenge. His mouth was turned downward in a scowl, but he gave me a sharp nod.

"You have my promise," I said to Crispin.

"Water first," he croaked.

Everyone waited while Oliver fulfilled that last request. There was so much hatred in Crispin's eyes that I half expected him to spit the water at Faulke. I think it was in his mind to, but he was too thirsty and he drank as greedily as Walter had.

"You were all fostered together at Pembroke," Crispin said at last to Faulke. "That is where you first showed your true colors. You pretended to be Lord Aleric's friend, but the entire time you were plotting against him. You conspired to steal his intended bride, Jeanne of Wentworth. You bewitched the girl, and then you killed her."

Faulke was slowly shaking his head from side to side, his expression a mixture of disbelief and outrage. His eyes locked with mine, and he spoke to me rather than Crispin. "I was never Aleric of Almain's friend. I was too far beneath his notice until the girl he wanted to wed became fixated upon me. I did not encourage Jeanne's attentions. She was spoiled and willful, and her father was willing to do as she entreated to make her happy. I knew Jeanne's father as well as Aleric's father would not be happy that I had ended their plans for a betrothal between their children. Alienating two powerful earls was not what I intended, but Jeanne said she would swear I had compromised her if I did not agree to the marriage."

I stared at Faulke in shock. That hardly sounded like the love match Avalene had once described. Somehow, I knew this was the real story of his first marriage. Jeanne and her father had forced him into it. Just as my father had forced him into our marriage. No wonder he had looked so angry that first day we met.

"Your brat killed her," Crispin hissed. "You had taken my lord's woman, and then killed her. He had his revenge with your next two wives. If he couldn't have Jeanne, then you were not allowed to have anyone. Not a wife, not an heir." He looked at me then, his face beyond the ability to smirk, but I had the feeling that was his intent. "One of his spies will see to you, too."

Everyone stared at Crispin in silence as the implication of his words hit home. Faulke was the first to react. He grabbed Crispin by the neck and slammed his head against the wall. "Tell me a name!"

Crispin managed to shake his head. His smile was truly gruesome. "I do not know the wench's name, but you trust her with your children. Aleric said she came with them to London."

Faulke's face went completely colorless. He stared at Crispin without seeing him, and I knew he was mentally cataloguing all the people who had traveled to London with the girls. At last he straightened and I knew he had thought of the most likely culprit. His gave Crispin's head a quick twist, there was the sharp sound of bones breaking in Crispin's neck, and then he turned toward me with a bleak look on his face.

"I need to find our children."

CHAPTER TWENTY-ONE

The Truth

"THE KING HAS DELAYED HIS JOURNEY TO THE Scottish border," Faulke told me that evening as he read through the latest messages from the Tower.

I looked to the place where Blanche used to sit with her hoop, and recalled how she would shout at Gretchen and Hilda when she tried to teach them French. Blanche could have been a good person, if not for Aleric's poisonous influence.

Everyone had gathered around the long table in my solar that night to discuss the shocking turn of events. Hilda and Gretchen, Richard and Gerhardt, Dante and Avalene, even Rami, who pretended to serve everyone ale while the pile of apples in the center of the table grew noticeably smaller and Rami's frame grew noticeably lumpier. The only soldiers standing guard were outside the solar doors. The men inside had somehow grudgingly come to trust one another.

"Blanche and Merewald are to be taken into the king's custody when we deliver our reports as to what took place here," Faulke said. "He wants Isabel and each man who was present to bear witness to the confessions of the dead." He glanced at me and I knew he would like to spare me that retelling, but there was no gainsaying the king.

"What will happen to the women?" Avalene asked. "How is this Merewald person involved?"

"Merewald was originally Faulke's first wife Jeanne's maid," I told her. I exchanged a look with Faulke and continued when he gave a small nod. "Merewald came to Hawksforth with Jeanne when her mistress married Faulke, and then she took over the care of Claire when Jeanne died. She blamed Faulke for Jeanne's early demise, and was somehow convinced that her mistress would have lived, if only Jeanne and Aleric had been allowed to wed."

Avalene huffed. "How could she be so misguided?"

"Aleric had a spy in his pay from the start of Jeanne's marriage," I said, "a troubadour that visited Hawksforth every few months to collect information. He fostered a friendship with the maid, and we suspect he worked hard to poison her against Faulke. After Jeanne died, he even convinced Merewald that Faulke would marry Claire to some lowborn Segrave to ensure that his daughter's inheritance stayed under his control. The troubadour delivered a promise from Aleric that Claire would marry Aleric's heir to Almain. That would make

Claire a great lady like her mother, and unite the houses as Jeanne's father had once planned. Merewald would be the hero. All she had to do was push Edith from the battlements, and put a little poison in Alice's food."

"Oh good Lord," Avalene gasped. "She told you all of this?"

"The confession wasn't that difficult to obtain." I shrugged slightly to disguise the shudder that went through me. "She started talking as soon as she was chained next to Blanche, with the battered bodies of Walter and Crispin still hanging from their manacles."

I looked at the others to gauge their reactions. Gerhardt was still translating my words into German for Gretchen and Hilda. Faulke and Richard were brooding. That was the only way to describe their dark moods. Who could blame them? They had nurtured a viper in their midst for years. No one had ever suspected Merewald.

"What a monster," Avalene declared. "How could anyone carry out those murders and then return to her victims' children to help care for them?"

"I asked that question myself and I still have no answer," I said. My gaze slid to Faulke and Richard, but I spoke to Avalene. "The woman looks perfectly normal, plain and unassuming, her devotion to Claire seemingly natural. Even her explanation of her crimes sounded perfectly sane, as if anyone in her position would do the same." I shook my head. "Everything was done for Jeanne, she claimed, and for Claire. She was so quietly deranged and so morally certain she had done the right things that she was able to hide the truth from everyone for years."

"Why does the king want her at the Tower?" Avalene asked.

Faulke provided the answer. "He wants her confession recorded along with the others. The spy will be found, the troubadour who claimed to speak for Lord Aleric. If a connection can be made, the king will decide if Lord Aleric will stand trial."

"The king has decided already," Chiavari said in a sure voice. "Almain has too many supporters to risk a trial, but Mordecai will make certain rumors of Aleric's treachery are carried to every keep. Aleric will die of some accident or common ailment in the coming weeks, and every lord in the realm will know why. His death will reinforce their fear that no man can escape the king's justice, no matter their rank."

He finished by taking an apple from the table and biting into it, seemingly unconcerned with Aleric's fate. The other men were scowling.

"He should be drawn and quartered," Richard announced, "his entrails spread before him as he dies."

"Aye," Gerhardt agreed. "They should tar and burn his entrails. They should—"

The point of a dagger landed in the middle of the table, its tip buried a fingernail length deep into the hard wood, its tang still vibrating. Gerhardt stopped talking midsentence as everyone turned their attention to Faulke.

"There are ladies present," he reminded Richard and Gerhardt in a mild voice.

The two men muttered apologies.

"So what will you do now?" Chiavari asked Faulke. "Your innocence in your wives' deaths will be known far and wide, once Aleric's guilt becomes common knowledge."

I felt another thrill of happiness that Faulke was finally free from the cloud of suspicion that had followed him for so many years, free of the impotent anger over rumors he could not dispute. His next words sobered me.

"Aleric's guilt will never be proven beyond a doubt," he said, "and that means my innocence will never be proven beyond a doubt. However, I assume more people will believe me now when I proclaim my innocence. As for what I will do?" He lifted my hand and kissed my wrist. His eyes never left mine. "I intend to spend a relaxing evening with my wife."

"We should leave for Hawksforth as soon as possible," Richard said with a sideways glance at Gerhardt. "What if Almain sets more spies against us? At Hawksforth, we can defend ourselves."

"Merewald proved we are vulnerable at Hawksforth," Faulke said. "We will remain in London until Aleric is no longer a threat. Anyone in his hire should cease their efforts against us when there is no longer the promise of pay."

My fingers were splayed on Faulke's thigh beneath the table, his hand atop mine. I gently pulled my hand free and nodded at Chiavari. "What about you and Avalene? What will you do now?"

"We have stayed in London too long." Chiavari looked around the room, then his gaze returned to his wife. "I promised the king we would remain at Ashland until Sir Roland's murder was solved. I will testify to the confession, and then we will set sail for Italy soon after. A ship already awaits our passage."

Avalene nodded, but her eyes were sad. She would probably be leaving England for good. Her father would visit her, but I doubted she would ever again see the aunt and uncle who had raised her, or any of the people she had grown up with. I knew all too well what it was like to leave behind everything familiar. I reached across the table for her hand.

"Faulke has never been on a pilgrimage beyond these shores," I told her. "I would very much like to show him the wonders of Venice. The journey will be sweeter, knowing we have a reunion with good friends awaiting us at our destination. In the meantime, you will see parts of the world that most Englishmen don't even know exist— mountains and seas, and cities that will take your breath away with their beauty. Just think of all the interesting new people you will meet."

I looked at Faulke and took my own words to heart. If I had never left Rheinbaden, if I had managed to stay hidden away at Grunental, I would never have known Faulke existed in this world, waiting for me to find him. How different both our lives would be. We were each a force to be reckoned with on our own, but when we turned together to face a challenge, we were like magnets, always stronger.

His eyes collided with mine and we both fell into one of our staring contests. I would never tire of gazing at him. His beautiful eyes, his handsome face, and especially the love for me that I could almost see radiating from him. He once said that he could give me no gift that I could not buy for myself, but he was wrong.

He had given me his heart.

EPILOGUE

In the coming years, Claire did indeed marry Remmington's heir, and they founded a long and prosperous dynasty. Lucy married Baron Tenby's heir, Albert, and bore him five children. Henry de Clare died young, before he and Jane could marry. Because her parents always encouraged her to follow her own heart, she became the prioress of Maldon Abbey.

As for the adults, Faulke and Isabel did not have one child, but instead had eight, an equal mix of boys and girls, who helped fill Hawksforth with love and laughter, along with the children of Gretchen and Richard, and Gerhardt and Hilda.

They all spoke Welsh.

ACKNOWLEDGMENTS

My family raised me to be a reader and a dreamer. "Life is limited only by your imagination." "Anything is possible if you work hard for it." Those statements were not always true, but I owe most of my successes in life to their inspiration.

However, I would not be a writer without the unconditional support of my best friend and husband. He is living proof that knights in shining armor still exist, and he is always ready to slay my dragons. His belief in me is unshakeable. Mine in him is the same. We make a good team. And exceptional children.

The entire staff at Random House also gets a loud round of applause. I always feel like I am working with the best in the business, and I am very grateful for their guidance and expertise. Junessa, you're a treasure.

Most of all, I want to thank my readers. It's still equal parts joy, exhilaration, and terror to realize other people will read my books. As a reader myself, most books I read live up to my expectations but some soar beyond them. You make me try harder to soar. Thank you for your continued support!